In the Witch's Shadow

Book One of the Kaulswyr Cycle

Costen Young

Dead Nettle Press

In the Witch's Shadow

Book One of the Kaulswyr Cycle

SECOND EDITION
Published in the United States by
Dead Nettle Press

Cover Design: Katherine Young
Map: Costen Young and Katherine Young
Interior Art: Costen Young

Print ISBN: 978-0-9894451-2-2
EBook ISBN: 978-0-9894451-3-9

To my family, friends and everyone else who helped make this book possible. It's been a long, continuing journey, but it's been infinitely richer for the company.

CONTENTS

Dramatis Personae

Cyrus Ulberath:	The last scion of House Ulberath, an unwilling hero
B'lantra Akspara:	A witch and an aspiring physician, engaged to Cyrus
Etienne Caulter:	A professional witchhunter
Teresa eta Caulteri:	Caulter's daughter
Celaan:	Empress of the fallen Aeore Imperium
Simon Barros:	A notorious warlock, consort to Celaan
Aeliraneth:	Renown scholar and infamous witch, mother to Cyrus
Kierahne:	A cloaked witch trained to serve the Illumentry
Etmos:	A professional witchhunter, handler of Kierahne
Dontarius Tankreed:	A rogue scholar, an opportunistic treasure hunter
Hendrick:	A Tekni researcher
P'talan:	A Tekni commander, former desert raider
Tarja del Armenijhan:	A Tekni commander, Dontarius' former lover
Helena:	A merchant woman
Pol:	Helena's husband

ROSHAN IGNATIUS KALEAN:	A nobleman, Master of the fortress of Ashenwall
MONTAVIAN GAVON:	Chief retainer to Rohan Ignatius
BOVASHAR BREGNA:	An Inquisition captain, Caulter's commanding officer
PETRU:	A witchhunter
ROMEI:	A Tekni insurgent
KAFKA:	An unfortunate Tekni insurgent
MARKOV ANSEF:	Sheriff of the village of Shrevnetska
NYSSE:	A water spirit
WILYAM AND PETAR:	Two brothers, deputized peacekeepers in the village of Shrevnetska
ENRIC:	A peacekeeper, Wilyam and Petar's friend
ASA OF THE MIST:	A beautiful but sadistic golden-haired witch
LYRA KAMANI:	Aeliraneth's physician and Cyrus' mentor
THE BALHAEGAST	A sanguine but sinister entity

CHAPTER 1

PORTAL

THE LIBRARY WAS FREEZING. It had been freezing the entire time he'd been exiled there. A fire crackled gently in the fireplace, though it put out far too little heat to suit him. Books on nearly every subject his young mind could imagine loomed over him. Polished reading tables sat perfectly spaced out over a tiled floor imprinted with a swirling pattern reminiscent of a winter storm. The bank of windows on the far wall would have let in a little light if the thick curtains pulled across them had allowed it. The outside was closed to him. The library was his one and only world right now— just as Mother wanted it.

Cyrus shivered and stretched his legs out to the coal box at his feet. The flame glowed through the iron slats, providing at least a tiny measure of comfort. It was the dead of winter, in the nine hundredth and eighth year since the Prophetess Ansala had defeated the Aeore and driven them back through the Wynding. Many of the better homes in the city of Targus had steam boilers in their cellars, piping heat up through copper pipes. Would it really be so hard to install one in the house? Mother could certainly afford it.

He put his head back down and tried to continue with his reading. The weight of the thick, leather-bound book dug into his leg as he pondered the meaning of the words on its vellum pages.

The Iriethan characters written there refused to coalesce into any sort of meaning. They were fighting him, as they often did. There were thousands of different ones, each with its own shifting definition and context, tense and appellation. They were subject only to the creator's need. The characters would twist their meaning if you weren't careful. To read anything, you had to make the characters do what you wanted them to.

Tonight they seemed to be in no mood to obey.

The clock on the wall ticked on, an unsubtle reminder that he was running out of time. Mother had never been known for her patience.

She paced back and forth in front of him, as oblivious to the chill in the room as she was to his growing distress. She was an elegant lady, tall and willowy, prideful and pristine. Her dark hair was intricately braided and pinned. The rouge that gave color to her pale cheeks had been specifically imported for her all the way from the islands of the West. Dyed in the bold burgundy and gold hues she favored, her dress was of the finest satin. The golden embroidery gracing the hem of her red velvet wrap glittered faintly in the light of the brass chandeliers hanging down from the arched ceiling high above. The attire matched the lacquered crimson fan she always carried with her.

Kassun and Bruel, Mother's bodyguards, stood dutifully near the windows, watching the proceeding with quiet disinterest. They were an imposing pair with their deep blue uniforms, their bristling mustaches and impassive, hardened faces. A pale, icy snowflake was embroidered on the shoulders of their coats, the symbol of Mother's house. Their swords and muskets were well kept, more than enough to ward away the intrepid and the curious when Mother went out and about.

Cyrus doubted Kassun and Bruel liked the cold library any more than he did, but both men would have surely curled up and died before complaining. They never complained. Now that he thought about it, they never said much of anything.

Maybe Mother had cast a spell on them.

She was Aeliraneth, Matriarch of House Ulberath, and she was a witch after all.

Father had long since disappeared. He'd been a great explorer, so Mother had said, and his ship had been lost to the grinding

2

ice of the Boundless Sea. Mother wouldn't talk about it, and after a few encounters with her fan, Cyrus had learned not to ask.

Many times he'd imagined what it would be like if Father returned. The door to Mother's estate would suddenly open, and a tall man would come through. He would have piercing eyes and maybe a red and yellow parrot like the pirates in the stories. He would smell like the warm sea breeze and have a thousand tales to tell. Things would change then. With Father home, Mother would be happier... and nicer. Maybe she would forget about Iriethan characters and endless lessons about things that had happened long ago.

He glanced up at the clock. It was getting late.

Mother's fan flicked out towards his face before he could duck away. The impact rocked his head back. His eyes watered.

"You need to be quicker with your translations," she said. "What have I told you?"

"That I should think quickly and act even faster."

"And what have I told you about distractions like the clock on the wall?"

"They get in the way, and I should ignore them."

"See that you do so from now on. Time is short, and I have things to do other than bothering with you. Now recite what you have read."

He looked down at the book and resigned himself to the beating he knew was coming. Mother demanded perfection with the translations, a feat he'd never quite mastered. He began reading aloud, expecting the crimson fan to come hammering down on him with every word. To his surprise, the fan never moved. When he'd finished, a ghost of approval played briefly across Mother's face.

"Your translation is adequate," she declared. She went over to one of the nearby reading tables, picked up the golden bell that sat atop and rang it. The door to the library opened, and one of the servants, Joana, came through bearing another great stack of dusty tomes. At Mother's direction, Joana awkwardly placed the books on the table and then departed.

"I'll expect these to be translated by the end of tomorrow," Mother said. "You're nearly ten, so you should be able to understand them. If I find your work acceptable, you'll be allowed outside again."

Cyrus' jaw dropped in outrage. Mother turned sharply and began to walk away. Kassun and Bruel stirred from their posts to follow her.

"Why?" Cyrus demanded, slapping one of the books off the table. "What's the point of any of this? I'm tired of looking at these stupid books!"

Mother whirled around. Anger flashed in her green eyes. The cold air of the room became suddenly charged. The clock on the wall sparked briefly and starting running backwards. The click of Mother's leather shoes on the tiles sounded like the tramp of doom as she came towards him.

He swallowed nervously. Now he'd done it.

She raised the fan to strike him and then reconsidered. "Do you remember what happened three years ago when I took you to the canal?"

"You had me walk out on the ice following that ley line. The ice cracked. You nearly drowned me."

"No, your own incompetence nearly drowned you. The ley line rejected you. I knew then you were no warlock, even if you could see the lines."

He frowned. Why did that matter? Warlocks had died out centuries ago. Witchcraft was for girls now. He'd never be able to command the storm like Mother, or cast any sort of spell whatsoever. As a witch's son, there was a whole world he could see, but never participate in— all the more reason for him to learn to duel and to shoot instead of wasting time with old books.

Mother knelt down so she could look him in the eye. Her momentary anger had dissipated, replaced by an icy contempt.

He almost preferred the anger.

"For those who aren't capable of power, knowledge is the only effective substitute. Properly used, knowledge can be power. Think on this as you're translating the books. I'll have Lyra supervise your work. If you want to see the sun again, make sure you don't disappoint her as you have me."

Mother walked away once more, taking Kassun and Bruel with her. He sat staring at the stack of books on the table, willing himself not to cry.

It wasn't fair!

Lyra Kamani stepped into the room a few moments later, ruefully shaking her head. She was a tall woman, with broad shoulders and large, calloused hands that looked better suited to farm labor than the medicine she practiced. Though the fabric of her green dress was rich velour, the cut was plain and functional; a far cry from the elaborate, brocaded gowns Mother so often wore.

Arakostrian by birth, Lyra lacked the haughty demeanor that characterized so many of her countrymen. Arakost had once been an empire rivaling even ancient Iriethan in size, and its people were loath to forget it.

Lyra was different though. There was a warmth to her that seemed like it would have been out of place in the cold, windswept lands of the decaying Empire. Curly brown hair fell down around her tanned face. Eyes, a deep hazel, almost seemed to blend in with a countenance that was just starting to show the first hints of age. The tarnished silver clover of Saint Rachael, marking her as an officially commissioned physician in the Northlands, hung around her neck.

"Your mother's in a foul temper tonight," Lyra noted.

Cyrus sighed. "I wasn't trying to make her angry."

"I doubt you're the real cause of it. Come look out the window."

He looked over to make sure Mother really had left, and then walked over and pulled back the curtain enough to peer out through the frost-streaked panes. The window opened out onto the front lawn of the estate. Snow filtered relentlessly down in the light of the colored lanterns set along the cobblestone of the drive, swirling round the hedges and the stone angels standing vigil on the manicured grounds. It often snowed or rained when Mother's temper turned dark. Beyond the confines of the estate, he could see the distant lights of the city of Targus. Mother had built the estate on a hill overlooking the city, strategically upwind from the smoke and the soot of the factories.

A pair of carriages clacked slowly up the drive and came to a stop at the foot of the wide marble steps that led to the front entrance. They were black and unmarked, pulled by equally dark horses.

Cyrus' brow furrowed. Visitors to the estate weren't all that uncommon, but they were usually the young men Mother fancied. She always had a parade of them, one to suit each of her many moods. The people getting out of the carriages were nothing of the sort though.

"The Illumentry?" he asked. "What are they doing here?"

"A very good question," Lyra said. "One I'd give more than a few silver sparrows to find out."

Cyrus watched as the men and women stepped down from the carriage. Geofri, Mother's secretary, went out to meet them. The Illumentry people were a dour bunch, their clothing as somber as their faces. They reminded him of school marms who'd bitten too hard into a lemon. The small red insignia of the lantern and the star, the Illumentry symbols, was visible on the lapels of their heavy coats.

The Illumentry revered Talast, the Northern Face of God. It was a hard faith, the Light in the Arctic Darkness, as harsh as the frigid tundra and icy peaks. They were always quick to remind everyone that their organization and technology had helped the scattered peoples of the north rebuild what was lost in the war with the Aeore.

"They're not here to arrest Mother, are they?" he asked in

alarm. "The Illumentry hates witches. They drag them off and put them in cages when they can."

Lyra shook her head. "Not your mother they won't. They're afraid of her, and with good reason. Besides, this lot doesn't look like they're up to arresting anyone. They didn't bring any inquisitors with them."

"I wonder what Mother is up to."

"Hard to say," Lyra said. "Look there. See that tall fellow with the silver beard— the one that looks like his only friend in the world just died? That's Aremis Finn, one of the Illumentry's best scholars on the Aeore lands. The prune-faced woman beside him is Matron Callia, head of the Illumentry archives here in Targus. Looks like it's going to be quite a merry gathering."

In short order the Illumentry visitors were escorted inside. Cyrus watched for a little while to see if anyone else would show up, but no one did. The snow continued to fall, quickly covering the drive.

"Come on," Lyra said at last, pointing to the stack of books Mother had left on the table. "I'll leave the curtains pulled back so you can look out, but I want you to get a little work done before bed."

He reluctantly picked one of the books up. Lyra was just as much of a taskmistress as Mother. The study of plants she'd made him undertake had been ruthlessly thorough, and Lyra hadn't settled for anything less than his best work. She'd been just as demanding with the mathematics and history, politics and etiquette she made him commit to memory. But Lyra had a gentleness to her, a kindness buried within her that made him want to learn. Her eyes were always smiling, even when she was angry with him. Her voice was always soft, even when she scolded him.

Lyra didn't bother calling him 'young Master Ulberath', which he hated, or 'young sir', which he despised even more. Unlike Mother, Lyra saw the value in his learning how to shoot a pistol and use a sword. They would practice whenever Mother wasn't watching, and he'd become passably good at both. Lyra had even taught him a little about lock picking. Where a doctor had learned about such things he had no idea, but he wasn't going to complain.

He stared down at the book he was supposed to be reading, but the Iriethan characters had resumed their endless attempts to frustrate him. After a while he couldn't stand it anymore. He put his lesson down and sauntered over to see whether any of the books on the library shelves were more interesting. Lyra gave him a stern glance, but didn't say anything.

The entire house suddenly shook. Lyra jumped to her feet. Bits of masonry cracked and fell from the ceiling. He thought he could hear distant shouting.

And smoke. He could smell smoke!

Cyrus jumped as the sharp crack of a gunshot echoed through the house. Another followed, and then another.

They hurried out of the library. Mother intercepted them as they came to the parlor. She grabbed Cyrus up and hugged him tightly.

They gasped at the sight of her. Her hair had come loose from the ornate pins and barrettes she'd bound it with. The rouge on her cheeks was streaked through with sweat and soot. Her gown was torn in several places, and along her side a bloody stain slowly spread its way across the fabric. The long scar she had on her forearm stood out against her pallid skin.

Yet despite her appearance, she showed no hint of panic. Her green eyes were steely, her jaw tightly set.

The parlor was in shambles. Stacks of books sat in forlorn piles near toppled shelves, and part of the high vaulted ceiling had caved in. The angry glare of flame flickered red against the windows. Smoke and dust hung heavily in the air.

His chest tightened when he saw the crushed and mangled bodies of the Illumentry men and women strewn out across the floor. Their blood spilled out, staining the lush carpet. Kassun and Bruel lay twisted and broken, their faces crushed to the point they were nearly unrecognizable. Brain matter leaked through their shattered skulls.

The electrocuted bodies of several creatures lay alongside them. They were misshapen things, with parts of animals and bits of machinery imbedded in their flesh.

Chimera? There were no such things… at least he'd never thought so until now.

"God's name!" Lyra exclaimed, making the sign of the spear across her chest.

Mother let go of Cyrus and abruptly shoved him away.

"Take him to the village of Shrevnetska. It's a tenspan's ride to the south along the Red Road," she said to Lyra.

"I know where it is," the physician said. "There's nothing there but a few sawmills."

"Don't argue with me. Just obey," Mother said, shortly. "We have no time. Use the cellar entrance by the library. Hopefully, it's still clear."

The house quivered as if some monstrous beast was stomping through it. Cries echoed above the crackle of the flames outside. Cyrus turned his face away and held onto Lyra's skirt. He knew those cries. Noreen, Daysus, even poor, simple little Joana— people whose faces he'd seen almost every day of his life. He covered his ears, but the noise wouldn't go away.

Mother gave him one last glance and then turned and hurried away. She wouldn't look back no matter how loudly he called to her. The rafters cracked and then came crashing down in a sea of plaster and smoldering timber, cutting off any chance for him to follow.

Lyra dragged him away, unconcerned about his protests. The rumbling continued from all around them as they returned to the library. Then from outside a brilliant blue bolt of lightning smote down, momentarily sundering the flames. The wind picked up, rattling madly at the windows. Sheets of icy rain began pounding down as if the heavens were crying out all their tears.

9

Mother had unleashed her witchcraft.

She wasn't the only one.

A mist began seeping under the door to the cellar they'd been hoping to use. The cloying fragrance of blooddrop flowers began to fill the library, overwhelming even the acrid odor of the burning timbers and smoldering books.

A woman with flowing golden hair appeared before them. She was beautiful: tall and fair, her skin porcelain perfect, her features elegant and shapely. Blue eyes gleamed. Richly tailored clothes sparkled. She might have passed for one of God's angels if not for the murderous expression stamped across her face. Blood that surely wasn't her own dripped from the sable gloves covering her hands. A cloth doll with a calico dress and yellow yarn hair sat on her shoulder.

She said nothing to them. The look in her eyes and the crooked smile that curled her ruby lips told them all they needed to know. Lyra put him behind her and backed away. The golden-haired woman relentlessly followed.

At last their backs touched the far wall of the library. There was nowhere left for them to run, and the golden-haired woman knew it. Lyra seized a jeweled letter opener from a nearby desk and held it defiantly before her.

The woman merely shrugged.

She swept in. In an instant, Lyra lay reeling on the floor and the woman's hand was around his throat. He flailed at her, trying to escape, trying to breathe. She slammed him back against the wall. His head swam. There was only her cruel smile and her blue eyes delighting in watching the life seep out of him.

The bones in his neck creaked and strained. A quick twist of her hand was the only thing he had to look forward to. Mother had abandoned him. There was no one left to break the woman's grip, no one to give breath back to his silently screaming lungs.

His eyes stretched over to an oddly colored oak panel along the wall. There was nothing particularly unique about it other than the discoloration that ran through its grain, nothing to indicate that it was special in any way.

His legs were going numb. His body seemed to be floating. There was only the pressure around his neck.

What was different about the oak panel?

Then he knew.

The Iriethan character: Meahveh the Portal. It shimmered reluctantly into view, silvery and thin, its lines running across each other in an intricate weave of curves and loops.

What was it doing there? Had Mother written it?

He called on it, demanding that it obey him.

A part of wall fell away behind him. He had the vague sense of Lyra moving, of her slamming into the golden-haired woman and knocking her away. Then he was falling through the opening he'd made. The pressure on his neck vanished. The golden-haired woman was gone, and only Lyra remained with him.

He felt the cold of the snow on his cheek. He took a breath and then began coughing, trying to get air back into his lungs. Lyra helped him to his feet. They were beside the line of thick pine trees that formed the boundary of Mother's estate.

The sky in the distance was lit up with the unholy reddish glow of smoke and flame. The estate was burning. For an instant he thought he saw the shadow of some great mechanical creature tearing through it. A cold, mournful breeze seemed to whisper through the pine's branches.

"Mother…"

"Don't worry about her. She can take care of herself," Lyra said.

"No, she can't! Take me back to the house. Now!"

Lyra shook her head firmly. When he tried to wriggle past her, she gripped his shoulders tightly. "No. We're going forward. That's the only way for us."

She held him close to her. "It will be alright

CHAPTER 2

PROPOSAL

GOSSAMER WINGS TICKLED THE STUBBLE along his angular jaw. Cyrus Ulberath's green eyes narrowed as the spring fairies buzzed incessantly around his face. His brow curled into the beginnings of a scowl. He swatted at the fairies, nearly dislodging the wrapped bundle of sallenden wood he carried on his bony shoulders. The cloud of tiny bodies deftly parted. They moved relentlessly in again, lapping at the beads of sweat on his pointy chin, pinching his lightly tanned skin and doing their best to undo the cord that bound his long, dark hair.

"Get! Find something else to do with your time," he said to them in exasperation.

He swore he could hear the faintest hint of malevolent laughter carried on the breeze swirling through the barely clothed trees of the Arkinwood.

He couldn't begin to guess what had riled the fairies. The sallenden tree had been felled not by the axe at his belt, but by simple old age. Maybe there was another storm coming, though he could see no signs of it in the sky.

He quickened his pace along the narrow earthen path that snaked through the forest. The fairies followed until the babble of the approaching Dry Run grew louder, and the burble of voices and braying animals interrupted the sylvan song of the forest. Cyrus allowed a smile to crease his face when they finally veered off into a nearby thicket.

The trees thinned as he crested a slight rise and started down into the next valley. The path descended in a broad, gentle curve before crossing the old stone bridge over the Dry Run. The village of Shrevnetska lay beyond like a child curled in the womb of the forest. The channel of the Run cut between the oak shingled roofs and stone foundations of the houses before flowing down to join the winding Dreyfus River. The white chapel of Ansala, the Illumentry's bastion in the village, sparkled in the sun. In the distance, a steamboat slowly chugged up the Dreyfus to deliver its load of coal to the new sawmill along the river's edge.

A faint ley line shimmered in the morning mists above. Lavender in hue, it was rail straight, like a shimmering string pulled tight across the sky. It was the only one around, a small and unimportant runt running north to join its larger brothers and sisters converging at distant Targus. The ley lines were leftovers from old Iriethan. For a witch, they were a valuable source of power from which to draw. For most other people, they were simply an old story.

He gazed at the scene before him and shook his head. It was peaceful. Tranquil. Suffocating.

The emerald green streamers and shimmering golden bows that were starting to dot the town in preparation for the festival of Greenleaf helped add some much needed color and life to the place, as did the amber lanterns and baubles in some of the windows. A new year had nearly dawned upon the lands of the Lanternlit, the nine hundred and eighteenth since Ansala had defeated the Aeore, God's Firstborn, at the battle of Cinder. The breach in the Wynding had been closed that day, and the Aeore had been forced back to their strange realm of Asylum.

Despite its pitiful attempt at pageantry, Shrevnetska was bereft and backwards. It was a storm-plagued town of logs and cabbages, so he'd said more than a few times to Lyra and B'lantra. Sadly it was also home, or had been for the last ten years of his life anyway.

He set the bundle of sallenden down when he reached the bridge and stretched, trying to get the stiffness out of his rangy, nearly scarecrow frame. The fragrant scent of the yellowish wood still clung to him, though it wasn't an unpleasant odor. It was certainly better than the smell of the gocochen dung that suddenly assaulted his nose. On its heels, the harsh braying of the large, feathery beasts of burden momentarily overwhelmed the splashing chatter of the Run's waters.

He brushed a few wood chips out of his hair and then noticed some of the sallenden sap had leeched out of the wrapping and had stained the white linen shirt he was wearing. His loose fitting black trousers, patched leather waistcoat and worn boots had fared no better.

"Shit! Dolece can cut her own damned wood next time."

He already knew better though. When next year's Greenleaf neared, Matron Dolece, the Illumentry's aged excuse for a cleric, would demand that he go after the sallenden wood once again. She would wave some silver sparrows in his face, insisting she was doing him a favor by offering him some honest work. He would probably trundle off into the wood once more, grudgingly grateful for the coin.

Dolece would burn the wood in the sacred hearth in the middle of the town square, just as Ansala had once done in the city of Calateph far to the north. Greenleaf was a holy celebration thanking God for deliverance from the Aeore invaders, she would say. After a long winter of being cooped up indoors, most of the revelers would ignore her. The corn whiskey and barley beer would flow, babies would be conceived in the strangest of places and Lyra and B'lantra would be busy patching up the drunks after they inevitably came to blows.

The pattern would be the same year after year, Greenleaf after Greenleaf, until Shrevnetska chewed up his youth and spit him back out old and gray.

As his mood darkened, Cyrus reached down into the pocket of his waistcoat. His fingers fumbled until he found the pair of crafted silksteel rings there. A subtle silvery white in color, they reacted to his touch, shifting from a soft, pliable weave to a light, warm metal and then back again.

It had taken him several days to painstakingly weave them from the webs the Arkinwood's sword spiders left behind, days more to cure them. Silksteel wasn't the easiest material to work with, and the spiders didn't help matters. Fortunately, the cuts and scrapes they'd left on his hands had healed readily enough, leaving B'lantra little the wiser about his efforts.

It had been worth it.

Today was the day he would finally present the silvery ring and ask her. Maybe by the time the next Greenleaf rolled around they could be gone from here. The villagers of Shrevnetska wouldn't miss them: a witch's son and a witch secretly sheltering in their midst. In turn, the two of them could forget Shrevnetska, provincial piss stain that it was, just like all the others who passed through it.

It was a hopeful thought as he picked the bundle of sallenden back up and trudged over the stone bridge to deliver it into Dolece's wrinkled clutches.

※ ※ ※

The house was quiet as Cyrus stepped into the kitchen. Only the winter sage and the basil hanging on their respective racks greeted him. Lyra, now Shrevnetska's resident physician, had already departed for the day, though that wasn't unusual. The only question was whether B'lantra had followed her mentor's example and left as well.

He hoped not.

One of her endless army of woodcarvings, a gargoyle— or at least what B'lantra imagined one to look like from the stories he'd told her— leered down at him from its place atop the shelves. Several more of her creations, including one depicting the banuken camels she'd grown up around, watched him from the corner of the room. On the wooden table in the center, a worn copy of *The Adventures of Sir Bennon*, his childhood hero, sat undisturbed, alongside yesterday's edition of *The Springboard*, Shrevnetska's fumbling attempt at a newspaper.

15

He studied the scene, trying to gauge whether B'lantra had already departed to start her nurse's rounds. She'd happily sleep the morning away if allowed.

A thin trail of steam rose from the kettle over the fireplace. The lingering scent of freshly brewed chala reached his nose.

Then his gaze fell on the lacquered brown and blue of the parquet 'fairy stone' board on the end table. The enameled wooden pieces were already set up in preparation for a game.

B'lantra was up at least.

He passed through the parlor and headed for the back step, carefully stepping around Lyra's favorite padded chair and some more of B'lantra's finished and unfinished carvings.

Several of the tapestries he'd woven decorated the walls. He studied them briefly, as he often did, looking for mistakes. There weren't any. He'd gotten surprisingly good at weaving over the years— not that it really helped him. The new machines coming out of places like Targus could spin a hundred tapestries in the time it took him to do just one.

Lyra's sword hung over the mantle. His brow curled suddenly. His sword, with its distinctive blue tassel, normally hung just below, and it was missing. It had been well over a tenspan of days since he'd last practiced with it. Had he put it back afterwards?

He shrugged. It could be found later.

The door on the far side beckoned him.

He frowned and found himself reaching down into his pocket again, not for the silksteel rings this time, but to the pair of brightly painted wooden blocks he always kept close. Mother had given him the opportunity to earn a whole set of them long ago. Only the two in his pocket remained. They were plain, except for when he was alone, and the convoluted Iriethan characters for energy and light shimmered into existence along the sides.

Lyra had saved them for him the night of the fire. He ground them together when he was troubled, like a nervous man might chew on his fingernails. It was a habit he needed to break. Mother was ten years burned, and the past was a thing best left alone.

Annoyed with himself, he once more reached for the rings. Asking for B'lantra's hand in marriage shouldn't be this difficult. If her habits held true, she would be just beyond the door, taking in the morning sun and organizing her supplies before starting her rounds.

What if she said no, or worse... demurred, giving him some vague words about taking up an honest trade or affording a family? She'd grown up a merchant's daughter. Such thoughts wouldn't be beyond her ken.

What if...

No.

He already knew her as well as a man could know a woman. The opportunity to present the ring had passed him by for three days now. Gathering his nerve, he opened the door and stepped through.

It's been months since the fire, and Mother hasn't returned. He's beginning to think she never will. He's not concerned about Mother today though.

The foreign girl is new to Shrevnetska, just like he is. She seems about his age, though she's small— more eyes and knees and hair than anything else.

He walks slowly, trying to work up his nerve to talk to her. Whenever he's near her, his heart begins to race a little. His knees feel weak.

Maybe she likes him too. It's hard to tell. Her big brown eyes light up whenever she sees him, though she never says anything.

He sighs. Girls are hard to figure out.

B'lantra of the family Akspara was sitting on the step just as he had anticipated, beautiful to his eyes, though she wouldn't have claimed as much herself. She was hardly an imposing figure. The entire length of her small frame would have barely come up to his chin if she'd been standing up. Her deep brown hair gently curled its way down nearly to her waist and lay freshly brushed over her shoulders. The purple glass bead that bound the single long braid that ran through her hair glittered faintly in the morning sun. Her skin matched the creamy white brown of her untouched cup of chala. The yellow and white healer's dress clung closely to her slender body, its hem gracefully flowing just above the top of the short black boots she wore. As he drew closer, he could smell the slight hint of lilac bloom enveloping her.

She turned when he came through. Her large brown eyes brightened. "I didn't know if I'd see you before I had to leave."

The trace of the lilting accent of her Trafari homeland to the south still lingered in her speech, though otherwise her diction was perfect. She'd picked up the Arakostrian tongue of the Northern lands far more quickly than he'd been able to learn her native Trafarga.

She studied him for a moment, and then her gaze unerringly found the stains the sallenden sap had left on his clothes. "I see Matron Dolece tracked you down and put you to work."

Cyrus brushed futilely at his shirt. "Apparently I didn't hide quickly enough. She got me just past Neska's store. Probably spent days planning the perfect time to strike."

B'lantra took a sip of her chala. "It wouldn't surprise me a bit. She's like an old spider that way."

Cyrus' hand slipped into his pocket as he came over to sit beside her. His fingers found the ring, and he drew it forth.

To his dismay, she'd turned away from him to focus on the worn leather medicine bag at her feet. Her delicate hands flitted, ruthlessly sorting and organizing the tools of her trade until they reached an ordered perfection not even the most disciplined army could match.

Her eyes flicked up at him. "What's wrong?"

His hand locked around the ring.

"Nothing, Bel," he replied, quickly. "Nothing's wrong. What makes you think anything's wrong?"

"You've been acting strangely for the last three days. And you only call me Bel when you have something on your mind."

"I do not. B'lantra just has too many syllables."

"Yes you do, and no it doesn't," she replied, giving him a gentle, but firm stare.

Cyrus took a deep breath. Without thinking on it anymore, he took the ring and slipped it onto her finger, hoping his hands didn't shake too badly.

A nervous tension rippled through him. His lips suddenly locked, and his tongue stood numb.

"Yes."

It took a moment for the word to register in his brain.

"Yes," she said again. The smile on her face was brighter than the morning sun.

She wrapped her arms around him in a surprisingly tight grip, kissed him and nothing else mattered. The world seemed to pause for them.

She finally released him and then excitedly turned to look at the ring, holding it up to admire it in the sunshine. "It's beautiful. Silksteel. You wove this yourself, didn't you? It must've taken forever!"

His pulse slowed to a dull roar.

"Not that proposing marriage is going to get you out of the game of fairy stones you promised me tonight," she abruptly declared.

"Oh," was all he could say at first, his mind still awash in the moment. "Umm… how did we suddenly go from marriage to fairy stones?"

"Well, the whole point of the game is to get your king to the center of the board to meet his queen, and you're always talking about how we're going to be king and queen of something."

"I suppose that's true," he said, his sense beginning to return. "Then again, maybe you're still mad because you lost the last four games."

"You do know that I let you win," she said, slyly.

He only had a moment to really think about it before she kissed him again. It was just as well. He did best when he just acted and dealt with the consequences as they came.

Her face suddenly fell in disappointment. "I have to go."

"Must you? Can't these people look after themselves for one single day?" he asked.

"It's only over to Urkasa and back. Soren's got that bad leg and needs to move about whether he wants to or not. There's Edrich's cough to worry with. And… and…"

Her eyes lit up with excitement again. "And I want to show Lyra the ring. She'll be so happy you asked me. Yes! You finally, finally asked me!"

"You knew I was going to?"

"I didn't have it down to the exact day and time or anything, but yes, I knew you would. Eventually." She reached over and gave his bound hair a playful yank. "It did take a little longer than I figured it would. It's not like I bite or anything."

"Yes, you—"

"That's beside the point."

"Well, I just wanted it to be… to be… I don't know…"

"I do. And you're sweet for trying so hard. It's another reason I said yes."

There was movement from the street behind her. Three men topped the slight rise along the alleyway that led past the step, two of them hulking giants, the third a wiry afterthought.

The first two came lumbering towards them: Wilyam and Petar, part of Shrevnetska's force of so-called peacekeepers. They were both blonde and heavily built; the nearly identical offspring of the mother unfortunate enough to bear them. Their bovine countenances lazily took in Shrevnetska's wooden buildings. Their dark green uniforms were stretched tightly over the bulging muscles in their arms and chests. Thick clubs hung down from the black leather belts at their waists.

The third man, Enric, came following afterwards, joining the brothers in their mindless chatter when he could; looking mournful when he was left out. His wide-eyed face was pockmarked and pinched, his gangly grin gap-toothed and jagged. In contrast to theirs, his uniform hung loosely off his scrawny frame, almost as if it resented having to touch his oily skin.

The sight of the three peacekeepers threatened to rip all the joy out of Cyrus' day. A stormy scowl darkened his face as they drew near.

The girl isn't on the edge of the village green like she usually is. She stands there every morning and stares sadly into the trees like she's waiting for someone.

He searches and finally finds her by the garden in the center of the village.

Wilyam, Petar and Enric have found her first. Petar distracts her while Enric steals the basket she's been using to gather herbs. Every time she tries to get it back, one of them slips around behind her and yanks on her braid.

They laugh at her when she tries to speak to them in her foreign language.

Wilyam gets tired of the game and throws her down. Petar kicks dirt on her.

Fire dances in the girl's eyes. For a moment she looks as if she wants to burn them to ash. She changes her mind and looks away.

He vaults over the short stone wall surrounding the garden. He's not completely sure why he even cares. He just knows he wants to protect her.

His feet trample the newly planted cabbages as he rushes over. "Leave her alone!"

His voice is shrill with anger and outrage.

Wilyam turns to him and sneers. Petar spits on the ground in front of him. Enric slides around to the side.

They forget about the foreign girl and charge him.

He smiles and readies his fists.

Little had changed between them in the years since. The trio spied Cyrus and B'lantra and quickened their pace. An enthusiastic snarl spread across their lumpy faces. Cyrus felt B'lantra grip his knee as he rose to meet them.

"Don't you dare," she said. "Not today."

"If they want to start trouble…"

"Then you'll walk away. I swear I'll bite you for real if you get into another fight with them."

"They're…"

"…not worth it."

He considered the idea and finally relented. The peacekeepers drew closer. Cyrus' eyes locked onto theirs. They returned his gaze without any sign of fear. There was eagerness in their faces instead.

Then they had passed on. He finally relaxed when they'd disappeared from sight.

B'lantra finished her chala and set the cup down. "That wasn't so hard, was it?"

Cyrus ran his hands over his face. The storm that had darkened his face dissipated almost as quickly as it had formed.

B'lantra looked up at the sun steadily rising in the sky above the rooftops. *Vashaenit!* I really do have to go."

"And I suppose I should climb up and fix our roof before I forget about it. I don't want to hear Lyra sniping about how it wasn't done," Cyrus said, sighing. "You haven't seen my sword lying around somewhere? It's not hanging up."

"Check by the bed, or in the closet. It's where you normally throw everything. If not, try actually cleaning," B'lantra replied. She hoisted the leather bag over her shoulder and gave him a final lingering kiss before setting out. "Be good while I'm gone. No fighting or lingering around Olaf's tavern."

"The roof and I will behave ourselves, I promise."

He watched her go and smiled before turning back to the house. He found himself still smiling, though the thought of climbing up on the shingled roof and working in the morning sun held absolutely no fascination.

✳ ✳ ✳

The wiry man stared at her in slack-jawed awe as she leisurely strolled out of the trees. He was a poor specimen: scrawny and gap-toothed, lost in a uniform that seemed far too large for him. From her perch in the trees, she had been watching him for some time. He was finally alone.

She reached out and stroked the yellow yarn hair of the rag doll that peeked out of her contoured pack. "Yes, Susanna. I think we've waited long enough."

She smiled at the wiry man. Her blue eyes glittered.

The shock of seeing her still hadn't faded from his face. He gazed longingly at her, drinking in her lithe figure. For a moment she thought he would fall to his knees in reverence. His hands hung limply at their sides. The club at his belt dangled impotently.

"Hello... hello there. Can I help you, madam?"

"Yes, I believe you can," she replied, twirling her golden hair around her finger. She pulled back the gray merchant's cloak she was wearing. The sword, with its silly blue tassel, was in her hand an instant later.

The wiry man's eyes widened.

She plunged the blade into his heart. His body quivered and then sagged to the ground without a sound. He gazed up at her with an almost doe eyed longing as the life drained from him.

His expression took some of the joy out the kill. There was none of the shock and terror she relished, no blind moment of panic or creeping angry realization that usually accompanied a victim's last fleeting moments.

It served her purpose, however.

She took the sword and hacked at the body a few times before ramming the tip of the blade into its chest a final time.

From her observations, Aeliraneth's son had made few friends in Shrevnetska. The villagers likely wouldn't need much convincing.

She tore her dress in a few select places and then rushed into the village.

"Help!" she cried in her best distressed-maiden voice.

CHAPTER 3

ACCUSATION

SOUNDS OF CONFUSION AND CHAOS echoed through the bright noontime air. From his perch along the shingled gable, Cyrus set down his hammer and paused to listen. There was no rhyme or reason to the cascade of voices, only a general sense that something was actually happening in sleepy Shrevnetska.

He scrabbled up the peak and peered out over the rooftops, trying to determine what it was. The chimneys and the painted spire of Ansala's chapel blocked his view, though judging from the sound, the disturbance seemed to be coming from the edge of the village, along the narrow grassy commons that formed a buffer between the buildings and the surrounding forest. Below him, a few of the villagers— fat Olaf in his beer-stained barman's frock, tall Gerda in her wax-covered chandler's apron— scurried toward their houses like rats retreating to their holes.

Cyrus slid down from the roof, landing gracefully on his feet beside the back step. More curious than cautious, he set off to see what calamity had beset Shrevnetska. It had to be more interesting than tapping shingles back into place in the midday sun.

He reached the painted white walls of the chapel, but didn't see anyone about.

The statue of the Prophetess loomed over him like some great weight about to crush him. He glared momentarily at it.

The Illumentry could keep its precious God. There were four Faces of God. Along with Talast, there was Brakeem in the South, ever changing like the shifting desert sands. Chulkan was the Eastern Face, raging like a blood red sunrise. And finally there was Kyento, the Western Face, supposedly serene and wise.

They were all equally worthless.

Lyra had said that they were all the same God, though that had never made sense. It defied logic that something could be one thing and many things at the same time.

Perhaps it gave people some sense of dull contentment to believe the world was an actually an orderly place, that things happened for a reason. He knew all too well how false that was.

The shouting he'd first heard started up again, drawing nearer with each passing moment.

Had something come out of the forest? In broad daylight? The Arkinwood wasn't always the most charitable neighbor.

A woman's scream— Clare Mironescu by the shrill sound of it— rang out. Timid and restrained, she had begun shyly flirting with him over the last year, much to B'lantra's annoyance.

He whirled around. Clare stared at him from a nearby door-way, face white as chalk, eyes three times larger than he'd ever seen them. He barely recognized her.

Whatever attraction she might have felt towards him had vanished. She slammed the door as he stepped closer. The frantic scraping sounds of a bar being drawn across it quickly followed.

Cyrus drew back, suddenly feeling exposed and vulnerable. He'd never been liked here, though Lyra's position as the village physician had helped shield him. He'd been careful to never let them find out he was Aeliraneth's son, but he'd long been used to whispers behind his back and stern, disapproving frowns whenever he walked by. A few even claimed the storms that periodically ripped through the village had started about the same time he'd arrived.

He shivered nervously. If something had happened... and if he was somehow blamed for it...

He stood in the shadow of the chapel. Could he debase himself enough to seek refuge inside? He'd almost rather stick his head in a hangman's noose than ask Dolece for anything.

"There he is. That's the one I saw!"

The voice cut through the afternoon. Cyrus didn't recognize it. Unlike Clare's panicked squawk, it was rich and passionate, almost beautiful in its intensity.

The woman pointing at him was as lovely as her voice. She was tall and lithe, with a face and figure so perfect that any artist worthy of the name would have given their soul to try and capture them. Blue eyes sparkled like a clear lake in the afternoon sun. Long hair hung down over her shoulders in exquisite golden waves. The torn lavender dress and gray cloak she was wearing seemed far too plain for her. A rag doll peered over her shoulder, like some mockery of innocence.

Cyrus could only stare.

Her eyes met his. Ruby lips curled into a subtle smile as Wilyam pushed past, the unwelcome shadow of his brother Petar close behind. Their clubs were out and ready.

Cyrus grimly readied himself, pride refusing to let him flee or seek refuge in the chapel. If Wilyam and Petar wanted a fight, he'd give them one. He'd be able to tell B'lantra he hadn't started it this time.

He barely noticed the golden-haired woman quietly disappear into the shadows.

"You're going to pay for what you did," Wilyam growled.

"What the hell are you talking about?" Cyrus demanded.

The peacekeeper answered with his club. Cyrus ducked under Wilyam's clumsy blow and then slammed his fist into the man's jaw. The impact of bone on bone sent a jarring shock up his arm, but it felt supremely satisfying nonetheless. Wilyam staggered away, blood pouring from his mouth.

Cyrus didn't have time to really appreciate the sight. Petar slammed into him, forcing him back against the wall of the chapel. The peacekeeper's hammy fists pummeled him with a series of quick and vicious blows to the ribs. Cyrus retained enough of his senses to finally bring his knee knifing up into Petar's midsection. The peacekeeper groaned and released his grip. Cyrus gave Petar's exposed shins a hard kick. The man buckled and fell.

Wilyam's large shadow loomed over him. Cyrus caught a brief glimpse of the peacekeeper's club coming at him. It was too late to do anything about it this time. The force of the blow rippled through him like storm winds through the grass. His arms and legs went suddenly numb. The stone steps of the chapel entrance rushed up to meet him… or maybe he rushed down to meet them. He wasn't sure which. His chin bounced off the corner of the steps, clacking his teeth together.

He tried to rise, willing his legs to support the weight of his body. They responded sluggishly. Then a second heavy strike to his spine removed any chance of getting his body to cooperate. Another blow came, and then another as he lay helpless.

"That's enough. I want him alive for now."

Cyrus tried to place the voice. It was aged and gruff, as unforgiving as the stone against his cheek.

"Take him to the cells."

Markov. It was Markov Ansef the sheriff—lank buzzard that he was.

Cyrus didn't know whether to be grateful the beating had ceased or whether to simply redirect his anger onto a new target. Markov had better sense than Wilyam and Petar, but he was no ally.

Soon it didn't matter. As he was seized and roughly dragged away, his body lost its fight to stay conscious.

❊ ❊ ❊

Soren sat quietly. The prescription B'lantra had painstakingly mixed for him lay untouched beside him. The curtains were pulled tight over the windows, just as they'd been all winter.

He was ignoring her, eyes intently boring into the framed line drawing on the shelf across the main room of the thatched farmhouse. The drawing was crude but functional, depicting a happy scene with his wife and children. It was all he had left of them beyond the headstones on their graves outside the house.

"Your leg is looking a lot better now," B'lantra said. "You won't be able to walk properly if you don't start using it soon."

"It hurts," he replied, a hint of irritation showing through his formerly placid mask. "Now leave me be, girl. You've done your duty."

"How about some sunshine then?" she suggested. "I could pull the curtains back, let in a little light. It's a nice day outside."

He only hunched up stubbornly in his chair.

"I'll do it myself then."

She walked over and deftly drew back the curtains. The afternoon sun flooded in, shimmering and bright. Soren blinked, like some cave creature dragged out of its hole.

"Put those back, damn you!"

"The draw string is right here," B'lantra said, holding it up for him to see. "If you want the curtains closed, then you'll have to get up, come over here and close them yourself."

He glared at her as she packed up her medicine bag. She was glad to leave the house, glad to feel the sun on her face again. The birds were singing in the distant trees, and the breeze held the scent of spring blossoms. It was a good day to be alive. If only Soren could be made to see that.

She walked slowly through the village and found a spot to sit near a half-empty hay wagon. Urkasa could barely even be called a village. It probably didn't have ten buildings to its name.

She began rummaging in her bag, daydreams intruding on her normally practical, organized mind. She jumped visibly when the shadow of another human being fell over her.

"Lyra. God's Face, you startled me!"

"Then pay attention to what you're doing. Save the idle fancies for when the work's done."

The older woman glowered down at her harshly before the lines around her wide mouth cracked into a faint smile. Her curly brown hair was shot through with streaks of gray. Her body had thickened a little over the last few years as age had crept over her, but she seemed to have little problem carrying the large bundle on her back.

"I wasn't daydreaming," B'lantra protested. "I was organizing."

"Call it what you like, dear," Lyra replied. "I understand you gave Soren some… encouragement."

"I'm not just going to let him sit there. He should be walking on that leg. I did everything right, but every time I see him, it's the same thing."

"The leg's not his real problem. His family is gone, but he remains. You don't just jump up and walk around happy as can be after that."

"What am I supposed to do with him then? Taking root in a dark room like some mushroom isn't going to bring his family back."

"It's mostly up to him now. I know you want to snap your fingers and make him better overnight, but you can't."

"Actually, I can," B'lantra said, before she thought better of it.

Lyra glanced quickly around. Her voice dropped to a harsh whisper. "You're not Aeliraneth, girl! You know what happens to witches. Do you want them to find you? How many times do you have to be told?"

"I didn't say I was going to. I just said I could," B'lantra said, petulantly. She stood up and pointed down the shabby street to a gangly red-headed woman walking pensively near Soren's house. "She goes every day to take care of him. She probably loves him. But he doesn't even notice her. He just stares at that drawing day in and day out. She lost her family too. They'd be perfect for each other if he'd only move on with his life."

Lyra relaxed a little. "And you might point that out to him, little matchmaker. But do it subtly and let him come to his own conclusions about things."

B'lantra sighed. "I'll… think about it. You might be right."

"It does happen occasionally, you know," Lyra said. "Now

come on. We're done here for the day. I'll be spending the night in Bremen for Andina's childbirth, but we can go back together as far as the fork."

B'lantra retrieved her bag and followed as they made their way out of the village.

As they passed the last house, Lyra finally noticed the silvery silksteel ring on B'lantra's finger. "Now I see why you're match-making and daydreaming today. Finally asked you, did he?"

B'lantra blushed. "You should have seen him. He was so ador-able, all tongue-tied. It was so sweet I didn't have the heart to tell him that if he wanted to marry a Trafari woman, all he had to do was make a bracelet and tie it around my wrist. After that, I just have to complete the *kala ganta*, our ritual of acceptance, and that's all there is to it."

"We're in Northern lands. A bracelet and a Southern ritual won't mean much to anyone around here," Lyra pointed out. "It might be best to stick to the Arakostrian tradition."

"It wouldn't feel right without the *kala ganta*," B'lantra insisted. Lyra's stubborn streak of Arakostrian propriety could be frustrat-ing at times. The physician had given her a home when nobody else would, treated her like a daughter— sometimes too much like a daughter.

It was her wedding after all, not Lyra's.

"I suppose you can do both if it makes you happy," the phy-sician conceded. She looked away for a moment. "Just keep your head on straight and don't get too wrapped up in everything if you want to go on to Denschen College in Erendel."

"You really think they'll take me?" B'lantra asked, inwardly relieved that the subject had changed.

"I think so. I'm just waiting on Mikela Greisz to reply to the letter I sent her. If she approves, then you should be fine. You'll have a silver clover of your own one day."

They walked onwards until they came to the fork and parted ways. B'lantra waited until Lyra was almost gone from sight, waved a final time and then turned towards Shrevnetska.

She walked the earthen path steadily until the village drew near. Two women came hurrying along, wicker baskets on their backs. B'lantra didn't immediately recognize either one of them, though with the drab blouses and skirts they wore, they could have seamlessly blended into any village within three days ride.

She didn't really pay them much attention until parts of the animated conversation they were having reached her ears.

"...doctor's son. Killed that scrawny peacekeeper just like that."

"Why'd he do it?"

"Had it in for him for a while now from what I heard. Some poor merchant woman saw the whole thing. He'd of killed her too if she hadn't run."

"They catch him then?"

"Got him trussed up in chains in the jail."

A queasy dread rippled through B'lantra. She quickly shielded her face and then ducked off the road until the two women had passed.

Cyrus. It had to be Cyrus. And Enric... dead?

Muttering curses under her breath, she frantically paced.

He wouldn't have done it. Cyrus was no pacifist, but he didn't believe in killing. It had to be a mistake.

"Please let it be just a rumor."

If not...

Lyra? Too far away. It would take too long to get to Bremen and back before dark.

Cyrus would have fought when they tried to take him. Wilyam and the rest of the peacekeepers were just looking for an excuse to attack him. Hopefully they hadn't hurt him too badly.

Her heart began to race.

Beregor Amstaad, the town's doddering burgomaster, would be only too happy to be rid of Cyrus. They'd take him to Ashenwall to stand trial before Roshan Ignatius, Shrevnetska's distant ruler. Northern justice. It would be a farce.

If they figured out Cyrus was the son of the Great Witch of Targus, it would be even worse. They'd save him for the Illumentry's witchhunters.

How was she going to free him? The jail was a miniature fortress of ugly stone, and the peacekeepers probably had Cyrus under guard.

"Ashte covan!"

Lyra's countless warnings about using witchcraft came floating back to her. She pushed them away.

❋ ❋ ❋

Cyrus stared around the gritty stone of the Shrevnetska village jail and tugged uncomfortably at the wrought iron collar around his neck. He yanked at the chain that ran from the collar to the wall, hoping that this time—maybe this time— it would pull free of its moorings.

It didn't.

He relaxed his hands and tried to see if he could pull them through the manacles around his wrists, but didn't have any more success than he'd had with the collar and chain. The only reward for his efforts was more scraped skin.

His hair had come loose from the cord that bound it and hung lankly over his face. Carefully reaching up with his bound hands, he tried to brush it away. He winced as the manacles accidentally grazed across his swollen left eye. His head pounded, sending throbbing waves of nausea through his body.

He was little more than a scarecrow mass of cuts and bruises. The peacekeepers hadn't bothered taking the silksteel ring on his finger. That was about the only good thing to be said for his situation.

Judging by the light streaming in from the small, barred window, the day was rapidly teetering toward dusk. With a little food and sleep, he'd be fine in a day or so. His body had always healed with unnatural speed. Along with his nightsight, it was one of the few advantages of being born from someone like Mother. It didn't make him any more comfortable in the meantime though, and if the beating he'd taken was any indication of the peace-keeper's plans for him, then he might not have a day or so.

They weren't even his worst problem. What did the gold-en-haired woman want? His life? If she wanted him dead, she'd hardly need the peacekeepers. It had been ten years. Wasn't that long enough to let the ashes grow cold?

Damn her! Damn Mother!

He eyed the door that led out of his cell, as if by glaring at it harshly enough he could somehow will his way through its heavy wood and reinforced wrought iron bands. The door just sat, solid and massive, blocking his way to freedom and almost mocking him in the process. He was a witch's son after all, not a witch it seemed to say. From behind its thick timbers, he heard the sounds of Markov and the peacekeepers shuffling around.

"You can rot in the pits of Hell!"

The shout was as much at the door as the men beyond.

In response, Markov's bearded face peered through the slot near the top of the door.

"Looks like he's awake."

The door opened. Wilyam and Petar came in, smelling like they'd been keeping the peace more at Olaf's tavern than in the rest of the village. It gave Cyrus some small joy to see Wilyam still tenderly rubbing his freshly split lip and Petar walking in with a limp.

He didn't bother to try and conceal the smirk on his face.

Markov came tromping in behind the brothers, his dark green uniform crisp and pressed, the pocket watch at his belt faintly clinking. Though he was growing a little older, his body showed few signs of age beyond his balding head. Lean and trim, he was as precise and orderly as any soldier. The spectacles on his face gave him a scholarly appearance, though there was nothing erudite in the way the man went about his business.

Enric was the only one missing from the sheriff's little band, though Cyrus found he didn't really miss Enric much at all.

Markov didn't waste any time with pleasantries. "Why'd you do it, boy? What in God's name were you thinking?"

"Do what?" Cyrus demanded. "You can't just lock me up on some woman's word. When Beregor finds out—"

"You think Beregor's going to help you after this? Hell, he might even decide to hang you here, save us taking you all the way to Ashenwall?"

"For what? What the hell is it you think I did?"

"You know damn well. You left your sword by Enric's body—tried to kill that poor woman so there wouldn't be any witnesses. Did you really think we wouldn't catch you?" Markov reached out and cuffed the side of Cyrus' already throbbing head. "The only thing I hate more than murderers is stupid murderers."

"I didn't kill Enric! I wasn't anywhere near him since this morning. That woman is lying to you. You can't believe—"

"I know all about this morning. Wilyam and Petar said you couldn't wait to start trouble. You've had it in for Enric for a while now. It's no great secret."

Cyrus opened his mouth to retort, and then gave up. Markov and the others likely didn't care. They were dogs that had found their bone and were preparing to sink their teeth into it. They wouldn't believe his story about the golden-haired woman. It would just lead to questions. It would lead them to finding out whose son he really was. The inquisitors wouldn't be far behind after that.

"Well?" Markov demanded.

"I don't have anything to say," Cyrus said, and miserably turned away as far as the chains would allow him.

"This is a waste of time," Wilyam said. He gleefully stared down at Cyrus like a boy hovering over a hapless griis-griis fly, debating whether to pull its wings off. "He'll get his soon enough."

"Agreed," Markov said. "Let him fester. We need to see to Enric. Go find Beregor and see if he still wants to send word to

Ashenwall. If not, we'll just set up the gallows in the town square. It's been a while since we've had a good hanging."

The sheriff gave Cyrus another look of disgust and then stalked out of the cell. Petar followed a moment later. Wilyam waited until they had left and then reached for the collar around Cyrus' neck and yanked it brutally downwards.

"Enric's wife was with child. Did you know that? Did you even care?" Wilyam demanded.

"I said I didn't kill him. What part of that didn't your pig brain understand?" Cyrus gasped.

"I understand just fine. I understand that I'm going to enjoy watching you hang. The best part is I get to see the look on your foreign bitch's pretty face when your neck snaps."

Wilyam used his heavy hand to grind the side of Cyrus' face against the dirty stone floor before he stepped back and then left the cell.

"Goat-raping peasant," Cyrus muttered once the door closed.

His head began throbbing more intensely. He reached into his pocket for the blocks. They were still there, apparently too unimportant for the peacekeepers to be concerned with.

He ground them together, trying not to think about how much trouble he was in. It was hard not to suddenly imagine the feel of the rope around his neck.

Finally, he put the blocks away and started to examine the manacles and the chain, looking once more for some weakness he could exploit. Finding none, he surveyed the cell again until he noticed a square nail sticking up from the loose masonry around the barred window to the outside.

If he could work it free, it might make a suitable lock pick. It was a slim hope, but it was the only one he had at the moment.

CHAPTER 4

A DARK DEPARTURE

THUNDER BOOMED THROUGH THE VALLEY, shaking the jail. Lightning split the sky. Cyrus shifted over and peered through the barred window of his cell.

Shrevnetska hadn't changed in the few hours he'd been unconscious, nor had the people in it. Kregor, the machinist for the nearby sawmill, walked by with his wife Olla. Their clothing was a perfect match for the drab town. B'lantra had complained more than once about the Northerners' almost vicious hatred for color, and he couldn't really argue with her.

News of his capture had probably spread all over town and was streaking its way to the neighboring settlements. Such was the way of things in places like Shrevnetska. Why had Mother ordered Lyra to bring him here? If there had been a reason, he could no longer remember it.

Of all the godforsaken places Mother could have picked.

The sky above was the only thing different. The red and gold of the sunset was streaked with a little purple, but it was fading, overtaken by a dark phalanx of approaching storm clouds. He watched them roll and tumble chaotically in the sky. The storm fairies came with them, dancing in the shifting wind currents. It was a fae storm, as the locals called it— the second one already since the cold of winter had broken.

Why had they plagued Shrevnetska? It was tempting to think Mother had something to do with it, but that was impossible. She was long dead.

The air changed, becoming laden with a sense of wild frenzy. The lithe fairies dove and swooped, sometimes in formation, sometimes haphazardly flitting about on their little bat-like wings. They were purple and black striped harbingers, nearly blending into the storm clouds behind them. Saffron sparks streamed out from their long, tangled hair. Lightning played back and forth as they drew energy in from the charged air and tossed it gleefully around.

The wind picked up, sending large drops of rain pounding against the walls of the jail. Through the trees a low bellow echoed, momentarily drowning out the sound of the rain and wind.

A troika most likely. The snaggle-toothed horrors would rise from their burrows deep in the forest, stirred up by the storm. It would probably be a wild night. The troika would hunt. The kurikai cats would prowl, and the fairies would rampage until tomorrow's dawn put an end to their madness.

As if he didn't have enough to worry about.

He turned his efforts back to the nail, working steadily at it until at last it came free. Taking his prize, he began to awkwardly work on the manacles.

It took him a moment to become aware of the song. Its sound hovered just above the cadence of the rain, soothing and peaceful in contrast to the growing fury of the storm.

B'lantra. She'd been so careful for so long.

"This has nothing to do with you. And this is the last place you need to be right now. I'll be fine."

From the adjacent room came the muted thump of bodies falling on the floor. The song dropped to a dull whisper and then finished with a pleasant flourish. Keys jingled. The door that had so infuriated him before now swung open. Lantern light flooded into his darkened cell.

The Trafari girl was soaked. Her dark hair lay wet and plastered over her face. Her yellow and white dress was dripping. The worn leather medicine bag under her cloak was drier, if not by much.

"Get out of here. If they find out—"

Her eyes locked onto him. She set the lantern down and swept across the room to embrace him before he ever got a chance to finish his sentence.

"Did you seriously think I was going to just leave you here?" she asked.

"Witchcraft, Bel? You'll bring the inquisitors down on us. If they find you, you'll hang right beside me… or worse."

At the mention of inquisitors a tremor of unspoken dread seemed to go up her spine. Her bottom lip started to tremble before she caught herself. "It was the only way I could get to you. Besides, no one saw me. They'll never know."

He could only hope she was right.

She quickly began using the key she'd taken to unlock the multitude of chains that bound him. The collar fell from his neck with a blissful clang. He took a few uncertain steps forward before stumbling and bumping up against her shoulder. She steadied him with surprising strength for her small frame.

"You look terrible," she concluded.

"I love you too," he said, managing a weak grin.

They made their way into the anteroom of the jail. Rain pelted in through the open door to the outside. Wilyam and Petar were splayed out over the floor like refuse someone had forgotten to throw away.

"I didn't know you could do that," Cyrus said, arching an eyebrow in surprise.

"I wasn't sure I could either," B'lantra replied. "The fire inside them kept flaring back up whenever I tried to dampen it."

"Where's Markov?"

"Checking in on the widow Anca last I saw, but he could be anywhere."

"And the golden-haired woman?"

"No one has seen her since they dragged you off. She's the same one you told me about, isn't she?"

Cyrus nodded.

"We need to leave while we can then," B'lantra said. "I don't know how long Wilyam and Petar are going to stay this way."

Wilyam stirred even before she'd finished speaking. He rolled over and blinked his eyes, as if he'd just awoken from a deep sleep.

"No, you don't!"

Cyrus swiftly moved in before Wilyam could get his bearings. A quick blow to the side of the head put the peacekeeper back down on the floor. Cyrus gave him a few more just to be sure.

"Was that really necessary?" B'lantra asked.

Cyrus glanced down at the cuts and bruises still covering his body and gave Wilyam another swift kick.

"Yes."

He turned away and then looked over the room, taking note of the swords and muskets neatly lined in their case by the wall and the key to the powder room on Petar's belt. He'd wanted a musket for a while, and now seemed as good a time as any to claim one.

Footsteps came through the door before he reached the case.

"*Vashaenit!*" B'lantra hissed.

Markov only hesitated for a moment. He ignored B'lantra and leveled his musket at Cyrus.

The Trafari girl's song was soft at first. Then it rose with fearful intensity. Markov's musket grew warmer. Flames danced along its length. The stock began to smolder. The sheriff cried out and threw the weapon down as if it had turned into a snake.

His astonishment turned to rage. "Witch! You're a damned witch!"

He ripped his sword from his sheath. B'lantra shrank back at his sudden fury. Cyrus rushed for the weapons case and grabbed up one of the swords there. B'lantra's song cracked and went silent. She frantically scrambled away from Markov. He followed. She hurled her lantern at him. Markov dodged and kept coming. Her eyes darted around for something else to defend herself. The only thing she found was an old broom.

Markov's movement was quick and clean. A strike from his

sword cleaved the broom handle in half. B'lantra stared at him in terror. He drew the blade back and prepared to run her through.

Cyrus pounced on him before he got the chance. Markov was an experienced fighter, and more agile than Cyrus would have given him credit for. He shifted his focus from B'lantra in plenty of time to parry Cyrus' attack. The witch's son pressed his advantage. Markov didn't panic. His retreat was smooth and orderly, just like everything else about him. A riposte nearly punched through Cyrus' guard.

Markov didn't let up. Cyrus began to tire. It had been too long since he'd put the proper time into sword practice. Every movement began to feel like he was slogging through sand. His body ached. It was already starting to recover from the beating earlier in the day, but it was in no shape for a prolonged fight.

Markov didn't intend to let it go that long anyway. His sword swept in. Cyrus was too slow to counter. The blade pierced the shoulder of his sword arm, barely missing his heart. Cyrus' weapon fell from his hand.

Markov stepped forward to finish him.

"Enough!"

B'lantra's hands shook as she held the blackened musket. "Put the sword down, or I'll put you down."

Markov stared at her. His spectacles gleamed in the flickering light of the room.

"You'll kill me anyway," he said with contempt.

B'lantra's gaze was frightened, but firm. "I won't if I don't have to."

Markov pursed his lips as he considered. "Alright. Have it your way, witch. You're not worth dying over."

Cyrus slid over and gingerly picked his sword back up. His shoulder burned. His shirt was already coated in his own blood. He pointed the tip of the blade at the sheriff.

"Time to see how you like it in chains."

"You won't get far, you know," Markov said as he was prodded towards the cell. "The inquisitors will find you. They always find witches. You'll wish you'd hanged."

"We'll do just fine," Cyrus replied through gritted teeth.

Inwardly, he didn't feel near as confident. Even if they managed to escape, their troubles were just beginning.

✳ ✳ ✳

Heavy sheets of wind and rain hammered down on her the instant B'lantra stepped beyond the doorway of the jail. Even sheltered in her cloak, the light from her lantern came perilously close to being snuffed out. Her heart began to race at the mere thought.

In the time it had taken her to free Cyrus, the storm had murdered the placid evening and raised a howling, rain-streaked murk from its corpse. The occasional shriek and bellow rang forth from the trees, and a barrage of crazed laughter filtered down from the storm fairies overhead. The gocochen and the jerukin oxen bayed miserably from their stables.

From inside it had seemed far less frenzied. The light coming from the doorway behind her suddenly seemed safe and comforting, even though she knew there was no going back.

"It's just dark is all," Cyrus said, as she nervously dug her fingernails into his arm.

He didn't mind it the way she did. The nightsight he'd been born with rendered it in a kaleidoscope of distinctive grays for him. She wasn't so fortunate.

He pulled the door to the jail shut and locked it behind them. With a quick twist he snapped the key off in the lock.

He was hurting. She could see it in his face, feel it with every breath he took.

"We need to get you tended to. You're in no condition to go anywhere," she said.

"I'll be fine," he insisted.

"No, you won't." She clamped down more tightly on his arm. "We can't just run blindly off in the dark. We need supplies…

a plan. And we have to find some way to warn Lyra."

"We'll go to the house then. We have a little time before those fools figure a way out."

He handed her the wrapped bundle of weapons and gunpowder they'd stolen from the jail, and they started forward. No one tried to stop them. Shrevnetska's residents were hunkered down in their homes like turtles in their shells. It would probably be daybreak before any of them dared to stick their heads out.

The journey would have been a brief, even pleasant, walk in other circumstances, but in the storm it seemed like it took forever. They slowly picked their way through a tangle of broken branches and flooded streets. Debris flew past them, clattering off into the night. The wind buffeted them mercilessly, moaning savagely as though the very existence of the village was an affront to it.

For an instant, B'lantra thought she heard a remnant of song carried on the wind's fury. It was strangely familiar, like an old tune she should remember. Almost as soon as she became aware of it, it vanished. Had it even been real? Sounds really couldn't be trusted in a fae storm.

At last the darkened house appeared out of the gloom, its oak walls weather-beaten and worn but still sturdy. Water poured off the roof, splashing manically down into an overflowing rain barrel. Just as Cyrus opened the door, her lantern finally gave out.

She gasped in terror as the darkness consumed her. Her body went rigid. Her song called to her. Flame. Beautiful flame. Flame would chase the blackness away and keep her safe.

"It's just the night, Bel. We're home. You know where everything is. It'll be alright," Cyrus whispered gently in her ear.

His voice helped. It was like a beacon on a stormy sea. She frantically grabbed at him as he pulled her through the door. She felt around to reassure herself that everything was where it should be. At last her fingers found the kitchen table. Cyrus sat her down in a chair. She then heard him going through the house drawing all the curtains closed.

"Did you hear anything outside?" he asked her from the parlor. "Like a voice on the wind?"

"I'm not sure," she answered, irritably. "Maybe I... No, never mind! Matches. I can't stand anymore dark!"

"We might not have any left. Stay put, and I'll see if there's some upstairs."

"That will take too long."

She hurriedly set the lantern on the table and began her song. Her voice was tight, her rhythm off.

"That's the hearth song, isn't it?" Cyrus noted. "Something about fires and the tea kettle when the old dwarf comes home."

She nodded without breaking the melody. A small ember sprang up on the end of the lantern wick and then ignited in a hot white flash. Flame burst forth, voraciously eating at the wick and already starting to search for its next meal. For an instant it thought about trying to escape the confines of the lantern case. B'lantra changed her tempo in time to stop it.

"Calm," she sang.

Her voice became gentler. The flame was new and didn't know any better. Like any child, it needed to be taught how to behave. It became calmer as her heart began to slow and her fears began to recede. Finally it stabilized, filling the kitchen with a beautifully flickering radiance. B'lantra brought the song to an end.

"You're amazing, you know," Cyrus said, blinking as his eyes adjusted to the sudden light. "Matches are few and far between until the spring traders come through, and here I have the one girl who doesn't need them."

B'lantra smiled briefly at the compliment, but then felt her mood darken again. "I'm not amazing at all. I panicked. I never thought Markov would... be so angry. He moved so fast and I... I couldn't think of any words for the song. I couldn't make it do what I wanted. If you hadn't stopped him..."

He gave her a kiss on the check. "You did just fine. I'm out of that damned cell because of you. We have a chance now. But ...

we can't stay here, Bel. The inquisitors will come looking for us."

She stared into the flame of the lantern. Suddenly its light seemed too dim. The shadows in the room felt larger and more frightening.

The inquisitors always came when word spread of a witch— like vultures drawn to a carrion feast. Black coated. Black cloaked. Pitiless. Merciless. The stories had left her clutching at her mother's skirts in terror when she was a child. They were the monsters of the night she had to hide from; monsters that could never be allowed to find her.

If they didn't hang her or burn her at the stake, they would turn her into one of the Sisters. It was almost better to burn.

She sighed and then turned to look at Cyrus. "Let's see how badly Markov and those other skish hurt you."

It gave her something to think about other than inquisitors and witches.

"I already said I'm fine," he protested, restlessly squirming as she began to examine the bruises and cuts dotting his body. He winced as she began cleaning the sword wound on his shoulder. "I'll be good as new by tomorrow."

"You're lucky you even have a tomorrow. If that blade had been a little farther over I'd be mourning you," she said, fishing into her damp medicine bag. She pulled out some ointment and applied it to the wound. "Stop fidgeting. I hate it when you do that."

"I wouldn't fidget if you'd quit poking and prodding me."

B'lantra continued her work despite his objections, stripping off his torn and sodden clothes whenever they got in her way. "We go through this every time you get hurt. I'm sorry my healing song doesn't work on you, but you'll just have to live with it. I swear you're going to break yourself one day, and I won't be able to fix it."

"I wasn't trying to get stabbed, you know," he groused.

She finished as quickly as she could. "There… you're fine. You might even live."

"Thank you," he said, a little reluctantly. "For everything. You really are amazing. Though I still can't believe you were going to shoot Markov."

"I wasn't really going to, but I suppose he didn't know that. I probably would have missed anyway. I hate guns."

"You may have to get used to them. We should probably get what we need and go."

"Do we even know where we're going?"

"Somewhere that doesn't have peacekeepers or inquisitors," he said. He dug out a battered traveling pack from one of the cabinets and began tossing food into it. "We'll figure out the rest on the way to wherever it is."

"That's not an answer," B'lantra said as she retrieved her own pack and began searching around to see what they could scavenge. It suddenly felt like she was a thief in her own house. "You don't know what that golden-haired woman wants or why she's trying to frame you for Enric's murder?"

He didn't look up from his packing. "I don't know any more now than I did ten years ago. I just know we need to be somewhere she isn't."

"She's not likely to make that easy."

"I know."

B'lantra stared around, trying to decide what to take and what had to be left. It amazed her to see how many things she'd collected in the ten years she'd lived in Shrevnetska. Her beloved carvings looked mournfully at her from the shelves. The baubles and knick-knacks glittered on the shelves trying to entice her to take a few of them with her. Her guitar, with its bright paint and colorful etchings, beckoned.

She was Trafari. She should know better. She'd spent her childhood selling wares from the back of a wagon. Space was precious. Each thing had to have a place or it had to be left behind.

"*H'vanna kriteph. H'vanna vantan.* Go swiftly. Go lightly," she whispered to herself.

45

They were things, and she'd never really thought about missing them. What had she gotten herself into? She hadn't thought it through, hadn't planned the way she should have.

Lyra wouldn't have approved. B'lantra cast a sad glance over at the physician's padded chair. Would she even see Lyra again? With any luck, the inquisitors would follow them and leave Lyra alone. There was no way to really be sure. The thought haunted her as she stripped out of the yellow and white nurse's dress and found a russet tunic and form fitting trousers.

She'd worked so hard to build a new life for herself here, tried so hard to learn the strange ways of the Northerners and get them to like her. The people of Shrevnetska held little love for Trafari beyond the bright wares they brought. They considered them thieves, gypsies and until recently, enemies to be vanquished. The Trafari revered Brakeem, the Southern Face of God— more than enough reason to dislike them. '*Straik*' was the less polite term, though it had been several years since any of the townspeople had openly uttered it in front of her.

She'd have to give up her plans to go to Denschen College. Her chances of acceptance had been tenuous before.

Now? It was almost incomprehensible that everything could be gone so quickly.

She sighed and gazed down at the ring Cyrus had given her.

Where would they go? There were few places in the world that would openly welcome a witch and a witch's son. Even her own people didn't want her. The Trafari caravans that came through … they knew. The subtle hand signs they made when she came near were clear enough. They wouldn't turn her over to the Illumentry, but that was as far as their charity extended.

She finished her packing and joined Cyrus as he stood in the kitchen by the fairy stone board. The pieces were still laid out exactly as they had been this morning.

"I guess we won't be playing again anytime soon." Her voice was suddenly choked.

He reached down and selected two of the pieces, keeping one and handing the other to her.

She tried to smile. "The king and queen, is it?"

"It's our game. Our rules. It's still ours no matter where we go." He pulled her gently to him and gave her a kiss on the cheek. "It will be all right."

She returned his embrace, then released him and shouldered her pack.

"I left a note under Lyra's pillow. I don't know what else we can do," Cyrus said. He stared at the front door. "Are you ready? It's going to be a long road."

"I grew up a wanderer, Cyrus. I can be one again." B'lantra took a last look around the house. "Now let's just go before I do something stupid like crying over a few baubles and carvings."

Cyrus checked the sword at his side and slipped an oil cloth over his newly acquired musket before slinging it over his shoulder. They set out, faces locked into the storm. B'lantra cradled the lantern, gently singing to it to keep it alight. Their old life slowly receded behind them, a retreating memory lost to the night.

CHAPTER 5

SCHEMES IN THE STORM

THE WOLFHOUND'S TAWNY FUR was raised nervously along its back, though it hadn't bared its teeth. From the corner of the old barn, it studied the company of men taking shelter from the storm. There were twelve of them, all heavily armed. The carriage they had brought with them was as black as their uniforms. The cramped steel cage it towed was carefully inscribed with a myriad of faintly shimmering glyphs.

Etienne Caulter watched warily as the wolfhound cautiously approached. It was large for its kind, almost unnaturally so. There was something he didn't like about the way its umber eyes flitted about. Intelligence lurked behind its shaggy gaze, far more than a hound should really possess. The company's horses snorted their disdain and stamped in warning. Undeterred, the wolfhound sniffed at the contents of the saddlebags they carried.

Caulter disabused it of the idea with an imperious glare. The wolfhound shrank back into the shadows. Charity wasn't the company's business, today or any other.

Myron, their carriage driver, pulled his pistol out and took aim at the crouching animal.

"Leave it," another man said. "It's not worth the bullet."

Caulter gave the wolfhound another glance and then walked away from the assembled men towards the exit to the crumbling barn. The storm outside almost seemed to intensify as he stared out into it. Rain pounded the old planks of the barn mercilessly. Lightning flashed, briefly lighting up the turbulent clouds behind. The wind picked up, trying but failing to rifle though his close-cropped brown hair and carefully groomed beard.

Caulter pulled his leather greatcoat more closely around his thick, muscled frame to make sure the silver pistols at his belt would stay dry. He still had his sword, but there was no sense in losing an advantage.

He might need every advantage he could get.

The weather was working against him, not so much because of the wind and rain, but for the enchantment it possessed. It confused his senses, blending scents together into a tortured jumble. Witches and fae creatures could easily hide, their smell washed away in the chaos the storm would bring with it.

From the reports he'd read, the entire area was periodically plagued by such storms. No official explanation had been offered. There were also plenty of accounts of fae activity, though that was hardly surprising given its proximity to the Arkinwood. Beyond the town of Shrevnetska and the old fortress of Ashenwall, there was little of interest.

The richness of the air almost hurt, but like the men he traveled with, he would suffer through it until it passed. Such was the lot of an inquisitor sometimes. Misfortune was simply another challenge to overcome, not a thing to cower before.

Still, the sad fact of the matter was that ill luck had stalked him ever since this hunt had started.

Another of the company came to stand beside him: Captain Bovashar Bregna. He was taller and thinner than Caulter. His hair was the color of sun-bleached sand and as yet unmarred by the streaks of gray that had begun to subtly creep into Caulter's. Only a few dimples broke up the continuity of Bregna's pale, aristocratic face. There was a faint silvery hue to his eyes, a side effect of the dose of silverworm he'd taken before the company had left their compound in Targus.

Bregna was young and talented. His rise to captain had been nearly unprecedented within the normally careful ranks of the Inquisition. The witches and fae they sought out were oftentimes dangerous prey, and ambitious hunters tended to die quickly.

He was also part of the ill luck as far as Caulter was concerned.

"We can't wait much longer, Lieutenant. Have the men prepare to move," Bregna ordered.

Caulter gave him a questioning look. There was no real advantage to going anywhere in the storm. Even an inquisitor would be vulnerable on a night like this. Surely their quarry wouldn't be going anywhere either. In truth, he wasn't even sure of the target. They had simply been ordered to travel south from Targus along the Red Road. Bregna was the only one who seemed to know anything more, and the Captain had been taciturn at best.

"How much farther are we going, Sir?"

"Far enough. This should be a simple hunt. Once it's done, I'm sure the alchemists will have a cure ready for your little… conundrum. What is she now, ten? Eleven?"

The brow of Caulter's broad, sun-beaten face curled. His square jaw tightened. That was yet another part of the ill luck. Admitting Teresa's existence to the Illumentry hadn't turned out the way he'd hoped. It had been a desperate gamble that the Illumentry alchemists, the best in the known world, could succeed in curing his stricken daughter when every doctor, healer and shaman he could lay hands on had failed.

It was a gamble that had gone poorly.

"She's twelve now, Sir."

"Well, twelve years too late to take care of a problem is still better than not taking care of it at all, I suppose," Bregna continued. "And there's also the matter of your… is 'wife' the proper word for such a woman?"

Ysolde was beyond the Illumentry's grasp at least. Caulter could take a small comfort in that.

"She's with God now," he stated, flatly.

"That solves a problem then. I imagine her kind would go to a god of some sort when they die, wouldn't they?"

"I'm sure they do, Sir."

Caulter said nothing else. The fae and the witches could have

Bregna. If the Illumentry alchemists were good on their word, then this was the last hunt he would undertake.

A faint rustle came from behind him. The sharp crack of a pistol being fired followed an instant later.

Caulter whirled around. The wolfhound had vanished. So had Myron.

"What happened?" Bregna demanded.

"It sprang from the darkness and took him," one of the men said. "I wounded it, but it fled off into the night."

"Shoot straighter next time," Bregna said, coldly. "Fan out, all of you. And stay in pairs."

Caulter's heart began to race before the silverworm in his body soothed his anxiety. He quietly cursed. He should have recognized the wolfhound for what it was: lupesku, a fae creature. It could assume several different forms, though it usually chose that of a wolf or large dog. They fed on livestock mostly, though they weren't above making a meal of an unwary traveler. On a normal night, the inquisitors would have quickly tracked it down by the smell of its enchantment and dispatched it. Tonight though, it had grown bold. The storm would make finding it far more difficult, a fact the lupesku knew well.

He drew his sword and cautiously crept out of the barn. Nicolai, one of the newer recruits, went with him.

The wind and rain lashed out at Caulter. In the distance, the trees bent before the might of the storm. The silverworm the inquisitors took saw to it that the darkness was no barrier to him. It enhanced him in other ways, giving him reflexes and endurance few men could match. It soothed his fears and dulled his feelings.

Emotion led to misjudgment. Misjudgment led to a quick end when dealing with witches and fae.

Caulter sniffed the air, but sensed nothing other than the chaos of the storm. The lupesku probably hadn't gone far. If it was like the others he'd encountered, the creature had a lair nearby. They would have to track it like any other hunters.

✳ ✳ ✳

The shelter of Shrevnetska was now a distant dream, lost hours ago to the storm overhead and the smothering embrace of the Arkinwood. Trees hemmed B'lantra in on all sides, clutching ever closer to the path she was on. The thick trunks were ancient and massive, like great giants holding court over the land.

The forest had been their unlikely ally so far, providing a cover for their escape and shelter from prying eyes. There had been no signs of pursuit from either the inquisitors or the golden-haired woman, though she had no idea how long that would last. They were headed to a cave Cyrus had discovered years ago. It would do for a start. At least it provided some shelter from the storm… and from the Arkinwood.

B'lantra nervously chewed her lip as she stared out into the night. A day ago she would have considered it insanity for them to be out here. The forest was filled with shrieks and cries. Every so often she heard the sound of something large and probably hungry crashing through the undergrowth.

Cyrus suddenly stopped. Even in the paltry glow of the lantern, she could see his face was troubled. He paced back and forth uncertainly, hovering just at the edge of the pool of light. His hand kept straying towards the pistols he'd taken from the peacekeeper's armory.

"What's wrong?" she asked.

The forest seemed to swallow the words up.

"This doesn't look right. We should've reached the cave by now," Cyrus said back.

Her voice rose in alarm. "You mean we're lost? How can we be lost? You know these woods."

"We're not lost. I know where we are and where we need to go. But the damned trees won't let us. I swear they're moving."

"They're rooted in place. How can they be moving?"

"I don't know. Why don't you ask them? Or better yet, burn a few of them down with that song of yours."

Her pulse began to miserably pound. The Arkinwood was an old forest, and despite generations of settlement little headway had been made in thinning it out. In fact, the denizens of the wood sometimes did a fair job of thinning out the people who lived near it.

She glanced anxiously back the way they'd come. There was only a thick tapestry of twisted boughs before her. The path they'd just traveled abruptly disappeared as if it had never been.

"It's gone!"

"That's what I've been trying to tell you."

She slid closer to him. "It's alive, isn't it?"

"It is tonight," he answered. "It gets better. Shine the light ahead. What do you see?"

She held the lantern tentatively forward. "Looks like the path we're following keeps going."

"Except this isn't the right way. I swear this path wasn't even here before."

B'lantra cocked her head suddenly as the song reached her ears. Its tendrils formed from the whisper of the trees. The creak of the branches above, the hiss of the wind ripping through the new leaves, the cries of the forest creatures— every noise of the night was a part of the song, but not the whole of it. The will and intent lurking within the sounds pushed at her mind. The cadence was fast and harsh to match the rising rhythm of her heartbeat.

"Do you hear—?"

"Yes."

"It's the same song I heard in the village."

Cyrus took her arm. "Come on. The Arkinwood won't let us just stay here."

The first stirrings came from the dark: the faint crackle of warping wood above the thrum of the rain, the whisper of the grass bending as something moved through it. It was all too easy for B'lantra to imagine the trees closing in, the roots inexorably pushing through the damp forest soil, the branches slowly reaching for her.

Cyrus pulled her away before she could think on it anymore. They fled down the narrow path that seemed to suspiciously open up for them. Several times they tried to turn off, only to find dense thickets blocking their passage.

The song continued to croon softly in the night, beckoning them onwards. B'lantra thought she should know the words, but she couldn't quite make them out. They teased her, hovering at the edge of understanding. She walked behind Cyrus, almost pathetically glad of the shield of light around her.

At last the trees thinned out, and they came to a clearing. The Dry Run pushed its way out of the forest here. It was prophetically named in the hot, dusty months when the sun scorched it to little more than a crying trickle, but it was anything but empty now. Emboldened by the pounding rain, its muddy waters surged out of its channel, rushing overtop the green grass and colorful spring wildflowers. The Karrak, Shrevnetska's old sawmill, stood beyond, revealing itself to her bit by bit with every flash of lightning overhead. A narrow strip of dry land led to the entrance.

Cyrus had taken her to see it in the bright sunshine once, but the Karrak looked far different than B'lantra remembered. It had been abandoned years ago when the loggers had pushed too deeply into the forest and angered its denizens. Retaliation had been swift and certain. From the stories still whispered around town, few of the workers had lived through the night.

It was a forlorn thing now, a hulking relic slowly being digested by the forest. Its dilapidated wooden walls seemed dark and twisted. There was a gaping hole in the roof that looked like it had been punched in by some great hand. The waterwheel skulked in the bubbling flood like a hungry predator waiting to spring out at them if they ventured too close.

"Can we go around?" she asked, leaning closer so Cyrus could hear her over the sound of the storm.

"Not unless you know how to fly. The water's moving too fast to cross, and the forest isn't going to let us go back," he replied.

"Whoever's singing that song wants us in there!"

"Staying here isn't going to help. Come on. You're the girl who doesn't need matches, remember."

At first she wondered how he could be so calm about everything. Then she felt him trembling against her. Saying a quick prayer to Brakeem and to Saint Rachael, she began her own song again to keep the lantern lit. Reluctantly they crept towards the mill. Out of the shelter of the trees, the rain poured down, prickling her skin. The wind snatched at her, threatening to knock her off balance.

They drew closer, walking along the narrow pathway that led over the waterwheel and the rushing water below. The worn wooden railing was slick to the touch. The door to the inside flapped helplessly in the wind.

She reached almost unconsciously for Cyrus' hand, trying to get her nerves to stop jangling. The dark pressed against her, building on the blind fear she'd had since childhood. It was a vicious predator with no purpose for its existence beyond leaving her terrified and vulnerable. It couldn't be reasoned with. Light was the only weapon that would work against it, and that was just a temporary victory. That just got you through another day. It was relentless, eternal. It would always win.

The flame in the lantern sputtered and threatened to go out. She changed the timbre of her song, her notes more a desperate plea to the flame than the encouragement she'd given it earlier.

If it went out…

God help her if it went out!

It was quieter within the Karrak. The flame blissfully perked back up. No monster of the night rose to devour her. Even the song that had led them here seemed to have subsided. Instead, the squeaks of rats moving through the ruins greeted her, as did the gentle coo of the birds nesting amidst the wooden rafters.

She peered around with the lantern, wishing its range extended farther. The spindly machines of the mill stood rusty and idle, their gears clogged with ivy. They loomed all around her, monsters in their own right, still and silent. Warped saw blades sat impotent, blunted teeth eternally lodged into the decadent wooden flesh of the decaying logs.

Cyrus stood beside her. His hand once again hovered near his pistols.

"Anything?" she asked.

He quickly shook his head.

Mindful of tripping and falling over the mass of tangled gears and rotted timber scattered around the muddy floor, she followed him as he cautiously moved farther away from the door.

She felt the presence before they'd gone more than a few paces, almost as if they'd stepped into another world. The hair on the back of her neck rose.

It was just an image: long, wild red hair almost like flame, eyes greener than any emerald in any story she'd ever heard.

Celaan. The name seared itself into her thoughts.

It was familiar.

B'lantra paused. It shouldn't be familiar. The name meant nothing to her as far as she knew. And yet just like the song in the night, it felt like a name she should know. It was almost as if she were meeting an old friend she'd forgotten— or reliving a nightmare that should have long since retreated into the opaque nothingness of her dreams. She didn't know which it was, and it only made the feeling worse.

It seemed an eternity before she could force herself to turn her head and look in front of her.

Celaan was sitting on a pile of cut timber underneath the hole in the roof, beautiful, though it was a beauty that didn't quite feel human. There wasn't really any other way B'lantra could think to describe her. Epic bards and poets might have found better words, but such things were beyond her skill at the moment.

The woman before her seemed unaffected by the rain, perfectly dry while the storm raged. Long fiery hair cascaded back over her shoulders. Her skin was a light bronze, like fields of wheat shimmering in the late summer sun. Her dress was a rich green to match the color of the forest outside. The fiercely glowing sigil of the Aeore, God's Firstborn, wrapped around her tall and elegant body. It was a crackling, writhing ribbon of energy.

It somehow reminded B'lantra of a snake coiling around her. The smile that came from the woman's red lips held about as much warmth.

❋ ❋ ❋

There were claw marks on the trees. Ten paces back there was a five toed footprint in the mud that had come from no natural animal. They were close to the lupesku's lair. The beast had returned, probably intending to devour what was left of Myron.

Caulter glanced around the darkened copse of trees they had come to. It was rocky here. There was probably a cave or burrow nearby.

He stopped suddenly. The ground was wrong. It felt hollow beneath his feet. As he shifted his weight he thought he heard the faint sound of a branch cracking.

"Let's be done with this then," Nicolai said.

The other inquisitor started forward.

"Wait!"

It was instinct that saved Caulter more than his inquisitor's training. He'd been a soldier long before he'd taken his commission as a witchhunter. The first rule of war was to stay alive. Instinct had told him to duck when Trafari marksmen had him set in their sights. Instinct had bid him lie in wait as Kyseri barbarians had overrun his watch post.

Branches cracked, loudly this time. Nicolai croaked in astonishment as the thin covering of branches and dirt gave way and he plummeted into the pit below. Caulter caught himself just before he joined him. Below him, Nicolai's cries suddenly went silent.

The trap had been well thought out. While some fae creatures possessed considerable intelligence, few of them had the foresight to set snares for their would-be hunters. The lupesku were an annoying exception. Caulter already knew what he would see as he looked down. Nicolai lay lifelessly at the bottom. The reddened tips of the sharpened spikes that had been set there poked up through his corpse.

Inquisitors were naturally resistant to the spells witches used and the glamours fae creatures employed. Sometimes it didn't help. It was why ambitious hunters died quickly. It was a lesson Nicolai would never learn.

The lupesku streaked from the darkness just as Caulter pulled himself back out of the pit. Freed from the need for deception, the creature had assumed its true form. It's large, sinewy body was covered in a thick pelt of coarse brown fur. Its snout was long and wide; its mouth filled with a set of gleaming fangs. Large pointed ears stood on its wolf-like head. It had four long and powerful arms. The smaller set ended in curved claws, much like a lion's. The larger set was cruder, better suited to digging than to grasping.

Caulter sidestepped its charge. Claws raked across his face. The lupesku turned and sprang again. Caulter wasn't fast enough to avoid it this time. It slapped the sword from his hand and then bore him to the muddy ground. He locked his hand around its throat to keep its fangs from tearing off his face. The same umber eyes that had characterized the wolfhound glared furiously at him. Its lower arms tore at him. Only the silksteel weave of his uniform prevented him from being eviscerated.

Even with the aid of the silverworm, the creature was far stronger than he was. Its fangs drew ever closer. Caulter snaked his other hand down to his pistol. He pulled it from its leather holster and pressed it against the creature's belly. It lurched upwards as he pulled the trigger.

Caulter quickly got to his feet and retrieved his sword. The lupesku gathered itself. Its side was soaked in blood, its breathing labored.

It charged at him once more. He was an inquisitor. It expected no mercy from him. He gave it none.

His blade pierced its heart. The lupesku stiffened. Its jaws snapped defiantly at him one last time before it sagged to the earth. Caulter felt no triumph, only the vague satisfaction of a job completed. He raised his sword and severed the beast's head from its body to keep it from rising again.

From behind him came the soft sound of black-booted footsteps approaching.

Bregna slid smoothly out of the darkness. "It won't be preying on anyone again."

"Nicolai didn't survive," Caulter said.

Bregna walked over to the pit and looked briefly down. "Unfortunate."

"We should see to him at least."

"Leave him. We have an appointment to keep further south."

"Sir?"

"You heard me. Gather the men back together."

Bregna turned and walked away.

Caulter cast a last look down at Nicolai. More ill luck.

Misfortune was simply another challenge to overcome, not a thing to cower before. It wasn't always possible. Such was the lot of an inquisitor sometimes.

CHAPTER 6

EMPRESS

HONEY, THE FLOW OF THE RIVER, the buzzing of the bees and the cry of the circling hawk: her voice was all of these things, sweet and melodic in a way that sent a chill down Cyrus' spine.

"Welcome, son of Aeliraneth. Welcome, child of the South."

The woman's song began again, gently playing even as she spoke as though it were a wound music box she'd merely set aside when company came.

Rising from the pile of timber, she came towards him. Cyrus met her gaze as defiantly as he could.

What was she? Aeore? She couldn't be. The Aeore were God's first creation, but they had rebelled against Him. So He cast them into Asylum until they repented. They'd only escaped once, back in Ansala's time. He'd heard no account of any Aeore on this side of the Wynding since. After the battle at Cinder, Ansala's armies had tracked down and slain any survivors. They'd taken a great deal of pride in it. The Wynding was supposed to be absolute, forever separating their realm of Asylum from the lands of the Lanternlit.

"Who are you? And why did you bring us here?" he asked, nervously.

"Celaan," B'lantra whispered.

"Very good," the woman said. Her eyes darted over to B'lantra. "There is a memory in your mind that is stirring from its sleep. You know me, girl. You would not be standing here if not for me. Ponder on that and see if your memory awakens."

B'lantra's brow wrinkled in thought. "Before, when I first came to Shrevnetska... no, I never saw you. I walked through the trees for days. I hid from the troika. It followed… I survived on my own. I never had any help from you!"

"Your every breath is a gift from me. But believe what you like until remembrance teaches you differently," Celaan replied, as if addressing an impertinent child. "I learned long ago not to expect gratitude for my actions."

Her gaze once again locked onto Cyrus. "I am Celaan, last empress of the Aeore."

"Were you part of the army that marched on Cinder? Have you been here all this time?"

"No. Such things are past. Your people may still shiver at the memory of a thousand years. Mine have long since moved on."

"How did you get here?"

"That is not important," Celaan said. She waved her hand around the dilapidated mill. "This ruin provides an ideal place to speak, does it not? Away from prying eyes and ears. The storms provide a welcome respite from my continuing confinement in the Arkinwood. It is a joy to take corporeal form, to use my own arms and legs again instead of those of others."

Her voice began to lose a little of its sweetness. "You have been indolent these last few years. That is a luxury you no longer have."

"That sounds like a threat."

"It is. But it is not I who threaten. She has found you once again. She will hunt you down no matter where you go."

"The golden-haired woman? One of yours? Was she doing your bidding when she killed Enric? Or when she tried to kill me ten years ago? Is that why we're here?"

"You are here because I willed it to be so. If not, you might already be in her grasp. She seeks the Heart of the Great Machine for her master. She seeks you because you are the one the Heart will answer to now that your Mother has gone. The Heart lies on this side of the Wynding. It must be returned to the Kaulswyr, the great machine in the nucleus of Asylum. Aeliraneth's burden falls to you now."

"My mother," Cyrus growled. He felt his face grow flush. "She's dead. I'm not bound to anything she promised you."

Celaan didn't waver. "The Heart touched Aeliraneth, and it touched you when you were little more than a thought in her womb. Your probabilities were set long ago."

"I'll decide my own life. I don't need you to tell me what it is."

"Beyond the Wynding lies an army of the corrupted. My people called them the Tainted. Asylum lies nearly in ruins. Without the Heart, the Kaulswyr will fail, and your precious Wynding will fail with it. The world you live in will fail soon after. The corruption will cut through it like a sword through paper, and there will be no Ansala to stop it this time. Both of our worlds depend on the safe return of the Heart."

Cyrus' brow furrowed. "How did you manage to lose something so important?"

He could see Celaan's impatience growing. Whether she really was what she claimed to be or not, she certainly fit the part. If Mother's mannerisms had taught him anything, it was that important people didn't like being questioned. They expected to be obeyed. He'd been given a task and was expected to dutifully carry it out. But if the so-called empress thought he'd just mindlessly follow her orders, she was mistaken.

"A thief stole the Heart for his own purposes," Celaan said. "When he tried to flee, I pursued him, as did your mother. When cornered, the thief activated the Heart's power. It was ripped from Asylum and came to rest on this side of the Wynding."

"Mother was part of your court?"

"Her intervention was timely," Celaan replied, tersely.

"So what exactly is this thing then, this all-powerful Heart that only responds to me?"

"It is an energy source— a sphere about the size of a clenched fist, pulsing with a dark life of its own. Heavier than a thousand mountains, light enough to float on its own in the right hands. It is the essence of the Kaulswyr, left for my people by God Himself.

The reality we live under was shaped by the Heart."

"And where is it? You don't know, do you? If you did, you would already have it."

"Your mother knew. She found the Heart and sealed it away. You need only retrieve it and complete the work she started. Seek the gear from the Bal-haegast. That will be your key."

"The Bal-haegast is a monster that kills anything it comes across. No one even knows if it's real. And even if I found the Heart, I couldn't return it. The Wynding isn't like some castle wall. It's a hard and fast barrier between the Lanternlit and Asylum. It touches all points, everywhere and nowhere at the same time. You don't just casually walk through something like that."

"Lesser people will always find reasons why something cannot be done. Greater ones will find a way to what they seek. Your mother met the Bal-haegast and lived. She found a way through the Wynding. Surely her son could do the same."

Cyrus' eyes narrowed warily. "It's not that simple, is it? Otherwise, why would you be cowering in some old mill in the middle of a fae storm? And if you think I'm going to just drop everything to go—"

"The thief that took the Heart still lives. He still seeks his prize. He took your mother from you ten years ago as well as your home. His servant takes away the life you have now. You have the opportunity to set right all the wrongs that have been done unto you and to House Ulberath. Will you not take it?"

"Vengeance?" Cyrus asked, bitterly. An angry sneer curled his lip. "I don't give a damn about vengeance. House Ulberath is ash. And I plan on leaving it in the past, just like my mother."

"You will seek the Heart, because in the end you will find you have no other choice," Celaan said. "I offer you a gift to keep you alive until reason catches up with you. It is a simple thing— a weapon of power from the Aeore armory of old."

The sigil around her body suddenly unwrapped itself like a serpent and burrowed into the damp ground. The earth all around the Aeore empress glowed, as if hot coals had been implanted underneath its skin. After a moment, the sigil returned from its subterranean voyage bearing a long curved sword.

The weapon was much like the radiant earth it came from, a long ruddy blade of deeply glowing embers. They flickered and danced faintly along the single honed edge. The hilt was wrapped in an onyx hide. A golden tassel dangled from it.

Celaan held the sword almost reverently as the sigil once again coiled its way around her. "This is Akestra, the Desire of Flame. When my people first began to suffer from the corruption, some sickened and died. Others changed as it consumed them, becoming the Tainted. I carried this blade when the first hordes broke upon my cities. I cut them down until the streets were blackened with their blood. I suffered from betrayal, but Akestra never failed me. I give her to you. You will have need of her soon."

Cyrus stared at the sword in awe. The blade shimmered almost like a living thing. The pulse of its ruddy steel quickened to match his excited heartbeat. Even after a thousand years, treasure hunters across the Lanternlit still sought out Aeore armaments left over from the war. He'd never thought to see an Aeore sword, let alone have one freely offered to him.

It was beautiful. It was power. Protection. He could face the golden-haired woman. He could face the inquisitors.

Anyone.

He could make his life what he wanted it to be.

The empress' song that had been quietly playing during their conversation intensified slowly in his head.

He stepped closer and reached out his hand for the hilt of the blade. Celaan calmly waited for him to take it. If there was any deceit or malevolence in her face, he didn't see it.

❋ ❋ ❋

B'lantra called his name again, though he didn't seem to hear her. Cyrus' face held an almost fervoured intensity. He was blind to her, blind to everything around him. Celaan watched him, a crouching cat waiting as the mouse drew ever closer to its claws. Her song filled the mill.

Frustrated, B'lantra took a step towards him. Her legs locked in place on the damp floor.

"Still as stone. Be a good girl."

Cyrus fingers were almost touching the sword. Celaan's eyes lit up.

No!

B'lantra called her song. The embers ignited inside her, and the first notes escaped her lips. Celaan's gaze turned on her.

"What do you think you are doing, little one? You are already mine. Now be still!"

An iron grip seized B'lantra, squeezing the breath from her body. Her song was cut off. The empress' presence was all around her. It pushed against her mind. It was in her mind! Her eyes widened in horror. It had been there for a long time, waiting for the right moment to reveal itself.

Celaan had done nothing to her, at least outwardly. It was her own body rebelling against her. Muscles she'd long thought her own to control now locked down, cutting off her breath. Her heart pounded against her ribs.

She fought it. She wouldn't stay silent. She wouldn't just mindlessly obey.

"Get out! Get out! They're my arms, my legs, my thoughts. Get out!"

"You defy me? I shaped you into what you are. You're nothing but a shallow reflection of something greater."

B'lantra forced her hands over her ears as if trying to block out the empress' voice. She writhed inside herself. From the dark places of her mind came thorns and brambles to snare her. She burned them away. For every one she seared, another came. Again and again until at last they gave up and slowly retreated to the obsidian veil of her deepest self.

Celaan's song broke apart, dissipating into the darkness.

✸ ✸ ✸

Cyrus quickly recovered and scrambled back. "Keep your damn sword. I don't want it."

Celaan glared furiously. The sigil pulsed with an angry, hellish light. "You do not question. You do not refuse. You obey!"

The empress' voice was harsh and cold, without any trace of the melodic sweetness it had carried before.

Standing imperiously before him, Celaan looked every bit a ruler of legend. "I had thought to leave my mark on you gently once you took my gift—to leave your will and your dreams intact. So be it. There are other methods I can use."

Cyrus pulled the pistol from his belt and took aim. Even now he hesitated to pull the trigger.

He barely saw the movement of Celaan's sword. The blade carved the pistol in half before he could even blink.

He stared numbly as the charred remnants of his weapon fell from his fingers. Celaan could have easily taken his hand off if she'd chosen.

It seemed she wanted him intact— for now at least.

Storm.

Celaan had said the storm had provided her a respite from her confinement. She must be feeding on the storm, using its energy to maintain herself.

Dawn.

Fae storms always ended at dawn.

If Celaan still controlled the trees, then they stood little chance of truly escaping her. But their odds were still better outside the Karrak. Maybe they could evade until then… buy time until sunlight broke the darkness.

How long until dawn?

He didn't know. It needed to be soon.

His eyes flicked back towards the door they'd come through. Grabbing B'lantra's hand, he turned and rushed towards it.

Celaan anticipated his actions. Her eyes flashed, the pupils narrowing to cat-like slits, knives of black amidst a hardened field of green. The door slammed shut. Her sigil uncoiled and lashed out at them, tearing through timber and machine alike to reach them.

"Liar! You said you needed us alive," Cyrus shouted at her.

"I need not kill you," the empress said. "I can break you in a thousand ways; reshape you to suit the purpose you were meant for. It was always going to be that way. The only question was by which method."

"You win. I'll find your damned Heart for you. Let B'lantra go at least."

"Neither you nor your Secondborn kin can be trusted without a whip at your back. And I shall provide it. If not by guile, then by force."

The sigil snatched at him, nearly severing one of the oaken pillars that held up the roof. A nascent thought suddenly churned through his head. He waited until the sigil came at him again, and then nimbly dodged away. It sped past him and wrapped itself around the pillar

Celaan realized what he intended, but not before her sigil had already sheared through the pillar.

Like a tree being felled the pillar toppled, pulling part of the roof down with it. Debris crashed in all around them. The world shook. He held B'lantra tightly and waited.

The rumbling slowly diminished. Dust rose everywhere around them, spreading up into the air before being beaten down by the rain that poured in from the enlarged hole in the roof.

The door they had come through was buried somewhere in the wreckage. He looked cautiously around. To his delight, he saw the broken oak pillar rising diagonally from the floor to precariously rest on the weather-beaten rafters of the sagging roof.

He grinned, stifling the urge to suddenly howl in triumph. It wasn't quite what he'd planned. He hadn't thought it through well enough to be completely sure what he'd intended.

It had worked out well enough though.

"Let's go," he said to B'lantra.

Her face was drawn and covered with streaks of caked dust and muck.

"Where's Celaan?" she asked in a choked whisper.

There was no immediate sign of the Aeore empress. It was hard to see anything amidst the debris, the rising dust and the falling rain. Had she been buried in the rubble or perhaps been forced back into her prison?

"Let's not wait to find out."

The pillar shifted uncertainly underneath their weight as they started to make their ascent. The surface, newly soaked from the pounding rain, was slippery, slowing their climb to a tentative crawl.

Celaan suddenly appeared from below, searching the wreckage. They waited, barely daring to breathe. She quickly found the wavering light from B'lantra's lantern. The ruddy sword they'd seen earlier, Akestra, came shimmering into being in her hands once more.

"Run!" Cyrus cried out.

The top of the pillar lurched against the rafters, threatening to spill them back down into the empress' clutches. Cyrus ran along the shifting surface as quickly as he dared.

B'lantra followed. The pillar shuddered beneath her. She lost her balance and fell. Just before tumbling into the gloom below, she managed to catch hold of the pillar. She hung there, clinging desperately with one hand while clasping her precious lantern with the other.

Cyrus reached back to her. "Come on. We're almost there."

She slipped as soon as she tried to pull herself back up.

"I can't!"

"Let go of the lantern!"

Celaan drew closer. Akestra crackled in her hands. Her sigil writhed, preparing to strike.

B'lantra glanced up at him, tears streaming down her face.

"Drop the lantern, Bel. I'll be right here in the dark with you. I promise!"

The Trafari girl reluctantly opened her shaking hand. The lantern fell. B'lantra quickly scrabbled back onto the pillar's surface. Tentatively, as if she were a damned soul walking into Hell, she began taking the last few steps up to the roof.

"I think not, little one," Celaan hissed from below.

The empress held her blade aloft and then hurled it at them. It sped towards them in a spinning red flash of sizzling energy. Cyrus stood transfixed, watching helplessly as the blade traveled its deadly arc. B'lantra sensed her peril and likewise froze, her breath caught somewhere between inhale and exhale.

They weren't the empress' intended targets.

The sword blasted into the pillar, shattering it into charred splinters. A scream started to form on B'lantra's lips just before she started to plummet.

Cyrus leapt towards her. His feet slipped from underneath him on the wet roof. He landed hard against the shingles. They groaned beneath him. He desperately stretched out his hand to catch her. At first he thought he'd missed. Then her nails grazed his arm, and her fingers met his. He closed his grip around them almost blindly. Her falling weight yanked him forward, nearly pulling him down with her. He felt the wet flesh of their hands sliding inexorably past each other. She cried out, frantically struggling to get purchase. His arm started to go numb.

He leaned down, his frame precariously balanced, to grab her with his other hand. He started to slip over the edge.

The sigil snapped at her, nearly snaring B'lantra's flailing ankle. Celaan patiently waited below like a hungry crocodile.

Cyrus braced himself as best he could. Before the sigil could strike again, he torqued his body around and tossed B'lantra up onto the roof beside him. His shoulder felt like it had nearly been ripped from its socket.

A moment later they began to slide down the sodden shingles. They toppled over the side of the roof, tumbling to the ground in a battered heap.

As breath slowly returned to his body, Cyrus coughed and wanly lifted his head. The storm had eased, fading from a torrent to a steady drizzle. The sky was lightening on the eastern horizon.

A miserable groan came from beside him. B'lantra lay next to him, bruised and worn. Her eyes were closed.

"Are we—?"

He brushed the tears from her face and smiled. "We're alive."

✻ ✻ ✻

Reluctantly B'lantra opened her eyes. Or at least she thought she did. It seemed an eternity since they'd fallen, though she knew it had only been moments. She blinked, hoping her sight had deceived her and there would be glorious daylight on the other side of her eyelids.

There wasn't.

The only comfort she could take was that the dark was a little less dark than it had been before.

She flexed her fingers and toes and then took a deep breath. It hurt, but not the stabbing pain that bespoke of internal injuries or broken bones. Her pack and her physician's satchel seemed to have taken the brunt of the fall.

Cyrus pulled her to her feet, and she groaned again.

They tottered away from the Karrak, sloshing through the rushing waters of the Dry Run as best they could. The current still fought them, but it had eased just as the storm had.

The night crumbled away with each step they took. The rain finally stopped, and the wind faded to a faint whisper in the trees.

A rumbling came from behind them.

The wall of the Karrak buckled as something crashed against it. Again it came. The wall burst outward. Celaan strode forth like some monstrosity being born from the mill's husk. Even with the dawn upon the world, she still was regal and terrible.

Her form was straight and tall in the infant morning. Akestra still gleamed with its hell light.

B'lantra splashed backwards into the water. Cyrus gasped in sudden bewilderment and fumbled for his sword. Celaan glided rapidly across the flowing current they'd stumbled through. The water hissed and bubbled as her sigil passed over it.

A dove cooed. Soft yellow light pierced through a hole in the clouds, glimmering off the water.

"Wretched girl. Do not think you will not have to honor our bargain when the time comes. Let suffering teach you obedience in the meantime."

The words bounced through B'lantra's brain, leaving a chill in their wake.

Celaan had vanished. B'lantra stood up, wet clothes clinging to her. The warmth of the sun on her face was joyous.

It was morning.

Light.

It would get her through another day at least.

CHAPTER 7

DECISIONS OF NECESSITY

ASA DROPPED DOWN FROM THE LIMB of the hawthorn tree when she heard the men approaching along the ruddy shale of the Red Road. It sounded like Bregna had brought an entire contingent with him. It wasn't part of the arrangement she'd carefully maneuvered him into.

The bejeweled rings on her fingers glittered as she caressed the yellow yarn hair of her rag doll. "Let's hope he remembered to bring what I asked him to, Susanna. I'll be very cross if he forgot."

The rag doll stared back at her from its place in her velvet handbag. There was a look of anxiety in its wide button eyes and hand-sewn face.

"Pretty Susanna. We'll be just fine. I promise I won't be mad at you— just Bregna if he doesn't bring us what we want. Just be quiet until I'm done. There's a good girl," she murmured.

Asa adjusted her clothing and patiently waited. She'd long since dispensed with the hideously drab merchant's garb she'd donned in Shrevnetska. The silk blouse she wore now was perfectly tailored to her figure, styled in the latest Erendel fashions. Its cloth shimmered faintly, shifting from red to gold to green and back again in the filtered light of the morning. Her soft leather leggings and high riding boots had been specially chosen to accentuate it, as had the green velvet cloak she had over her shoulders.

Gradually the clip-clop of horses' hooves and the creak of a carriage grew louder. The inquisitors rode into view. They pulled up when they saw her.

Bregna had brought the silverworm just as he'd promised. She could sense it writhing within its little glass vials in the black carriage behind him.

Bregna was a glory seeker whose ambition far exceeded his meager grasp. Even so, it had taken nearly a year for him to agree to her offer— an entire year of nights in his bedchamber subtly breaking his inquisitor's discipline. It had been quite delightful watching his once firm nobility and resolve slowly crumble under her touch. Her offer had been a simple thing gently whispered in his ear: the location of Aeliraneth's son in exchange for a small sample of the silverworm. He'd agreed only after they'd arranged to meet well away from the prying eyes of the Conclave officials.

The inquisitors guarded their silverworm zealously. The secret to its manufacture was unknown outside a select few in the Illumentry. It was their one hedge against their quarry and their greatest weakness. The silverworm didn't let go of the inquisitors any more readily than they let go of it. The more they used it, the more trapped within it they became.

She gave Bregna a smile. He would return with neither Aeliraneth's son nor the silverworm. She hadn't quite decided his fate afterwards. Bedding a witch was a grave sin for an inquisitor. Rather than killing him, it might be more amusing to watch him being led to the gallows, a disgraced and broken man.

Bregna's face remained impassive, though his eyes carefully surveyed her cleavage and the tight fit of her clothes.

"Hello again, darling. I see the storm didn't delay you for too long," she said.

"It would take more than that wickedness to stop us. I do hope for your sake you haven't brought us on a fool's errand," he replied, sternly.

"Always obsessed with duty and honor. I really shouldn't have expected anything else from you," Asa pouted, batting her long eyelashes. "As for me, I like pleasure with my duty. So let's get to my pleasure before we get to your duty."

Bregna nodded and stepped down from his horse. He walked

back to the black carriage, opened the door and retrieved a well-crafted wooden box. He returned and set it down a short distance in front of her.

Several of the other inquisitors gaped in astonishment. One of them, an older man with a thick frame and trimmed beard, stepped forward.

"Sir, you can't simply hand over—"

"I certainly can, Lieutenant. You're welcome to lodge an official complaint. I doubt you'll find the Conclave very sympathetic once I explain my reasons to them."

The other inquisitor reluctantly stepped back.

"Problems?" Asa inquired.

"None that concern you, my dear. Now where is Aeliraneth's son hiding?"

"You'll find him in the town jail of Shrevnetska. The sheriff and his men placed him under their protection at my... suggestion," she told him.

"Excellent. Come and claim your payment then."

Asa sauntered over, ignoring the armed men bristling all around her. They breathlessly watched her approach as though the box were a trap they were just waiting to spring.

"There is just one thing," Bregna said. At his subtle gesture the other inquisitors moved to surround her.

Asa kept the bright smile on her face. Bregna had no intention of parting with the silverworm it seemed. He was far more of a duplicitous little serpent than she would have given him credit for. He'd shown little hint of subtly while he was 'taming' her in the bedchamber.

"It's not that I don't trust you, but I would feel much better if we had Aeliraneth's son in our actual custody before I turned over the silverworm. You'll accompany us to Shrevnetska, of course."

"Of course," Asa said, innocently. The cycle of betrayal had started for both of them.

She called the mists to her. They came, billowing out of the earth like a swarm of insects. The Red Road was almost instantly swallowed up in a thick gray blanket. Had the inquisitors been normal men, she could have easily crushed them within its folds. Instead they resisted her with unexpected resolve.

"That's not very nice of them, is it Susanna?"

"Witch," one of the men called.

He loomed out of the mist, his pistols drawn.

Her sword appeared in her hand. It was far different from the crude weapon she'd used to butcher the wiry man back in Shrevnetska. Glyphs of ancient power danced along his blade. It was a tenuous like the mist: a single-edged weapon of Aeore make, perfectly balanced and weighted for her stature.

"Surrender yourself, witch. Your spells have no effect on us," the inquisitor said when he spotted her.

Asa effortlessly closed the distance between them. He trained his pistols on her. His fingers moved to the triggers. Her sword separated his head from his shoulders before he could complete the motion.

"Some of us don't need spells."

She glided towards the box of silverworm. The remaining inquisitors reacted quickly, forming a stout wall between her and her prize. Bregna stood amongst them, coldly confident.

At her command, tendrils of mist swirled around the box. Before the inquisitor's eyes the mist enveloped it. A moment later it had vanished.

Bregna scalded her with a look of fury. Asa only laughed and blew him a kiss from her ruby lips. As the inquisitors bore down on her, she stepped back into the mists. They stopped their advance, looking wildly around for her. They found nothing other than the mist and the dripping forest of the early morning.

Much to Asa's disappointment, they wasted little time with dismay. Like marionettes, they mechanically stripped their fallen comrade of his weapons and equipment and proceeded onto their next goal.

Having long since resumed her perch in the hawthorn tree, Asa watched them go. They would find Aeliraneth's son soon enough. Once they did it would make it much easier to keep track of him. The mists allowed her to find almost anyone if she desired, anyone except Aeliraneth's son. It had taken her nearly ten years to finally run him to ground. Perhaps he had some sort of charm that allowed him to stay hidden. Whatever his method, she would extract it from him once he was suitably broken. Arranging his confinement in the jail meant he wouldn't be going anywhere until the inquisitors arrived.

"Not that they'll be keeping him for very long, of course," she said to Susanna.

The doll looked at her in disapproval.

"Don't give me that, Susanna. You know I don't like it." She gave the doll an angry shake. "And don't start crying either, you stupid little bitch. I don't want to listen to it!"

Her face softened after a moment, and she once more patted it on the head. "I'm sorry, Susanna. But you know you shouldn't talk back like that. There, there. Dry your tears before someone sees you. Now let's see what Bregna brought us."

Inside the box were several rows of glass flasks, each containing an opaque silvery liquid. She held one up to examine it. The silver compound twisted and churned in response, almost excited by the prospect of being picked up and used.

"The finest blend from the finest alchemists of Targus," Bregna had promised when she'd made her offer to him.

She had no use for it personally. Simon did however. He'd sought it for years now, though he'd never fully explained why. She was seldom interested in his technical reasons. Very little of what he did was without merit or purpose. That discipline had served him well in life when he'd commanded Celaan's armies. It served him equally well in death.

In the meantime, there was Aeliraneth's son to concern herself with. His suffering had only just begun.

✳ ✳ ✳

The fire crackled contentedly in the center of the cave, throwing shadows against the rough rock walls. The day outside was bright and warm, though Cyrus hadn't ventured outside much since he'd awakened. The night had left him and B'lantra both weary and woeful. The Trafari girl lay nearby, curled tightly into her blanket, a shapely lump amidst their scattered and slowly drying belongings.

He stared into the fire, trying to focus his scattered thoughts, and found himself grinding the wooden blocks together. Para-octet the Spark and Doraghe the Flame, the Iriethan characters for energy and light, shimmered along the sides.

Mother. Aeliraneth. The Great Witch. Hellspawned bitch.

He sits in the serene stillness of the grounds outside the manor house playing with the toys Lyra discreetly gives him. Playtime and toys aren't allowed. They're yet another distraction, so Mother claims. The book he's supposed to be studying sits beside him cheerfully ignored.

Mother appears without warning. She stares down at him. Her face had twists in anger when she sees the toys. The crimson fan quivers.

The beating he's expecting never comes. Instead Mother holds out her hand and presents him with the first of the blocks.

There are more, she says. Seventeen more are scattered around the grounds, each one carefully hidden. He will have to be clever to find them all. He can eat and sleep again when he has.

It had been four long, hungry days before he'd finally laid hands on the last one. He'd won, beaten Mother at her game, though no praise had been forthcoming.

"You said you wanted nothing to do with your mother, but I see you haven't gotten rid of those old blocks," Lyra observed from the cave's entrance.

Caught unawares, Cyrus dropped the blocks and bolted up, frantically grabbing for his musket.

Lyra's lined faced cracked into a smile. She set down the bundle she carried and came over to sit down by the fire.

"I wasn't expecting to see you again," Cyrus finally stammered.

"Obviously. And you looked pretty silly with that crazed look on your face."

His expression contorted into a frown.

"You might as well take that sour look off. I've known you nearly all your life, and I'll see fit to tease you if I want. Now come sit with your poor old foster mother. She's been worried about you."

Cyrus relented. "I'm a little roughed up, but I'll manage."

Lyra hugged him tightly as soon as he was within reach. "I figured you'd come here. A fine mess you've gotten yourself into. I doubt a few words from me or anyone else is going to get you out of it this time."

Cyrus looked away. "You shouldn't get in the middle of this. You'll be safe once I leave here."

"So you're going to leave and take all your troubles with you, are you?"

"What else do you want me to do? I didn't plan it this way."

"You never do, little hero. The rumors are already spreading about the murderer and his daring escape during the storm. They say witchcraft was involved, so I daresay B'lantra had a hand in it despite my warnings."

Cyrus hesitated, trying to figure out where to begin. He told her the story as best he could: being thrown in jail, his escape, the flight through the storm and their encounter with Celaan.

Lyra listened intently. She was quiet for a moment even after he finished, seemingly lost in thought. "Celaan means 'She Who Transcends' in the Aeore tongue. Their names are as much titles as anything else."

His eyebrows arched up in surprise. "How the hell could you possibly know that?"

"Despite the many times you may have mumbled it under your breath at me, I'm not some pot scrubber in an apron. I was the occasional scribe to Aeliraneth, as well as physician, errand girl and… keeper of unruly children," Lyra replied, giving him an almost wistful smile. "Celaan is some sort of holy figure to the Aeore, but I really don't know much more than that. Your mother wasn't always forthcoming about her plans— or anything else for that matter."

"Mother's dead, and so is House Ulberath," Cyrus said, pointedly. "And I'm not about to rake over the ashes. I'm not sure where we'll go. Maybe Erendel. It's ten times the size of Targus. They revere the Western Face of God there— Kyento— so the Illumentry doesn't have much of a foothold. We can blend in so they never find us."

"Erendel isn't the worst place you could go. You might not find that as easy as you think though. Even in death, Aeliraneth isn't the kind of woman you just casually toss aside."

"Well, if Mother wanted this Heart of the Great Machine, then it was for all the wrong reasons."

"You don't know that."

Cyrus poked the fire with a nearby stick, watching as a few sparks wafted up. "I know Mother. That's all I need to know."

"You don't know her as well as you think. No one did."

Cyrus jabbed at the coals until the stick began to blacken. The fire crackled almost as if in protest. "Fine. What about this Heart that Celaan nearly us killed over? I know about the Kaulswyr and the Wynding, but what would this 'empress' want with this heart? There has to be more to it than just preserving the Wynding. What is she even doing in the Arkinwood?"

The sudden intake of air against his teeth was sharp. "The night of the fire Mother told you to take me to Shrevnetska. She knew Celaan was waiting there. She planned it!"

Lyra held up her hand before he could continue. "If that's true, then she had her reasons. And it wasn't just to hand you over to some Aeore in the Arkinwood. She put too much time into you."

"Don't I know it! Like the shepherd puts effort into the lamb before it's taken off to the slaughterhouse."

"She was harsh with you, and I couldn't always stop her. But she loved you in her own way. Aeliraneth wasn't the villain you make her out to be. I would have ended up at the end of a rope if not for her."

"She saved you? Why? And how did you end up about to be hanged?"

Lyra shrugged. "Maybe she had need for a physician who wouldn't ask too many questions. Maybe she felt sorry for me. I never understood why, and I didn't ask too closely. I was once one of the better physicians in Targus. Let's just say that people have vices, and those vices sometimes put them in places they shouldn't be. I saw a lot more of the underbelly of Targus than I really wanted to in those days."

Cyrus' eyes widened. "That's why you keep the sword and know about locks. I thought it was just something you picked up along the way."

"I used those skills to earn a living for a time. They caught me eventually. On the day of my hanging, your mother simply walked up to the judge and offered two golden coins for my release. They didn't argue with her. Even then she was feared. They even gave me my silver clover back. So no, your mother isn't the villain you make her out to be."

Cyrus irritably snapped the stick he was holding. It didn't sound like the mother he knew. "Saving you was the one good thing she did. The rest of it was for the attention and the power. She was always more interested in being at the center of it— all the wonder of being the one witch strong enough to defy the Illumentry. The men came flocking to her too. You think I don't remember, but I do. Hell, any one of them could've been my father. I'll bet she didn't even know who it was."

"It's done. Brooding about it now doesn't help," Lyra said, impatience beginning to creep into her tone. "You're old enough now so it doesn't matter who you are, not who your father was."

"That doesn't mean I'm not right."

Lyra spied the wooden blocks lying nearby and seized them up in her calloused hands before he could stop her. "Why do you still have these if you despise her so much? I'd think you'd want to get rid of any reminder of her whatsoever. Here... let me help you on your way."

With a flick of her wrist she tossed the blocks towards the fire. Cyrus cried out and leapt up, snatching them away from the flame's grasp.

Lyra arched an eyebrow in response. "I see you do care. At least a little bit."

Cyrus puffed his cheeks and let out an exasperated sigh. "I don't know. She's my mother... but I... you can't hate and love somebody at the same time."

"Some people have managed to do it for years it would seem," Lyra noted.

B'lantra grumbled miserably and sat up, blinking sleepily at them both. Cyrus spotted a large bruise along the side of her face as well as an assortment of scrapes and cuts.

"Looks like you're the one in need of a doctor," he observed.

B'lantra rubbed her jaw and tilted her head to the side, reaching up to massage the stiffness out of her neck. "I think one of your knobby knees attacked the side of my face when we fell."

"So the princess is awake at last," Lyra said. "And was up past her bedtime by the look of her."

B'lantra's crossness fell away. She threw back her blanket and leapt up to embrace the physician. "I thought we'd never see you again!"

"I'm not that easy to get rid of, dear," Lyra said. "Now let's get you tended to."

She went over to retrieve her bundle. Her supplies weren't as ruthlessly organized as B'lantra's were, but she seemed to know exactly where everything was. Her hands moved in perfect rhythm, sometimes gentle, sometimes firm. She kept her attention firmly fixed on her patient, reaching out and snaring whatever ingredients she needed without even looking.

"Now you know how I feel," Cyrus said, a smirk working across his face.

"Unlike you, I can actually sit still," B'lantra retorted. "So what were you two arguing about? I thought I heard some sort of squabble. And something about Erendel."

"I was thinking that's where we should go," Cyrus said. "It's a long way, but we could probably head west to Anadyne and catch a steamer from there. Or fly. They say they're even started using hot air balloons now."

"Absolutely not," B'lantra said, firmly. "I'm not about to fly up in one of those things. The steamer doesn't sound so bad. There used to be a ferry that would take you across Lake X'anca near Ba'ket. We rode on it a few times when I was little. The cinders from the boiler would fly up in the air and burn holes in your clothes if you weren't careful."

Her brown eyes lit up. "If we're going to Erendel… Lyra, do you think Denschen would still—?"

The physician shook her head sadly. "You made your choice. Denschen College is closed to you now."

B'lantra lowered her head. "I couldn't just let Cyrus stay in there. I couldn't."

"I know. You made the right choice. But there are consequences even for the right choice," Lyra said, softly. She forced a smile. "Just because the college is closed to you doesn't mean the city is. It has its share of problems, but it's a beautiful place. You'll do fine there."

B'lantra turned to Cyrus. "What about Celaan and everything else? Can we really leave it all behind just like that?"

"Do you really want to get involved with some Aeore empress?"

"No, I've had enough of Aeore. Asylum must be a wretched cesspool if it has someone like her ruling it."

"She's trapped in the Arkinwood, so she said. If we leave soon, we can clear the wood before nightfall. She can stay there and rot."

"Celaan's not the only one. Our quest to make enemies has been a rousing success," B'lantra said, glumly.

"The inquisitors are probably in the village already, poking their ugly snouts about. I had better go and have a word with them," Lyra said as she finished her work on B'lantra.

"You don't have to do that," Cyrus said, urgently. "Just stay away from them. They're inquisitors. They—"

Lyra put her hand up. "I'm no witch. Dolece and her chapel priestesses will see to it they can't touch me. If you had bothered to study them, you would know the inquisitor's limits. Arakost relies on them, but they also fear them. Even the Illumentry is wary of its creation. They're not completely above the law, despite what they'd like you to believe."

"I still don't like it."

"There's nothing you can do about it now." Lyra said. She gave B'lantra a knowing look, reached into her bundle and pulled out a lantern and some oil flasks. A moment later she abruptly hopped up from where she'd been sitting. "I've tarried here long enough. You two need to be off if you want to make it out of the Arkinwood before dark."

She slung her bundle over her shoulder, and they walked her to the entrance. They weren't going to see her again, at least not until everything had been fixed. The thought weighed heavily on Cyrus all of a sudden.

"Take care and… well… I mean…"

"I'll be fine," Lyra said. "I may even take a notion to retire to Erendel and have you tend to me in my dotage when this is all over."

Cyrus tried to smile, but the result was bittersweet at best. "We'll come back. You'll see. We'll be king and queen of something. We'll come back and tell you all about our adventures."

He couldn't be certain Lyra believed him. He wasn't even sure he believed it, but it felt good to say the words. Maybe if he said them enough, they'd come true.

"And I'll be eager to hear your stories. Be well."

Lyra walked away without saying anything else. She was Arakostrian at heart, and farewells weren't a thing to be lingered on in the Empire, no matter the sentiment. Cyrus could only wish it was that simple for him. Lyra slowly disappeared, bundle and all, into the trees

He watched her go and then found he was once more grinding the blocks together.

CHAPTER 8

SHADES OF MERCY

B'LANTRA COULDN'T BE SURE whether Helena was even aware of her surroundings anymore. The woman lay on a thin bedroll beside the wagon, her glazed eyes staring uncertainly up at the sycamore trees growing along the Red Road. Her face was pale, almost corpse-like. Her bedraggled, blondish hair was soaked with sweat. The gashes the troika had left in her leg and side had been difficult to stitch closed.

Helena was lucky to still be alive.

How long she would stay that way remained to be seen.

B'lantra had a nauseating feeling the woman was dying despite all her efforts. It was probably venom. The spittle that dripped from the troika's snaggled jaws was caustic, but not normally poisonous. Even that had its exceptions though.

It was wrong to hate any of God's creatures, so the blessed scrolls of the Galagax, the Trafari answer to the Illumentry's Litany, clearly said. Every beast had its own nature. You could take advantage of that nature once you understood it, but you could never alter it. Thus, there was no profit in wasting hate on something you couldn't change.

Brakeem would simply have to overlook her failing. When it came down to it, no scroll, no matter how blessed, would change her opinion on troika.

The old stone well beside the shabby house beckons them as they clack along the Red Road.

Matri's been told it's a stopover for traders coming up from the south. They're thirsty. So is Thule, their jerukin ox. His massive head hangs low.

She hands Patri the bucket, and he goes to see if there's any water in the well. The trees stand heavy and dark all around, so different from the plains and steppes she's been used to.

The growl comes. Patri screams. The huge shape stands over his body. Its three little red eyes are wild and hateful. Thule is next. Matri throws her off the wagon and tells her to run.

She runs through the trees with the sound of cracking bones echoing behind her.

B'lantra blinked her eyes and tried to refocus herself. They were nearly two full days from Shrevnetska now, and the journey had been unexpectedly quiet until they'd come across the distressed merchant family by the side of the road. The troika's assault had been swift, judging from the account of Helena's husband and the tracks around the wagon. The attack was unusual so close to the road, but not unheard of.

She'd have to make a decision on Helena. If it was troika venom, then it was incurable by mundane means. That left only witchcraft. Her song was hardly subtle. There was no way the merchant family wouldn't know it for what it was. After seeing Markov's reaction in the jail, she was reluctant to try it again. The inquisitors might still be tracking them, and a story of witchcraft would draw them like moths to a flame.

Vashaenit! She bit her lip as she thought.

She'd played the role of the witch far too much for her own comfort in the last few days.

Behind her Cyrus stood somberly with Helena's husband, Pol, and one of his sons. Two younger children clutched at their father's legs.

"Is Helena going to be alright?" Pol asked. "She's not looking much better."

"I'll do all I can," B'lantra answered.

"I'm sure you will," he said, stiffly.

His upper lip curled, and his brow wrinkled ever so slightly as he gazed back at her, taking in her face, her skin and the glittering bead in her uncovered hair. He didn't trust her or her skill. She could see it lurking in his face— subtle, muted, but there. He wanted someone taking care of his wife who looked like him, who was born to his customs and lands, not a foreigner with strange looks and unknown secrets.

He was fortunate she was here at all. It would have been so much easier for her to offer up a few empty prayers and continue on her way.

She did her best to quiet her resentment and forced a smile for the benefit of the children. Her bearing told a different story, however. Pol saw it, and his shoulders slumped. He turned away and began murmuring a plea to Talast.

Cyrus came over and knelt beside her. She urgently clasped his hand.

"You know what will happen," he whispered to her, as if he already knew what she was thinking.

"I can't just leave her... Not after—"

"I know, and I love you. Do what you have to."

Helena began shuddering. Her teeth were clenched in pain. Beneath the bandages, her skin was starting to blacken.

B'lantra sighed and felt her hands starting to tremble.

She'd known since she was a child that witchcraft was something she had to hide, and Lyra had always been quick to remind her. She'd been the girl who could hear the fairies speak, who noticed the murmurings in the night and perceived the ley lines crossing overhead. She'd known of these things even before she'd truly known what a witch was.

Not one in ten thousand could say the same, so it was said.

A witch saw the things others dismissed simply as shadows, heard the things others ignored as simply noise. To be a witch was forever separate and apart.

It was to be a cursed descendant of the Bathael the Usurper, she who had poisoned Ansala and tried to steal her glory in the days after the Prophetess' victory over the Aeore. Thus said the

Litany. Even the Galagax agreed. None of the four Faces of God had any love for her kind. Ansala herself had been a witch, but that was before Bathael had acted. In retaliation, Ansala had spoken the Bane, renouncing her own power and casting down every witch and warlock from their lofty perches. Now there were no more warlocks, and every witch born was a thing to be shunned and feared.

B'lantra had always been careful to never let the villagers know what she was behind the casual smiles she gave. Her reticence had been broken in the last days. Now she would have to break it one more time.

"I'll see if I can distract them," Cyrus said, speaking in the Trafarga language she'd taught him.

"You can't," B'lantra replied. "They'll know. Just keep them away until it's done."

She closed her eyes and began the song as quietly and as quickly as she dared. She immediately felt the inner torch of Helena's body. She could see all its myriad details: the flow of blood through the tiny capillaries, the beating of the heart though its chambers, the kidneys and liver as they desperately tried to filter out a poison they had no defense against. Lyra's careful training had shown her how they all connected.

Above them sat a dark intruder, hunched and hungry. Its tendrils reached out to snuff the flickering flame. B'lantra pushed at it, driving it back, striking and searing it until grudgingly it faded away. She then enjoined Helena's flame to grow, just as she'd done with the ember at the end of the lantern wick a few nights before. The battered cinders sprang forth and enkindled once more.

Flame was flame, no matter if it was inside or out. It was alive. It grew and consumed, lived to hunger and hungered to live. It could be encouraged or dampened. Outer flame was harder to master without the ready vessel of the body to contain it, but it was really no different to her.

An angry murmuring came from near the merchant wagon. She heard Cyrus' musket being cocked.

The family knew what she'd done.

What she was.

B'lantra opened her eyes and jerked herself back to her surroundings. Her song died on her lips. Pol had grabbed up a club from the back of the wagon. His oldest son, a ruddy faced boy of perhaps fifteen or so, nervously held a hatchet in his hands.

"Necromancer. What have you done? Get away from her!" the merchantman cried.

Cyrus kept the musket trained on him. "What she's done is save Helena's life."

B'lantra quickly gathered her supplies back up, not bothering to organize them. There had been a thought in her mind that maybe— just maybe— the family would accept what she'd done without questioning it too much.

Raas t'abulden. Road stupid, as Patri would have said. She should have known better.

Pol stepped forward.

Cyrus' finger reluctantly moved to the trigger. "Don't. Just don't. You'd think we robbed you instead of helped you."

B'lantra briefly turned her attention to Helena. The color had begun to return to the woman's face, and her breathing had eased.

"Hurry up, Bel!"

"Got it," B'lantra said, snatching up her pack and medicine bag.

Helena coughed and sat up, gasping like a drowning woman breaking the surface of the water. One of Pol's daughters, a young raven-haired girl, suddenly darted between the would-be combatants. She locked her arms around Helena's neck, nearly knocking the woman back down onto the pallet.

B'lantra smiled. There hadn't been time for her song to completely restore Helena, but the remaining wounds could heal by themselves now that the poison was gone. Pol and his family could see to it from here.

With the merchant family occupied, she and Cyrus hastily retreated into the surrounding trees.

"I hope that was worth the trouble," he said when they finally stopped to catch their breath.

"It was," B'lantra replied. "You know it too."

At least some stories in the world would end well today, and she'd had a part in making sure they did. It had been her choice, and it had been the right one.

* * *

The scent of witchcraft hung thickly in the air, both cloying and brilliant. It seared at Caulter's senses like a maddened thing. It had been an unexpected blessing after their failure to apprehend Aeliraneth's son in Shrevnetska.

Perhaps his luck was finally turning.

Witchcraft had been used, and it had acted as a burning signal flare, drawing the company inexorably in its direction. It was still fresh too, though it hadn't come from Aeliraneth's son.

The scent tugged at Caulter, urging him onwards to ravenously seek and to find, and to kill if need be. His years of disciplined training as a soldier waged a silent battle against the instincts the silverworm had instilled in him.

It was a war all inquisitors fought, a price for being what they were. He'd quailed six years ago when they'd first forced the silverworm upon him. The liquid had oozed from the flask and coiled around his arm like a serpent. The Conclave templars had held him to stop him from fleeing. Their hands had locked around his chin to keep him from screaming. Etienne Caulter had been changed that day. He often felt like he was simply a shell walking around in the man's body and sharing his memories.

He'd known fear in his life. And feeling. Even love.

They were distant things now, half remembered and sometimes even missed, but no longer important enough to keep him from doing what must be done.

The price was worth it. It had drawn them back to the Red

Road after their encounter with Lyra Kamani, the hellcat physician in Shrevnetska, had nearly destroyed their hunt. It had led them to the merchant family and soon to the completion of their mission.

Caulter couldn't help but feel a trace of sympathy for Pol, the merchantman cowering against the side of his rickety wagon. There was a troika bellowing from somewhere beyond the trees, probably intending to return to finish what it had started.

Bregna stood before Pol, coldly glaring. The captain had probably contemplated a hundred ways to end his miserable existence.

Caulter was surprised at himself for letting the interrogation go on as long as it had. It galled him to watch. The inquisitors had limited authority over the common folk, as the physician in Shrevnetska had so caustically pointed out. Bregna was a menace, and more to the point, a traitor. Allowing silverworm to fall into the hands of an outsider, let alone a witch was an unconscionable crime, worthy of a swift and painful execution.

It didn't matter anymore. He'd said it to himself over and over ever since he'd met Bregna. Teresa was the only thing that was really important. If the Illumentry alchemists could cure her, the Conclave could deal with Bregna as they saw fit.

She sits on the bed staring at the music box he's given her. She starts to wind it up. Her gray eyes harden. He's leaving her at the orphanage, and she knows it.

"I thought we were going to get me a sword so we could practice."

She's in no shape to practice anything.

Her dark hair is lank against her thin face. Her complexion is an ashen reflection of its once rich coppery hue. The mysterious scar that appeared on her forearm when she was two stands out along her increasingly scrawny frame.

"You're leaving again, aren't you?"

He nods.

Her face contorts angrily. For an instant she looks like she'll take the music box and hurl it across the room.

He leaves the room. Why does she have to make things so difficult?
He has to go. The Conclave has an assignment for him, and he can't
refuse it. She's nearly twelve. She should be old enough to understand.

He'd have to work with her once she was better. She might
have inherited her mother's looks, but she had none of Ysolde's
elegance or gentle grace. Teresa was far too wild and headstrong
for her own good. He'd put her aside too often, moved her around
too much. She needed stability, a real home. He would keep
teaching her how to use a sword, of course. And a pistol. But it
would be his only concession to her whims.

As he looked in front of him, he saw Bregna had already
grasped the front of the merchantman's coat. His other hand
hovered near the engraved silver knife at his belt.

"How long ago?" the captain demanded.

"Not long. You can still catch them, Sir Inquisitor."

Beads of sweat rolled down Pol's cheeks, mixing in with the
thin layer of road grime on his round face. Behind him, his children all stared blankly, the youngest clinging desperately to her
mother's neck.

Bregna released his hold on the merchantman and pushed
him roughly back against the wagon.

"Which way?"

Pol numbly pointed towards the trees.

Bregna's gaze turned to the blondish woman sitting tersely
on the wagon seat. "So, the witch that was with him healed this
woman of her wounds? She was expiring, and the sorceress called
her back from the brink of death? Caulter, have you ever heard
of something like this before?"

"No, a witch that can heal is highly unusual. It's been years
since we've had a reliable report of one who could."

"But can she heal or is she merely conjuring demons in human
form?" Bregna said. A cold smile formed on his thin lips as he
regarded the blonde woman. "I can smell the stench of enchantment on her. Perhaps further investigation is warranted."

The merchant's face grew even paler. "Please, Sir! She's no demon. She would have died rather than be treated by that vile witch. She—"

Bregna's fist flew. The merchantman spun around and collapsed over in a bloody, whimpering heap. The inquisitor captain drew his knife and moved towards the woman. She regarded him in nearly uncomprehending terror. The child clinging to her began crying.

Caulter reluctantly moved. Events had gone far enough.

Bregna's face lit up with rage as Caulter yanked him away from the woman on the wagon. The captain struggled against him. Caulter bore down using his weight and superior leverage. Bregna's fist slammed into his ribs. Caulter shrugged it off. He latched his hand around the captain's throat and squeezed. It was tempting to simply snap his filthy little neck, but he wouldn't. Not yet.

The knife flashed. Caulter saw it coming. He'd been in too many battles in too many places not to. He caught Bregna's wrist before the knife could do any damage. With a quick twist, it lay on the ground.

He heard the other inquisitors moving in. The click of a pistol being cocked back followed.

"You've just signed your own death warrant, Caulter," Bregna hissed. His eyes flickered over to the rest of the inquisitors. "Take this traitor away and put a bullet in his thick skull!"

Caulter didn't release his grip. A hand reached out and seized his shoulder. The cold barrel of a pistol tickled the skin on the back of his neck.

"We're inquisitors, not highwayman. We don't murder travelers on the highway. We're the people's protector, not their executioners. We go into the dark so they can stay in the light. We seek evil so they may know goodness. We—"

"Do you think quoting a few bits from the Commission Oath is going to save your worthless hide?" Bregna demanded.

Caulter waited. Even with the silverworm, doubts began to

creep in. The woman on the wagon was hardly worth it. The inquisitors were supposed to dedicate their lives to the principles of the order. It was an ideal that didn't always have a place in reality.

The muzzle of the pistol withdrew from the back of his neck. The hand released his shoulder. Caulter allowed himself a quick sigh of relief. He'd gambled once again and won this time. He could have almost laughed at the muted outrage racing across Bregna's face.

The captain shot the merchant family a shriveling glance.

"Let them go."

Caulter relaxed his hold. Hopefully, that would be the end of it.

"It seems the men have found themselves a new hero," Bregna growled. He lowered his voice. "We don't have to be enemies, Caulter. Work with me, and we'll both get what we want."

"Does your ambition have no end? Do you have any comprehension of what you've already done?"

"Do you have any comprehension of what's at stake? Aeliraneth understood the meaning of the old Iriethan characters. The blonde witch claimed she taught her son. Think of what that would mean to the Conclave."

"You had relations with the witch to get that information."

"That's a sin we share, Caulter. Don't let your self-righteousness keep you from forgetting that."

Caulter shoved Bregna away and picked up the captain's knife. He stared at the blade for a long moment. "I dealt with my sin, Bregna. Yours is still running free with the silverworm."

"Do you think the Illumentry alchemists will really waste time trying to cure your brat? The sad truth is that you're not important enough to them."

Caulter paused.

"But if we were to return with the son of the Great Witch in tow, you suddenly become a hero— not just to these men but to everyone," Bregna continued. "You suddenly become important enough for the alchemists to fall over themselves curing her."

Caulter flicked the knife at Bregna. It landed between the captain's feet, its handle quivering

"Alright," he said at last. "Both Aeliraneth's son and the witch he's with gain ground on us. They may elude us altogether if we tarry here."

Bregna put the knife away. "Given your great wisdom in such matters, how do you suggest we capture them? The scent is still fresh. They're on foot, so they can't have gotten far."

Caulter ignored the derision in the captain's tone as best he could. "The Red Road curves around. We send some men after them to flush them out. The rest of us can ride around and intercept them when they emerge on the other side."

The troika bellowed again.

Bregna shook his head. "I've a better idea. We'll use that beast to our advantage."

"What are you talking about?"

"You of all people should understand the importance of gathering information on one's target, Caulter. They were clever enough to escape the village jail. The sheriff said the witch could call fire, and the boy fought like a demon. Perhaps he's exaggerating to cover his incompetence, perhaps not. That beast gives us the perfect opportunity to learn what they may be capable of. The witch may well turn out to be an unforeseen gift."

Caulter raised an eyebrow, but said nothing further. Caught up in confronting Bregna, he'd momentarily forgotten about the witch and her healing ability.

What should he do with her?

He'd slain witches when required or witnessed them broken and turned into weapons by the Illumentry. He'd simply accepted it as God's will. Perhaps coming across this witch was also God's will.

He pondered on the decision he was going to have to make and then realized his thoughts were already turning to how he could pry her from the Illumentry's grasp. If Bregna's scheme failed, it might be the only chance Teresa had.

The only decision that remained for him was how he could turn the situation to his desires.

Plans turning through his mind, he quickly joined Bregna and the other inquisitors as they rode off in the direction of the troika.

CHAPTER 9

THE NOOSE TIGHTENS

THEY WALKED HAND IN HAND through the meadow, the late afternoon sun shining warm and bright upon them. The ground sloped to the Dreyfus River, covered in a patchwork of yellow daffodils, white crocus and a dozen other flowers B'lantra recognized. She thought about listing them and their effects on the body just to show off for Cyrus, but she doubted he would appreciate it. Lyra had spent years drumming information like that into his head.

"Look at the flowers. They're beautiful, aren't they?"

They really were.

The witchcraft she'd used on Helena had left her bone tired, enough so that she'd be hard pressed to use it again until tomorrow. There was also a good chance they were still being hunted. Erendel seemed like a distant dream they might never see. The flowers made it easier to forget their problems, and to just pretend for a little while that everything was still right with the world.

"I was just thinking about the flowers... and possibly hoping you wouldn't notice and start reciting every flower name you could think of," Cyrus said.

"Who says that's what I was thinking?" B'lantra asked, indignantly. "It could have been anything. You don't know."

"Just an idle guess," he replied. He leisurely took her in with his eyes. "No lectures about flowers or the effects of distilled essences, please. You're the only flower I'm interested in right now."

"That's surprisingly romantic coming from you, Cyrus. I don't think the best poets of Erendel could have put it any better."

It really wasn't all that surprising when she thought about it.

At heart Cyrus was a gentleman and a scholar, though he would have probably thrown anyone who called him that straight into the mud. He might try to hide his upbringing, but it peeked out at unexpected times: in his table manners, in his sense of right and wrong, and in his ability to gently redirect their conversation with a heartfelt compliment.

It was a side of him she wished he'd show more often.

"Look up in the sky," he said. "I think our lonely village ley line has found a friend."

She followed to where he'd pointed. The singular line that ran overtop Shrevnetska continued its northward journey, but now it was crossed by a larger one following the westward trail of the sun. It reminded her of two ships briefly passing each other in a vast blue ocean, perhaps journeying to one of the islands of clouds dotting the horizon.

"We'll see more of them as we go north," Cyrus said.

B'lantra could only smile.

She stands in the grassy commons, watching the evening sky. The ley line shimmers—purple against the reds and yellows of the sunset. It's alone like she is. Can she really be the only person that sees it?

She sees the strange Northern boy watching her. He glances up into the sky. His eyes go straight to the ley line before they focus on her. He's not like the others in the village. He's aware— like someone who can see color when everyone else around them can only see in black and white.

He hasn't said anything to her since he saved from her Wilyam and his stupid friends. It still scares her how close she was to unleashing her fire against them.

He slowly walks across the grass to stand beside her. Again, he glances up into the sky and finds the ley line. She looks up at it too before lowering her head.

They stand in awkward silence.

Finally, she can't stand it anymore.

"You can see it too, can't you?"

He stares at her. Maybe it's her words. She still doesn't speak the Northern tongue very well. Patri hadn't finished teaching her. He never will now.

He nods. Then his eyes light up with excitement. "You mean the ley line, don't you? The purple ribbon in the sky."

She laughs. The words tumble out of her. Northern tongue. Trafarga. It doesn't matter. After so many days of fear and silence, the words won't stop.

She tells him about the k'ziani, the swirling sand fae that sometimes appear on the horizon at dusk. He tells her about the stings, the corrupted machine spirits that haunt some of the old graveyards in Targus.

She'd found home in a way… in a place far removed from the lands she'd grown up in.

B'lantra took another look at the flowers and wrapped her arm around his waist. "I almost wish we had time for other things. We did bring a blanket after all."

"Well, flowers do need to be pollinated," he said, grinning. "But I'm afraid the flower will have to defer that pleasure for the time being. I saw a bog fairy nest about halfway down the slope, and that's a little too close for my liking. Besides, I'd like to make Vershanon's Inn by nightfall if we can."

"There? Are you sure it's safe?" she asked. "It's the only stop on the road until Ashenwall. The inquisitors might be watching it."

"We need supplies before we turn west. A lot of people come through there, even Trafari caravans. We should be able to hide easily enough."

"Maybe. I suppose if we're together it might just work out."

"We've been inseparable for years now, ever since you walked out of the Arkinwood that one spring day. It was a day like this, if I remember right."

"You were standing beside the bridge over the Dry Run when old Gregori found me and carried me across. I still remember the look you gave me."

"It was love at first sight."

"You would have been just as happy if it had been a troupe of jesters or a trader from Arakost. At least until Lyra found you and put you back to work," B'lantra teased.

Her smile suddenly fell away.

The large shape moved deliberately through the trees at the edge of the meadow. It would have been twice the height of a man if it hadn't been hunched over. She could see its long claws and the jagged club it carried. Its oily gray-green hide almost blended into the surrounding foliage. It was half-way through its spring molting, and strips of skin hung from its body like trailing wisps of paper. From its mouth jutted yellowed fangs, a few broken off, others razor sharp. A long, filthy mane of lank hair flowed over its heavy shoulders and down its back.

It had been a long time since she'd been so close to one of the creatures. She could have happily spent a lifetime never having to do it again.

Cyrus immediately saw the look on her face. "What's the matter?"

Her hands shook.

"Troika," she whispered.

❋ ❋ ❋

Asa laughed softly to herself as she lay underneath the beech trees, Susanna tucked beside her. The events she'd so carefully arranged were coming together even better than she'd expected. She'd come far since being sacrificed to the waters, grown since she'd been sold like a filthy gocochen.

Her thoughts churned. She'd been a burden for a family that didn't want her. Father had eventually found someone who did.

A pair of gocochen and ten silver sparrows for her. The transaction had been simple and smooth, as if she were nothing more than a pair of shoes at the market.

She'had to leave her sister Arellia behind. Perfect little Arellia, Father's great pride. Perfect, sweet Arellia, who'd always gotten everything she ever wanted. With the mill closed and work scarce, he could only afford to keep one daughter, Father said. Her buyer would be good to her.

She sits on the bed looking out the window. The sheets are softer than anything she's known. The curtains flutter as a breeze blows through the window. They look like real silk.

Her buyer must have a lot of money.

He enters the room and locks the door behind him. He's a tall man with dark hair. She's been too nervous to really study his face.

He unloosens his belt and sits down beside her.

Her skin prickles as his hand slides up her back.

"Pretty thing," he whispers.

He tells her to unbutton her dress.

Her buyer hadn't been able to keep possession of his prize. His skull had been caved in when another man from another family wanted her. The blood feud had carried on for nearly a year before they decided it was no longer worth the time and money.

She stands at the edge of the pier overlooking the lake. The wood is rough beneath her bare feet. The chain weighs heavily around her neck. The iron weight it's attached to has a crack running along its length. They couldn't even be bothered to use a new one. Her wrists are bound tightly together.

It's evening. The sunset is red like blood.

"Too pretty to live," the judge declares. He's an old man with a tight, brown cap and a long, white beard. "Let the harlot that started this war pay the price for her poisonous ways."

The assembled nobles murmur their agreement. It's all about power to them. Power to shape their own lives and those of others. It's how the world works. She knows that now.

She stares at the water below. It laps the pier supports, gray and cold.

Susanna watches, clutching her little yellow-haired doll. She's five now. Sweet little daughter her buyer had given her that night in his bedchamber.

Susanna she cherishes. Susanna she's never wanted.

Susanna looks more like her than she does her father. Blonde hair. Rosy cheeks. Her expression is cold.

Little bitch! She doesn't care. None of them care.

One of the soldiers comes to stand beside her. He lifts the weight and throws it into the water. There is a splash and then a horrible pull around her neck.

She falls.

The water is just as cold as it looked.

It had been a good bargain she'd made as the waters enveloped her. It had been the only one she could have made. Nysse, the water spirit, certainly thought so. It offered a new life. Power. All it wanted was Susanna.

It was a good bargain.

Asa ran her hand down, carefully smoothing out the wrinkles in the doll's calico dress. "It was alright, wasn't it Susanna? My friend liked you."

The doll looked sadly at her.

"I'm sorry if Nysse hurt you, my darling. It had to be done. Mother couldn't just drown, you know. It had to be done."

Almost unconsciously Asa reached up to the silken kerchief around her neck. The skin underneath was bruised and blackened, the marks the chain had left just as fresh as the day it had first been wrapped around her. Along with the matching marks around her wrists, it was the only blemish on her otherwise perfect skin.

There were other ways to make a witch than a simple accident of birth. Nysse had given her the mist to command, and allowed her to heal even the most horrific injuries in time.

It had also prevented her from healing the marks on her skin, a simple reminder that what had been given could also be taken away.

It was a situation that was unacceptable.

Sensing movement from over her shoulder, she turned. The chimera fluttered towards her, its lidless, bloodshot eyes boring into her. Bat-like wings fluttered in excitement.

It was an annoying little creature, with parts from various beasts that never would have come together naturally. From its hairless round body to its rat's tail to its oversized ears, it was an abomination, neither natural nor fae. She could have crushed it in the palm of her hand and had thought about doing so more than once.

On the heels on the chimera's appearance, the morning grew still. Three crimson stones seared themselves into existence on the earth. The nearby blades of grass shriveled in their wake. Lines of pulsing energy leeched out from the stones connecting them in a triangular array of ruddy light. The air between them shimmered and then fell in on itself, revealing a dark, pulsing channel. Energy briefly sparked along its sides before clearing.

It was an Aeore technique, developed in Asylum long ago. The Aeore used it for communication and for transport. It had allowed them to easily outmaneuver the besieged Iriethan forces during the time of Ansala.

Asa stood up and adjusted her hair and clothing before discreetly tucking Susanna away in her handbag.

Her Simon had come to call.

※ ※ ※

The creature paused and sniffed the ground. Its three piggish red eyes stared around. It probably couldn't see them from this distance, but it wouldn't be long before it caught their scent.

"Get ready to run," Cyrus whispered.

The sound of voices suddenly carried up the slope, laughing and chatting: two girls playing some sort of game down by the Dreyfus. The troika stopped sniffing the ground and raised its body up. Its misshapen head cocked to the side taking in the sound of the girls' voices. With a grunt of what sounded like pleasure it began creeping down towards them.

Cyrus slipped off his pack and brought out his musket. He'd figured on hunting small game with it, not hungry troika. The monsters should have gone back to their lairs in the deep woods after the storm, but then little else had gone right in the last few days. Why should this afternoon be any different?

"One bullet isn't going to stop it. You'd need a whole company," B'lantra whispered.

"I'm not going to just let those girls get eaten," he snapped.

"We need a plan first."

"There's no time for a plan."

The look she gave him was so withering and devastating it amazed him that the grass didn't shrivel around her. He couldn't be quite sure whether the quietly hissed stream of Trafari profanity that followed was directed at him or the troika.

She was right though. He had no idea of what he was going to do; only that he had to do something. He thought once more of the ruddy, flickering embers that had danced along Akestra's edge as Celaan had held the sword in her hands. The weapon would have likely made short work of the troika.

He didn't have it. He'd made his choice, and all he had was his skill and his luck. It was a poor substitute.

A single musket might not stop the monster, but maybe he could lead it off if he could get its attention…

He took aim and fired without giving it any more thought. The shot was true, slicing neatly through a cluster of leaves and striking the troika on its flank. Any normal animal would have been crippled. The troika merely yelped and turned, trying to find the source of its sudden pain. A growl erupted from its throat.

Cyrus threw down the musket and pulled his pistol from his belt. His next shot found its mark as well. The bullet tore into the heavy muscles on the creature's shoulder, but it didn't slow it down enough to do him any good.

It came charging at him, closing the distance far more quickly than he'd imagined. A sidelong glance towards the edge of the meadow told him he'd be run down before he reached the relative safety of the trees.

So much for leading it away.

"Get out of here!" he ordered B'lantra.

He unsheathed his sword and sprang forward to meet the monster. Its club came crashing towards him in a blur. Cyrus twisted out of the way, barely in time. The club pounded into the earth, flattening the grass and leaving a gaping tear in the flower-covered skin of the meadow. He moved around, desperately hoping for an opening. For all its size, the creature was surprisingly agile. Again the club came careening towards him. Again he dodged. The monster grunted in frustration.

Cyrus finally saw his chance and stepped forward, thrusting the sword into where he guessed its heart lay. The troika was unfazed. Much to his dismay, the tip of his sword blade barely penetrated its thick hide. The stroke sent a numbing shock up his arm. Its claws flashed towards him. He turned, trying to avoid them. Not enough!

It hardly touched him, but the force was still enough to send him spinning to the earth. The troika stood over him and raised its club, preparing to turn him into pulp.

B'lantra's song cut through the air. He had a vague sense of her dropping her pack and charging towards the troika. A red shower of sparks ignited around its muzzle, singeing and burning it. It howled in rage and stumbled backwards, slapping angrily at the cinders boring into its flesh. The song faded quickly away. B'lantra had used her last inner reserves of energy for the day.

"Move, idiot!" she cried.

He got to his feet and staggered away. "I told you to get out of here!"

"I never agreed to that," she said. Her eyes were wide and her face was drawn.

An idea whirled though his head. "The bog fairies! If we can lead it towards them, they'll take care of the troika."

"And us too! Are you mad?"

"It's a plan, isn't it?"

"Not a very good—"

"Come on!"

They made a frantic dash for the tree line. The troika recovered and let out another ear-splitting bellow before charging after them. It relentlessly gained on them.

At last they reached the trees. The smell of its rancid breath and the sound of its snarl were just behind them. Its club struck, cracking through the branches overhead. Claws slashed out, catching the sleeve of B'lantra's tunic and tearing it away. The creature paused long enough to snuffle at the torn shreds of cloth before resuming its chase.

They continued on, weaving their way down the hillside. They could hear it behind them, tearing its way through the trees and the undergrowth, doggedly following.

"Shouldn't... be... much... farther," Cyrus gasped.

They drew closer to the river, passing through a lush patch of tree ferns. They suddenly found their way barred by a gaping cliff that cut its way up the hillside. The ground dropped off, with only a sheer, moss-covered fall before them. Cyrus hadn't counted on the cliff. He looked around frantically before he finally spotted a narrow trail cutting back at an awkward angle from the cliff face before continuing down the slope. It was treacherous and steep, better suited for nimble-footed mountain goats than for people.

Was there another way down?

The troika gave him no time to think on it further. It loomed out of the tree ferns. Its red eyes were angry and maddened, White foamy slobber was splattered across its muzzle.

Its club hammered down.

Cyrus pushed B'lantra out of the way and dived for cover. The blow flattened the ground where they'd both stood. Splinters of wood and chunks of rock flew everywhere.

He rolled quickly and came about. The creature had focused on B'lantra. Its claws hungrily reached for her. She backed away, then lost her footing and disappeared over the edge of the cliff.

Her scream carried downwards even as he raced over to try and catch her. He couldn't. There would be no repeat of his feat at the Karrak. He barely caught a glimpse of her flailing form spiraling downwards into the trees and rocks below.

This wasn't how he meant for it to go!

He stared blankly. It had all happened so quickly.

The troika gave a grunt of disappointment, then turned and glared at him. Its hairy nostrils flared, taking in his scent. Standing so close, the stench of rotting meat and dung that rose from it made his stomach want to tumble over the cliff after B'lantra.

With a vengeful howl it came at him. Once again he found himself sprinting down the slope just out of the reach of its claws. For a brief moment he thought the steep trail down the slope might be too much for it, but the troika proved to be nearly as agile as he was.

He kept running.

B'lantra?

There was nothing he could do for her right now.

The first bog fairy flew past his face. She was a beautiful and an ugly creature at the same time, no larger than his hand. Her body was in perfect tiny proportion, lightly clad in garments that looked as if they'd been sewn from oak leaves. Her wings were delicate and light, long pale gossamer streamers that kept her aloft with a grace no bird could match. Her warty skin was an almost iridescent blue-green, mottled through with long streaks of black. The bulging purple eyes that dominated her face watched him malevolently. She held a barbed spear tightly in her hand, its tip dripping with what looked like poison.

Fixated on him, she didn't notice the troika until it was too late. She let out a piercing scream and tried to veer away. Before she could escape, the monster's hand shot out and seized her, crushing her tiny body in its grip. It stopped long enough to gulp down her mangled remains.

The fairy's alarm cry had gone out, however. Cyrus edged

carefully away as more of her kind skimmed past his face. Behind him a great mound of hardened earth jutted from the ground. A strange yellowish moss grew over parts of it, giving off a faint light. The smell of rotting vegetation wafted past him. From an opening in the mound, fairies poured forth. In an instant the air was full of them. The troika bellowed in annoyance and swatted at them. Some were mashed by its club or ripped apart by its claws, but more came to bolster their ranks.

Several of them began spinning strands of golden fiber around the monster, binding its arms and legs. Others moved in to plunge their spears into its body, hobbling it. The troika's roar changed to a fearful, whining whimper as it succumbed to the fairies' sheer numbers. It toppled over, covered in an angry, buzzing horde.

Cyrus moved away, hoping they were too busy to notice him. The troika would be eaten alive, and he had no desire join it. The shrill pitch of the fairies' triumphant cries summoning their weaker sisters to the feast echoed in his ears.

Once he was beyond the earshot of the bog fairies, he called B'lantra's name, hoping the sound of his voice would draw her attention and not the notice of something less pleasant.

No answer came in response.

He made his way down the slope, glancing around occasionally to make sure nothing was creeping up behind him. The sun was sinking towards the horizon, and the shadows were lengthening noticeably.

He would need to find her before dark— before something else found her.

"Damn!"

He'd thought for years about what it would be like when he and B'lantra finally left Shrevnetska. This wasn't the way he'd imagined it.

CHAPTER 10

THE NOOSE CLOSES

VIOLET EYES BORED INTO ASA like two cold and distant stars. Simon Barros, once General of the Aeore Imperial Legions and consort to the Revered Empress Celaan, had been a gangly, almost awkward man in life, and it still showed in his ghostly form. He towered over her, a translucent scarecrow. His craggy face was firm, with a strong jaw, a hawk-like nose and a commanding gaze. His beard was full. He wore a richly appointed coat, trimmed with golden thread and the insignia of the rank he'd once had. Underneath the coat, his form fitting armor looked as pristine as it had the day he'd died. Celaan had specially commissioned it for him in honor of his victory at the Falchon Plains.

Warlock. Scholar. Savior. Simon Barros had been all of these things. Though no Aeore, he'd been their one hope against the Tainted. His strategies had worked when no others had. He'd stood on the threshold of victory, only to see it snatched away from him.

He had loved. That was the only real fault Asa could find with him. Love was simply a word one person used to gain power over another.

Before her, Asa saw the man who had talked to her, listened to her and told her that she could be more than a wealthy noble's fleeting trophy. She saw the man who had lifted her out of the waters, and convinced the Aeore to let her join them rather than killing her.

The water connected all things, so Nysse said. It flowed everywhere, even to Asylum. Eddies in the current would open up

109

from time to time. You could travel them if you had the skill, even though the Wynding. Your journey would never end in the same place twice. After she'd made her bargain, Nysse had brought her to Asylum and the Aeore Imperium.

Simon had found his way to there from the Lanternlit years before, and had already earned the Aeore's admiration. With his help, she had become strong enough to spit back in the face of a world that had spit on her. There in battle with the Tainted, she'd earned the Aeore sword she carried.

Simon grew nearer. The grass withered with each step he took. The leaves blackened and curled away from his presence. The birdsong from the trees had gone suddenly still. He was a blighted thing, a haunted thing, a gliding, aching patch of dark within dark, quiet within quiet. On the other side of the portal that had opened, his laboratory stood. Its machines quietly hummed. The misshapen chimera went dutifully about their tasks. Asa noted a spidery, lion footed one standing almost mournfully over a pile of bodies that hadn't yet been removed. It seemed Simon's search for a new form to wear wasn't going well.

"I expected you to report in by yesterday at the latest."

The voice was deep and commanding. It had a certain gentleness to it, but underneath lurked the harsh tone of authority that made soldiers snap to attention.

"Unfortunately, events delayed me," Asa said. "The storms in the area proved troublesome."

It was a half-truth at best, and she suspected Simon was well aware of it. He didn't question it however, beyond a slight rise in one of his eyebrows. "And what of the silverworm? You claimed a bold plan to procure it, yet I have seen nothing other than your absence."

She had been gone too long and he'd become impatient. Like any bristling beast, he would need to be soothed.

"I have something better than a bold plan, dear Simon."

She radiantly held up the box of silverworm for him to see.

His violet eyes softened immediately as she knew they would.

The chimera swooped down and took the box from her in its scaly claws, clucking to itself contentedly as it flew back and hovered over his shoulder.

"Shall I ask how you managed to obtain it?" he asked.

"It was a small matter of convincing some of the inquisitors to part with it," she replied, demurely.

"Well done. You are as resourceful as you are lovely."

"What is it you intend to do with the silverworm?"

"The technical details would no doubt bore you, and I know how much you hate being bored."

"Your plan for them has to be more interesting than the inquisitors themselves. I found them disappointing."

"You shouldn't need to deal with them any further. In fact, now that you have the silverworm, I prefer you leave them be."

"How does this help bring down the ward around Aeliraneth's old estate? That is the last hurdle between us and the Heart of the Great Machine is it not?"

"You're invited to witness exactly how it will help," Simon said. There was an almost childlike eagerness under his impassive mask as he gestured towards the portal. His tone suggested it was more of a command than a request.

"Thank you, but the portals always make me queasy. Might I beg your indulgence to remain at large a little longer?" Asa asked. "There are some loose ends remaining in regards to my obtaining the silverworm. It would be best if they were tied up."

"Do you require some assistance, my dear?"

"It's a minor matter, but one that shouldn't be left unattended."

She kept her eyes straight and her shoulders square, the perfect model of a loyal and dedicated subordinate. Simon was more perceptive than most men, but he tended to lose himself in his work.

"Very well, Asa. I'll expect to see you soon. Our moment of triumph is nearly at hand. I wouldn't want you to miss it."

Simon turned and glided towards the pattern of red stones, the chimera close behind. In a moment, he and the stones had disappeared, leaving only the burned grass as a reminder of their presence.

Asa glanced carefully around. Just because Simon had departed didn't mean the chimera had. It served as his eyes and ears, and despite its ungainly appearance, it could be remarkably subtle if it chose.

When she finally judged it safe, Asa retrieved Susanna from her handbag.

"Events have quickened a little it seems. I won't be able to play with Aeliraneth's son as much as I'd like. No matter."

She called the mists to her. They swirled round, comforting and soothing in their embrace.

The doll gave her a questioning look.

"We're going back to Shrevnetska," Asa said. A slight smile curled across her lips. "Mother's feeling a little sick, you see. I think I need to see a doctor."

❊ ❊ ❊

The evening birds were cooing their welcome song to the coming night as B'lantra opened her eyes. She sat up and then almost immediately wished she hadn't. Her head throbbed and her body ached. She gazed at the slope, tracing the path of broken branches she'd left in her wake.

There was no going back that way.

A quick assessment found a lot of scratches and bruises, a growing knot on the side of her head, but no broken bones or sprains. The physician's satchel at her side was surprisingly intact, having somehow managed to take less of a beating coming down the slope than she had. The lantern Lyra had given her hadn't been so fortunate. Her clothes were torn and muddied; her hair was a tangled mess.

The light was fading, the sun barely above the horizon. At first she was hesitant to call out for Cyrus, but even when need overcame caution, she was rewarded only with the sounds of water flowing and frogs croaking. It was most likely from the Dreyfus, and that seemed as good a place as any to start looking for him.

If he was still alive, that is.

The memory of the troika swirled back to her. She shuddered. Of course he was still alive. Cyrus would have found a way. He always did.

If not…

No. The idea wasn't even worth contemplating.

"If you'd listened to me, come up with some sort of plan, this wouldn't have happened."

She really couldn't fault him for intervening. He couldn't have refused, any more than she could have just left Helena to die. It was the same reasons that had compelled him to protect a scrawny foreign girl when it would have been so much easier to just turn his back. He had always been her knight protector and she his princess, even though they both laughed at those very same characters in the stories they read.

For all his good intentions however, his stupidity had gotten them into a fine mess. If he'd hated the lectures she'd given him before, wait until she found him again.

Once she set out, it didn't take her long to find the trail that paralleled the Dreyfus' course. It was a little muddy from the storm, but still passable.

She called him one more time and again received no answer. Where was he?

The patter of footsteps came towards her from down the path. Was it Cyrus? No, the steps were too heavy to be Cyrus.

They were gone almost as soon as she became aware of them.

She carefully surveyed the trees around. There was nothing, not even a squirrel to keep her company. The calls of the evening birds seemed to have vanished.

Night was coming. Her stomach began to churn as the reality of her situation set in. Nervously, she found a sturdy branch near the water's edge and softly began her song. Her craft was nearly as bedraggled as she was. Flame reluctantly sprouted from the end of the branch. It was enough to keep the darkness at bay at least, though she wasn't sure how long she could maintain it.

Warily, she proceeded on, wishing she had more to defend herself with than the paring knife at her belt. Again she heard what she thought were footsteps. Again she looked around and saw nothing.

She was no warrior, nor even an experienced hunter. She had only her wits if there was a troika or something even worse lurking nearby.

She turned and fled down the path when the footsteps came again.

A man slid smoothly out of the trees blocking her progress. There were other figures closing in on her. Her song quivered. The flame from her torch seemed to grow dim.

Black coats. Black uniforms. The monsters had found her!

B'lantra froze. A clean-shaven man with sandy colored hair approached her. His aristocratic face had a triumphant sneer on it.

"I am Inquisitor Captain Bregna. You will cease your wickedness and surrender."

She turned to run.

"There's nowhere for you to go."

The voice came from another man behind her. He was older with a slightly graying beard.

"I am Inquisitor Lieutenant Caulter. You stand accused of witchcraft. You are ordered to come with us and submit yourself to God's judgment."

B'lantra's torch fell from her limp fingers.

They'd tracked her. Trapped her. Stupid! The escape from Shrevnetska would never have been that easy.

This is what Celaan had meant. This was the suffering she'd been talking about. The song that came to her was instinctive, a nearly blind primal fear.

Bregna leapt at her. The fire she called forth lashed out towards him in a red-yellow wave of heat and light, striking frantically. The flames seemed to slide away from him.

The movement of his hand was more of a blur than anything else. Her head snapped around from the force of the blow, her song strangled. The ground rushed up to meet her, knocking the breath from her body as it slammed into her.

She tried to get up, to crawl away and hide.

A heavy boot drove into her back, crushing her down to the ground again. The soft muddy earth of the path pressed against her face. She tasted blood in her mouth. A hand reached down and grabbed a fistful of her hair, using it to yank her head back up.

"I don't think we want to hear any of your song, witch," Bregna said.

Her vision swam in and out. The inquisitors were all around her now, staring down. Their expressions were cold and empty.

B'lantra willed the song to come to her. Bregna's hand came down sharply across her face once more. Lights flashed dully inside her skull.

"Bring the witch-locks. That will keep her in check."

The iron manacles, engraved with dully glinting golden glyphs, burned when they bound her hands with them. It felt like she was being smothered. Her flame called to her like a lost child wailing in the night and then went horribly quiet. She was barely aware of her body heaving and writhing. Eventually the pain subsided down to an empty, miserable ache.

A few tears streamed down her bruised face.

"We've been dealing with your kind for a long time now. We know how to defang a serpent," Bregna said. "Now tell me where Aeliraneth's son has gone."

"I'm not telling you anything," B'lantra said. She tried to spit in his face. Blood ran down her chin.

His grip on her hair tightened. "No one's going to come running to help you. There's just you and us until the hangman takes you or the Conclave breaks you. Now answer my question, witch. I won't ask so nicely again."

"No!"

Cyrus was still free. Maybe he'd find some way to stay that way. Bregna drew back his hand again.

"The boy will be easy enough to find. If she's to be broken, the Conclave will want her as unspoiled as possible," Caulter said, quickly.

"Don't worry. She's not going to be spoiled," Bregna replied. He took B'lantra's physician's satchel and handed it to Caulter. "We'll see if this will lure Aeliraneth's son out."

He turned to the other inquisitors. "You two take her away in the cage we brought. Secure her in the dungeons of Ashenwall, and we'll join you once we have him."

"Witches are supposed to go to Calateph and the Conclave when they're first captured," Caulter said.

"The roshan of this province will want to see them first. Since you're so fond of proper protocol, you'll know that it requires we inform the local ruler that we're arresting two of his citizens on suspicion of witchcraft," Bregna said, coldly. "Besides, it's a long way to Calateph. We wouldn't want them misplaced along the way, would we Caulter?"

Caulter's expression darkened. "We'll have Aeliraneth's spawn in a few hours."

As she was being taken away, B'lantra watched Bregna lean closer to Caulter. "You've grown soft, old man. If you really cared about the Trafari witch that much, then perhaps you should have just cut her throat. It might have been kinder and quicker in the long run."

❋ ❋ ❋

Cyrus waited sullenly in the darkened meadow.

Damn it! Where was she?

B'lantra's discarded pack was still lying amidst the daffodils, near enough to his own. He'd searched everywhere he could think of, called for her as much as he dared without drawing the attention of the inquisitors, bandits or worse.

He hated just standing around. The inaction had already set his nerves jangling almost more than he could take. He'd have to make another pass through the woods.

A branch crackled near the edge of the tree line.

B'lantra?

No, something else.

The man was watching him from the trees. Cyrus stepped back at first, fearful. The black coat and cloak were plain to see. The man mockingly held up a battered leather satchel.

B'lantra's medicine bag!

The man retreated beneath the trees. Furious, Cyrus grabbed his musket and sword and bolted after him.

The trap was sprung. Three men glided out of the trees towards him. There were probably others already moving to cut off his escape.

Two of them began to flank him, while the one in the center calmly continued his advance.

"I am Caulter, Inquisitor Lieutenant of the Illumentry. Cyrus of House Ulberath, you are ordered to come with us and—"

Cyrus reached for his musket. It was tempting to just shoot Caulter down then and there, but he wouldn't. Murdering was for thieves and thugs.

If he could wound Caulter, then maybe…

He wasn't really sure what he was going to do.

Caulter sensed his hesitation and closed in quickly. Caught off guard, Cyrus instinctively brought the musket up. Caulter wrenched it from his hands before he could fire. Cyrus fell back, frantically grabbing his sword. The inquisitor gave him no quarter.

Cyrus barely had time to parry a series of quick thrusts. His own riposte was slow and clumsy. Caulter warded it off easily.

Caulter calmly waited until he had overextended himself and then flicked out his sword. Cyrus' own weapon went spinning out of his hand. Blood welled up from a long cut along his wrist.

Caulter advanced again.

Cyrus was forced back, weaving and dodging to avoid the shining blade coming relentlessly after him. Caulter drove him into the waiting arms of the other inquisitors, and they stepped in to seize him.

He fought their grip, flailing and kicking, punching at their pale, ghoul faces over and over again. It was hopeless. For every one he knocked away, another seemed to take his place.

"That's enough," he heard Caulter say.

Cyrus shook his head, trying to regain his senses and found Caulter's sword point leveled at his throat.

"It's a wonder you survived that troika at all."

"What have you done with B'lantra?" Cyrus demanded, still struggling against the other inquisitor's grip.

"The witch is under our protection. She's presently unharmed and will stay that way provided you give yourself up without any further incident," Caulter answered.

"Like hell she will. I know about your kind!"

The blade didn't waver from Cyrus' throat. "Then you already know there's no point in continuing this. You have my word: she won't be hurt if you surrender yourself. Think carefully, boy. Your alternatives aren't particularly good."

❋ ❋ ❋

Night had settled across Shrevnetska. The faint sounds of hammer and saw still rang out as the inhabitants worked to repair the damage the storm had left in its wake.

Lyra walked slowly into the kitchen of her house. The emptiness hit her almost immediately. B'lantra would have been near the hearth, making some of the strange Trafari food she liked, while Cyrus would have been by the table reading one of his silly stories. They would have been talking and laughing with each other, sharing hopes and dreams, planning the big things they would one day do.

Everything was silent and cold now. The house felt larger and lonelier than she'd ever remembered it. The unfinished wood carving of a wide-eyed falcon that B'lantra had been working on still sat in the corner. Cyrus' leather bound edition of the latest exploits of Sir Bennon still lay on the shelf, half unread. The way events had unfolded, neither would be completed anytime soon.

It seemed only yesterday the dark-haired Trafari girl had been carried across the bridge into the village. Only yesterday that Cyrus had been charging around playing soldier, giving any and all a brooding little boy's scowl.

Only yesterday…

"I'm getting old and sentimental, and I have too much work to do for that nonsense," she chided herself. She was Arakostrian, and she should know better.

They would be fine. She hoped to Talast and the rest of God's Faces they would be. The inquisitors had been driven from the village like the dogs they were. The rest was up to Cyrus and B'lantra.

Her chair, normally her little piece of comfort in an unpredictable, chaotic world, didn't feel as relaxing as it normally did, even after she'd lit the fire in the fireplace and sat down in it. Her knitting sat ignored in her lap, the pointed needle impaling the beginning of a red sweater. Instead, she idly stroked Saint Rachael's silver clover around her neck and contemplated.

The presence in the room was suddenly overwhelming. Lyra bolted up out of her chair. Still in its battered leather sheath, her old sword hung over the mantle. How long it would take her to reach it?

"It wouldn't do you any good, even if I let you get to it," the voice purred from the darkened corner of the room. The shadows seemed to grow longer.

"Who are you?" Lyra demanded.

"I'm hurt that you wouldn't remember. We have such history together, you and I. Aeliraneth's handmaiden, who thought she could elude me and start a new life with a son that wasn't hers."

The intruder came into the light, her heeled boots gently clicking on the floor. The fire's ruddy glow reflected off her elegant, perfect features. The fabric of her clothes almost shimmered, shifting from red to gold to green. From under her arm, a yellow haired stitched doll stared.

"I am Asa of the Mist. I was sent to make sure none of Aeliraneth's servants survived the attack on the estate. One by one, I tracked down those the fire didn't consume. Last year I found Janus the gardener, bless his old heart. Imagine my surprise when he told me the most valuable servant of all was still alive."

"Pity Janus couldn't keep quiet. He always was a talker," Lyra replied, doing her best to keep her voice firm.

"I managed to persuade him to spill his secrets," Asa said. "In the end, it wasn't the only thing of his that spilled."

"If you're going to try and kill me, the least you can do is not talk so much," Lyra snapped. "That is why you're here, isn't it?"

"All in good time. Tell me, how is your little cretin of a foster son these days? He should be all grown up by now," Asa asked. The sweetness of her tone belied the menace written all over her face. "I understand he's even gone off and gotten himself a little girlfriend. How nice. I'm sure they make a lovely couple."

"They had to leave suddenly. They never did say where they were going. Tragic, really."

"Oh, that is a shame. I suppose the Trafari girl the inquisitors just captured will be freed once they realize they have the wrong person. And the young man they apprehended has nothing to worry about. Of course, neither of them will stay in the inquisitors' hands for long. I'm sure I can find better uses for them."

"Leave them alone!"

"And just what do you think you're going to do about it?"

Lyra raced for her sword. Mist seeped up from the floor. Her hand grasped the hilt, and she ripped it from the mantle.

Asa already had her own weapon ready. The glyphs along

the blade glittered. An Aeore weapon. Lyra already knew she couldn't win.

She attacked anyway.

Asa easily parried.

"Not bad… for a decrepit doctor."

The golden-haired woman's sword sliced out, neatly severing Lyra's blade. The mist reached out from the floor and seized the physician. Asa smiled as it pulled Lyra back and flung her to the floor.

To Lyra's surprise, Asa put her sword away. "Don't worry, old woman. I'm not here to kill you. As a matter of fact, I'm here to help you."

Lyra glared at her.

Asa clicked her tongue in disapproval. "Such manners are quite unbecoming. Especially for someone who was raised in Arakost. Surely you want to see your beloved foster son again. We're going on a little journey, you see. I expect we'll meet up with him quite soon."

The mist thickened.

Lyra stretched out her hand. Her fingers found her knitting needle an instant before the mist consumed her.

CHAPTER 11

MACHINATIONS AND MALICE

THE HORSE STUMBLED ON THE ROCKY GROUND, causing Cyrus' chin to bounce off its flank yet again. Though more open than the lands near Shrevnetska, this section of the Red Road was littered with steep ravines on either side. He felt the change in the horse's gait as they passed over yet another oaken bridge spanning the gaps.

He grunted in irritation as the wooden blocks he'd earned from Mother dug into his side. The inquisitors had searched him thoroughly, but with the Iriethan characters temporarily vanished from them, the blocks had proved too uninteresting to be bothered with. They'd let him keep them, and now they pressed incessantly against his ribs with every step the horse took.

He once again hurt from his latest beating, though the bruises and cuts he'd suffered were beginning to heal up nicely. They usually did, no matter what he did to himself. B'lantra had told him on many occasions the ability made him reckless, but it was one of the few parts of Mother's legacy to him that actually had any use.

The inquisitors had bound him and slung him over the back of one of their horses like a sack of meal, shifting him to a new horse and rider every so often. It hadn't really been important to him. The side of one horse was much the same as any other from his viewpoint.

They'd only brought one set of something they called witch-locks, and since those were being used elsewhere, presumably on B'lantra, the inquisitors had resorted to ordinary rope to secure him. It made a potential escape attempt easier, if only just.

The morning mist still clung to the ground in places, wrapping around the rocky cliffs and bogs, enjoying its brief reign before the sun grew strong enough to burn it from existence. Birds chirped overhead. He envied them their freedom.

The company had ridden hard all night. Cyrus had felt every bump and jog along the trail, although they probably hadn't purposefully tried to make it uncomfortable for him. Other than maybe their Captain Bregna, they didn't seem the type. It was far more likely they simply didn't care about his comfort one way or the other.

He was little more than a package to be delivered. In truth, he'd probably ceased to be a man in their eyes as soon as the words 'witch's son' were attached to his name.

From what he could gather, they were headed north to Ashenwall, home of Roshan Ignatius, the reclusive lord of Shashanka Province where Shrevnetska lay. The roshan and his fortress at Ashenwall had always been a distant thing to the village, ignored and mostly forgotten about except for the tax collectors that came through twice a year. While it mostly left them to their own resources in the event of trouble, it was an arrangement that suited Shrevnetska and the surrounding villages well enough. And given the roshan's conspicuous absence from the village's life, it must have suited him as well.

B'lantra was being taken to the fortress as well. Apparently the inquisitors intended to present them as trophies to Roshan Ignatius before taking them on to Calateph, the capital of Arakost.

By gocochen, it was a four day ride from Shrevnetska. With horses and the way the inquisitors were pressing, they would probably cover the distance in about half that time. That left him less than a day to devise a way to free himself.

He craned his neck over. The inquisitor he was riding with kept a small knife in a pocket of the saddle. Of course, even if he could get to it there was no way he'd be able to cut his bonds, throw the rider off the horse and gallop away before they stopped him. He'd have to figure that part out after he had the knife.

The inquisitor glanced warily down at him as he moved. His name was Dorza or something similar. Cyrus couldn't remember exactly. With his pale skin, closely-cropped hair and nearly expressionless face, the man didn't stand out from his comrades much anyway. In response to Dorza's watchful look, Cyrus put his head back down and stared at the ground passing underneath him, waiting for his chance to come.

The inquisitors rode on through the morning before coming to an abrupt halt at the start of a long oak suspension bridge that crossed a deep gorge cut by one of the Dreyfus' tributaries. Cyrus noticed the mist around them had thickened instead of dispersing the way it should have as the sun rose higher in the sky. His captors saw it too, and a jittery edginess swept through them.

"Careful now," Bregna ordered as the company started to cross. "Every man on alert. Haefin, issue out the witchbane."

Nothing happened for a long, quiet instant. The mist grew thicker, swirling around them, binding them in a writhing gray blanket. Wispy tendrils crept out like fingers.

Touching. Searching.

The heavy planks of the oak bridge creaked. The inquisitor's horses snorted nervously.

Cyrus strained against the ropes as he tried to look around. The blocks suddenly felt warm against his chest, almost as if they were being heated.

Had the golden-haired woman—?

The mist suddenly locked onto the bridge. It pulled. The bridge shook. The planks splintered and cracked.

"Ride!" Bregna screamed.

The mist tightened its grip like some great crushing hand. The bridge started to give way. Dorza urged his mount onwards. The horse lurched forward, nearly throwing Cyrus off.

Screams and cries echoed. Cyrus had the vague impression of men and animals tumbling down into the rocky depths below. The harsh crack of splintering boards rippled through the morning.

The horse leaped just as the planks of the bridge collapsed beneath it.

Cyrus barely had time to gather himself. Everything had happened so quickly he could scarcely believe what he was witnessing. The mist continued to relentlessly whirl around them. The ruins of the bridge were quickly enveloped in its folds.

Along with Dorza, only Bregna and Caulter remained.

Three. Only three left.

Cyrus turned his body and carefully reached for the knife in the saddle pocket. Dorza was distracted, maybe he wouldn't—

"Don't even think it, witchspawn."

Cyrus didn't have time for disappointment. The mist seized the horse they were on and ripped it to the ground as if it were nothing more than a toy. Cyrus was pitched onto the damp ground, his senses reeling.

The animal cried out in terror. The mist quickly gobbled it up, smothering the life from it.

"You might be immune to my charms, but your equipment and your horses aren't. You see, there are other ways to deal with witchhunters," a sultry woman's voice said from the mist.

Cyrus caught a flash of golden hair.

Dorza suddenly stiffened. Blood spurted from his mouth. The feeble mewling that poured out of him was enough to nearly make Cyrus retch. As he toppled over, the golden haired woman pulled her shimmering sword from his back. The weapon was Aeore make, much like Akestra.

Cyrus could faintly smell her perfume. Blooddrop flowers. It was a sweet, almost spicy fragrance. The small crimson flowers were the last to bloom before the snow, harbingers of cold and death. Perfume made from them looked like nothing so much as blood in a flask. The fragrance suited her perfectly.

Her blue eyes found him. Ruby lips sneered down.

"Don't go anywhere, pretty pretty."

"The silverworm isn't enough for you?" Bregna demanded.

"Hello again, Captain," the golden-haired woman said as she turned. "One good betrayal deserves another, don't you think? I've come to claim your prize from you."

Cyrus crawled away, hoping her blue eyes didn't find him again. The knife he'd been thinking of stealing earlier still lay in its place behind the saddle of Dorza's slaughtered horse. He wriggled desperately towards it

The blocks burned hotter against his chest.

He shimmied overtop Dorza's lifeless body, trying not to stare at the man's vacant face. Quickly, he pulled the knife from its sheath and began trying to cut the rope that bound his hands. It seemed to take forever.

The battle continued to unfold nearby. The golden-haired woman was lithe, fluid and deadly fast; flowing, like living water given form and purpose.

She was murderous grace.

The sword in her hands whirled and danced. It was tenuous like the mist all around, but real enough to send Bregna staggering back from her onslaught. He was already wounded, holding his side, his fingers red with blood.

Caulter fired his pistols. Gun smoke curled up, merging with the mist. The bullets missed their mark. Caulter cursed and drew his sword.

Another strike came from the mist sword. Bregna fell to his knees. Like a cat prolonging the kill, the golden-haired woman was merely playing with him now.

Cyrus didn't stop to watch the rest. He cut though the last remaining bit of rope and raced for one of the surviving horses. Desperation and need overcame the numbness in his legs.

The animal reared as he climbed onto it, nearly slinging him off. It needed no urging from him to run.

Lyra had taught him how to ride long ago in the tame confines of Mother's estate. He was grateful for her lessons now. It took all the skill he had to maintain even a minimal amount of control over the animal as it galloped away. Mostly he just held on, letting the horse choose the path of their flight, more worried about being thrown off its back than where they were headed.

✳ ✳ ✳

The cage creaked endlessly on. Ever step brought her closer to Ashenwall. B'lantra sat, caught halfway into the world and halfway into a dream. Dark, tenuous things gnawed, tormenting her at the corners of her thought. She tried to think of pleasant things: making tonics with Lyra, listening with Cyrus to a traveling storyteller or sitting on the seat of the wagon watching a colorful new town slowly come into view.

She had to hold onto those things. Savor them. The Illumentry would try to take them from her. They would take everything she was. She wouldn't remember Cyrus or Lyra. If she tried hard enough maybe she could keep a small piece of them, hide them in a place no one else could find them.

She wanted to feel angry, but it was hard to really feel anything at the moment other than exhaustion.

B'lantra suddenly felt the empress in the shadows of her mind. Celaan had been there all along, watching her, seemingly amused with her plight.

"You knew this would happen? You caused this?" B'lantra asked, her voice a choked whisper.

I caused nothing. Your own choices brought you to this. Think on the woman Helena you saved. You said to yourself that it was the right choice. Do you feel that way now, knowing what it led to?

"I don't know any more. Why is this happening? What do you want from me?"

I want only that which you promised me so long ago. You gave yourself to me. In return you received ten years of life you would not have had otherwise. I am merely collecting on a debt, you see. We have important things to do, you and I. Things that must be done for the good of all.

"I'm not your slave."

"They will kill you."

"You're just offering death of a different kind."

"The boy can be broken and still be effective. You are more delicate. I am part of you now. Stop fighting me, and this can all be over for both of us."

"No," B'lantra repeated. "I'll kill myself before I let you or the Illumentry have me."

She blinked, and the empress was gone.

Had Celaan always been there, watching her, manipulating her thoughts and instincts? Was she being punished because she'd openly disobeyed?

Maybe Celaan had never been there at all.

Why was this happening to her?

Witch.

That was her answer, and it came bitterly. One word. One word and everything she'd ever wanted became meaningless. They'd taken her wedding ring. They'd taken her song, her future. Witches didn't get married. They didn't go to Denschen College.

Tears welled up before she choked them back. She wouldn't give the inquisitors the satisfaction. It was one small way to defy them. It was the only way she could think of right now. The bars of her cage were thick. The witch-locks had left her song dead to her.

The rhythmic creaking of her cage suddenly ceased. Had they stopped? The waking world promised to be no better than the dream world, but she cracked her eyes open nonetheless. The light of the afternoon was almost blinding. The sky was a clear, cloudless blue, its solidity broken only by a trio of shimmering ley lines leisurely crossing overhead. A windmill slowly creaked in the distance. There were a few flowers growing nearby. Images of the meadow she and Cyrus had walked across barely a day before flashed by, a bitter contrast to the cruel reality of the now.

A man wearing the black uniform of the inquisitors was

approaching the wagon. His dark skin was stretched tightly across the prominent bones of his face and his gaunt body. Amber eyes mechanically studied the other inquisitors before briefly washing over her. Behind him stood a black carriage nearly identical to the one that pulled her cage.

"Hail, Inquisitors. Where are you bound with this newly captured witch?"

"Hail, Sentinel Etmos. We are bound for Ashenwall by order of our captain. We are to secure her there and await his arrival."

"You're part of Captain Bregna's detachment, then? A rising star that one. I wasn't aware that his commission covered this region, nor was I aware of any report of arcane activity in the area."

"She wasn't the primary focus of our mission, merely a fortunate happenstance. I'm not at liberty to discuss anything further," the inquisitor said.

"I understand," Etmos said. "Some secrets are best kept that way." He gave B'lantra another curious glance.

The door of the carriage behind him silently slid open and a woman slid out. B'lantra froze.

An Illumentry Sister!

In days gone by, witches had been simply hunted down and burned. In some of the more backward hamlets they still were. The Illumentry wasn't so wasteful. From the whispered tales she'd heard, it broke the witches it captured, reshaping them into hideous forms with no trace of their humanity. Everything they had ever been was brutally erased leaving only a shell the Illumentry could make use of.

Burning them alive would have been a kinder fate.

It was hard to tell anything about the woman. She didn't seem deformed or monstrous. Her face and body were mostly concealed under a crimson cloak embroidered with silvery glyphs. Only her tattooed hands protruded from the folds of the cloak.

Even though her face was hidden, B'lantra sensed the Sister was studying her.

"Where did you obtain this witch?" she asked, stiffly. Her voice was husky and cracked like that of an old woman.

"Near the village of Shrevnetska, Sister. She was masquerading as a healer. She may have been hiding there for years spreading her poison."

"Poison, is it?" the woman wondered. "Let's have a look at this poisoner of Shrevnetska."

"We don't have time for this, Kierahne," Etmos said, sternly. "Get back in the carriage until you're called for."

"Indulge me, Sentinel. It won't take long."

Kierahne came towards the cage, her boots and cloak swishing in the grass.

B'lantra didn't raise her head to look. She only waited, hoping the inquisitors, the monstrous sister and everything else would fade into the netherworld dream she'd been having.

"That's no good," Kierahne said.

Her hand snaked between the bars and gripped B'lantra's chin. The bones in her hand crackled with her movement. B'lantra shrank away, but the woman's grip was strong. Her long fingernails pressed against the Trafari girl's skin until she was forced to meet the sister's gaze.

The face under the cloak was startling. It was almost… human. Kierahne was no more than a few years older than she was, even though her voice made her sound much older. She might have even been pretty once. Her eyes were round and soft. They'd perhaps been a deep brown, but the color had faded. Her nose, probably once delicate and straight, now listed slightly to the side from where it had been forcefully broken and improperly reset. Her lips were deep and full, but marred by irregular tics that gripped the side of her face. Fine white scars, maybe from a scalpel, ran across her face. Her head was shaved, and every inch of her skin was covered in elaborate, colorful tattoos and markings. A few of them B'lantra recognized from Lyra's stories about Aeliraneth: glyphs of power and of control.

"A little defiance left, I see," Kierahne said, almost sadly, as B'lantra still fought against her grip. "That won't last long. They'll try to break you of all those silly dreams and hopes. Don't let them. They'll tell you that you won't need them anymore. And they'll find a good use for you too… once they've made you into what they want."

"That's enough, Kierahne. I said it's time to go. We have business down south," Etmos said. The markings on Kierahne's body flared up, and a spasm of pain shot across her face.

"Find me after they're done with you. I'll do what I can to help you," she whispered and then turned away.

B'lantra's cage started to creak. They were moving once more. She went back to her dream, caring little whether the cloaked woman and her gaunt handler stayed or left. She tried to make the dream pleasant, to put Cyrus and Lyra, meadows and song in it. It was important to hold onto those things while she could. The broken, marked face of Kierahne kept appearing whether she wanted it to or not.

❄ ❄ ❄

Once he was certain the witch had gone, Caulter blinked his eyes and sat up, dropping his appearance of death. It had been years since he'd had to feign death in order to survive, not since the final days of the last crusade against Trafaria. It had been cowardice then, and it was cowardice now, but it had kept him alive at least.

The mist had faded as surely as the witch had. Only the morning sun and the skittering of the rabbits in the rocks greeted him. If not for Dorza's corpse and the mangled remains of his mount, Caulter would have been tempted to think it had all been a bad dream. Only a single horse remained alive, standing a short distance away nibbling at some of the forest flowers.

The bridge they had crossed over was a shattered hulk. Caulter went over and took a quick look down into the ravine it had spanned. The men he had ridden with were scattered all around, their bodies broken and twisted on the jagged rocks far below. The golden-haired witch had chosen her location well. Acting together the inquisitors might have been able to kill her. The witchbane they'd brought with them would have paralyzed and then swiftly ended her. Even a scratch would have probably been enough. Now the witchbane was lost along with the rest of the company.

Damn her!

She'd effortlessly evaded the shots he'd fired at her. The Aeore sword in her hands had nearly run him through on several occasions. Only his skill had saved him— his skill and blind luck. She'd thrust him aside with startling ease. He might as well have been one of the pallid griis-griis flies that seemed to infest this region for all the effort it had taken her.

Where had she gotten her hands on an Aeore weapon? Along with her other abilities, it made her a frightening menace.

"Next time I'll take your head!" he growled, looking once more at the crumpled forms of the men below.

The silverworm swiftly diluted his anger.

"Teresa."

In truth, the golden-haired witch was no longer his concern. She'd been more interested in Aeliraneth's son than slaughtering the men who'd captured him.

Let her have him. The Trafari girl was his goal, and he knew where she was bound. The only question was how to get her out of Ashenwall.

He began reloading his pistols as he pondered.

A feeble groan came from nearby. Caulter turned. Bregna knelt on the ground trying to get to his feet. The side of his silksteel uniform was soaked with blood. There was a faraway, almost haunted look in his pale eyes.

"Caulter," he said. "Help me up. We still have time. We can find the witch and recover both Aeliraneth's son and the silverworm."

Caulter finished reloading his pistols and walked over to the fallen captain. "There were twelve of us when this hunt began. We're all that's left other than the two you sent to Ashenwall. What time is it you think we have?"

"She didn't kill me when she had the chance. It's a mistake she'll live to regret. We'll rally the Conclave. Hunt her down. We'll raze this whole wretched region to the ground if we have to."

"No, Bregna."

"What are you talking about? Help me up. We're losing ground on her."

"Did you wonder why she spared you?" Caulter asked. His voice was filled with cold contempt. "It's because you weren't worth killing. It was more fun to watch your fall from grace. You'll be led to the gallows, and she'll be there to watch."

"Don't be a fool. We can still win."

Caulter shook his head. As a plan formed in his mind, he eyed Bregna's coat. It was a little tattered, but its rank insignia would serve him well.

He took out his pistol and pointed it at Bregna's head. The captain's face twisted furiously.

"What do you think you're doing?"

"Saving you from a humiliation you brought on yourself," Caulter replied as he slid back the hammer and pulled the trigger.

CHAPTER 12

MAIDEN IN THE MIST

GRIIS-GRIIS FLIES SKIMMED JUST ABOVE the surface of the water. This early in the year their bodies were still a pure white. Their monotonous drone filled the air. Frogs croaked, their calls intermingling with the stream's gentle babble as the water flowed under a crudely constructed wooden bridge. A mournful cry rang out overhead, coming from some bird Cyrus didn't recognize. The area teemed with life, but it still felt like a lonely and forlorn place.

On the other side of the stream, beyond a stand of marshlands, one of the spidery Iriethan towers loomed. The land was coated with them in some places, though even the best scholars hadn't been able to discern their function. The tower was a thin black spire of interlocking strands of fibrous metal, its top surrounded by a swirling vortex of clouds. It listed now as the land around it had shifted.

Sitting on a nearby log, Cyrus studied the tower for a moment and then turned his attention back down to the blocks he'd earned from Mother. They were cool to the touch. The characters still shimmered just as docilely as they always had. They were the child's toys they'd always been.

So why had they flared up?

They'd reacted to the golden-haired witch's presence. Perhaps the blocks were supposed to protect him.

If so, how?

He'd had them before, and they hadn't helped. The only thing saving him then had been the portal he'd found. Maybe there was some command word Mother had neglected to mention to him.

Maybe they needed to be in his possession. Now that he thought about it, Lyra' had them in her apron pocket when they'd faced the witch in Mother's library.

He shook his head and began chewing on some biscuits he'd found in the saddlebag of the horse he'd acquired. It would take more than a couple of child's blocks to stop the golden-haired witch. He'd pushed the horse hard. With luck, he'd been able to outrun her.

The blocks did lend some credence to the story Celaan had spun for him though. He'd been so determined to reject the empress, so determined to rule his own fate. What if Celaan had been right? What if getting the Heart of the Great Machine was the only way to dictate his own life?

Even if he found it, what then? He couldn't just blindly run off to Asylum with it. There was more to it than that. Celaan was probably no better than the golden-haired witch. Maybe he could play them against each other, using the Heart as leverage. They could keep whatever power it contained. He wasn't Mother. He didn't need power like some sort of drug. It would be enough to use it to secure a future for him and B'lantra.

But how to get it?

Seek the golden gear from the Bal-haegast, Celaan had said. What golden gear? What did it have to do with anything?

Too many questions. Too few answers.

The Bal-haegast? He began grinding the blocks together.

The stories were as old as time, an old woman, or group of women living near a dark and forgotten pool. They were said to be leftover spirits of creation. Time didn't apply to them. They saw everything: future, present and past. It would be dangerous. The Bal-haegast were said to eat the unwary, and pretty much anyone else who crossed their path, but if anyone or anything would know about something like the Heart, it would be them.

He mulled the idea. According to the stories, the pool was a few days ride east of Ashenwall.

He frowned and then angrily grabbed a nearby bit of rotted wood and tossed it into the stream. Why didn't he fly up to the moon while he was at it? He was wasting his time even thinking about it while B'lantra was in Ashenwall. Getting her out would take all the skill and luck he had. By his reckoning, he was still a full day from the roshan's fortress, though he didn't know what he would do once he got there.

The unfortunate inquisitor who'd owned the horse before him had left an extra uniform neatly folded in the saddlebag. If he was lucky, it would get him past the gate guard and into the fortress.

The rest he'd just have to work out as he went along.

His odds weren't particularly good. He'd likely see B'lantra again, just before they tied a rope around his neck. Maybe the roshan would be feeling charitable and would be kind enough to hang them together.

He ground the blocks together more fiercely before he forced himself to put them away.

It was marsh country along this section of the road, and it was best to be through it by nightfall. Judging by the sun and the lengthening shadows streaming out from the Iriethan tower, he wasn't going to make it.

He finished his biscuit and prepared to move on.

Mist erupted out of the stream and started to encircle him. The painted blocks began to heat up once more.

Cyrus cursed and ran for the horse, scrambling onto its back and frantically turning it towards the wooden bridge.

Too late.

The golden-haired woman stood blocking his path.

Cyrus quickly turned the horse around and prepared to gallop back the way he'd come.

The mist snared him. Its grasp was like that of a lover gently wrapping around his midsection, though far stronger. He was ripped out of the saddle and sent tumbling onto the damp ground. Cyrus rolled in the direction of the fall and came gracefully to his feet. He wasn't a particularly skilled rider. He'd mastered falling off a horse far more quickly than he'd learned the finer nuances of controlling one. The horse bolted off into the evening only to find itself corralled by the mist.

"I told you not to go anywhere, pretty pretty," the golden haired woman said with an amused smile on her shapely face. "Your animal left a trail of broken branches and prints even a blind man could follow. You should really be more careful if you want to stay hidden."

Cyrus pulled the knife from his belt. She seemed to take no notice.

"Such a handsome young man. My, how you've grown since I last saw you."

The gleam in her eyes was predatory.

She sauntered towards him, just as she had years before. She hadn't aged at all. She'd towered over him then, a preening mass of blood and death. He was taller than she was now, but even so he felt the same fear that had gripped him as a child. The faint clip-clop of her heeled boots lightly sounded above the babble of the stream as she walked over the log bridge.

"What do you want?" he demanded.

"You are Cyrus Ulberath aren't you — the one and only son of Aeliraneth, the so-called Hellspawn of Targus. What wouldn't I want with you?"

The same smell he'd noticed earlier, blooddrop, wafted by him, swirling in the mist that surrounded them. A yellow-haired doll peeked out at him from the elaborate silk handbag she carried.

"We weren't properly introduced the last time we met. I am Asa. We have some things to discuss."

"I have other business!"

Asa looked like a cat about to pounce. "Yes, that bluster worked so well with the inquisitors, didn't it?"

"You're the one that killed Enric. All this happened because of you, just like it did ten years ago."

"Was that his name? I didn't really bother to find out," she said, casually. "But this isn't happening because of lovely me. Not really. Your mother began it when she involved herself in affairs that were none of her concern. Celaan began it when she forgot what she was fighting for and tried to merge with the Kaulswyr— as if that flame-haired whore were worthy of being a Keeper. No, I'm simply bringing it all to a desirable conclusion."

"Mother's dead!"

Asa laughed. "Not quite true, but close enough. You're still very much alive however, despite my earlier efforts."

"What does this have to do with me? I'm no witch."

"You mean other than cleaning up annoying loose ends that should have been taken care of years ago? The wards on your mother's old house remain, blocking access to the secrets within— the Heart of the Great Machine, for example. You could be useful in helping remove them."

"You'll get no help from me," he said, stubbornly.

"You're assuming I'm asking for your help, pretty pretty," Asa said. Her blue eyes narrowed dangerously. "I'm not."

Cyrus glanced around. He was trapped. The mist surrounded him. He wasn't Mother. He had no frost or lightning at his beck and call. All the inquisitor's swords and guns had done them no good. What chance did he have?

Cyrus gripped the knife more tightly. "Stay away from me. I don't want to have to hurt a woman."

"My, how very gallant of you," Asa said. The mist reared up in warning. "But I think I'm quite safe."

She held her arm out straight towards him and opened her hand. The silver chain unwound. The tarnished clover of Saint Rachael at the end of it gently swayed.

Cyrus stopped. A numb horror crept through his entire being like frost spreading across a window pane in winter.

"I think you might recognize this," Asa said, coolly.

"How… what have you done?" Cyrus stammered.

He'd forgotten Lyra. It had never occurred to him that she wouldn't be safe, that she wouldn't be there waiting for him when he got back.

His chest tightened painfully. The blocks began to burn against his skin.

"Oh, don't worry. She's well. I haven't damaged the old bag… much," Asa assured him. Her silken laughter played through the evening. "Would you like to see her? I've thoughtfully brought her along with me."

A battered form emerged from the mist, vague at first, then taking shape and substance. Curly hair. A yellow and white dress. Hazel eyes defiantly peering from a lined face. Only her bundle was missing.

Cyrus gasped.

The mist parted enough for him to see her. Strands of mist coiled around her, binding her tightly. The aging physician glared at Asa.

"Now, shall we discuss things in a more civilized fashion, or would you still prefer we resort to violence?" the golden-haired woman asked sweetly.

"Let her go!"

"I'll be more than happy to— once you've retrieved the Heart of the Great Machine for me. Do that and I might be inclined to forgive you both for all the trouble you've caused me."

"Caused you? You destroyed any life I had in Shrevnetska. The entire Illumentry wants me captured or dead. B'lantra's in Ashenwall. All because of you."

"I haven't even begun to destroy your life, my dear," Asa said. She glanced over at Lyra. The mist surrounding the physician tightened its grip. "Shall I show you what true destruction of your life means?"

Cyrus lowered the knife. "Fine."

"Don't look so sad. What you have to do is quite simple. Your mother found the Heart of the Great Machine and concealed it somewhere in her estate. When the estate burned, a ward sprang up preventing all further entry. You're going to remove it for me."

"I'm not Mother. I'm not even a warlock. What makes you think I can remove anything?"

"Aeliraneth knew she was dying. She also knew you were her only heir. The ward is like any other lock. It just needs the proper key. In other words: you."

"What if I can't?"

"Let's not ruin a pleasant conversation by stating the obvious."

"Don't you dare listen to her!"

Lyra strained against the mist bonds. "It goes on and on. The demands will never end. She'll kill me anyway, don't you see."

The mist sizzled. Lyra grimaced in pain.

Asa walked closer and put her hand on Lyra's shoulder. "Be quiet, old doctor. Let's have the young man decide, shall we?"

"Decide this!"

Lyra slid the knitting needle out of her apron pocket. With a quick turn of her body, she buried the point of it into Asa's chest. The doll fell to the ground. Asa hissed and staggered back, clawing at the hilt of the needle.

"Get out of here!" Lyra cried.

Asa grimaced as she plucked the knitting needle out. No blood flowed. Only water trickled out before the wound closed itself over. The water bubbled, changed to steam and then absorbed back into Asa's body. Her face was hard, the sweetness vanished.

Cyrus was finally able to force his legs to work. Asa was faster. The sword appeared in her hands even as he raced towards Lyra.

The golden-haired woman's movement was quick and clean. Lyra's eyes widened. The blade penetrated. Asa's lips curled into a satisfied smile as the physician went limp.

"Let's see how you like it," she said, as she pulled the blade back. She held out Lyra's silver clover in triumph.

The knife fell from Cyrus' trembling fingers. He watched the silver clover swing back and forth... back and forth. The moment seemed to drag out into a wretched eternity. He couldn't think or feel. He couldn't breathe.

It wasn't possible. It couldn't be. Lyra had always been there… always would be there…

The mist seized him an instant later, holding him rigidly.

Asa reached down and picked up the doll.

"Don't worry, Susanna. I'm fine," she said. She examined the hole the knitting needle had left in her tunic. "The handmaiden's gone and torn my beautiful shirt. I guess we'll have to extract a price for that, won't we?"

"You bitch!" Cyrus croaked before the pressure of the mist around his throat cut off any more words. He flailed helplessly. Tears were forming in his eyes, no matter how hard he tried to fight them.

Asa walked up to him and gently caressed his face before running her fingers lightly over his chest and down to his groin. His skin crawled.

Why couldn't Asa have just killed him instead? He stared helplessly at the physician's form. There was nothing he could do now. Lyra was turned away so he couldn't see her face. It was the only blessing available to him.

The blocks seared at him. Energy and light.

"It seems all this unpleasantness has cost me a hostage. How unfortunate," Asa said. "You have other people you care about. There's that pretty little Trafari girl. Would you like me to find her too? I might keep her alive for years, unlike the old doctor. Of course, she won't be so pretty when I'm done with her."

He would have cursed at her, screamed his sudden rage and hate at the top of his voice, but the mist's grip around his neck prevented him from doing even that.

The blocks erupted, surging in response to his agony.

Energy and light. Para-octet and Doraghe. How to use them?

He didn't know. He could only imagine striking Asa down again and again. He could only envision the energy streaking outwards, searing her over and over. He could only see the light hitting her, boiling her flesh away until nothing remained.

Not her hateful smile. Not her smug face. Not her voice whispering into his ear.

Nothing!

Nothing mattered except breaking her into tiny mewling bits.

He could imagine it. He could see it.

He blindly dug at the blocks, trying to tear them away from his skin. They scorched his hand as he touched them.

The Iriethan characters burned with a brilliant glow.

He flung the blocks at Asa without thinking.

The light coming from them was a dazzling white. The mist released him.

Asa tried to run.

He thought he heard her scream.

The blocks exploded. He was suddenly sailing through the heavens, unfettered by gravity before ground and stream came rushing up to meet him. He landed hard, skidding on the damp earth before coming to a stop amidst a stand of cattails.

※ ※ ※

Cyrus found himself lying amidst the rushes and the cattails. Night had come, although he couldn't immediately figure out where the evening had gone.

Then he remembered.

He jumped up, expecting to find Asa bearing down on him. There was nothing around him other than the moonlit stream and the marsh beyond. Saranor, the red moon, had risen. The Iriethan tower gleamed at him in the reddish light.

The blocks?

They had scorched him before he'd thrown them. Though he felt no pain, he hurriedly looked down at his hand, anticipating blackened and blistered skin. Strangely, he found his palm dirty, scraped, but otherwise unmarred. The pocket of his waistcoat where he'd kept the blocks was likewise intact and whole. It was as though the blocks had never been, their energy spent in the flash of light that seemed to have saved him.

Had Mother foreseen what would happen and given him the blocks to protect him if she no longer could? It was hard to believe she would have bothered to take the time, but it seemed she had.

No, it wasn't hard to believe when he thought about it. Lyra had been right. Mother had put a lot of time in him. It wasn't out of love. He refused to believe that. Mother had been honing a tool to use. He was a contingency, a fallback. It was all he'd ever been to her.

Somehow he knew he should probably feel grateful for being alive, but he couldn't bring himself to feel much in the way of gratitude at the moment.

Asa had vanished as completely as her mist. The hint of blood-drop that had accompanied her had vanished as well, and only the humid, slightly rotting smell of the marsh remained.

"Bitch! I hope it hurt!"

He shook his head. He might have driven her off, wounded her, but she wasn't dead. He wasn't going to be that fortunate. The whole damn world was out to get him. Maybe God really was real and had joined in for the fun. Nothing had gone the way he'd wanted it. Nothing was the way it was supposed to be.

Why should things change now?

On his way back to the stream, he found Lyra's clover lying on the ground beside the doll that Asa had carried. Angrily, he kicked the doll away, and then stared at the clover. He hesitated a long moment before he picked it up, as if somehow by leaving it there he could pretend it wasn't real— that there was still a place waiting for him when he'd finished his adventures and returned in triumph.

Lyra's body still lay a short distance away, cold and still beneath the moonlight. His stomach knotted fiercely up. It was all he could do not to retch.

"I'm sorry," he whispered.

It was poor and inadequate. He should have… should have…
Damn! There were so many things he should have done.

He forced his legs to move. Memory upon memory hammered down on him as he neared the body, threatening to drag him down into an abyss with them. Every thought, every image— pleasant or not— hurt and kept hurting. His knees suddenly felt weak and tried to give way. There were tears flowing down his face before he even realized it, refusing to stop despite his efforts. He bowed his head and clutched the clover to his chest.

His sobs swiftly subsided. He could almost hear Lyra's voice in his head, scolding him. He had to move on, she would have said. He had other things to deal with, and people who needed him. She'd said much the same in the cold, hungry days after the fire in Targus.

Would Lyra go to Heaven? Was there even such a place? Maybe she'd be doomed to wander the Inbetween Lands, the spirit world between Heaven and Hell. Those who'd lived imperfect lives were often condemned to the Inbetween Lands for a time.

Damn all four Faces of God if Lyra didn't go to Heaven.

The memories flared back up again.

It wasn't fair!

He screamed it aloud to the marsh, his voice echoing through the night.

And finally he let them go— not because he wanted to, but because he had to.

It hurt too much.

Thoughts of Asa, beautiful and savage, flickered through his mind. Was she really dead? There wasn't a body. There was no way to really be sure. She was just gone, denying him any satisfaction he might have taken from spitting on her corpse.

He put the clover around his neck and stared down at Lyra.

"I told you we'd come back. That we'd tell you all about our adventures…"

The words felt empty now.

There would be no more telling. There would be no more drilling of facts and figures into his head. There would be no more faint smiles or Arakostrian propriety. No more lessons on swordplay or lock picking.

No more…

"Stop it!"

He gazed up at the sky. How was he going to see to Lyra? He had no shovel, no wood to make a pyre. In Arakost the dead were often placed in cairns because the ground was too frozen to dig. He looked around. There weren't even any decent stones nearby.

The world hated him it seemed. At the moment he hated it right back.

B'lantra would be in Ashenwall by now. There wasn't time. Hopefully, Lyra would understand.

He sniffed and wiped his face one last time. There was only forward for him now. He turned away and walked down the narrow road.

"Don't think. Don't remember. Just move. Just do."

He found the horse a little ways down, chewing nervously on some dogwood flowers. After a little coaxing, he calmed it down enough for it to let him climb onto its back. He continued forward to the roshan's fortress, not stopping to look back again.

CHAPTER 13

ASHENWALL

THE LIGHT WOOLEN BLANKETS SLID DOWN over Dontarius Tankreed's bare body as he sat up. He stretched out his hand and gently felt the warmth of Ketrina, the gunsmith's wife, curled up next to him. Silky smooth skin, honey-blonde hair playfully teased down over her shoulders and sultry curves in all the right places, it was pleasantly tempting to wake her up for one last round. She would probably be more than willing. His body was delightfully sore from her willingness.

The gunsmith was bound to be back soon though, and the man would have plenty of weapons within easy reach. Ketrina's willingness wasn't worth the trouble. She'd already given him the information he wanted.

Dontarius went over to the washbowl on the table, splashed a little water on his face and then ran his hand through his light brown hair. He glanced in the mirror on the stand beside the washbowl. His skin had a healthy glow to it, his jaw line was firm, and his blue eyes were bright and clear. Young, bright and moderately handsome, he was the very image of an up and coming Illumentry scholar. He had a bright and prosperous future before him, so he'd been told.

And why not? It was an image he'd carefully crafted over the last three years, and he certainly didn't lack the skill to maintain it. When he grew tired of it, he could easily craft another.

He'd done it before.

Without another thought, he began searching for his clothes. Even in the dull light, he could make out the small red insignia of the lantern and the spear on the front of his dark blue coat. He quickly found the matching trousers, shirt and waistcoat, as well as the leather satchel he stored his pens and other paraphernalia in.

He checked the exquisitely made Arakostrian crossbow he kept folded in his coat pocket, and then slipped out of the house with the silence of a practiced thief.

His horse was still tethered to the post outside. It looked impatient, nickering in irritation as he approached.

"Sorry, boy," he said, as he pulled himself up on the saddle. "Women have a way of occupying your time."

The horse ignored him for a long, annoying instant, even after he'd tapped his heels repeatedly at its sides. Finally, it grudgingly obeyed him and began trotting away from the house.

After a short journey, Dontarius came to a stone signpost along the side of the road. He turned off and guided the animal along a narrow path until a large gray rock blocked any further progress. A man in a green, wide-brimmed hat came up to meet him.

"Good morning to you, Hendrick. I trust you didn't have to wait long."

Hendrick was a lean and wiry man with an unkempt air about him. His long beard was untrimmed, and his bushy eyebrows nearly obscured his beady, narrowly set eyes.

"Long enough. Have you got the shipment of weapons ready for us?"

Dontarius nodded. "From what my source told me, it will be arriving later today. At least two hundred muskets and an ample supply of powder and bullets, all fresh from the foundries of Targus. There are even a few of the new repeating rifles they've been experimenting with."

"I'm betting your source was that lonely gunsmith's wife."

"Does the source matter as long as the information is good?"

"Are you sure it's good?"

"Yes, I'd say it was quite good," Dontarius said with a grin.

Hendrick waved his hand dismissively. "Bah! A few copper crows will buy a whore like that in any tavern."

"Jealous?" Dontarius inquired. "Just because you haven't dipped your candle into the wax pot in years doesn't mean the rest of us can't enjoy life."

The bearded man gave him a dark look. "Make sure they put the shipment where we can get our hands on it. It won't do us any good if we have to fight through half the roshan's guards to get to it."

"I'll advise Gavon to have them stack it by the gate in case of fire. Romei will open the gate from inside. All you have to do is get in, take the shipment and get out."

"We might do a little more than that if we get the chance."

"You'll just bring the Illumentry down even harder," Dontarius said. "I wish Kestrel would listen to me. Or even that strutting fool P'talan."

Hendrick angrily pointed a knobby finger at him. "They're done listening to the likes of you. Have many of us have they locked up for wanting to do things a different way? The Illumentry was founded to bring the light of knowledge to the darkness, not add more shadows."

Dontarius waited patiently while Hendrick continued his diatribe. He'd heard it before and didn't necessarily disagree with any of it. The Illumentry had been formed in the chaos and desolation following Ansala's defeat of the Aeore. It had helped reassemble the war-torn peoples with an eternal promise that with faith and hard work the greatness of old Iriethan could be restored. Scholarship, frugality and practicality helped form its precepts. Sacred duty, personal enlightenment and ordered harmony helped make up its creed. The fact that men weren't living in caves or mindlessly hooting as they smashed each other's skulls in with rocks was a testament to its success.

The Illumentry wasn't always a kind and generous mother though. She was a hoarder as well as a preserver. The masses were taught only what the provosts deemed it necessary for them to know, and though the Illumentry was rich in scholars, those scholars were only permitted to study within prescribed limits. Deviation from the order of things resulted in unpleasant consequences.

The scholar and engineers of the Illumentry had a right to be frustrated, but nothing good would come from open war. Hendrick and the other dissidents, the Tekni, had changed from the secretive society of rogue scholars and inventors it had been years ago, and not for the better. Their frustration had turned to hatred, though as of yet they lacked the means to carry out their plans

"Are you finished yet?" Dontarius asked when it became clear that Hendrick's ranting was going to turn into a lengthy lecture.

The other man scowled at him. "I'm wasting my breath on you anyway. You'll never understand."

"I'm trying to maintain a balance so we can work in peace. That's why I'm telling you about the weapons. You don't want full scale war. You know what it was like in the days after Cinder. Is that what you want?"

"You're a bloody coward!"

Dontarius held up a hand. "I don't have any more time to argue with you. I need to be back inside the walls before they fuss too much. Be safe, Hendrick."

Hendrick's expression softened a bit. "You as well, Dontarius. You're not a bad sort, even if you are an idiot."

Dontarius smiled and turned to go.

"We'll not hide in the shadows much longer. Things are going to be changing very soon," Hendrick called after him.

Dontarius only nodded in response, trying to think of books, Ketrina's curves and other, happier things as he made his way back to the road.

※ ※ ※

It was morning on what would possibly be the last day of her life. B'lantra normally relished the coming of a new day, but it was hard to take much joy in the sunshine. Her cage creaked endlessly onwards. The land was open here, with only a few copses of trees marring the waves of grass. The wind blew chill. She pulled her torn cloak closer around her to retain some warmth.

A group of pilgrims, with their gray cloaks and colorful lanterns, proceeded along in front of them, making their yearly trek towards the holy city of Calateph for the festival of Greenleaf. The inquisitors carefully guided the carriage through their scattered ranks. Their springtime hymn to the glory of Ansala's defeat of the Aeore rang in her ears. She tried to shut it out, just as she tried to shut out the pilgrims' staring faces. Did they feel sympathy for her? Condemnation? Maybe they would see the injustice of what was happening to her. Maybe they would cheer if the roshan decided to hang her.

B'lantra wasn't sure she cared anymore.

They topped a slight rise, and Ashenwall came into view. She watched the roshan's personal emblem, a golden hawk on a crimson background, fluttering proudly from one of the old towers. Trails of steam poured out from some newly-installed brick chimneys, probably from a boiler somewhere in its depths. The fortress had been aptly named, built into the jagged hillside that jutted out behind it. The steep slopes behind it provided it with a natural defense on three sides, and the monstrous outer wall presented would-be attackers with a formidable behemoth of stone to contend with. In its prime, Ashenwall would have deterred all but the largest armies.

Now it was just a remnant of an earlier age. Wind, rain and the passage of time had worn down the battlements and turrets. The fortress had been designed to repulse arrows and swords, not the monstrous artillery a modern army could muster. It wasn't completely without its defenses. Here and there the blunt muzzles of cannons, newly arrived from the foundries of Targus, glared ominously out over the grassy approach.

There was little need for them. The last crusade against her people had ended nearly twenty years ago, and neither the rump of the Arakostrian Empire nor the Trafari Kajanate had any great desire to repeat it. The Kajanate was embroiled in its own internal struggles, and the Empire was afraid of overextending itself and losing yet more territory, just as they had lost Targus. In the absence of war, the fortress had slowly transformed itself into a trading post of sorts. The gates stood open, manned by a squadron of bored sentries.

The raucous sounds of trading and haggling accosted her as they passed through. Colorful tents and booths were set up all through the stone courtyard. Animals brayed, and children darted in between tents playing some sort of game. There were people from all over: stoic Arakostrians with their long beards trimmed flat at the end like coal shovels; short bandy-legged Nurengarns with their swarthy, grim faces; even a few finely dressed Erende-lers strutting around with an arrogant cast to their sallow faces. A momentary hush fell over the crowd as their carriage entered. B'lantra felt the stares bore into her. It only lasted a moment, before interest turned elsewhere. A ragged witch girl in a cage was hardly a reason to delay important business.

Their carriage finally came to a halt in a more isolated section of the courtyard. A fancy looking man in a burgundy coat, tan breeches and pointy shoes of fine leather approached them. His wide brimmed hat was tilted at an awkward angle, with an over-sized green feather sticking up from it. Despite his finery, the man looked ill at ease, as if the world was a constant source of worry to him. B'lantra took an instant dislike to him. Cadaverously thin, with a long hooked nose and a balding head of yellow hair, he seemed like a gangly stork that was trying to pretend it was a peacock.

In short order, her cage was opened. The inquisitors waited for her to exit. When she refused they reached in and roughly dragged her out. The man came forward to inspect her while the inquisitors held her.

"A messenger informed us of your arrival. You couldn't have brought her through the side entrance?" he sniffed.

"Our orders were to bring her to the fortress and present her before the roshan, Executor Gavon. The front gate was the most expedient route," the inquisitor replied. "Our captain expressed his hope in the roshan's cooperation."

"And your captain will have it," Gavon said. He cast a disdainful glance at B'lantra. "Are you sure she's safe?"

"She's quite harmless in her present condition. The manacles around her wrists have been specifically enchanted to prevent her from causing any trouble."

Gavon sighed. "Very well. Bring her along. I'm sure we have a cell suitable for her."

B'lantra kept her eyes to the ground. She was beaten and cowed, apparently docile. The inquisitor's grip on her arms had grown slack. The pistols in their belts beckoned her.

Gavon walked closer and stared down at her. "Rest assured, witch, that I do not like having the business of Ashenwall interrupted by your ilk. Cause me any further trouble, and I will make it a point to ensure you are disposed of in a most egregious manner."

"Ashte valan, skish!"

B'lantra brought her knee up into his groin. An almost effeminate shriek poured from his lips as he buckled over. She snatched the pistol from one of the inquisitors and tore out their grasp.

Where would she go? What would she do?

She had no idea. She just ran.

Colors and sounds blurred around her. The manacles clinked as she moved. People screamed as she stumbled into the courtyard. With her bound hands, she pointed the pistol wildly around.

The gate. Where was the gate she'd come through?

"Stop."

The command was firm, without any sense of malice to it. The glyphs around the manacles flared. A spasm of pain shot through her, numbing her legs and bringing her to a sudden halt.

One of the inquisitors calmly approached her. There was some sort of silvery disc in his hands. B'lantra strained. Why wouldn't her body move? Sweat and tears ran down her face.

The gate was close. It had to be.

"There's nowhere for you to go. Put the pistol down."

The inquisitor slid his fingers along the side of the disc. The manacles grew heavier, forcing her arms down with them.

"No," she declared.

She flicked the pistol up. One shot. That's all she had. She awkwardly aimed. The silvery disc in the inquisitor's hand became her world. Destroy that and she might have a chance of escape.

The other inquisitor slammed into her, bearing her to the ground. Her body felt as if it had been impregnated with lead. She cried out in pain and frustration as he forced the pistol from her grasp.

"That will be enough from you," he said.

Unlike Bregna, he didn't raise his hand to her. He didn't even seem angry at her attempt at escape. There was no emotion to him at all, just a cold brutal efficiency.

He pulled her to her feet and started to take her away. The assembled crowd of traders began clapping. B'lantra could only hang her head.

Why shouldn't they be happy? One more witch bagged. One more menace removed from the world.

Gavon stomped over to her. Unlike the inquisitors, his face was florid with embarrassment and rage.

"You… you… you're going to pay dearly for this outrage, mark my words. I'll see you hanged, burned and drawn and quartered…. all in one day!"

"The problem has been contained, Executor, so let's not do anything rash," one of the inquisitors said, coldly. "She's property of the Illumentry. Now and forever."

❋ ❋ ❋

Above the din of the market, Dontarius heard his name being called. Executor Montavian Gavon, chief amongst the roshan's retainers, and also chief amongst Dontarius' personal annoyances, came hurrying over to intercept him. The executor's face was flushed, and there were hints of dirt on his normally pristine trousers. It was hard to tell what had befallen Gavon, though judging from the snickers of the other servants, it must have been hard on his dignity.

Dontarius waved cordially. "I trust the morning finds you well and happy."

Gavon fixed him with an icy stare. "The day does not find me well and happy at all. I've been most foully accosted by the Trafari harlot the inquisitors brought in. Her barbaric assault will not go unpunished, mark my words."

"The Trafari girl was a witch then? Yes, that would certainly explain how she managed to assault you even while under the watchful eye of the inquisitors."

"It's unconscionable. The Inquisition's reputation is completely undeserved if they can't better manage their property. Their new Captain Caulter was almost as rude as the witch. I intend to make a formal complaint to the Conclave in Targus."

Dontarius did his best not to smile. "I wish you success then. I'm glad to see that your… umm, injuries… were not severe. Now if you'll excuse me—"

"You are most certainly not excused. Roshan Ignatius has requested your presence. He was most displeased to learn that you were not to be found within the walls."

Dontarius frowned. It was rare the roshan requested an audience with anyone outside his inner circle. Even after spending months here, he hadn't glimpsed the man more than a handful of times. It had worked well up until now. The less notice some of his activities drew, the better.

He followed Gavon across the courtyard and through a maze of rooms and corridors, until they passed under a low archway and into the upper gardens.

It was easy to see why the roshan would want to spend his

time here. The vibrant reds of the tulips and the bold yellows of the daffodils stood out brilliantly in the morning sun. Elsewhere, the cherry trees posed gracefully in their elegant white-blossomed coats. Only the bristling guards, with their wiry mustaches, square jaws and copious armaments cast any gloom on the scene.

Roshan Ignatius Kalean, Master of Ashenwall, stood in contemplation underneath a large statue of Voctor the Just, disciple of Ansala. His coat and trousers were of dark red velvet trimmed with gold. Beneath them his starched white shirt gleamed like newly fallen snow. His dark shoes were polished to an almost mirror-like perfection. The quality of the ensemble did nothing to conceal the squat, heavy frame of the man who wore them.

"Your Lordship, I have brought scholar Dontarius Tankreed as you requested," Gavon announced.

Dontarius studied the roshan, wondering what had prompted the man to summon him. The stories said Ignatius had been a man of vigor and energy in his youth, leading his armies to countless victories. They also said he was a bloated sluggard who'd long since dug his own grave with a knife and fork. Judging by his appearance, the reality was somewhere in between. There was no denying Ignatius' considerable bulk, but there was quite a bit of thick muscle remaining on his frame. His hands looked strong enough to easily snap a man's neck.

Ignatius glanced over, an annoyed expression on his rotund face. "I sent for you some time ago, Dontarius. I don't like to be kept waiting, even in such a pleasant place as this."

Dontarius shifted his weight from one foot to the other. He was already off to a bad start with the roshan. The day was taking a decidedly unpleasant turn.

Ignatius intertwined the fingers of his hands. "I've just had a most interesting conversation with one of the inquisitors, an acting captain Etienne Caulter. He informs me that Cyrus Ulberath, the lost son of the Great Witch Aeliraneth, has been found. The inquisitors had captured him, and he was to be brought here to be presented to me. It was just a formality, of course. They had no intention of leaving him here."

"I notice you're speaking in the past tense, Your Lordship."

"The inquisitors suffered some misfortune on the road, and the young man managed to escape their custody. They have formally requested my assistance in helping locate him."

"I assume Your Lordship judged it an Illumentry matter and respectfully declined."

"On the contrary, I assigned every available man to assist in the search."

"I see. Well, I'll be happy to assist, though I am hardly an experienced tracker."

"I have other assignments in mind for you. I understand you were quite the admirer of Lady Ulberath."

"Your Lordship?"

"I make it a point to know as much as possible about those who reside within my walls. I've had several conversations with Executor Gavin. Your name has come up quite often."

Dontarius paled. He cast a quick glance over to Gavin. The smirk on the executor's face was obvious.

"Aeliraneth's work is well known in the scholarly community," he said, quickly. "She designed the aqueducts of Arathul. Many of the basic models for the factories of Targus came from her. She knew the old Iriethan script fluently when even the best of us could only translate a few characters. She was a remarkable— if very conniving and evil— woman."

Ignatius' jowls quivered. "She was a damned sorceress! And the powers wouldn't act against her because of the secrets she possessed. How they adored her! Aeliraneth knew the secret of reading the Iriethan characters. Think of what it would mean if she passed that knowledge to her son. How many treasure troves of ancient learning are out there, barred because no one can read the symbols to open them? How many ancient stores of weapons lie unused? Too many to count."

"That knowledge would indeed be valuable," Dontarius said.

"With the assistance of my men, I'm sure Cyrus Ulberath will be quickly caught. It gives us our opportunity. I want you to befriend him. He'll be frightened and angry, full of resentment towards the Illumentry. The voice of a friend may persuade him that he would be best off here. If he were to claim sanctuary within my walls, it would be callous and cruel to refuse."

Dontarius lowered his gaze and thought quickly. It was just another petty power grab— one he really didn't want to become embroiled in. Ignatius was one of a hundred different nobles and merchant princes competing to fill the growing void left by the Arakostrian Empire's decline. Such people were beggars in many ways, all fighting over the scraps of an increasingly bare table. It didn't end well for most of them.

"I'm not really sure I'm the right person—"

"Nonsense, Dontarius. Your morals may be questionable, but your skills aren't. You used to be a relic hunter, did you not?"

Dontarius tried to keep his face as innocent looking as possible. He'd been a lot of things in his past, some of them not so pleasant, and the fact that the roshan might have some inkling of them was troublesome. If events turned sour, it could easily turn out to be more than troublesome.

The roshan reached into the inner pocket of his coat and retrieved a battered red moleskin notebook.

"Recognize this?"

"No, Your Lordship. I can't say that I do," Dontarius said.

Inwardly, he winced. It was foolish for men who took the sorts of risks he did to keep a journal. It was simple, stupid sentiment. He'd written his feelings, his memories, his loves and his losses in it. He'd also kept most of the notes he'd made and the inscriptions he'd copied over the years. It was damning enough to earn him a lengthy sentence in the northern mines.

It had been his one weakness, and the roshan had found a way to exploit it. They must have realized some of his activities and searched his quarters. Likely Gavon had something to do with it. Damn! He'd thought himself so smart, so far ahead of everyone else around him.

The Illumentry took a dim view of relic hunters. Outwardly, they maintained that it was a desecration of sacred sites, and a danger to public safety. Entire villages had been razed when ancient war machines were unearthed and carelessly activated. High-ranking Illumentry scholars and engineers were the only ones capable of understanding and containing such eldritch dangers, so the official story went.

"Let's not fool ourselves. Of course you recognize it," Ignatius said. He chidingly clicked his tongue. "You seem to have an unhealthy fascination with the ancient city of Marithandri. It is my understanding that the Illumentry has banned such inquiries by holy edict, yet you've gone to great lengths to discover its location."

Despite the calm veneer he tried to maintain, Dontarius could guess the alarm on his face was obvious. Finding Marithandri, an ancient Iriethan city rumored to lie untouched somewhere in the icy wastes of the Frostshear Mountains, was the unspoken dream of relic hunters across the Lanternlit. The Illumentry had claimed the city as its own, though no one knew its location. Their edict forbade any search for it. Even the name had been stricken from its official records.

It was why Dontarius had taken on the guise of an Illumentry scholar in the first place.

"I'm sure your superiors would be displeased to learn of your prior activities. I'm equally sure you wouldn't like the results of that displeasure," the roshan said as he put the notebook back into his coat pocket. "Find out what secrets Aeliraneth's son has, and you're welcome to keep your past doings as dark as you like. Do we have an understanding?"

Dontarius bowed. The day had not only taken an unpleasant turn, it had careened off into an abyss.

"We do, Your Lordship."

"One other thing," the roshan said. "If you need anything, please be sure to speak with Gavin. I'm sure he'll be quite keen to assist you."

The gleam in the executor's eye practically lit up the morning.

Dontarius hurried from the garden once he'd been dismissed. The spring breeze was cool on his face, but he found himself sweating anyway.

He was involved in the roshan's plans whether he wanted to be or not, so he might as well take what advantage he could. Aeliraneth had taken so many secrets to her fiery grave, and this could be the breakthrough he'd dreamed of for years. He needed time, both to figure out a way to gain the trust of Aeliraneth's son and to recover his notebook. Hopefully the Tekni would wait a little longer before doing anything reckless.

That was yet another worry to add to his growing list. If the roshan had been thorough enough to dig up the past, what else did he know? Did he know about the Tekni? Perhaps he knew and simply didn't care.

He noticed one of the guards casually following him. The man was doing his best not to be noticed, but his intent was plain.

Dontarius sighed. It might be a long while before he saw the outside of Ashenwall.

CHAPTER 14

CONVERGENCE

CYRUS TOOK A DEEP BREATH and stepped out of the shadows, trying to look confident. In the daylight he might not have gotten even this far. Earlier he'd seen patrol after patrol leave Ashenwall until he'd begun to wonder if there was anyone left in the fortress at all. They were probably looking for him— at least that's the only explanation he'd been able to come up with. Fortunately, the side entrance to Ashenwall was probably the last place they'd expect him to turn up.

The guards snapped to attention when he saw the black uniform. Children were taught from an early age to respect the authority of the inquisitors. With luck, they would only see the uniform, not the man wearing it.

"Sir Inquisitor, I heard your company was attacked. Captain Caulter will be pleased to know you're still alive."

Cyrus nearly cringed. Caulter and the rest of the inquisitors were dead at Asa's hands, or so he'd thought. If Caulter was still breathing, then getting B'lantra out of Ashenwall would become a lot more difficult.

"Yes, I did survive," he answered, a little uncertainly. "Are there any other of my company within the walls?"

"Only Captain Caulter and the two escorting the witch that I know of, Sir."

The guard was looking at him a little too closely, the beginnings of suspicion forming on his face like fluffy clouds dancing in before a storm.

"That will be all, guardsman," Cyrus said.

He could already feel their eyes upon him. The black inquisitor

160

uniform he wore didn't fit him properly, and with his long hair and stubbly chin he didn't really fit the crisp image of an inquisitor. He couldn't stay in the uniform. Caulter knew his face, and walking around in the black garb of the inquisitors would surely draw his attention.

The guard hesitated. "Sir Inquisitor, your uniform seems… ill fitting. Is everything in order?"

Cyrus fixed him with the cold, imperial stare he'd seen the inquisitors use. "Everything is in order, guardsman. Now let me pass unless you want to explain to my captain why you delayed me here."

He waited, anxiously hoping the guards wouldn't examine him too closely. Their blue uniforms were crisp and clean, their muskets and short swords polished and kept. Still, they had a comfortable, bored look to them that suggested the worst thing they'd had to worry about for a while was their commander's inspection.

After a long, agonizingly slow moment, the guards opened the heavy doors for him. Cyrus quickly led his horse through before they had a chance to think on it any further.

He passed along a broad, tall tunnel large enough to bring a wagon through. The stonework was immaculate, each block lovingly shaped and placed. He glanced nervously around in the dim light, taking careful note of the arrow slits spaced along the walls and the murderholes standing ready along the ceiling. Properly manned, the defenders could swiftly turn the passageway into a killing ground.

Beyond the tunnel, he came to a large square guard room. It appeared to be blissfully empty. There was a stairway leading up to what he guessed was the main part of the fortress.

He left the horse behind and started to make his ascent. He climbed for what seemed like forever until at last the faint yellow glow of lantern light appeared from around a corner up ahead. Peering cautiously around, he saw only a single guardsman standing watch in front of a thick, iron banded door. He gathered his nerve, then straightened his shoulders and walked confidently around the corner.

As before, the guard saw his uniform and immediately jumped to attention.

"Sir. I wasn't expecting to—"

"Where is the witch that they brought in?" Cyrus demanded before he could finish.

"She was still in the dungeons last I knew. I heard Roshan Ignatius interrogated her, but I don't know what became of her beyond that."

Cyrus nodded coldly.

"Was there anything else, Sir?" the man asked.

Cyrus' fist caught the sentry squarely in the jaw. Another blow left him sprawled on the floor. He quickly dragged the unconscious man back around the corner into the darkness, glancing warily around to make sure no one had seen.

After he'd stripped the guard's uniform and weapons and put them on, he regarded the prone man lying at his feet. It would be simpler just to cut his throat and be done with him. He sighed and discarded the thought. He was no murderer, and killing the man really couldn't be called anything else. Instead he took the guard's belt and bootlaces and used them to bind the man as best he could. It was no real substitute for rope, but it would have to do.

He proceeded through the door and warily moved down the empty corridor beyond. It was warmer than he'd imaged. A set of copper pipes gently clanked along the tops of the walls, letting out a puff of steam every so often. The rumble of machinery came distantly from below.

Much to his dismay, he quickly found an endless progression of stone archways, alcoves and closed doors. It might take hours to find his way down to the dungeons.

He reached down and checked the knife at his belt.

One of the inhabitants was bound to know their way around…

❋ ❋ ❋

"This is foolish, Romei. You should wait. Or better yet, not do it at all," Dontarius hissed quietly from atop the battlements.

"We're not waiting any longer. It happens tonight. There's too great an opportunity with most of the soldiers out looking for that witch's brat of yours," Romei answered from the shadows.

The man was no scholar. He was one of the new sorts the Tekni had been recruiting: a killer— cold and efficient. A native of Nurengar, the former Imperial province west of Arakost, he was short and squat, used to sweltering summers and achingly long winters. The brown-eyed, brown-haired Nurengarn were as harsh as their environment, and Romei was no exception. The only things the nation seemed to produce were wild men and wheat.

The guard the roshan had assigned to follow him never stood a chance. The kill had been quick and clean, the body dumped into the midden heap before Dontarius had even had a chance to object. Now, standing in the shadows within reach of the guard's killer, he felt more than a little unease rippling through him. He glanced down the wall, but the distant sentry wasn't paying him very close attention.

"It was supposed to just be a raid," he said to Romei. "I had them put the guns and the powder close to the gate so you could be in and out, not storm the whole place. You don't have the men or the weapons to fight a war against the Illumentry."

"You're wrong, Dontarius. We've made some new friends. Powerful ones. We have the men we need, and soon we'll have the weapons you brought us and a fortress to call our own."

"You'll never get enough men through those gates to take the fortress before they can turn the cannons on you."

"We don't need to get through the gate. The tunnel's done. That idiot of an inquisitor captain had them send soldiers out all day. Now's the perfect time."

"That tunnel was months away from completion. There's no way you could have finished it."

Romei chuckled. "I told you we have some new friends."

Events seemed to be unraveling more rapidly than he'd feared. "The Illumentry will crush you. Their Divine Light will raise a rallying cry and every army in the Lion's League cities and in Arakost will descend on you."

"Let them come. It takes their attention from Targus and the rest of the League cities," Romei said. "By the time they take back Ashenwall, we'll already be in control there."

Dontarius could almost see the eager grin on his face. "Tell them to call it off. Once they recapture Aeliraneth's son, I can get him to trust me. Who knows what secrets his mother taught him?"

"They won't find him. Probably hiding somewhere if he's smart. We're coming. I'm telling you this because Tarja still sees some value in your worthless hide. But don't try to warn anybody."

Dontarius thought he could hear the faint scraping of a knife blade being drawn from its sheath.

"Tarja's here?" he asked.

"Don't get your hopes up, Dontarius. She's done with you."

Dontarius angrily shook his head and then walked away.

Romei was an idiot. They all were. The Tekni had made up their mind, and nothing he could do would change that now.

He'd tried to play both the Illumentry and the Tekni sides and keep them from each other's throats. He'd enjoyed the power his Illumentry status had given him, especially when he could use it to impress his way into a pretty girl's bed. Tarja had been one of his conquests, though in the end it was hard to tell who had conquered who. He'd enjoyed the intrigue and mystery of the Tekni society and genuinely appreciated the opportunity to interact with like-minded colleagues.

He'd also betrayed both those organizations when he'd felt it necessary. No one advanced when both sides were intent on destroying each other.

Tarja hadn't understood that. Despite her brilliance, she was an idealist. She viewed the world through a lens of black and white, good and evil. It had made leaving her that much harder.

How had the Tekni become strong enough to challenge the Illumentry? He would have to find out later. If Romei had been telling the truth, then Ashenwall was about to become the opening act of a play he had no interest in seeing.

He walked back towards his quarters, lost in both his thoughts and the quiet hush of the night.

He barely noticed the single guardsman walking up behind him. The man appeared a little ragged looking, which seemed strange given Gavon's attention to detail, but that was the executor's problem, not his.

In an instant, the man's knife was at his throat.

"The witch girl they're keeping in the dungeons. I want to know how to get to her. Tell me if you want to stay alive."

✻ ✻ ✻

"Bovashar Bregna sends his regards."

Inquisitor Petru was reaching for his knife.

From the door to his temporary quarters, Acting Captain Caulter whirled around. He caught Petru's wrist an instant before the blade imbedded itself in his chest. His elbow flashed out, catching his attacker in the face. Petru staggered backwards, blood dripping from his nose. The knife clattered to the stone floor.

Caulter drew out his pistol. "What the Hell's name do you think you're doing?"

Petru's hand raced towards his own weapon.

Caulter mechanically shot him down before he could reach it. Smoke swirled. The sharp crack echoed through the empty corridors. Petru flew backwards and lay motionless on the floor.

Caulter looked around to see if anyone had noticed, but this part of the fortress was still as stone. He regarded the body for a moment and then dragged it back into his quarters. A quick search revealed the glimmering key to the witch-locks. He shoved the body under the small bed in the sparsely furnished room. It would take a while for it to be discovered.

165

"Wasteful," he murmured.

He'd intended to get the key from Petru anyway, though he hadn't planned on murdering him to get it.

Why had Bregna wanted him dead? From the moment he'd been assigned to the hunt, the former captain had made no secret of his disdain. There had to be more to it than that.

Caulter pursed his lips. With any luck, he would be gone with the Trafari witch before it made any difference. Roshan Ignatius had eagerly accepted his request for aid in tracking down Aeliraneth's son. Caulter had watched the wheels turning in his greedy little mind, imagining all the great secrets he could force Cyrus Ulberath to reveal.

He picked up the scarlet cloak he'd purchased earlier in the day and stuffed it into a leather satchel. It wasn't an exact match for a Sister's cloak, but it was close enough for his needs. From his experience, the common people learned to quickly look away when they sighted an inquisitor. It was doubly true for Illumentry sisters. It was best not to draw the attention of someone who could turn you to ash with a mere gesture, especially when they had Illumentry sanction.

There were a few other preparations to be made before he could go get the Trafari witch, but with Petru dead, the only thing in his way now was the other inquisitor, Vladimir.

Would he be any different than Petru?

Caulter left the room and locked the door behind him, praying Vladimir would be more reasonable.

✳ ✳ ✳

"How do I get to the dungeons? I'll not ask again," Cyrus repeated, bringing the knife closer to the scholar's throat. The man hadn't been his first choice of victims, but he was certainly an easier target than one of the guards.

"I know where she is. Hell, I'll even take you there if it will help keep me alive," his new prisoner squeaked.

Cyrus brought the knife away from the scholar's throat and

pressed it against his back instead. "Why not? You might make a good hostage. Now let's go to the dungeons, shall we?"

"I'll make an excellent hostage. My name is Dontarius. Of the Tankreed family. Roshan Ignatius himself has a personal interest in my welfare. Executor Gavon also pays great attention to my affairs."

"Then do as you're told, and you can be happily reunited. Try to run and they'll be mourning your passing," Cyrus replied, trying to sound menacing.

"You came in here for a witch?" the scholar inquired.

"You talk a lot for someone whose life is in danger."

"You'd be amazed how often just talking can solve all sorts of problems."

"Since you're so keen on talking, then tell me why all the soldiers suddenly decided to ride out. I've barely seen any since I got here," Cyrus said.

Dontarius squirmed a little. "An inquisitor captain came riding in and said he'd lost a valuable prisoner. He persuaded the roshan to organize a manhunt to recapture him."

It was as Cyrus had guessed. Caulter had done him a favor, though the inquisitor probably didn't see it that way.

They began to slowly walk down the corridor. The murmur of voices grew louder and then faded away again. Cyrus relaxed a little when they passed from the edge of his hearing.

So far his hastily constructed plan seemed to be working. With any luck he could slip in and steal B'lantra from under the roshan's nose while they looked for him elsewhere.

Of course, he'd have to find some way of getting by Caulter. That would be the hard part. And there was Dontarius. What should he do with—?

With surprising agility, Dontarius suddenly twisted out of Cyrus' grip. The scholar reached into his coat pocket. Before Cyrus could even blink, he found a crossbow pointed at his face.

He could only stare in shock. The weapon was finely made,

with some sort of clockwork mechanism that allowed its four glistening bolts to be quickly fired in succession. It was an assassin's weapon mostly found in Arakost, where silently eliminating a rival had become a way of life.

Dontarius studied him for a moment and then his face broke out into a grin. "God, it seems, has a warped sense of humor. I was waiting for you, wondering if I'd ever get the chance to talk to you. And here you are where I least expected it. I'm very happy to meet you, Cyrus Ulberath."

Cyrus felt the pit of his stomach drop. "I can tell."

To his surprise, Dontarius put the crossbow away. "I was already making plans to free you once they brought you here. I never expected you to come here on your own."

"Why would an assassin want to help me?" Cyrus growled.

"I'm not an assassin. I'm just a scholar who appreciates finely crafted weapons. I knew your mother… well, sort of. I met her when I was a boy and attended her lectures in Taveron Hall in Targus. She was so far ahead of any other scholar it was pathetic. I took a moleskin notebook with me and copied every word she said. I'd be honored to help her son."

"What makes you think I need you? If you want to help, just point me in the direction of the dungeons," Cyrus said, his eyes narrowing suspiciously.

"You'll find yourself there all too quickly if you're not careful. The inquisitors won't let their new acquisition go easily."

"And you're willing to kill inquisitors just to help me?"

"I never said I was going to kill them. Like I said, you'd be amazed how often just talking can solve a lot of problems."

Cyrus frowned. The one man in the whole damn fortress who was willing to help was probably an assassin.

Lovely.

❈ ❈ ❈

Executor Gavon waited until the voices had faded before he poked his balding head out from behind the corner. His gaunt fingers fluttered with excitement before he gathered his courage and followed them.

If Dontarius and the witch's son found him, they would surely try to kill him, and there might not be time to summon the guards. He would wait a little longer and gather evidence so convincing that even Dontarius couldn't talk his way out of it.

He could personally see to the interrogation of Aeliraneth's son and get the reward for any information the wretch revealed. Better yet, he could also make sure that Dontarius was hanged for his crimes. It seemed fitting punishment considering the disruption the scholar's antics caused the orderly world he'd spent so long building.

He crept along behind them like a mouse following a trail of breadcrumbs.

❋ ❋ ❋

Cyrus had to admit that Dontarius was as good a talker as he'd claimed. They'd passed two sets of guards already. Dontarius' quick wit had left the guardsmen smiling and relaxed, so much so that they'd taken little notice of the ragged looking sentry accompanying him.

They hadn't needed Dontarius' prodigious charm once they'd made it down to the dungeons. From there, they'd discovered that B'lantra had been moved from the interrogation room, and at first Cyrus had despaired of finding her. But with the scholar as a guide, they'd finally come upon a single inquisitor standing watch outside a closed door.

It had to be where they were keeping her.

Now Cyrus lurked anxiously in a dark corner, waiting as Dontarius approached the inquisitor. If the scholar was going to betray him, this was the time.

So far, it seemed Dontarius had kept his word. Over the rumble of the boiler, Cyrus listened to him spin a colorful account of how a man fitting the description of the escaped witch's son had been killed, and the roshan had requested the inquisitor come and help identify the body. It seemed to resonate with the black uniformed man, and in mere moments both Dontarius and the inquisitor were walking towards him. Cyrus readied himself and pounced.

He quickly found himself on the dirty stone of floor of the dungeon with the inquisitor's knife poised above his throat. It took all his strength to keep the blade from coming down and piercing him. It was a fight he wasn't going to win. He struggled and strained, but the blade crept ever downwards.

The inquisitor suddenly stiffened and collapsed onto the floor beside him. Cyrus sat up, gasping for breath, trying to figure out what happened. Dontarius stood over the man's body, a heavy sap in his hand.

How many weapons did he scholar have on him?

"That went well," Dontarius said, cheerily.

"Thank you."

Dontarius smiled in satisfaction and patted the sap. "Talking is the best way to solve problems, but not the only one."

Cyrus went and tried the door the inquisitor had been guarding. Finding it locked, he searched the unconscious man's pockets until he found a set the keys. He took a deep breath and unlocked the door.

Hopefully B'lantra was behind it. Hopefully she was alive.

He tried to quiet his rushing thoughts.

She would be alive. She had to be!

The inside of the cell was cramped, with only a straw pallet, a chamber pot and a small table with a tin pitcher of water on it.

"Cyrus?"

The voice sent his heart soaring.

He looked past the chains that bound her, seeing only her, living… breathing. For an instant it was enough. Then the heavy chain and collar holding her and the manacles binding her became all too real.

"You're not supposed to be here. You can't be… how did you

get here?" B'lantra's voice was a fractured remnant of what it should have been. She glanced wildly around. "Where are they? Where's the inquisitor? They were here... they'll come back and find you too. You've got to go!"

"It's alright. They're not here right now."

He tried the keys first on the inscribed manacles. When none of them fit, he moved to the iron collar and the chain binding her to the wall. The lock turned, and chain and collar fell to the floor. He carefully helped B'lantra up and then held her close to him.

She tried to cry. Her shoulders heaved against him and her body shook, but no tears would flow. "I dreamed about you. They didn't want me to, but I did. I put you and Lyra and stories and sunshine and everything else in that I could think of. They took the ring you gave me. I'm sorry. I tried to stop them. I..."

"The ring's not important. I've got what I came for," he whispered to her.

Even after all she'd been through, he thought he still detected the faint smell of lilacs on her. It was one small thing about her, one of a hundred small things he'd missed. He found unexpected tears running down his checks.

B'lantra looked up and lifted a grimy hand up to wipe some of them away. "You shouldn't have come. If you were free, you should have just run."

He laid his forehead against hers. "Did you seriously think I was going to just leave you here?"

"That inquisitor is going to wake up, and all of this will be for nothing if we don't hurry," Dontarius chimed in as he stood watch over the door.

B'lantra tensed at the sight of the scholar.

"It's alright. He's a friend," Cyrus said in her ear. "At least I hope he is."

"Did you find a key for these manacles?" B'lantra asked hopefully as she staggered over to the pitcher of water on the table.

Cyrus shook his head.

"Let me take a look. I've had some dealing with locks in my time," Dontarius said.

The scholar came over to examine the manacles while Cyrus tried to help B'lantra with the pitcher.

"I can do it myself," she said between sips. "I can walk. I'm supposed to be taking care of you, remember."

"There's nothing I can do about the bindings," Dontarius announced. "We'll have to cut them off with something when we get the chance."

"They're specially made by the Illumentry alchemists for use on witches. As such, they require a certain key."

They turned in alarm.

Caulter stood blocking their way out, grim and efficient as ever. He carried a leather pack over his shoulder. His sword was at his side, and the pistols at his belt were plain to see.

CHAPTER 15

SILENCE OF THE STONE

THE INQUISITOR HADN'T DRAWN A WEAPON. Not yet at least. Cyrus grimly raised his musket before he had the chance. Caulter fixed him with a cold stare in response.

"You're more resourceful than I would have given you credit for. After what she did to my company, I would have expected the witch to have secured you quite easily."

"She failed."

"Obviously. I'd be curious to know how you managed to escape, but I don't have time right now."

Caulter stepped into the room.

"I will kill you," Cyrus warned.

Caulter raised an eyebrow, but otherwise didn't show any reaction. "You don't have the stones for it, boy."

"Where are your men?" Dontarius wondered. "Where are the guards down here for that matter? You didn't bring some of the roshan's soldiers with you?"

"My men are dead except for the one lying out in the hallway. I didn't spend time getting rid of the roshan's guards just to bring them all with me again," Caulter replied.

"You had them tromping all over the countryside... for what?"

Caulter paid no more heed to the scholar. Instead he reached into the pack he was carrying and brought out B'lantra's battered physician's satchel and an embroidered crimson cloak. He tossed both of them at her. "The satchel is yours. You might need it. Put the cloak on."

"What kind of game is this?" Cyrus demanded.

"It's no game, boy. I'm taking the witch with me. You can

173

come or stay as you please. It's no longer of any concern to me."

B'lantra put the satchel over her shoulder and then held up the cloak Caulter had thrown to her. "This looks like… an Illumentry sister's cloak?"

"Not quite, but it will be enough to convince the roshan's men. Put it on."

"Why? What do you want with her?" Cyrus asked, shifting to keep himself between Caulter and B'lantra.

"We're going north to an orphanage in Targus. My daughter Teresa is there. She has a wasting sickness, and you're going to cure it," Caulter said, ignoring Cyrus and looking directly at B'lantra.

She glared at him. "You arrogant ass! You think I'm going to help you? After everything they did."

"That was Bregna, not me."

"That's no excuse. You treat me like some kind of disease— like some animal— and then expect me to cast spells for you when suddenly it's convenient!"

"You'll help me," Caulter said, calmly. "You'll help me because you want to leave here and be free again, and you can't do that without me. You'll help me because you want your lover to live. And you'll help me because you trained as a physician, and right now there's a sick little girl who needs you. After that, where the two of you go is of no interest to me."

B'lantra's eyes continued to scorch the inquisitor. She bit her lip. Finally, she closed her eyes, breathed deeply and slowly put on the cloak.

"We can't trust him, Bel!"

"It's practical, Cyrus. We don't have any choice unless you have some brilliant plan for escaping you haven't told me about." She gave him a wan smile and leaned wearily against his shoulder. "And I know you well enough to know that you don't."

"I take it you've already made the necessary arrangements to leave Ashenwall," Dontarius said.

"I've horses in the stables beside the gate. We'll simply ride out. You're already wearing Illumentry clothes, and the witch's son has the uniform of the roshan's men, so your presence doesn't complicate things."

"What about these manacles on my wrists? Do you have the key for those?" B'lantra asked.

"No," Caulter said, shortly.

"So we're just supposed to put ourselves in your hands like sheep to a shepherd? Not even an apology?" Cyrus challenged.

Caulter's voice was hard. "Most witches are mad, hateful things like that golden-haired woman. And that doesn't count the fae creatures lurking in the dark places of the world. So no, I'll not apologize for it. Many people sleep easier because of what we do."

Cyrus gritted his teeth in disgust. It galled him to have anything to do with Caulter, but it seemed like the best option they had. If the man could help them escape, then curing a sick girl was a small price to pay for their freedom. The real question was whether it would stay a small price.

✳ ✳ ✳

Gavon watched from the shadows. At first he'd been fearful that the inquisitor captain was going to steal his glory, but that threat had passed. The man had other plans, and it appeared he was intent on stealing the roshan's newest prize.

It couldn't be allowed.

The inquisitors were always treacherous, their motives always hidden. Ignatius would need to know of their betrayal. And it would be Executor Gavon— quick-witted, loyal and efficient— who brought the conspiracy to light.

He had to hurry though. If he waited too long his quarry would escape. Chuckling to himself, Gavon made his way back out of the dungeons to seek out the guard captain and the roshan.

✳ ✳ ✳

They moved down yet another deserted hallway and through a carved archway. It was painfully quiet, and the sound of every footstep they took echoed in Cyrus' ears. The hallway seemed as though it would never end.

What guards they passed were more like statues than people, wordlessly letting them by. Reddish moonlight showed through the windows, adding to the quiet desolation that seemed to have overtaken Ashenwall. He caught a brief glimpse of the courtyard below. The traders and shopkeepers had vanished, leaving only a ghostly stillness behind.

Caulter walked along with intense, single-minded purpose, seemingly unconcerned with anything that didn't directly affect his goal. Even Dontarius seemed to feel the tension and had been quiet for once.

Something was building in the silence. Trying to ignore it, Cyrus found himself brooding instead. Under the uniform he wore, Lyra's silver clover hung around his neck. He'd have to tell B'lantra what had happened, and he had no idea how he could even begin to form the words. Maybe it was a secret he could keep a little longer. Instinctively he reached for the wooden blocks and then curled his fist when he found them absent.

B'lantra began to hum, a bright little melody against the grimness of Ashenwall. He put a hand against her shoulder. She startled, interrupting her tune.

"What's that you're humming?"

"I don't think it has a name," she whispered back to him. "I just want to be out of this place. I swear it's like some kind of silent scream locked away in stone."

"We'll be out soon," he assured her with a confidence he didn't completely feel.

They proceeded on until they came to another archway, this time with the statues of two smiling, but oddly solemn cherubim flanking it. In the dim light, it was hard to tell whether they were intended to be cheerful or not. The smiles were there, but they seemed strained somehow, more as though two carefree lives had been bound into servitude rather than any sort of joy in service.

"This way," Caulter said. "The courtyard and the gate should be close."

The dull thump of booted footsteps came, at first distant and then rapidly drawing nearer. In the stillness of the stone hallway, it sounded like the pounding of a thousand horses.

"I wonder if our luck has run out or whether it's simply a patrol," Dontarius said.

"If it is, then it's the first one we've seen. Strange that they seem to be coming straight for us," Caulter observed, checking his sword and pistols.

"Should we hide?" B'lantra asked.

"There's nowhere to hide here unless we can find some way to become part of the wall," Dontarius said.

A group of the roshan's men came into view.

"Come on. They haven't seen us yet," Caulter whispered.

It was too late.

"Halt! Surrender yourself, Inquisitor Captain. Give up the witch and the boy!"

The words assaulted the silence. Caulter drew his pistols in a smooth motion and fired. The crack of the shots split the air. The flash momentarily pierced the gloom of the hallway. Two of the soldiers cried out and fell to the floor.

"Run!"

Cyrus didn't move at first. His feet seemed rooted into the floor, no more mobile than the stone cherubim.

One of the roshan's men raised his musket, pointed it and prepared to return fire. B'lantra and the others turned to flee. The gunner pulled the trigger and then staggered from the weapon's recoil, his aim compromised. The blast tore through the cherub right beside Cyrus. Its bittersweet expression disintegrated into a thousand pieces.

His ears rang. Caulter grabbed him by the front of his guardsman's uniform and shoved him down the hallway.

"I said run, you fool!"

After a moment's confusion, the remaining soldiers began their pursuit.

The silence of the stone had been broken.

Murmurs and whispers came as the inhabitants of the fortress began to awaken. A few poked their heads curiously out of their doors, while others cautiously stepped out to see what all the commotion was. They were plowed over by the fugitives and the soldiers chasing them, adding to the sense of growing chaos that seemed to have erupted.

Rounding a corner, the little company came to a set of wooden doors held by two puzzled guardsmen.

"Sir!" one of the guards said, recognizing the insignia on Caulter's coat. "What's going on? Are we under attack?"

It seemed that the order to arrest them hadn't gone out to all the soldiers in the fortress.

"There are Tekni spies in the fortress dressed as the roshan's men," Dontarius said, smoothly. "They're trying to assassinate the inquisitor captain. Hold these doors against them while we get him to safety."

The guards looked at each other in bewilderment and then scurried to obey. The doors opened inwards, and the fugitives found themselves at one end of a long rectangular chapel. The direction they'd come from appeared to be the only way out.

Once they were inside, Cyrus and Dontarius shut the doors and barred them, leaving the astonished chapel guards to deal with the pursuing soldiers.

"That will take them a bit to sort out," Dontarius said with a satisfied grin.

The light, almost airy feeling of the chapel was a sharp contrast from the heavy stone corridors they'd traveled through. Through a line of large arched windows spanning the left wall, Saranor, with its ruddy deserts and shimmering cold ice caps, gleamed at them. Banks of colored lanterns hung down on thin chains anchored to the ceiling. There was a row of carved wooden benches in the center, and on the far end stood a stone statue of the Prophetess, clad in ancient armor, a spear in her outstretched hand.

On the right wall stood a long mural showing the vast army of Aeore invaders pouring over the green fields near Cinder. In their dull, bronzed armor they looked almost like insects. A few stalwart disciples were all that remained of Ansala's once mighty army. Voctor stood with his sword held high, challenging his Aeore enemies to battle. Navi readied the turrets for one last stand as the Aeore gunships bore down. Rachael used her healing droughts to strengthen both the defender's bodies and their resolve. The fallen lay scattered around, their blood drowning out the wildflowers that grew on the fields. Angels descended from the heavens, bearing away the souls of the dead. Above the carnage of the battle, Ansala stood, poised to plunge her spear into a great spidery machine at the top of the hill.

"The soldiers will come to order soon enough. Try and find something else to block the doors with," Caulter said.

They searched around, but found only the benches. Dragging them across the tiled floor of the chapel, they braced them against the doors.

"What happened to simply walking out?" Cyrus asked, bitterly. "This isn't going to hold long. They'll probably have the gate barred against us as well."

From the other side of the doors they heard a chorus of angry, voices.

"So we're still trapped? There has to be some way out. How did you get in here, Cyrus? Can we get back out the same way?" B'lantra asked.

"That's on the other side of Ashenwall," Dontarius said. "We'll never make it there without being surrounded and caught."

Caulter studied the room. "I didn't have time to look over the fortress plans. Is there a way out of here, scholar?

Dontarius absently tapped his finger against his temple and then grinned. "There's supposed to be a passageway behind the statue of Ansala. Priestesses used to use it sometimes. It goes down a few sets of stairs and then comes out onto the backside of the courtyard."

"Then lead on. We've no choice but to fight our way out now," Caulter said.

From the other side of the doors, the voices seemed to have quieted. The first shove came against the door. The makeshift barricade shifted but held.

They were halfway across the length of the chapel when Cyrus caught the first glimpse of movement from behind the statue, followed by the flicker of lantern light. Soldiers came issuing forth from the passageway they'd been hoping to use. They quickly swept up and around the stone statue of the Prophetess, blocking the way forward. Through the windows, the claret light of Saranor made them look almost like demons surging out of some gateway from the netherworld.

The fugitives skidded to a halt. The soldiers stood their ground. From their ranks, a massive man in richly appointed clothes appeared, moonlight and lantern light alike taking their turns sparkling off the jewels imbedded in his clothes. Despite his outfit, the man's bearing suggested he was anything but foppish.

A gaunt, nearly hairless retainer, wearing a ridiculous plumed hat, hurried up beside him. "See, Your Lordship. See? It is as I told you. Dontarius has betrayed your trust and seeks to help the witch escape. The inquisitor captain too."

He practically shook with excitement, like a puppy presenting a chewed offering to its master.

"So I see, Gavon. You have done well," the bejeweled man replied.

"Roshan Ignatius. And just when I thought things couldn't get any worse," Dontarius whispered in apprehension.

"You didn't think your betrayal would go unnoticed, did you Dontarius? I merely asked you to befriend Aeliraneth's son, not aid in his escape."

"Your Lordship, please… I can explain—"

Ignatius cut him off with a wave of his hand and a withering look. "It's far too late for your forked tongue now, relic hunter."

Gavon's face lit up with joy.

Outside a bell began tolling loudly and rapidly. Ignatius cast an irritated glance in the direction of the clatter but otherwise paid no attention. Some of his guards stirred uneasily.

"Your Lordship, the alarm bell…"

"Ignore it. We have the source of the alarm right here," Ignatius said. The ends of his thick lips curled up into what Cyrus could only guess was a smile. He turned his attention back to the fugitives. "Captain Caulter, I've heard that you also conspired against me. In the interest of maintaining a cordial relationship between my domain and the Illumentry, I will overlook this incident and release you with no further harm. Turn the witch and Aeliraneth's son over to me and all will be forgiven."

Cyrus felt an empty pang of dread seize him. Caulter couldn't possibly be willing to die over this. He would leave them. He'd brought them all this way—allowed them to actually think they might have a chance at life again— only to crush those hopes when the moment came.

"No," Caulter said, coldly meeting Ignatius' gaze.

"What?" Ignatius rumbled.

Cyrus was surprised as well.

"No," Caulter repeated.

"Take them," Ignatius ordered.

The soldiers came at them. Again, Cyrus hesitated to fire his musket. Maybe he wasn't cut out for war.

He brought the weapon up in time to parry a sword thrust from one of the soldiers. It only saved him for a moment.

They quickly surrounded him and tore the musket from his grasp. He caught a brief glimpse of another soldier coming in towards him, sword raised. He tried to wriggle away as the blade descended. A burning line of fire ripped down his side. His breath was torn away. He fell, the blurry sight of blue uniformed men all around.

Then there was another flash of movement and the creak of a leather coat.

Caulter.

The inquisitor drove the soldiers back with a flurry of kicks and sword thrusts before dragging Cyrus up.

"The girl! Keep her alive!"

Caulter threw him back in the direction of B'lantra before unleashing another onslaught against the soldiers.

The doors behind him creaked and groaned as the men on the other side slammed against them. Each time the barricaded doors gave a little more.

"They won't hold much longer," Dontarius cried.

"Cyrus!"

At first he couldn't understand why B'lantra's eyes widened in alarm or why she suddenly looked so upset, and then pain lanced through him again. He gasped and put his hand to his side. Blood dripped through his fingers.

"I'm fine," he told her.

"Like hell you are!"

Cyrus looked over to Caulter. The inquisitor still fought, but wouldn't be able to keep the roshan's men back much longer.

A way out. They needed a way out.

※ ※ ※

Caulter parried the sword thrust from one of the soldiers and then deftly sliced the man's throat open.

He was an inquisitor, and today the rabble before him would learn what that meant.

He snatched a pistol from another opponent's belt, shoved him back and shot him down.

His plan was unraveling. There were more soldiers coming up the stairway. He'd worked to empty the fortress as much as possible, but perhaps he hadn't been thorough enough.

Or perhaps the roshan wasn't as stupid as he'd first appeared.

He couldn't hold. He'd thought at first to punch a path through their ranks long enough to get the witch down the stairs and to the courtyard, but the roshan had too many men with him.

His sword found the innards of another one of the soldiers.

The roshan was close. If he could get to him, the Master of Ashenwall might make an excellent bargaining tool.

Caulter rolled forward and closed in on his new target with calculated precision. One of the roshan's defenders frantically tried to ready his musket and squeeze off a shot before he got there. Caulter cut him down before he ever got the chance.

Was swordsmanship truly such a dying art in this age of powder and bullets?

His answer came quickly, when instead of curling up into a frightened ball as Caulter had anticipated, Ignatius calmly picked up a sword from one of his fallen men.

Caulter's surprise lasted only an instant. He pressed the attack against the roshan as hard as he could. Inwardly, he felt a sense of growing desperation.

The first rule of war was to stay alive.

He was no longer sure it was possible.

❋ ❋ ❋

He would have to get his hands dirty. There really wasn't any other way around it. The witch-locks had left the Trafari girl nearly helpless; Aeliraneth's son was already wounded and Caulter looked like he would be overwhelmed soon.

It had been some time since he'd killed anyone, and Dontarius didn't relish the thought now. Eliminating an opponent was best accomplished through the use of politics and position rather than brute force. Still, if they couldn't find a way to win here, all the politics and position in the world wouldn't save him from the hangman's noose.

Besides, the chaos presented the perfect opportunity to retrieve the notebook Ignatius had taken from him. It was a pretty good bet the fat bastard still had it secured in his coat pocket.

Dontarius pulled out his crossbow, debating how best to use it. The obvious target would be the roshan, but he couldn't get a clear shot. He surveyed the carnage around him until he finally spotted the thin chain suspending a bank of lanterns from the ceiling.

He aimed and fired. Just like in the stories that circulated in cheap taverns, the lanterns crashed down, flattening the hapless men below. Glass and sparks scattered everywhere. The light in the chapel dimmed precipitously.

Dontarius weaved through the soldier's surprised ranks before they could recover. He reached the roshan just as one of Caulter's blows staggered him. Deftly, he snaked his hand inside Ignatius' coat until he found his prize.

❋ ❋ ❋

Cyrus' eyes stopped on the mural on the wall. The moonlight played off it, and for a moment he could almost imagine the Aeore armies in motion, crashing and pounding against the disciple's defenses.

Because of the moonlight…

He traced it back to the windows.

"Damn it! I should have seen it sooner!"

He spied his musket lying abandoned on the floor. He ran over to it, ducking under the sword of one of the soldiers to reach it. Cyrus swiftly slammed the wooden stock into the man's face and then turned it towards the windows.

The force of the shot nearly knocked him on his back, but it was enough to tear a gaping hole in the windows.

"What are you doing?" B'lantra demanded.

Instead of answering, he snatched her up and threw her over his shoulder. She flailed at him as he climbed through the hole.

He jumped. Her hoarse scream lingered in the air.

CHAPTER 16

THE FLAME'S JUDGMENT

WHEN CYRUS FINALLY WORKED UP the courage up to open his eyes, he saw brown-gold straw piled into the back of a wooden wagon rushing up to meet him. B'lantra's hands clutched at him as they fell. He plunged down through the top layers until the straw's bulk was thick enough to bring him to a stop.

He lay stunned, sprawled with the Trafari girl in the back of the wagon, like kitchen refuse hurriedly tossed away by an overworked housewife.

B'lantra groaned miserably beside him. "I've been falling a lot lately. It needs to stop."

"Are you hurt?" he finally asked.

"I've a few cuts is all. Did you know there would be a wagon filled with straw to catch us, or were you just hoping?"

"I saw a few wagons in the courtyard earlier. The rest? Well..."

"Ugh! And I'd just gotten over being mad at you over the troika."

He grimaced in pain. The sword wound burned like a hot iron being set to his flesh. He tried not to let it show on his face. It was his own fault for getting cut, and B'lantra had enough to worry about without fretting over him.

The wound didn't escape her notice.

"It'll be a lot worse if we don't find a way out of here," he said.

The dull sound of the alarm bell tolling intruded on his consciousness. They struggled through the straw and off the back of the wagon. Screams and shouts crashed in on them from all sides of the courtyard, as though the deathly silence inside the fortress had been merely a prelude to something greater.

Soldiers of the roshan, scribes and servants ran in all directions. There were other men and women already in the courtyard, pursuing or being pursued by the fortress' inhabitants, killing them or being killed in turn. The invaders were well armed, their muskets and swords clean and well maintained. There seemed to be no rhyme or reason to their dress. The only thing they had in common seemed to be a raging desire to slaughter as many of the people inside as possible. They had breached the walls somehow, even though a contingent of defenders still held the main gate. Lanterns burned sporadically around the darkened courtyard, manic fireflies in the night. The alarm bell from atop one of the towers continued tolling its call for help.

From above them, Dontarius fell in the straw with a heavy thump. Caulter followed a moment later.

"Tekni! You knew this would happen, didn't you? That's why you were so willing to leave," Caulter accused before the two men had even climbed out of the wagon.

"You haven't helped," Dontarius shot back. "I'm not the one who sent the soldiers out on a pointless manhunt!"

"Enough," B'lantra said, trying to make her voice heard over the din of the battle. "We need a way out of here."

"There isn't one unless that gate opens," Caulter said.

From a passageway in the adjacent wall, the soldiers they'd just fought came streaming out. They suddenly stopped and gaped at the carnage going on in the courtyard.

"What are you waiting for?" Ignatius roared, bursting through the door behind them.

He took in the battle unfolding around him, and his heavy face contorted in astounded rage. His eyes flicked back and forth, taking in details, watching movements, gauging positions. He began issuing orders at a rapid clip.

Cyrus had to admit that the man seemed to know what he was doing.

Across the way, a company of his gunmen had formed a firing

line on top of the walls. Their muskets cracked off like clockwork, mowing down a group of Tekni attackers as they came into the light. Elsewhere, the newcomers blasted through servant and soldier alike to overrun one of the guard towers. Invader and defender fought each other in a whirling cascade of motion. A Tekni woman screamed as two soldiers rammed their bayonets into her flailing body. A Tekni soldier stopped long enough to cut the throat of a hapless stable boy.

This was war. Cyrus had read about it, even dreamed about it as a boy when battles and knights, great armies and brave soldiers had captured his imagination. Seeing it was another thing all together.

Cyrus cursed aloud, wishing he could find some way to get the images out of his mind. Whatever the two sides were fighting over, this wasn't his war.

A high-pitched whirring echoed across the courtyard like some infernal machine winding itself up. Beams of yellow light suddenly streaked across the battlefield, ripping the darkness asunder. They slammed into a squadron of the roshan's men who'd taken temporary cover behind a wagon loaded down with barrels.

The wooden barrels exploded in a rain of scalding liquid as if boiled from the inside out. The men sheltering behind them were cast aside like dandelion fluff on the wind. The beams continued their path of destruction, leaving a charred black streak on the stone walls until finally tapering off.

Two large men came into view carrying even larger packs of strange apparatus strapped to their backs. Electrical coils shimmered, and blue sparks dancing along their lengths. Brass knobs turned as some set of internal gears wound hidden springs back into position. A thick cable snaked around the back, connecting to a thick metal tube each of the men carried in their muscled arms. The contraption slowly charged itself back up.

The roshan's men fell back, all except one. Whether brave or suicidally stupid, he held his ground and quickly reloaded his musket. He fired just before the apparatus reached full capacity. The bullet tore through the skull of one of the men. His strange weapon sparked madly as he toppled backwards.

The roshan's soldier had little time to savor his triumph. The other Tekni man unleashed the full force of the beam against him. Like the barrels, the soldier's body blew apart from inside, showering the ground in a rain of flesh and blood.

Cyrus stared in horror as he and B'lantra tried to take cover. To his relief, the Tekni giant turned his attention away.

"Brakeem's name," B'lantra said. Her face was ashen as she began murmuring a prayer in Trafarga.

The roshan's men did their best to muster a counterattack. The sound of musket fire went on and on. Smoke hung heavily through the courtyard.

Caulter suddenly twisted and fell. A stray bullet had ripped a gaping hole in his leg. The roshan's soldiers came out of the darkness and bore down on him. Cyrus went to help even before he realized what he was doing. He despised Caulter, or at least he'd thought so up until now. He grabbed the inquisitor, pulling him up and trying to help him away.

Caulter's disdain was obvious, although he didn't refuse the aid. "Idiot! You should have left me."

Before Cyrus could worry about whether it had been the right decision, the roshan's soldiers were set upon by a larger group of Tekni fighters. Seeing their clothes, some of the Tekni broke away from the main group and came at both inquisitor and witch's son, bayonets ready.

Dontarius quickly stepped in front holding his arms up. "P'talan, it's me! It's Dontarius. I'm on your side, dammit!"

P'talan was a tall and rangy man, dressed in a loose-fitting, but functional, array of deep red and yellow silks. He was Southern, with wild black hair and brown eyes. He raised a wickedly sharp hand axe and made ready to bring it down on the scholar's skull before recognizing him and stopping.

"Dontarius! You *skish*! Romei said you'd be hiding under a chambermaid's skirts, not outside."

"I've got him. I have Aeliraneth's son with me. Help me get him out of here before he gets killed and we lose everything!"

"I don't give a damn about your prize," P'talan said, glaring contemptuously at him.

"What about Kestrel? Maybe I can talk to him."

P'talan spit on the ground in front of Dontarius. "He's leading an assault against one of the towers. You're on your own!"

He dashed off. The other Tekni followed once they'd finished slaughtering the roshan's men.

"What was that?" Cyrus demanded. "Did you intend to hand me over to them after we escaped?"

"I was trying to get them to help us, but they have their own agenda. We'll be killed if we stay here," Dontarius replied uneasily.

Cyrus ran a hand down his face in frustration. "Noticed that, did you?"

"I see now," Caulter said, pain showing through his normally stoic demeanor. "I wondered why the gunpowder was stacked so close to the gate. You had them stack all of it there, didn't you Dontarius? You thought they'd just take it and leave."

Cyrus looked over to where the gunpowder was kept. "Is that enough to blow through the gate?"

"Probably, but we've no way to set it off without getting ourselves killed," Dontarius answered.

Cyrus glanced at the fallen Tekni giant.

"Maybe we don't need the gunpowder."

B'lantra seemed to guess his thoughts. "You can't just rush in. You'll get killed. Stop trying to—"

The idea had taken root and grown. His mind was set.

He gave Caulter over to B'lantra before she could protest any further and then frantically sprinted towards the Tekni man's body. With any luck, the roshan's soldiers and the Tekni would be too busy killing each other to notice him.

B'lantra was right— not that he'd admit it to her. He'd acted without thinking, the way he always had. But what else was there to do? Someone needed to do something, so why not him when he was the one who could see what needed to be done?

Pain from the sword wound pierced through him again. He winced. It would be fine. If he could move, then it couldn't be that bad.

He reached the body. The coils still gently sparked. Steam still trailed from the end of the tube. The knobs were soaked in blood and brain matter, but otherwise intact. Hopefully, the weapon still worked.

He quickly undid the leather straps on the pack and tried to lift it up. It was heavier than he'd imagined, so instead he set it down, took the tube and pointed it the direction of the gate.

How to fire it?

Despite their ornate design, the controls looked simple enough to use. He pursed his lips. Who would have thought Mother's stupid lectures on physics and electrical theory would have actually done him any good?

He flipped what he guessed was the charging switch and then grimly smiled as he heard the whirring start back up. Sparks flew along the coil, slowly at first and then with growing strength.

All he had to do was wait and then fire.

❈ ❈ ❈

He was trying to play the hero again.

Idiot!

B'lantra's fingernails ground into her palms. Countless times in the brief moments since they'd been reunited he'd thrown himself into harm's way without thinking. The thoughtless part was the worst. Did he care so little for his life or any they could have together that it simply didn't bother him?

No, that wasn't it.

He was doing it for her. He would have fallen on a thousand swords or fought a thousand dragons for her. He was out in the open, a sitting target. He was going to die for her if she didn't do something.

What?

The witch-locks still clung to her wrists. Her song was still dead to her.

She felt Caulter pressing against her. His face had the same pallor as the walls of the fortress. She looked down in astonishment at the glimmering key he pushed into her hand.

Her mouth fell open in outrage. Her chest tightened as her heart began to pound even more furiously.

"You… had this the entire time? Liar!"

He hadn't trusted her! He'd risked their lives because he couldn't bring himself to put faith in a witch.

Fool! Stupid, idiotic, pointless arrogance!

As if the entire fortress trying to kill them wasn't bad enough.

Hands shaking in fury, she brought the key up to the manacles.

✳ ✳ ✳

One of the roshan's men staggered towards him, wounded and bleeding, his bayonet leveled. Cyrus sidestepped his charge, and brought his fist crashing into the man's skull. The soldier dropped.

The Tekni weapon showed ready.

Another soldier attacked from behind, grappling his arms.

"That's it! Don't let him go."

It was Gavon. The retainer crept out from behind the wagon he'd been sheltering under, holding a long curved knife in his hand. The bright green feather in his hat bobbed as he shuffled closer.

"Hold him. Hold him. His Lordship will be so pleased to learn I'm the one who captured the son of the Great Witch."

The executor stepped closer.

✳ ✳ ✳

The key finally turned. The manacles fell from her.

She called, and the song answered.

"Leave him alone!"

Hot, vengeful blue flame burst out like a caged animal newly released. It snapped viciously at Gavon and the others, scorching them away from Cyrus. They fled yelping into the night.

She wasn't done.

Fire spread forth on its own accord, eagerly lapping at wood and stone and flesh. A surge of power ran through her. She felt the flame, inside and out, clean and cleansing.

The memories came from all directions. Bregna stood over her again, a cold smile on his face. The cramped cage creaked endlessly on. The seemingly endless dark and lonely time chained to the wall without hope or sunlight to protect her still stretched out before her.

Her anger grew.

Burn. It could all burn.

"This is hate. This is what it means. To cast down your enemies. We can make them pay for everything you have suffered. I will help you. Call me. Be mine and I will help you."

The words echoed through her head.

It was wrong to hate. The scrolls of the Galagax were quite clear on that. But she did hate. She was a witch and she hated. She sang and she hated.

The flames went where they wanted to, without her will or her consent. Clouds shot across the sky to blot out the moon. The ground of the courtyard shook and ruptured. A great serpentine body of fire ripped forth, painting the night with a burning red. It had a woman's face and a hundred grasping arms and hands. It was filled with a triumphant malice at being set free.

"Celaan."

B'lantra sang on.

The fiery arms shot out in all directions, swatting aside the roshan's soldiers and the Tekni attackers alike. They smashed stone and crushed wood, searing and scorching anything that moved. Wood turned to ash. Metal melted like butter into simmering pools.

Stone cracked. Flesh burned.

The combatants momentarily forgot their grievances with each other and scattered. There were screams, curses and prayers before God heard all around.

The Tekni giant charged his weapon up. The beam lanced out, boring into Celaan's fiery body. It only served to intensify the flames.

"What do you little things know of war? Let me show you!"

One of her hands came down, a great burning hammer flattening anything underneath it. B'lantra thought she heard the Tekni man scream. There was a brief flash of blue sparks and the beam abruptly ceased.

She had a vague sense that she'd opened a door that wouldn't be so easily closed. She was standing in the Karrak all over again, listening to the empress' dark song. She felt helpless to stop it. She wasn't even sure she wanted to.

She wasn't a tiny thing scared of the vast night. Not any longer.

She was a witch. Unbound. They had reason to cage her. They had reason to fear her. They had made her suffer in the dark, and now she would bring that suffering right back to them.

Burn. It could all burn.

"Turn the cannons! Turn the cannons round on it!" Ignatius shouted, motioning to some of his men.

Few of them heard him.

Celaan considered, as if trying to decide which of her many potential targets she should obliterate next. And then her hollow eyes fell on Roshan Ignatius, waving his arms and trying to get his soldiers to come to order. She reached for him, a sickly grin crossing her burning countenance.

Ignatius sensed his peril and tried to flee. Celaan seized him, crushing the air out of his body, choking off his terrified scream as she lifted him up into the air. His body began to smolder and burn. Flames streamed across him, choking off his cries. Celaan squeezed until he was nearly unrecognizable, half-cooked pulp between her fingers and then flung the smoking corpse across the courtyard. The remains of Roshan Ignatius Kalean, Master of Ashenwall, splattered off the far wall and slid down, leaving an ugly red smear behind.

"The gate! B'lantra, can you hear me? Destroy the gate!"

Cyrus' words were plaintive. B'lantra looked around trying to pinpoint where they had come from before she found him, waving his arms like the roshan had done before him and pointing.

He seemed distant to her now, a thing she thought she ought to care about. Why? The flames were what counted. They were searing and bright, comforting in their embrace— her eternal shield against the night so it would never trouble her again.

Celaan's song had subsumed her own. It danced in her head, filling her thoughts.

The empress' gaze fixed on Cyrus.

"There you are. You will not get away this time. You will obey this time. I will break you. Reshape you into what I need."

He was important to her. B'lantra tried to remember why. What could make him more important than the beautiful flame? The question gnawed at the back of her mind. She glanced down at her hand almost before she realized she was doing it.

Something was missing. What was it?

The song was there. Her song. Celaan's song. They were nearly the same now, both calling out a hymn to the flames.

Cyrus tried to escape, but staggered over some rubble and fell. B'lantra's brow wrinkled in concentration. What was missing?

Her finger… and the ring that had once been on it.

He'd given it to her, asked her to spend the rest of her life with him.

Celaan's hands, still red with the roshan's lifeblood, greedily reached out for Cyrus. The blood boiled and bubbled as it dripped down from her fiery fingers.

No.

Celaan was using her. B'lantra suddenly understood her rage

for what it was. Everything around her was seared and scarred. The stonework was a choked ruin. Tears flowed from the dying. Fierce battle cries had changed to fearful whimpering and pleas for divine forgiveness. Piles of ash stood where hay wagons and buildings once were.

Was this a world she wanted to live in?

She changed her song, deliberately… painfully, ripping it back away from the darkness and rage that dominated. It was her song, and she would use it the way she desired, not the desires of something else.

It worked both ways. Celaan was part of her, linked to her. If B'lantra could be directed, then she in turn could direct.

She willed the fiery manifestation away from Cyrus and to the gate. Celaan fought, writhing and squirming incessantly until B'lantra thought her mind would crack. The empress tore at the song, trying to force the melody apart and take it back for herself.

"You wretched thing. You dare betray me!"

"I'd be betraying myself if I didn't."

Celaan unwillingly lurched toward the gate. The burning hands smashed: once, twice and again. The wood of the gate smoldered and then ignited into flames. Its iron bandings began to boil away.

The gate held up against another blow. And another. It finally splintered, buckled and finally shattered, its smoking timbers falling away, its supports crumbling into a growing pile of debris and dust.

Celaan began to lose focus and diminish, shrinking gradually back into the earth from which she came.

"Go. You're not wanted here," B'lantra told her. "I don't need you anymore."

Celaan lashed out a final time, twisting B'lantra's song, burning it like she had the gate.

"Then I take back my flame until you prove worthy of it."

B'lantra screamed. The song surged, wild and free, and then collapsed altogether. The flame inside her began to wither.

Then Celaan was gone. The song was gone.

And she was just B'lantra.

✳ ✳ ✳

The Tekni fighter ran towards him. Cyrus braced himself, but the man simply pushed his way past and fled through the broken gates.

Fires still burned. The courtyard was a ravaged waste. He cast an anxious glance back at the stacked gunpowder.

Already some on both sides were regrouping and beginning to form plans for continuing the slaughter. Murmurs and cries came from all around the beleaguered fortress. Some had thought they'd seen a vision from God. Others thought the gates of Hell had opened up before them. Cyrus couldn't really disagree with either opinion.

B'lantra was at the center of it somehow. He found her staring at the carnage that had been wrought. She gazed blankly at him for a moment and then, recognizing him, clutched at the front of his guardsman's uniform with surprising urgency.

"I tried… I tried to stop her. This isn't what I wanted. But I made her do what I wanted. I made her do what I wanted…"

He held her to him. "Yes, you did. You smashed the gates. We're free, but we need to leave now."

Her eyes lit up. "Free? We can go? I can still hear it all. The roshan. I remember him… and the others."

"Don't worry about the roshan. He won't stop us. We just need to go," Cyrus urged, turning her quickly away before she caught sight of the steaming mass of broken bones and entrails that had once been Roshan Ignatius.

The sound of horses' hooves pounded towards them. They spun around in terror. Two riders leading a third horse came towards them. One wore torn blue clothing, the other a long dark coat.

"There you are! Thought I'd lost you in all this," said the man in the blue clothes. He was dirty and disheveled, soot and ash covering his face.

Cyrus glared at him. "Who are you planning to try and sell us to now, Dontarius?"

"I figured we could cover more distance with horses than on foot is all. Unless you'd rather walk and take the chance on being caught again."

Cyrus grunted in irritation and then reluctantly climbed up on the horse. He turned and helped B'lantra clamor up behind him.

"I don't know how to ride," she told him. "Lyra was going to show me, but she didn't get the chance."

Cyrus' face fell at the mention of Lyra, but he tried to put on a smile for her. "Don't worry. Just hold on, and we'll be fine."

The other rider groaned a little and stared up at them, face white with pain. His lower leg was caked in dirt and blood. He grimly hung onto the neck of the horse to keep from toppling off.

"He's still here?" Cyrus asked.

Dontarius shrugged. "Caulter? He wouldn't let me out of his sight for an instant."

They maneuvered the horses around the debris and then sped away, quickly outdistancing anyone who came near. The fires still burned near the gate, coming ominously closer to the stacked gunpowder. A few of the combatants from both sides had noticed their coming peril and were trying to beat out to flames.

The little company didn't wait to find out how it would end. Turning their horses, they galloped through the gate and out onto the plain beyond.

CHAPTER 17

WOUNDS OF WAR

TWO DAYS HAD PASSED since the fires of Ashenwall. It felt like no time at all. It felt like forever.

B'lantra was glad of the shelter the fire's light provided. It flickered serenely and peacefully, a sharp contrast to the wild and uncontrolled burn at Ashenwall. She tried not to think about the fortress. There was a safety and security in forgetfulness, of letting memory fade until it had no power over her.

Her song had been stolen though, and that was something she couldn't forget even if she wanted to. In some ways it was worse than the witch-locks. That had been like a suffocating hand around her throat, choking off her voice. Now there was only a mournful and tuneless shade with no notes left to strangle.

It was frightening to think that she couldn't light a lantern or heal an injured body when she wanted to. She'd always been wary of doing it, but never unable.

The flame was her friend, her companion. It would always be there to protect her from the dark.

And now it wasn't.

That was the growing fear, the demon chittering ever louder in the back of her thoughts. It would tear at her, telling her what an empty, cold shell she'd become. It would remind her how incomplete she was until she called the empress again like a lost cub bleating for its mother.

"I take back my flame until you prove worthy of it," Celaan had said.

B'lantra angrily poked the fire with a nearby stick.

She sits huddled near the wagon, the thin blanket pulled tightly against her small chin. Matri and Patri are asleep. They don't feel the weight of the night like she does. The fire has nearly burned out. The red embers give only a faint glow. She can hear the forlorn whispers of the spirits lurking near the ancient ruins where they've camped. Patri says she's just imagining it, but she knows better.

She sings. Patri says it silly to be afraid of the dark. He taught her a song about daylight and sunshine so she wouldn't be afraid. She looks to the lantern hanging off the side of the wagon. Patri put it out before they went to bed.

She sings. The wick of the lantern glows. Soon there is light. The spirits stop whispering. She is safe. She can sleep.

The flame was hers. It had always been hers, ever since she could remember. The Aeore empress was no mother taking a misused gift back from an ungrateful child.

It was theft!

B'lantra looked out into the night. A trio of ley lines ran overhead, straight and true, almost mocking her with their presence. She could still see them at least. Maybe that meant there was hope of getting the flame back.

But how, without becoming the very thing she'd fought at Ashenwall?

The night didn't seem prepared to yield any answers.

From beside her, Cyrus reached out to pull the small brass pot away from its spot by the fire. The aroma of brewed chala floated past them. He poured it into a wooden cup and wordlessly offered it to her. It was bitter without the milk and sugar she liked in it, but she was lucky to have it at all. From the looks of the contents of their saddlebags, it seemed the horses Dontarius had stolen had belonged to a traveling spice merchant. She'd quickly found the small pouch of chala, but beyond that and a few apples, there had been little of use. Ground pepper did little good without something to sprinkle it on.

They were two days out of Ashenwall now, heading east. Cyrus had deliberately chosen the direction, though he'd been reluctant to tell her why. Something was eating at him as surely as the loss of her flame gnawed at her.

They'd taken turns sleeping, unsure of the new company they found themselves in. Dontarius didn't appear to care where they went. He'd been smiling and cheerful in the sort of false way a banker might be before he swindled you out of your savings and cast you into debtor's prison. Likely he expected Cyrus to lead him to some fabled treasure. He would be disappointed if she had anything to say about it.

Caulter was still with them, grim as ever, though he was fading with each passing day. She'd refused to help him. He was an inquisitor. The enemy. Cyrus had said there was some good in him, but he was naïve about things. She couldn't look at Caulter and not see the Bregna's fist coming across her face or feel the iron cage creaking around her. The sooner they were rid of him, the better.

Cyrus shifted around and then grunted uncomfortably—probably his sword wound flaring up again. He wouldn't allow her to look at it, and it was getting worse instead of better. There were circles under his eyes, and his cheeks were sunken.

"I'm fine," he said as she reached for her physician's satchel.

His tone was harsh. Startled and hurt, she drew her hand back from the bag.

"Why won't you let me help you?" she demanded. "It's what happened at the fortress isn't it. Celaan—"

"No, it's not you. It's everything else."

"What everything else? And why are we heading east?"

He glanced over at Dontarius and Caulter.

"The world's not going to let us just go. It's got to be made to," he said quietly in Trafarga.

"So what are you saying? That you're going to listen to Celaan and find this Heart of the Great Machine for her?" she asked, her jaw setting sternly.

He leaned in closer to her and lowered his voice. "Seek the

golden gear from the Bal-haegast. That's what Celaan said. We're blind. We're groping around in the dark about things, and it's going to get us killed."

"And the Bal-haegast won't? *Ashte covan!* You don't even know if it's real," she hissed back.

"I know everything trying to kill us is real. You know the stories as well as I do. The Bal-haegast lives in a pool. And that pool is only a few days ride from here."

"It's a monster, Cyrus. It eats people. Even if it is real, you'd have to be insane to go anywhere near it. You're wounded as it is."

"Give me another alternative. Tell me another way to learn the truth about what's happening."

"A *skish* is bad enough without stepping on it."

"This *skish* will step on us if we don't do something."

"You always get this little twitch on your face when you try to hide something from me," she accused. "You met that golden-haired woman. You never said how you escaped from her."

He reached over and took a sip of her chala. "It's a long story. I promise I'll tell you the whole thing when we're farther away from Ashenwall. Right now I just want to sleep."

"Is this before or after we get eaten by the Bal-haegast?"

He lay down and shifted closer to the fire. "I love you and I'm not going to argue with you anymore. Now get some sleep. We can't stay here much past dawn."

"You make me angry, and now you want me to just go to sleep. I'm going to at least check on that wound of yours."

He reached out and firmly pushed her hand away. "I said I'm fine. You can look at it tomorrow in the daylight if it makes you happy."

He turned away in response to her angry glare.

She waited, but heard only the sound of his ragged breathing. Damn him!

She lay down, and pulled the scarlet cloak more closely around her. Sleep didn't come easily.

✷ ✷ ✷

It was late afternoon of the next day before Caulter finally fell off the horse. He lay on the muddy ground, breathing heavily.

Cyrus had been walking for a little bit to ease his back and legs, sore from a day spent on horseback. B'lantra sat tensely in the saddle, still angry with him.

He hurried over to Caulter almost as soon as he saw him fall. The inquisitor's eyes were barely open, his teeth clenched. His arm flailed, attempting to grab hold of the dangling stirrup from the saddle above him and use it to pull himself back up. He swatted at Cyrus in a pathetic effort to ward him away.

"I need a true surgeon, not some witch's brat!"

The corners of Cyrus' mouth curled up in frustration. Caulter had managed to keep up with the rest of them, sometimes lagging a little behind, but never letting them leave his sight. He wouldn't be able to do it any longer, no matter his resolve.

B'lantra got off the horse and came to stand beside him.

"He could use your help," he said.

B'lantra crossed her arms. "I said no. He would have turned us over to the Illumentry without a second thought if he didn't need us."

"He also saved both of us back in that fortress."

"We wouldn't have been in that fortress at all if not for men like him. You think he's going to thank us? No. Let him die."

"What happened to the girl who risked everything to save a dying woman on the road?"

"Ashenwall happened."

He shook his head and handed her his knife. "If you want him dead, then gut him and be done with it. The result will be the same, and at least he won't have to suffer."

Her eyes widened.

"Go on," he said. "It ensures he doesn't follow us."

"You know I can't just… why do you care so much anyway? He's just as much your enemy as he is mine!"

"I care about the girl who stopped to help a merchant family when she didn't have to. This isn't like you, Bel."

"And hiding things from me isn't like you," she shot back.

He put his hand to his chest before he even thought about it. Lyra's clover around his neck suddenly seemed like a dead weight dragging him down.

"Fine. We treat him enough so that he'll live, and we put some distance between us and him. We can talk then. If that doesn't work for you, then use the knife."

B'lantra looked imploringly to the heavens before rolling her eyes in weary frustration. "We're going to have to stop somewhere then. I can't do anything for him here."

"There's a farmhouse somewhere up ahead. I saw it when we topped that last rise," Dontarius suggested, edging his horse closer to them. "I didn't notice anyone about either. Maybe it's been abandoned. Let's see…"

The scholar reached into his satchel and pulled out a spyglass of burnished brass and carved oak. He carefully unfolded it and then peered through one end of it, making adjustments to the round knobs along the middle of the instrument as needed.

"Ahh… there it is. No one home. No chimney smoke. Nothing. Strange given the time of day, but I suppose we shouldn't question our luck."

"What else do you keep in that bag? I don't suppose there's a full-course dinner in there?" Cyrus asked.

"Nothing your stomach would agree with, sadly enough," Dontarius answered, folding the spyglass neatly back up and putting it away. "Not unless your mother taught you how to chew up brass when you were younger."

"A lot of homesteads keep herbs and supplies on hand in case the doctors can't get there. We might be able to find something in case I don't have what I need," B'lantra said, and then cast a worried glance over at Cyrus. "I'm going to have more than one to treat."

"I'm fine," Cyrus repeated. B'lantra would keep nagging him until he finally gave in. If he hadn't gotten cut… if he would have just taken the Aeore weapon Celaan had offered, then maybe Lyra…

There were so many could haves and should haves.

He sighed. "Help me get him back on the horse, Dontarius. You might as well be useful if you're going to gawk."

After helping the inquisitor back up, they rode slowly towards the farmstead, staying close beside Caulter to keep him from toppling off his mount again.

Cyrus thought of Lyra again and her clover around his neck. He pushed the thought out of his mind just as quickly.

How would he find words to tell B'lantra anyway? Words were for men like Dontarius who could spin beautiful tales at will. He didn't completely trust the scholar, but he envied him that much.

✳ ✳ ✳

The fire burned contentedly in the hearth, throwing shadows around the large farmhouse kitchen. The blackened teakettle slowly worked its way to a boil. Yet even with the hearth lit and the teakettle bubbling, the place didn't feel right.

It was too quiet, too still, too…

B'lantra couldn't put words to what it was.

The table in the middle of the kitchen was set, as if for tea, but the tea had long since grown cold. The butter had been left out and had melted down to a soft, squishy mass. Scones had been taken out of their tin and sat atop brown earthenware saucers. Hungry as they were, they'd thought at first to gobble some of them down, but a quick glance at the light skin of mold that was just starting to form had dissuaded them.

The upstairs had been no better. Bedrooms lay empty. The colorful patchwork quilts they had adorned them were still crumpled up from use instead of being folded. Closets were full of clothes that no one remained to wear. In one of the rooms they'd even found an empty cradle. Glass from a nearby broken window covered the knitted blue baby's blanket that had been left there.

It was eerie and unsettling, an open question with no ready answers.

The house wasn't without its charms, however. There had been a treasure trove of food, clothing and just as importantly to her: many of the healing herbs she needed to replace the dwindling supply in her satchel.

Despite her objections, Cyrus had insisted on going out to scout around. He'd barely spoken to her at all, except to make painfully obvious observations about what they'd found in the house. When those had failed to placate her insistence on checking on his wound, he had fled outside. She didn't understand it. He'd said he'd tell her what was troubling him, yet he'd evaded instead of answered her. It was as close to a broken promise as he'd ever come with her. She'd have to more forcibly confront him when she got the chance. He'd really left her no other option.

Though she and Cyrus had been almost reluctant to disturb anything in the house, Dontarius had proceeded to move right in, helping himself to the contents of the ladder, the barrel of beer in the cellar and the family's small library. He sat happily in a chair near the fire, much more interested in the book in his hand and the mug beside him than the world around him.

Like Cyrus, he'd been difficult. In fact, he'd been worse than difficult. Cyrus, despite his stubbornness, had at least tried to be useful. Dontarius didn't seem to be good for much other than letting words endlessly spew forth from his lips.

Caulter stirred feverishly on a pile of blankets they'd made for him and then began to toss and turn with a surprising amount of vigor for a gravely injured man. His face was almost ghostly. The dark lines under his closed eyes stood out against his pallid skin. Even though he still wore the black inquisitor uniform, it was hard to imagine she was staring at the same man who'd so coldly manipulated events at Ashenwall.

All for her it seemed.

B'lantra took a deep breath. Her needle and gut were ready, the water was nearly heated, and there was plenty of material for bandages. She expected no thanks at the end, and despite her training as a physician, she couldn't help but think it might be better if Caulter never woke up.

He was everything she'd always feared, and here she was trying to save his life. The irony was thick enough to make her want to vomit.

The teakettle began to whistle. She waited, expecting any moment for Dontarius to put down the book he was reading and go tend to it. Her brows knitted together in anger as the whistling continued unabated.

"Dontarius, the teakettle. Take it off and bring me some hot water over here."

There was no answer.

"Dontarius!"

"I heard you. There's no need to shout," he said, leisurely putting the book down and reaching over for the kettle.

"I'll shout a lot louder if you don't hurry up."

He brought the kettle over to her with exaggerated slowness. She bit her lip when he set it down on a stitched cloth pad beside her, willing herself not to slap the smug expression off his face.

"I actually found something the family left," he said, showing her a crumpled note filled with nearly illegible scrawling.

She glanced at it, trying to make sense of it. "A golden owl? They talk about following it. Why would they be so obsessed with it?"

Dontarius shrugged. "I don't know if it means anything. It's probably rubbish. Likely insanity took the family. Too much lead in the pipes maybe."

"Go find Cyrus just in case. He's been gone long enough," she said, using another of the pads to lift up the kettle and carefully pour some of the water into a small ceramic basin beside her.

"I doubt he's managed to get very far."

"Now!"

He departed as if he'd just been stung. She closed her eyes for a moment and tried to refocus herself before setting in to work.

Caulter's leg wasn't as mangled as it might have been. The bone was intact, though the skin and muscle had been badly torn by the passage of the bullet. It wasn't beyond her skill to fix. Infection and the fever that followed had reduced Caulter to his current state more than anything else.

"Which unfortunately means you'll survive," she murmured.

Caulter's eyes flew open. An instant later his knife was out of its sheath and at her throat.

❋ ❋ ❋

Dontarius breathed a sigh of relief once he'd cleared the farmhouse's painted green door. The Trafari girl was an irascible shrew, plain and simple. It was amazing that Cyrus could put up with her as artfully as he did. The charms that lay beneath her dirty and battered clothes must be impressive indeed.

He chuckled. If Cyrus was any kind of man, he probably had ways to keep her from talking too much in bed.

Not that there was anything wrong with opinionated women. Tarja had been that and so much more. And unlike Tarja, B'lantra didn't seem inclined to fling knives into the innards of things that annoyed her. Yet despite that obvious advantage, there was something about the girl that grated on him.

If he were going to continue his new partnership with Aeliraneth's son, he'd have to find some way of making friends with her. Why did she have to make it so difficult? True she'd been through a rough time, but she was hardly unique in that regard, and there was no need for her to take out her misery on him.

She was also a witch, though he didn't find that fact particularly worrisome. Despite what he'd seen at Ashenwall, the language of her body spoke of fear rather than aggression. She was closer to prey than predator. Like any weapon, witchcraft ceased to be effective if the wielder feared it.

Besides, witch or not, she was still a woman, and women were something he'd long since learned to manage.

Perhaps things would settle down once Cyrus and the inquisitor had been tended to. They could then turn to important matters like the Iriethan characters Cyrus undoubtedly knew how to read. He might well be the key to finding Marithandri whether he knew it or not.

Dontarius relaxed for a moment in the sunshine, taking in the early afternoon air. The yard reminded him of the land around the gunsmith's house, though this was busier. It was a true farm, unlike the gunsmith's paltry attempts to keep a few animals around for meat and eggs.

It was also rapidly starting to fall into disrepair. A flock of chickens roamed wherever it pleased, relentlessly pecking through the garden in search of seeds. The cows and pigs had already muscled their way through the oak fencing that was supposed to keep them in. Rakes and hoes stood abandoned by the oak tree in the center of the yard, spots of rust beginning to form on their iron heads.

The whole situation did seem more than a little odd. Dontarius scratched at the stubble growing on his chin and tried to think. What could have possessed the entire family to just leave so suddenly?

Surely not a golden owl.

There were no preparations for a journey as far as he could see. It was as if the family had simply wandered off into the hills.

Or had been spirited away.

Stranger things had been known to happen. Every place had its share of unwanted supernatural guests to conveniently blame for every malady from baby's teething pains to curdled milk.

He chuckled to himself. It was daylight still, and the prospects of running into a ghost or spirit out here were unlikely at best.

He strode across the yard with a little more purpose to his step than he'd shown in the kitchen, stopping when he reached the low stone wall that marked the boundary between the yard and the fields beyond. There was no sign of Cyrus. The only answer to his calls came from a flock of crows sitting in a distant elm tree.

He frowned. Aeliraneth's son was impulsive, and probably more wounded than he was letting on. Maybe allowing him to wander off by himself hadn't been such a good idea.

CHAPTER 18

WITCHBANE

THE EDGE OF CAULTER'S BLADE HOVERED just above her skin. His eyes were glazed, feverish. The knife shook in his hand.

A few days before, B'lantra might have been startled or even terrified. Now she didn't even flinch. "If you want me to leave you to die, I'll be happy to."

"Have you come to treat me or finish what the bullet started? Witches are ever unpredictable things."

"You're not in control anymore," she said. She didn't bother to hide the sense of triumph in her tone. "You don't dare kill me, not if you want me to save your precious daughter."

"I'm not the one who's lost control," he said, his eyes clearing. The knife became steadier in his hand. "I was a fool to give you that key."

She glared at him indignantly. "You were a fool for keeping it as long as you did."

"I've set loose a monster."

"You've never used an incantation. You have no idea what it's like— what it is or isn't. All you know how to do is beat and break!"

"Have you ever seen another witch?"

"Not until I saw Kierahne on the way to Ashenwall," B'lantra admitted.

"Then you're not even aware of what you are. You don't understand your craft— what it is or isn't. Every witch has a singular talent. It manifests in childhood, usually through stress or trauma. It grows as they find new applications for it. Your ability to heal is simply an aspect of your flame. To you, burning and healing are

210

two parts of the same thing. Eventually, even the best intentioned witch will find ways to use their craft as a weapon. You think you're the first one who could burn armies and tear stone apart?"

"I wouldn't have burned anything if you'd left me alone!"

His gaze was harsh. "For every one that just wants to be left alone, there are ten who want to bend the world to their will. We're the only thing stopping them. When they get loose, things like Ashenwall happen. How many people did you burn?"

"You brought me there. You set this in motion. It's your fault, not mine!"

"So you destroy to stay alive?"

"I'm not going back in that cage. I'm not becoming Kierahne."

"I'm sure that golden-haired witch would say the same thing if you asked her."

B'lantra's chest tightened. "Don't you dare compare me to her! I don't see her sitting here trying to help you."

"I'm taking you to Targus one way or another. You're the last hope Teresa has."

"That's asking a lot. Targus is crawling with Illumentry people and inquisitors."

"You didn't seem to think I was asking a lot when you were chained up in Ashenwall. But if your freedom from that fortress or from the Illumentry isn't enough for you, then I know a way for you to regain some measure of mastery over your craft. I'll provide it for you in exchange for doing what I ask. It serves both our interests."

"What makes you think I need any help?"

"Your craft is diffused. Nearly broken. You couldn't use it right now if you wanted to."

She gasped. "How did you know—?"

"I can smell it on you. You reek of witchcraft, but the scent is different now. I've seen it before in Illumentry witches when they use their craft too readily. The Illumentry alchemists have something called a focusing stone. It helps realign a witch's energies and keeps them from burning out too quickly. I know where to obtain one."

She stared at him. Unbelieving. Untrusting. "You let me refocus long enough for me to remain useful to you. It's still all about control."

The ends of Caulter's lips curled up slightly. It was the closest thing she'd ever seen to a smile cross his face. "Is it worth a little control to have your craft back?"

"Your leg is still in need of treatment. The infection won't cure itself," she finally said, lowering her gaze.

He studied her before he finally withdrew the knife. "I'll take that as a yes."

❋ ❋ ❋

The trail of footprints came to an abrupt end at the edge of a narrow, winding stream that cut its way through the trees and rolling hills. Cyrus studied the ground, but found no other signs of the farm family's passage. There had been at least five of them, three adults and two children.

Beyond the stream the land sloped upwards, the trees around the river thinning before giving way to long stretches of fields covered in tawny winter grasses. He'd be unlikely to pick up their trail, even if it was there to find.

He didn't really want to investigate anymore. It was becoming difficult to really think of anything other than the weakness in his body. The afternoon sun had been gentle when he'd reemerged from the farmhouse, but now the raw heat on his face was starting to curdle his insides.

He'd wandered a good ways from the house, more than he really should have. The farmyard and the barn were well beyond his sight now. Even the mournful grunts and bays of the few remaining farm animals had faded away.

It was time to return and have B'lantra look at the wound on his side. It wasn't going away. He'd taken a beating during their escape from Ashenwall, but he should have recovered by now.

He was always had before, so he hadn't given the wound the attention it deserved. What was wrong? Why wasn't it healing?

No matter how carefully he tried to keep it from her, she'd notice the clover eventually. He'd have to tell her how he'd allowed the woman who'd been like a mother to both of them to die. How he'd left her body to the crows.

He put his hand to the clover and sighed. He'd tried to never keep secrets from her, and now was a rotten time to start.

He turned around and began to walk back, concentrating on putting one foot in front of the other, and not how long the return trek suddenly seemed. Sweat rolled down his cheeks from the exertion.

The pain of the sword wound surged again, making his eyes water. He gasped and fell to one knee. The world around him began to mercilessly spin. He felt his stomach heave.

The subtle movement above him came quickly, as did the faint flapping of wings that accompanied it. He was too busy retching to notice at first, but then he sensed it and weakly raised his head. Spittle dripped from his lips.

The golden owl regarded him curiously from its perch in the tree, its wide-eyed stare far more discerning than any bird he'd ever seen. It was a small creature, barely two hands tall. Its golden feathers looked downy soft to the touch. Its delicate ebony beak and claws were cruelly sharp.

Its eyes were what drew his attention. There were a deep blue within blue that seemed to pull him into their endless depths. They were ancient: eyes that had seen the land change a thousand times over, eyes that would look on the world long after he'd departed it.

Cyrus wiped his mouth on his sleeve and tried to clear his thoughts. He was ill, poisoned maybe.

It was just an owl. That's all it could be. What was it doing out in the daylight?

The owl turned away suddenly, spread its wings and took

off from the branch. Cyrus stared in dull rapture for a moment as it silently glided across one of the adjacent fields. It was like watching a sunbeam come to life. He painfully pulled himself back onto his feet and began to follow it, though he couldn't really conceive of a reason why he should.

It settled onto another tree branch and patiently waited for him as he stumbled along behind it. It flitted away when he drew near. Again he followed. His legs grew more leaden with each step. It was hard to breathe, hard to think.

At last his legs gave out, and the ground lurched up to meet him. The clouds and the sky seemed to crash in on him, refusing to snap into focus no matter how many times he blinked his eyes. It took most of his effort to lift his head back up.

The golden owl had disappeared as mysteriously as it had come— flitting sunlight rippling through the branches for an instant, and then passing.

Where had the wretched creature gone? Why couldn't he find it?

In its place, a shadow fell over him. An enemy? He tried to rise and grab for his sword, but succeeded only in throwing himself back onto the ground.

"Easy. Let's get you back to the house. You're a bit of a mess."

He thought he could hear the cows and pigs. Was he near the farmyard?

The shadow descended.

❉ ❉ ❉

The back door to the farmhouse slammed open. The sound of heavy footsteps came stomping across the wooden floor. B'lantra reached nervously for her paring knife.

Dontarius burst into the kitchen, his face flushed from exertion. Cyrus' limp body dangled over his shoulder.

She leapt to her feet, eyes wide with shock.

"He's alive," Dontarius said, assuaging her worst fears. "But not by much."

B'lantra spread out some of the remaining blankets near the fire and had Dontarius carefully lay Cyrus down on them.

"What happened?"

The scholar wiped his brow and sat down, still breathing heavily. "He was like this when I found him. He was babbling about some forest spirit, though I didn't see anything."

"An owl?"

"Maybe. I couldn't really understand what he was saying."

She hurriedly stripped off the battered guardsman's uniform he'd been wearing and then suddenly paused when she saw the clover— Lyra's clover— hanging around his neck.

"What haven't you been telling me?" she whispered to him.

"He's no physician. What's he doing with that?" Dontarius asked.

"It's not his. It's… never mind… I'll deal with it later," B'lantra replied. She carefully took the clover off his neck and put it in the pocket of her tunic.

The wound was ugly. An inflamed, blood soaked gash ran from just under Cyrus' armpit diagonally down across his ribs, swollen and oozing, the skin around it blackened and dying. Heat radiated from the wound as if he was burning from the inside out.

"Stupid man," she snapped at him. He was unconscious and probably beyond hearing her, but it didn't stop her. "Why didn't you show me this? Stupid, stupid, stupid, stupid! *Ashte covan! Calcato!*"

She calmed down, wiping the sudden tears from her eyes and quickly gathered up a collection of ointments, oils and herbs.

"Go to the well and get me some more water."

Dontarius didn't argue with her this time.

The wound was like nothing she'd ever seen. There were no descriptions of anything resembling it in the books Lyra had lying around the house, nor had the elder healer ever mentioned something like it during her apprenticeship. It was more than an infection, more than just the damage of sharpened metal cutting into flesh. It had to be a poison, something on the sword that had cut him.

She stared at the wound, panic boiling just underneath her skin. She'd had her song to rely on the last time. That was the only reason Helena was still breathing. The song didn't work on Cyrus. It never had, and she'd never understood why.

What was she going to do now?

Caulter sat up. "The poison used is *ahalacaster*. Most people that know about it just call it witchbane. It's quite deadly to your kind. Your lover might not be a witch, but he is a witch's spawn. It didn't work immediately as it would on a witch, but it eventually felled him."

"Why would the roshan's guards have something like that?"

"Why do you think? The roshan probably got it from one of the other inquisitors. He heard there was a witch loose in his fortress, panicked, and used a resource it takes the Illumentry alchemists days to make."

"There must be an antidote for it... something."

"There is."

She waited, but he didn't speak.

"What more do you want from me?"

Again silence.

"What is it? Tell me? Do you want me to grovel? Is that it?" she demanded, turning on him in fury. Her speech slipped into Trafarga before she even realized it. "If Cyrus dies because you wouldn't help, you can be damn sure I'll return that favor for your Teresa!"

He held up his hand. "Letting Teresa die won't do your lover any good."

Surprise momentarily replaced anger. Did he understand her native Trafarga? He must. How?

"From what I can see, you have everything you need within easy reach," he finally said. "All except one item: *Aniacun bavari*. You'd know it as golden cape."

"I know what it is," she snapped. "It's poisonous. Bog fairies use it to paralyze and kill their prey."

"You're correct. It grows year round, so you shouldn't have too much trouble finding some."

"How is one poison supposed to cure another?"

"It doesn't. But if used properly it can draw out other poisons. Like attracts like, here just as in the real world."

"I can't just leave Cyrus."

"You'd rather send the scholar out on his own then? Your lover is slipping away from you. Think carefully."

"He might be dead by the time I got back."

"Leave your bag here. I'll tend him until you return."

Her eyes narrowed suspiciously. "Why would you even bother to help him? He's nothing to you. You deal in death, not healing."

"I deal in a lot of things," he said, his expression as cold as ever. "Keeping Aeliraneth's son alive serves my interest at the moment. Now help me up, girl."

She hesitated for a moment and then walked over and held onto Caulter as he awkwardly got to his feet. He limped across the kitchen and eased himself down onto a chair near Cyrus.

"Where has that layabout scholar gotten to? He could have fetched half an ocean by now."

"Did I hear my name being so charitably mentioned?" Dontarius asked, striding back into the kitchen with a dribbling bucket in each hand. "I see a near death experience hasn't improved your temperament, Inquisitor."

"You get to be useful again," B'lantra informed him.

Dontarius arched his eyebrows skeptically. "What exactly am I being volunteered for this time?"

He bowed, almost mockingly, after she'd explained. "I'm always happy to help a maiden in distress."

⁂

B'lantra walked purposefully along, diligently scanning for signs of her quarry. The golden cape wouldn't be close to the house. The farm family would have dug it up if they'd had any sense. It was poisonous, enough so that it often tainted the ground where it grew. Its tiny, worm-like tendrils would drill into the soil, leeching water and minerals until the earth around it was nothing more than a husk. Once sated, it would spread its sail-like spores out for the wind to catch. Fortunately, many of its would-be children never found a safe haven.

It would be in a damp, shady area, and so they'd headed out in the direction of the nearby stream. Dontarius walked beside her, his longer legs easily enabling him to match her pace. After she'd spurned his few attempts at conversation, he'd been quiet for the most part. She'd brought him along mostly to avoid having to go alone, though the scholar was far from an ideal choice for an escort.

They found the stream readily enough, but much to her dismay the only things the area could offer were a surprised herd of deer and some orange lichen growing up and around a rotting tree stump.

"Let's try downstream a little ways. There should be some nearby," she said.

Dontarius shrugged and followed her. "I assume this golden cape is something easy to see."

"I already told you what it looks like. It has a large golden cap and usually grows in clumps. Think of it like a big, poisonous pile of gold coins."

"I'll bet there have been some severely disappointed treasure hunters over the years."

They proceeded swiftly along, their journey punctuated by the drone of the griis-griis flies and the shrill croak of the spring frogs. The water flowed sluggishly through this part of the stream, leisurely lapping over the brown stones of the stream bed.

At last, the golden glint caught her eye.

It grew a short ways down the stream, clumped up beautifully in a heap amidst the gnarled roots of an ancient willow. The feathery caps overlapped each other, glittering in the evening sun. The ground around it was already parched and cracked, but so far the massive willow was more than holding its own.

B'lantra smiled for the first time in what seemed like days. Right now, the plant was better than any treasure she could have asked for. She was fortunate too. Despite Caulter's assurance, the golden cape looked to be the only one of its kind around.

"There is it," she said triumphantly to Dontarius. "I told you it looked like gold."

He didn't answer. She felt the sudden void of silence close in on her.

❋ ❋ ❋

The owl's large blue eyes seemed to follow him no matter which way he moved. Dontarius stood enraptured. There was a sense of awe that clung to the creature, an immensity that surrounded it even though he could have comfortably held it in the palm of his hand.

He was starting to wonder if it was even alive. It hadn't once moved in the time he'd been observing it. Maybe it was some sort of golem or automaton left over from the ancient days. It was certainly too lifelike to be a statue. It could be Iriethan, possibly older.

It seemed as good an explanation as any, though all of the constructs he'd ever seen had been clearly mechanical in nature. One didn't need to see an Iriethan steam golem for more than an instant to know it for what it was. Still, the Iriethan had been a subtle people, and it wasn't beyond the realm of possibility that they'd created something as elaborate as the owl.

He drew closer. The owl's eyes narrowed.

Or had they?

It was hard to tell if it had shown any reaction. The shadows in the trees seemed to grow a little darker as he approached. The air rapidly started to chill around him, but he didn't let it deter him. He was a scholar after all, not some superstitious rube. He'd best make his observations while he still had some light to work with.

He reached out to it, curious to see how it would respond.

Its thoughts briefly touched his. It was aware!

Its wings suddenly rippled into motion. Its gaze seemed to tear through his soul, examining everything he was and would ever be.

It found him inadequate.

He was an affront. An insect unworthy of its presence!

It came at him before he could even think to withdraw his hand or to shield his face. He fell back, the image of clawed sunlight tearing through his brain.

It was all over in a moment. He found himself sitting on the ground, blinking as if he'd stared at the sun too long.

The owl had vanished. The branch it had been resting on still quivered, but otherwise there was no sign it had ever been there at all.

"There you are."

He turned and found B'lantra standing a short distance away, glaring irritably down at him. He hurriedly got back to his feet, brushing himself off and casting a sheepish glance at her.

"Where have you been? I found the golden cape, but then you disappeared."

"I saw something."

He was no longer sure if what he'd seen had been real or delusion. Either way it was gone, and right now he was more than satisfied to leave it that way.

"What did you see?"

He looked away in embarrassment. "I got lost. That's what you want to hear, isn't it? The addle-brained scholar got himself lost instead of being useful!"

She seemed more taken aback than angry as his outburst, and for a moment he felt guilty about uttering it. Then, mercurial as ever, she shrugged and motioned him to follow her.

❋ ❋ ❋

The golden cape was almost hers.

B'lantra pushed her way past the suddenly subdued scholar

and impatiently approached the willow tree. The shadows were growing ever longer, steadily merging into inky pools almost before her eyes. They'd be lucky to make it back to the farmhouse before the night closed in.

She drew her knife and reached out to sever one of the stems. Caulter hadn't said how many of the caps he would need, so it was best to harvest as many as she could.

The crackling of the bark came slowly, barely intruding on her consciousness. It was probably the wind rustling through the willow's branches.

"B'lantra!"

The thick root loomed above her, its end razor sharp, like the talon of some giant bird. She opened her mouth to scream. Dontarius yanked her away an instant before the root came stabbing down, brutally goring the earth where she'd knelt.

She staggered back into the stream bed, the knife falling out of her hand. Several more of the tree root talons ripped themselves from the earth, their points just as sharp as the first. They hovered menacingly over the golden cape, a thick tangle of poised razors, daring her to try to make her way into their midst.

She brushed her hair out of her face and tried to catch her breath.

"We'll have to find some golden cape elsewhere," Dontarius said. "There's nothing but death here."

"Where? There's no time to look around. Look at the sun!"

"Maybe tomorrow—"

"He'll be dead by tomorrow!"

The scholar's face grew ashen. His eyes widened.

A small golden owl sat perched in a crock between two of the trunks, glaring malevolently at them. B'lantra could feel its power, sense the reverence the trees and the stream held for it. Its very presence sent a hushed shiver down her spine. It had been there from the beginning. It was a piece of God, long since cast away, but never forgetting.

The eyes that looked on her were knowing, yet unknowable. They were haughty and imperious. Alien.

"It won't let you come near, Lady Witch. An offense has been committed against it, and reparations must be made."

The words were spoken in Trafarga.

CHAPTER 19

KODA

S HE WHIRLED AROUND. The man coming through the trees was tall and rangy much like Cyrus, though older and heavier. It was the southerner she'd seen at Ashenwall.

The scars of numerous battles creased his frame. His face was craggy, with dark eyes, high cheekbones and a thick black beard. Dark, curly hair, just as wild and untamed as she remembered, flowed down to his shoulders. The hand axe at his side and the musket slung behind him looked no less lethal than they had at Ashenwall. His bearing spoke of a lifetime of fighting for survival. On his back he carried a battered rucksack.

He was probably Surani, B'lantra guessed, from one of the tribes of the Da'Gebron wastes that lay south and east of her homeland. She'd grown up with the countless stories of the Surani raiders of the deep deserts. They were handsome, charming and competent: equal parts dashing hero and ruthless adversary.

"P'talan," Dontarius said, a mixture of both surprise and annoyance crossing his face. "Why are you here?"

"Scouting," the newcomer replied, smoothly switching his speech to the Arakostrian tongue B'lantra had become accustomed to.

"Never mind that. What do you mean an offense was committed?" she demanded. It was hardly a fitting greeting, but time was precious.

P'talan gestured towards the owl. "Isn't it obvious? Your new friend here committed blasphemy. He tried to touch the spirit with unclean hands and an unclean soul. In retaliation it blocks you from your goal."

"I wasn't aware that you were a purveyor of otherworldly lore, P'talan," Dontarius said, folding his arms defiantly.

"The desert teaches many things. Fortunately for you, one of those is patience," the raider replied, giving him a black look.

"Patience? You? I'll have to remember to tell the stonecutters to include that on the monument they're no doubt building in your honor. Besides, I never touched it."

"But you tried, didn't you? It's a sacred thing, scholar. It's not one of your machines to be torn apart and examined."

"What's the wretched thing doing here anyway?"

"It was always here. It's just that some are too blind to recognize it for what it is."

"Enough!" B'lantra said in frustration. "You two can fight later. Do you know what kind of reparations the spirit wants?"

"There are two possibilities. One would be to sacrifice the one who offended it," P'talan said. He grinned when he saw the look of horror spread across Dontarius' face. "But since there's a remote chance your friend's rapier wit might be missed, there's also the rite of Kasa'nekt."

"I thought the Numer Circle banned that ages ago."

P'talan smiled. "Perhaps in your wet and comfortable Trafari cities, but not in the desert. What kaja wants to leave his pretty fountains and flowers and go enforce it?"

"Exactly what is this rite?" Dontarius asked.

"Life, death and rebirth," B'lantra told him. "It can be used to call dark things."

"An old superstition if ever there was one," P'talan said, reaching into his rucksack. "It sounds far grander than it really is. The first part is blood. Since you are the offender, scholar, would you care to donate some?"

He seemed amused as Dontarius drew back.

P'talan shrugged. "No? Then I'll fix what you and your books and machines could not."

He took the knife from his belt and made a small cut across his palm. He held it above the ground and a few red drops splashed down into the sandy soil.

"Life."

He reached into the rucksack again and took out a whitened jawbone. B'lantra couldn't begin to guess what animal it might have come from. The raider laid the bone down amidst the drops of blood.

"Death."

His hand went to the rucksack a final time and drew forth a flask of oil in a ribbed vial of blue glass. He opened the stopper and poured a few drops out carefully around in a rough circle. The scent of spring flowers wafted up into the evening air.

"Rebirth."

"That's it? That's your great ritual?" Dontarius scoffed.

"Take a look," P'talan replied quietly, pointing toward the tree.

B'lantra turned her head. The owl was disappearing with the fading sun, and the roots around the willow had become still again. The golden caps of her prize beckoned to her.

"Mara'kat."

"You're welcome," he said, bowing gracefully before her.

She blushed, then quickly turned away and walked towards the willow. When no movement came from the roots, she stepped forward, retrieved her knife and deftly sliced away as many of the caps as she could carry.

"A curious thing to be foraging for," P'talan noted, putting the vial and the jawbone back into the rucksack. "I didn't think to ask you why you needed something like golden cape. Or your name for that matter."

"B'lantra of Gu'Daan, of the family Akspara," she said in Trafarga. It had been a long time since her family name had meant anything to anyone around her, and she didn't bother adding all the generally flowery descriptors than went along with it. "And the golden cape is for my beloved."

"P'talan of the sands, of the clan Destomil," he replied in

turn. "That beloved wouldn't happen to be the Northern man I saw you with at Ashenwall, B'lantra of the family Akspara? Or perhaps Princess would be more appropriate."

"Possibly," she said, looking away in embarrassment. "Now if you don't mind, I need to return. He's very ill."

"I'll go as well if it pleases you. I'd like to see what sort of cure is made from something as deadly as golden cape."

She really couldn't refuse. What reason would she give when his actions might well have saved Cyrus' life?

"If you insist. The evening is coming, so I won't turn down an escort," B'lantra said, reaching down to light her lantern.

"What are you up to, P'talan?" Dontarius asked, suspiciously. "It's not like you to be quite so generous with your time."

"I only wish to see the result of my efforts. I've given you my aid and asked nothing in return. Is that not enough?"

"You mean you haven't asked for anything yet. But I'm sure you will," Dontarius said.

He leaned in closer to B'lantra. "Don't trust him. I know him well enough to know he's up to something. He didn't just stumble across us."

She'd had all she could stand of Dontarius. "I know what I'm doing. P'talan found a way to be useful. It's more than you can say."

"Fine," he hissed angrily. "If you don't want to listen, then you're on your own. God help you."

A gentle, reassuring look slowly spread across P'talan's face. "Shall we go?"

❋ ❋ ❋

Caulter ran the whetstone slowly down the blade of his sword, more out of habit than for any real need. The nicks in the blade had long since been smoothed out.

He waited patiently. The clock on the wall ticked on, but there was no sign of the Trafari witch returning. The final red-gold embers of the dying sun peeked through the window.

He continued sharpening the sword, ignoring the dull ache

in his leg. Acknowledging it wouldn't make it go away any more than becoming agitated about the passage of time would speed the girl's return.

He was a soldier, and waiting was what soldiers spent most of their time doing. Waiting for death. Waiting for glory. It was inevitably all the same.

At his feet, Cyrus lay still. Only the faintest hint of breath escaping from his lips told Caulter that his charge hadn't already passed beyond. He'd carefully cleaned the wound and done his best to keep the boy warm. He'd even managed to get a little water down him during a brief moment of lucid consciousness.

Cyrus was losing the fight against the witchbane, though that was to be expected. The Illumentry alchemists were very good at what they did.

Once the Trafari witch returned with the golden cape, he could make a crude but effective version of the poison. The plant was just as much a part of witchbane as it was a part of the cure. It would be ironic if she wound up contributing to her own destruction, but then all witches contributed to their destruction one way or another. It was simply a matter of time.

He sensed rather than heard the movement in the darkening farmyard. It wasn't the witch and the scholar returning, nor was it the missing farm family.

The door to the farmhouse creaked and then opened. Footsteps came across the hallway. There were several of them, doing their best to be quiet.

He calmly drew his pistols and waited for them.

Waiting for death. Waiting for glory. It was inevitably all the same.

He didn't pull the trigger when the door opened, or even when the first man appeared in the doorway. The intruders hesitated for a moment and then burst through the door in a quick wave. They were heavily armed men of a stripes and sizes, from older, grizzled fighters to fresh faced farm boys whose beards had barely grown in. What they all shared in common was a hungry, almost desperate, air.

They drew back at first when they saw his pistols and his uniform. Then they took note of his wounded leg, and it seemed to bolster their courage.

Caulter cocked the pistols as they moved closer. He drew a steady bead on the nearest one: a scar-faced, bandy-legged Nurengarn who looked all too eager to tempt fate.

※ ※ ※

As she drew near the farmhouse, B'lantra could sense something was wrong. There were fresh horses in the stables and too many lanterns lit within the house. New footprints marred the damp earth of the yard.

Dontarius shook his head in weary resignation.

B'lantra's heartbeat picked up. For the first time since she'd laid eyes him, she was starting to think the scholar might have been right about something.

P'talan seemed strangely at ease, gazing casually up as the stars poked out and Saranor rose above the oak tree in the center of the yard.

During their return trek, the Surani raider had been exceedingly gallant towards her in the exaggerated, formal manner of the Trafari aristocracy. It had been amusingly quaint, if a bit strange. His stories of battles and conquests, of loves lost and won on the moonlit sands of Da'Gebron had filled her with wonder and an almost sad sense of homesickness.

He was too casual now, too unconcerned about the changes that had taken place in the yard and the house.

"What's going on, P'talan?" she asked, warily.

"Your Cyrus is most likely in a bad way. You probably shouldn't delay tending to him," was all he said in response.

The sound of raised voices reached her as soon as she passed through the front door. P'talan suddenly reached out and clasped her arm.

"Let's see what all the fuss is about, Princess."

He led her down the hallway to the kitchen door. The voices behind it were louder now, coarse and angry.

As B'lantra came in, she found Caulter and several Tekni soldiers staring each other down. The Tekni's swords and muskets had already been drawn. They seemed uncertain whether to attack or not, but they hadn't backed away either. Caulter stood by the chair she'd left him in, his face wan and sweating. His pistols were at the ready.

"And here we are," the raider said in satisfaction. "All the lost sheep returned nicely to the fold, I believe."

"I warned you," Dontarius said, quietly.

B'lantra turned on P'talan in outrage. "You lied to me!"

"No. I said I was scouting, and I was," he replied in Trafarga. "You were too concerned with your own problems to ask what I was scouting for. Did the philosopher Fa'boule not say: *failure to discern on your part does not constitute a fault on mine*'?"

"And Fa'boule was burned at the stake for defrauding the Kolmat Autarchy," she snapped back.

"Leave the girl and go if you value your lives," Caulter warned.

"I think not," P'talan replied.

At his signal, the Tekni moved in.

B'lantra looked to Dontarius. He was so proud of his honeyed words. Surely, he wouldn't let this go any farther. The scholar merely met her glance and then disdainfully looked to the ceiling.

"You said you knew what you were doing," his eyes seemed to say.

She was on her own.

Ripping her arm away from P'talan's grasp, she boldly stepped between the would-be combatants.

"Stop this!"

From her pocket she pulled out Lyra's silver clover and held it aloft. "Tonight this is my house— a house of healing. There will be no bloodshed in here!"

At her utterance, everyone in the room suddenly stopped and stared at her. A pall of breathless silence overtook the room.

P'talan walked over and fixed her with a harsh glance as if reassessing her status and authority. Her resolve began to waver. Her flame had been doused in the fortress courtyard, stripped and smothered. Whatever she'd been then, she was now just a tired, bedraggled girl standing amidst a group of armed killers.

She stood her ground anyway.

"I invoke the right of Healer's Sanctuary under the Tamaka Koda."

There was no way to know if P'talan and the Tekni would honor it or not. Caulter... she had no idea.

If the Surani raider was half the romantic storybook figure he looked, then the silver clover in her hand would mean something, and he would recognize her claim. Physicians had always been granted sanctuary, even amidst the interminable struggles between rival merchant houses that sometimes engulfed Trafari life. Even during the crusades twenty years earlier, the invading Arakostrian soldiers had usually respected the symbol of Saint Rachael.

After what seemed like an agonizing eternity, P'talan lowered his eyes and bowed slightly. "If you want to invoke Tamaka, I will honor it for now, Princess. And now, Healer. If you keep adding titles, then I'll soon be at a loss for what to call you."

"Physician is the only title I ever wanted," B'lantra said, stiffly.

P'talan laughed, and she noticed his eyes surveying the length of her body. She felt suddenly self-conscious and adjusted the front of her tunic before realizing it.

"Then tell your witchhunter to stand down. You have some work to do in your house of healing."

"You can sit back down, Caulter. We have a truce for now," B'lantra said.

Caulter stirred. She thought for a moment he would open fire regardless of any arrangement she'd made, but the inquisitor was staring at P'talan. The Surani raider returned his gaze. They were sizing each other up like two tomcats.

Finally Caulter readjusted himself and casually checked the condition of his pistols as if the matter was no longer a concern to him. B'lantra breathed an inward sigh of relief.

"Are you sure about this, P'talan? There's only the wounded witchhunter here. We can—" one of the Tekni began.

P'talan held his hand up. "It will do for now. Only a fool fights a woman in her own kitchen."

Cyrus drew a rasping breath and pitifully twitched. B'lantra quickly shifted her focus and knelt down beside him. She held his limp fingers in hers and made a silent plea to Saint Rachael.

"Don't you dare die on me."

She rose, and turning to Caulter, pulled out the golden cape. "I've done my part. Now it's time to do yours."

Caulter looked around the kitchen. "We're fortunate we're not somewhere out in the wilds. We have most of what we'll need, and we'll trust your skill to make up the difference."

❋ ❋ ❋

Cyrus slowly opened his eyes and found he was lying atop some blankets on the floor. The knitted white wool was scratchy against his cheek. The vague memory of not being able to move his arms and legs crept through his mind, but he found they responded to his commands once again.

It took him a moment to recognize B'lantra's voice singing softly of sunshine and springtime. She was sitting beside him, wearing a dark blue linen dress. Once she noticed he was awake, she put aside the piece of scrap wood she'd been whittling on. Her hair had been freshly washed, and she'd replaced the cracked glass bead at the end of braid with a hastily carved wooden one. Her skin was clear and bright, the cuts and bruises that had covered her well on their way to disappearing. The faint scent of lilac once again clung to her.

He didn't need to look in a mirror to know he wasn't in as

good a shape. His hair felt sweaty and lank against the back of his head. A quick run of his hand across his chin revealed several days of growth.

He took an experimental breath, half expecting to feel pain shooting through him. To his pleasant surprise, he found only a dull ache. He'd been stripped down to the waist, and there were bandages all along his side.

The teakettle over the hearth began to whistle. He started to rise to tend to it, old habits directing his actions more than conscious thought. B'lantra's hand moved, faster than he would have imagined possible, settling on his bare chest and gently, but firmly, pushing him back down.

"No, you don't. You're going to stay right there until I say you can get up."

"Come on, Bel—"

"Too many people went to too much trouble to keep you alive. Stay put. You need to start thinking more about what you do," she said as she got up and went towards the hearth to deal with the teakettle. There was more than a little anger in her tone.

"Well, it didn't quite go the way I expected it to," he admitted.

"No, it didn't. You can't keep throwing yourself at everything. We have hopes and dreams, you and I. Where does it leave them if you get yourself killed because of stupidity?"

He lies in the ravine beside the sycamore, staring up at the cracked branches he's left in the wake of his fall. The sun filters through the leaves. The tree seems to be mocking him. Who was he to think he could climb it when no one else in the village ever had?

His breath comes in short, painful bursts. His leg is twisted underneath him. He can see bone and blood sticking up through it, though he can't really feel it.

A moment later the strange foreign girl that wandered out of the woods a few days ago is staring down at him. The braid in her long hair tickles his nose as she leans over him and looks at his mangled leg.

She looks up at the tree and the broken branches. Her eyes scold him.

She says nothing as she climbs out of the ravine. It seems a long time before she returns with Lyra and a rope.

B'lantra came back and set a mug of tea and some water in a wooden cup beside him. She allowed him to sit up and then waited until he had sipped some of the water and started carefully on the tea before she held up the silver clover.

"I want to know why you have this."

He put his hand reflexively to his chest and found it was gone.

"She would never part with it, not even to give to you. You've been holding something inside you ever since Ashenwall. What was it? Where's Lyra?"

He lay back down miserably on the woolen blanket before he finally spoke. The pain was still there, resurfacing all over again. The passage of days hadn't dulled it as much as he'd wanted. The words came out, choked and bitter. The memories threatened to drown him where he lay.

She was calmer than he'd expected her to be. The lines of her brow furrowed, and her jaw tightened, but no fit of hysteria burst forth from her. Maybe it was just the way of things. Lyra was gone, and no amount of tears would change that.

B'lantra was practical. He wasn't.

"And why didn't you tell me? I could understand while we were inside Ashenwall, but you've had two full days since then!"

"I... couldn't find the words is why. I couldn't think about it—didn't want to think about it. If I had been there... I should have stayed. I could have done something! I could—"

Her hands clenched. "No! Don't you dare blame yourself! Don't you dare become another Soren wallowing in your house like a damned mushroom! It wasn't your fault. I know you don't believe that, but it's true."

"But if I'd... I didn't mean for it to—"

"Asa tore through a whole company of inquisitors. What were you supposed to do?"

"I don't know. Something."

He closed his eyes as another barrage of memories welled up from somewhere in the back of his mind. Maybe he should have just stayed asleep. The waking world was certainly no ally today.

B'lantra leaned over and gave him a kiss on the cheek. "Let it go. I know you tried. You always try. That's why I love you. And… and I wish more than anything we could go back and do everything all over again and maybe get it right, but we can't."

She took a deep breath. "We have other things to worry about."

❋ ❋ ❋

The first creak of movement came against the floorboards outside the kitchen before B'lantra could continue. P'talan came striding in, Dontarius and a couple of the Tekni soldiers on his heels. He briefly bowed to her before turning to Cyrus.

"I see you're awake and recovering. I'm glad my effort in helping to obtain the golden cape wasn't wasted."

Cyrus carefully turned himself on his blanket. "I doubt you did it out of the goodness of your heart."

"The proper response would be thank you. Your healer did most of the work, I'll admit. I merely provided some assistance along the way," P'talan replied.

A scowl began forming on Cyrus' face.

B'lantra groaned inwardly. She'd told him countless times about the sometimes subtle ways with which Southerners conducted themselves. A look or a gesture, a slight rise in tone or change in posture said as much as any bluntly worded statement.

P'talan seemed momentarily taken aback. "Ahh, yes. The famed Northern manners. I had hoped your time with the princess might have given you some *bara'kahn*, some merchant sense as we call it. But perhaps not."

"Why were you hunting for us?" Cyrus demanded.

"Your new friend Dontarius has mentioned on several occasions the value of someone who knows the ancient Iriethan characters. He seems to believe you're one of the few who does. After his eloquent appeal during the battle for Ashenwall, a decision was made to offer you our protection," P'talan said. His eyes shifted over to B'lantra. "And to you also. A witch who can devastate an entire fortress is certainly worthy of a proper escort as well."

"We were going elsewhere. Where exactly do you mean to take us?" B'lantra asked carefully, trying to suppress her outrage.

She placed a cautionary hand on Cyrus, digging her nails into his skin just hard enough to make her point. It was *bara'kahn*, and P'talan was negotiating with her as an equal, although he really didn't have to. Any sign of distress on their part simply gave him more bargaining power.

"For the moment I'll keep my own counsel as to our destination. I can force you to come with me, but it saves me time and effort if you do so willingly," the raider said.

"We appreciate your offer, but I'm afraid we must decline," she replied, as smoothly as she could.

"You should reconsider," P'talan said. There was just a touch of harshness creeping into his voice. "Tamaka provides consideration for a healer, but if the healer were to commit an act of aggression, which is a likely result of declining our offer, then the Koda would be annulled."

"If a witch who can devastate an entire fortress is worthy of an escort, then there is risk in angering one. Perhaps I invoked Tamaka merely to spare the lives of your men," B'lantra said.

The Tekni soldiers that had come into the room with P'talan began to murmur anxiously amongst themselves. The raider remained calm. "If you could do that, then you would have done it already, and we wouldn't be speaking so pleasantly."

The Koda was looking more and more like a deal with a *k'ziani* sand demon. "We'll accept your kind offer of protection. But Cyrus isn't going to be ready to travel for some time, I'm afraid."

"Arakostrian regiments will cross the Maidenskar from the north and fall upon us if we stay here a more than a few days," P'talan said. His eyes narrowed. "I'm sure as a practitioner of

Saint Rachael's arts you can restore him to health in that time."

"We're not going anywhere with you," Cyrus blustered. "You can count on that!"

"Your lovely princess did go to a great deal of trouble to arrange the Koda between us, so you should thank her by honoring her efforts," P'talan noted, seemingly unperturbed. "So rest up and get well. You'll need your energy for the journey ahead. I'll have men standing close by… if you happen to need anything."

Chapter 20

Sojourn

Her jaw was set tightly, her brow furrowed the way it always did when she heard something she didn't like. Cyrus had seen that look from her a lot lately.

"There's no way to know if Asa is truly dead, and Celaan said something about some hidden master she had. Unless you know of some ancient tomb we can stop at and pick up a magical sword, we really don't have a weapon we can use against her. Mother's blocks are gone."

"Witchbane? We don't even know if it will hurt her, but we know damn sure what it did to you!"

"I'm not going to coat a sword with it and cut myself."

B'lantra shook her head. "Not to sound selfish, but what about me? It's called witchbane for a reason."

"I'll keep it and I'll handle it. All you have to do is run when I tell you to."

"And that's your idea of a plan, is it?" B'lantra sniffed.

Cyrus patted her arm and grinned. "You said I needed to think about things more, so here we are."

"Do you want her dead that badly?" she asked him suddenly.

"Of course I do, Bel. Don't you?" he answered, his grin fading, his eyes narrowing in anger.

"Vengeance is a bad basis for a plan."

"This isn't vengeance. It's survival," he said, emphatically. "I'm not losing you like I did Lyra."

B'lantra got up from beside him and began slowly pacing. "Even if I thought it was a good idea— which I don't, by the way— I don't know how to make witchbane."

"Caulter probably does."

"He's not going to just give that knowledge away."

"After what you told me about that focusing stone, I can't say I trust him," Cyrus said. "But he may not want anything. Asa nearly killed him too."

"I guess I brought it on myself. You would have to pick now to actually listen to me," B'lantra said. "Ugh! Let's get this over with then. I've already spent more time around Caulter than I want to this morning."

Cyrus gingerly made his way back to the kitchen, B'lantra reluctantly trailing along behind him. Caulter was still sitting on his blanket as they entered, almost as if he'd never moved. Lately he'd seemed more a statue than a man.

"My leg is fine, girl. You already checked it this morning," he growled.

Cyrus couldn't bring himself to attempt much in the way of beginning conversation. "We have other business. I want to know how to make witchbane."

Caulter raised a questioning eyebrow. "Are you suicidal then? After all the trouble she went through for you? There are easier ways to meet God."

"It's not for me. It's for Asa— the golden haired woman that nearly killed both of us."

"What about your lover then? Witchbane is fatal. It is quick and certain, not a thing to be taken lightly," Caulter replied.

"And you've used it many times, I'll wager," B'lantra said, shivering even though a fire burned in the hearth nearby.

"There aren't a whole lot of options," Cyrus said. "Look what she did to your lot."

Caulter's expression didn't change much, but he nodded his head slightly in what Cyrus guessed was some sort of approval. "It's better than just charging in and getting yourself killed, which is what I would have expected from you."

"So you'll help then."

"Perhaps. But I want to know why you're going east. I want to know why that witch was hunting you, son of Aeliraneth. You're not important enough on your own. So what did your mother have that they want so badly?"

Cyrus glowered at him, but acceded. There was little to be gained by hiding the truth.

The inquisitor listened to the tale stoically for the most part.

"From your description, this thief that stole the Heart sounds like some sort of warlock."

"Warlocks don't exist anymore," B'lantra said.

"That's a convenient truth for the Illumentry. Warlocks exist, though they're rare enough to be legends. It was some lingering effect of the Aeore weapons from the war, so they say. Witches and warlocks were the backbone of Iriethan. What better way to ensure an enemy could never rise again? There was one— Simon Barros, about a generation ago. He disappeared before we could run him to ground. Some rumors even claimed he found a way to cross the Wynding and escape to Asylum," Caulter said.

"You hunted him like any other witch then?" Cyrus asked, incredulously.

"I didn't, but others did. The Conclave feared him, and with good reason. The list of his crimes is as long as your arm."

"So he found his way into the Aeore lands and stole the Heart. Mother must have tracked him down. Celaan was telling the truth after all."

"The pieces certainly fit. I doubt this Aeore empress of yours was telling you everything. Commanders only tell their would-be soldiers what they need to know in order to accomplish their task. Nothing more is required or desired."

"It's even more reason to seek out the Bal-haegast then."

"I agree."

Cyrus was almost stunned by the words. He'd expected Caulter to argue with him, or at the very least give him the cold, disdainful stare he'd come to hate.

"I'll begin the witchbane this afternoon," Caulter said. "Now leave me unless you have some other business."

Cyrus turned and irritably made his way back outside. He felt like a servant who'd been summarily dismissed. The morning air was pregnant with a fine, misty spring rain, forcing him to search around for a dry place to sit.

"I told you it was a bad idea," B'lantra said before he'd even had a chance to settle.

"He agreed to do it, so I don't see what's so bad about it," he countered.

"Don't you? He's going to make a poison that will kill both of us—with our blessing!"

"What else can we do? We can't just wait around here and do nothing."

"I don't know," she said. "It may not even make a difference if we can't get away from P'talan and his lot."

A clatter came from across the farmyard. As they looked over they saw two of the Tekni soldiers walking across the fields, headed for a wooden shed near the stables. One of them had a freshly shot deer draped over his burly shoulders.

"Lovely," B'lantra groused. "Just what the morning needed was a bloody deer carcass. I hate venison."

Cyrus suddenly grinned and glanced over at her medicine bag. "You know how to cook it though, don't you?"

"Yes, but..."

Her words trailed off as she took his meaning. "As a matter of fact, I do. I even have all the 'spices' right in the kitchen."

❋ ❋ ❋

B'lantra stopped cutting up the winter vegetables and stared out the window onto the fields beyond the farmyard. The afternoon had brightened after the rain, but the only thing of interest was a flock of crows pecking at a forlorn scarecrow.

She was a woman surrounded by over a dozen men, and naturally the cooking duties had fallen on her. It was annoying at best, but she'd resigned herself to putting up with it for the time being.

It was probably safer as well. Aside from Cyrus, the lot of them could have probably burned water, and none them, Cyrus included, knew how to make a proper cup of chala.

The Tekni had been afraid of her at first, but as time had passed and they'd seen no indication of witchcraft from her they'd grown more relaxed. She'd become no different than any other woman in their eyes. How much of a threat could she possibly be?

P'talan strode into the kitchen, still looking every inch the desert raider. His eyes locked onto her almost as soon as he crossed the threshold.

"The blue you're wearing suits you," he said in Trafarga.

B'lantra blushed in spite of herself. "I borrowed a dress from one of the bedrooms. It feels a little strange taking it without asking, but there's no one here to ask."

"Then there's no point in letting it go to waste," P'talan said. "I imagine you're used to the yellow and white of the healers."

"I am. But circumstances don't always allow for what one is used to."

"I suspect you'll find a way to adapt. I have to admit I was surprised when you invoked Tamaka. You couldn't have known that I would accept."

"I've seen too much killing lately, so I could only hope you would see the advantage of it."

"It was a brave thing to do, though I almost didn't agree."

"So why did you?" B'lantra asked.

"Because life doesn't always present opportunities, and nothing is served by letting them pass," he answered, again letting his eyes caress her and leaving her feeling a little flattered, but mostly flustered.

She looked away and concentrated on the vegetables she'd been cutting. "You're talking about what happened at Ashenwall. 'A witch that can devastate an entire fortress.' I believe that's how you put it."

"There is that," he said. "The wrath of a witch is truly a sight to behold. But even so, you've been on your own recently, without guidance or protection. Perhaps we can help each other."

"You don't fear a witch's wrath?"

He stepped in closer to her. She swore she could still smell a faint trace of the wind and the sand on him. "I'm from Surin. You're Trafari. Neither one of us should have these irrational fears about witches the way Northerners do."

"Brakeem has no more love in his heart for witchcraft than does Talast. There's many a kaja that hunts and traps us just like the inquisitors," she said.

"True, but it depends greatly on the kaja. Brakeem's mood shifts like the sands, and everything is not always what it would seem. In some places, witches have risen to become advisors or consorts. They're a power in several Surani tribes."

"Those are the exceptions though. How many are so lucky?"

"Perhaps, though there are not many witches to begin with. So how did a flower of Trafaria, a princess even, end up becoming a healer in the frozen north?"

She wasn't a princess, and he knew it just as well as she did. Still, there was no reason to totally shatter the illusion. "My parents were traveling north on business. They were killed by troika in the woods near Shrevnetska, and the people of the village took me in."

"Strange that they would do so. There's been little love between the Northerners and us ever since Fa'boule made the false crown out of straik-gold for the Arakostrian emperor."

B'lantra smiled. "I imagine the emperor must have looked pretty silly when the rains came and the crown melted on top of his head."

"They say his face was stained for weeks afterwards. But now they call us 'straiks' and thieves and gypsies. Don't you ever grow weary of that and want to go back home?"

"Not all the Northerners are like that. Lyra, my teacher back in Shrevnetska, gave me a home. Treated me like a daughter. I couldn't ask for more than that from anybody, Trafari or not."

P'talan's eyes lit up in understanding. "That's the healer who owned the clover you held up, isn't it?"

"Yes," she answered. Lyra's memory hurt still. She'd put on a brave front for Cyrus, but the pain lingered.

P'talan's hand gently brushed across hers. "I've heard Saint Rachael's healers don't give away their clovers, so I'm sorry for your loss."

"Thank you," she said, demurely edging her hand away.

Before she could think on it anymore, another of the Tekni fighters came in and motioned to P'talan.

"If you'll excuse me, I have some things to attend to. Be well, Princess," the raider said.

Once he was gone, B'lantra found her fingers running across the bead in her hair. It was wonderful hearing Trafarga, and once again talking to someone who remembered the same colors and sounds she did. There was a whole land she missed more than she'd known, and P'talan was her first link to it in a long time.

He wanted something from her, possibly the power she'd unleashed at the fortress, but other things as well from the look in his eyes. He could have easily made her body a part of the condition for his help. He might still do so if the opportunity presented itself.

It was the Southern way, the way of the merchant that ran through all parts of life in one fashion or form, to take advantage of opportunities. Maybe she'd been absent from that way for too long and had lost her *bara'kahn*. That might have to change if they were going to survive.

She glanced around, but none of the Tekni soldiers seemed to be paying her any attention. Carefully, she brought out the ingredients from her physician's satchel and started assembling them. As far as the Tekni knew, dinner tonight would be no different than it had been the previous two nights.

There was no reason for them to suspect anything. She was a woman, after all. How much of a threat could she possibly be?

❋ ❋ ❋

"Keep your eyes off her while you still have them!"

From the other side of the stables, Cyrus advanced on the Surani raider. His hand hovered near the hilt of his sword.

P'talan studied him with wry detachment and put down the brush he'd been using on the chestnut stallion beside him. A couple of the nearby Tekni soldiers slid protectively around their captain.

The raider casually waved them away.

"And what offense have I committed onto you?" he asked in Trafarga.

Cyrus was momentarily taken aback. He'd been expecting his challenge to be answered with swords or with fists, not with words. P'talan switched back and forth between his native language and the Arakostrian tongue of the Northern lands with surprising ease, much as B'lantra did.

"You know damn well what offense you've committed, *skish!*"

His own Trafarga was stuttered and a little awkward, but functional enough if P'talan's reaction was any indication.

Anger flashed in the raider's dark eyes, but it quickly passed. "Do you truly know what that word means amongst my people, Northerner?"

"It's a sand grub, so what? Fits you well enough."

"It's found mostly in the Da'Gebron wastes. They're foul little things about the size of your foot, skittering around in clumps on their spiky legs. Fat, bloated bodies and a thin shell outside. The smell of them is enough to make a man retch for days. *Skish* is the sound they make when you step on them."

"Is there a point to all this?" Cyrus demanded.

"It's also a deadly insult and not a word to be used lightly. There have been blood feuds between houses from utterance of it. If you were a Southerner, a follower of Brakeem, my honor would demand I take your head. As it is, you're simply a child speaking of things he doesn't understand."

"We'll see who the child is!"

Cyrus drew his sword and quickly closed on the raider. The techniques Caulter had unleashed in Ashenwall flashed through his mind. He'd seen them. Now all he had to do was use them.

P'talan pulled the hand axe from his belt and met the charge. The flat of his hand quickly found Cyrus' wounded side. P'talan used the opening to shove him away.

"You're not completely unfamiliar with the blade," the raider said. "It's a pity you don't have the wisdom to match. You have no *bara'kahn*, no understanding, and yet you still have designs on a flower of Trafaria."

"I know her a lot better than you do," Cyrus growled, still clutching at his side.

"Do you really? Your Trafarga is barely adequate. You've never set foot in our lands. If you desire her so much, then where is the *Ma'ganta* bracelet on her wrist?"

"*Ma'ganta?* What are you talking about?"

"You don't even know that?" P'talan sneered. "The *ma'ganta* is a pledge between a man and the woman he chooses. Brakeem's Covenant it's called. There are no words needed. He simply ties it around her wrist if she allows. Perhaps you should bother learning something about where a woman comes from before you claim you know her. It might give you some wisdom before you tell me what I should or shouldn't do."

"Let me give you some wisdom about Northerners," Cyrus said in Arakostrian. His voice was clear and commanding. His bearing was proud. His gaze coldly burned through the raider. "Our land is cold, our vengeance colder. *Ma'ganta* or not, I'll kill you if you touch her."

P'talan regarded him, taking in his battered appearance and the way he still held his arm to his side.

"Maybe you will. Then again, maybe you won't," the raider

said. His expression still held mirth, but the condescension had fled from his tone. "The future is an uncertain thing. One thing that is certain is that if you're well enough to fight, you're well enough to travel. We'll be leaving at dawn tomorrow."

The Tekni soldiers had closed in around them once more. One of them moved in and took the sword from his hand.

"Where are we going?" Cyrus demanded.

The raider smiled. "The future is an uncertain thing."

❋ ❋ ❋

They sat beside each other on the porch of the farmhouse as the sun dipped down towards the tree line.

"From the stars we came…" B'lantra intoned in Trafarga, reciting the Kamer rite for the departed in Southern fashion.

"…to the stars we return," Cyrus finished.

He turned his attention back to the flame of the small candle that sat amidst the twisting chalk patterns she'd spent the last hour painstakingly drawing on the ground. Both their hands lay clasped around Lyra's silver clover.

"*Ah-men,*" they recited together.

And that was it: they'd said their farewells to Lyra and it was time to move on.

Simple.

Only it wasn't.

B'lantra was still calm. She felt the loss, though no great bout of tears or wailing had erupted since he'd told her. The rite was more for her benefit than his at this point. If anyone deserved to be in Heaven, surely Lyra did, but the world was unfair in so many ways.

The more he learned that truth, the less he liked it.

It was as if by going through the Kamer with B'lantra, he'd once again ripped open all the wounded misery he'd felt watching Lyra crumple to the ground B'lantra had said the wound needed reopening, that it was festering inside and needed to be cleaned. Lyra might have said the same thing if she still could have.

Maybe they were right, but even now he didn't feel much better.

B'lantra turned her face away from him and took a deep long breath, wiping some sudden tears away.

"It's done."

They sat in silence for a little while, gazing out over the yard. Out of the corner of his eye, Cyrus saw a couple of rabbits scurry through the neatly planted fields and past a forlorn scarecrow. It really wasn't that much different from Shrevnetska in some ways. The serenity almost seemed strange after all the chaos of the last few days.

"What do you suppose the Bal-haegast will tell us?" B'lantra asked after a while.

"I have no idea. Maybe where this Heart thing is, so we can find it and be done with all of this," he replied.

She smiled, wearily. "I guess we'll find out together. It's nearly time for dinner."

"Maybe you could just order the Tekni to let us go. I heard them calling you Princess."

B'lantra shook her head. "That's something P'talan started because of my name. There's a Trafari legend about a princess named B'lantra who got lost and is trying to find her way back home. If you help her on her way, then you'll be blessed. It's just an old story, so doesn't mean much anymore. But P'talan is Surani, and maybe the old customs die down harder in the desert."

Cyrus laughed. "So you're not exiled royalty then?"

"No, I'm a merchant's daughter," B'lantra said. "Matri thought the name was pretty. Patri thought it would get people to buy more off the wagon."

"So they buy something just in case, huh? Strange custom, but I guess it works."

She gazed purposefully at him. "Maybe this mess will be over soon, and I can show you all the customs there. I'd like to go home. Let them make all the evil signs at me they want. I don't care anymore."

"I think I'd like that too."

The ruddy plains and white sparkling ice caps of Saranor began to rise. The ley lines crossed in the sky, shimmering like celestial beacons. And dancing out of the oak tree in the center of the yard came a white filament of streaming light.

"Look, there's a moon fairy. And another over there," he said.

Two Tekni soldiers walked under the tree, blissfully unaware that anything out of the ordinary was happening.

The fairy daintily rose on her gossamer wings. Her skin was banded with lines of gold and crimson in places. Elsewhere it was a milky white to match hair that flowed away almost like dandelion seeds blowing in the wind. She emitted a soft yellow glow, ringing out against the purple sky of evening. Soon she was joined by others, twisting and swirling upwards around the treetops in a gleaming chorus.

"They're beautiful," B'lantra said, laying her head on his shoulder. "It's hard being a witch. But sometimes… you see something like this, and it almost makes it worth it."

He held her close, glad to be enjoying something with her again. It seemed a long time since they'd had the chance.

They sat for a while, watching the private light show provided for them.

CHAPTER 21

HUNTERS AND HUNTED

THE I-WE WAS HUNGRY. Empty. A squirrel squeaked and then fell silent, sensing its peril as the I-We landed on the branch of the oak tree. It needn't have bothered. Squirrels weren't important. The memories of such things, vapid and fleeting, were beneath notice.

The I-We searched across the length of the yard to the farmhouse structure, distantly sensing the memories inside. Some were hot and vibrant, others cold and violent.

All were better than the emptiness that gnawed.

The I-We stretched its wings and preened its shadowy black feathers. Its ochre talons gripped the branch. Prey had returned to the house. There had been too many cool nights since the I-We had felt warmth and life, enough to range far from the lovely pool that was home.

The Sunlit Owl had told the I-We that the offspring of the Aeliraneth prey was inside. It had come, as the I-We knew it must. The I-We would deal with it soon.

The Sunlit Owl saw many things. It was proud and stern… but kind; provided the prey showed it the respect it felt it was due. The prey thing designating itself P'talan had used the proper ritual, and so it slept now. The Midnight Owl had come in its place now that the sun had departed. The Sunlit Owl knew hunger as only a distant thing.

It sought. The Midnight Owl hunted.

I and We, as it had always been since the Creation.

Silently and patiently, the I-We waited until one of the prey things left the house. The prey called itself Kafka and considered itself part of a collective called the Tekni. Like many of the other prey, it was eager to fight another collective called the Illumentry. The prey was pair-bonded to another of its kind that it called Anne. It had a memory of saying goodbye to an offspring, Mikel. It had sent them away from the coming fight between the Tekni and Illumentry collectives so they wouldn't be damaged. It worried about their safety, and so it was restless.

The Kafka prey wasn't like the I-We. It was alone inside its mind, as all prey were, sharing shadows of their true memories by the noises they made.

I-We tested the memories. They were dry and unappetizing, but hunger remained. The emptiness gnawed.

The I-We called to the Kafka prey, in the dark, underneath the silent stars. It changed its face, so the prey might know it.

"Anne! God's name, you scared me coming out of the dark like that. What are you doing here anyway? How did you get here?"

"Thank God I found you. There were bandits on the road, Kafka. They attacked our wagon. Mikel and I got away but he's hurt. I— I couldn't carry him any farther. You have to come help me with him before it's too late."

"Let me get some of the others. We have a doctor with us."

"There's no time. I think… I think he's dying. Please, this is our son! He wants to see you one last time."

The Kafka prey was trusting, and it followed in the dark until the I-We was ready to feed. It didn't resist at first, but then it began to sense the danger it was in and tried to run.

It was too late.

The I-We sampled and then devoured the memories one by one until hunger began to fade a little, and emptiness was filled for a time.

The Kafka prey whimpered as its true memories were ripped out. Its body shook. Blood poured from its eyes and nose. It fell to the ground, quaking and convulsing before it expired— empty now as the I-We had been.

✳ ✳ ✳

Cyrus waited at his seat at the table, impatiently nibbling on one the scones B'lantra had baked earlier in the day. The smell of Trafari cooking filled the dining room. He glanced down at the steaming bowl of venison stew in front of him and swallowed as his mouth began to water. B'lantra had outdone herself. It seemed a shame to let it go to waste.

His eyes flicked around the table.

The Tekni were assembled, chatting idly as they enjoyed a mug of the farm family's beer. The smell of the stew had drawn P'talan and all but three of the Tekni soldiers into the kitchen.

The Surani raider sat across from him. P'talan stirred at the stew with his spoon, and nodded approvingly to B'lantra as the aroma of the meal cascaded over him. To Cyrus' annoyance, P'talan began murmuring a lengthy grace.

It wouldn't take long after they began eating. Afterwards, the worst thing he and B'lantra would have to contend with would be stepping over their slumbering bodies.

At last the grace was over. Did the raider really have to thank every single Face of God for the meal? Cyrus spread some more butter over his scone and finished it off with a bit of cider.

P'talan scooped up a mouthful of stew. Following his lead, the men reached for their bowls. Beneath the table, Cyrus gripped the leg of the chair in anticipation.

The door to the outside flew open, tearing the jovial air of dinner asunder. One of the Tekni solders, Gerimain, burst in. He was a large man with arms that looked more akin to tree trunks than human appendages. His face was ashen, and his mustache was bristled up like a frightened cat.

"He's dead! Kafka's dead."

"What! How long ago?" P'talan demanded, casting aside the spoonful of stew.

"He's not even cold yet. Not a mark on him other than a little blood on his face. He was just lying there. Daan is missing too."

P'talan clenched his fists and then let loose a string of Trafari curses. His gaze fell harshly upon Caulter, though he didn't say anything. Caulter merely glanced calmly back at him.

"Keep an eye on all of them. If the inquisitor moves, kill him," P'talan ordered.

He stalked out of the house with Gerimain, presumably to see Kakfa's corpse for himself. They waited, tensely. Cyrus slowly got up from his chair and walked over to B'lantra. The Tekni watched him closely. He saw one slide his hand ever so slightly towards his musket. They had been relaxed before, almost friendly. Now any pretense of warmth had fled from them.

P'talan stalked back in. "I wanted you all to witness this. I didn't break the Koda. My people are the ones who suffered the grievance. Despite my doubts, I spared the witchhunter. Now my people are dead or missing, and justice will be done."

He turned on Caulter once more. "What secrets are you hiding out in the dark, Illumentry filth?"

"If you can't keep track of your men, then maybe they should find themselves a competent commander," Caulter replied, coldly. The inquisitor's gaze was almost reptilian.

Cyrus stepped between the two. "One of your men is dead, and your response is to start a fight and get more of them killed? Even I know better."

"You defend a witchhunter?" P'talan demanded. "He's a blight on this world, and you should know that better than any, witch's son. Can you look at him and honestly tell me he wouldn't strike at us if he had the chance? What if there are Illumentry sisters in the woods picking us off one by one? No. The witchhunter dies!"

He shoved Cyrus aside and pulled the hand axe from his belt. The inquisitor rose to meet him. B'lantra stepped forward, only to be restrained by two of the Tekni soldiers.

The faint click of a crossbow bolt being drawn back brought the rising chaos in the room to an abrupt halt.

"I think that will be quite enough from everyone."

Dontarius moved with a speed and grace Cyrus hadn't thought him capable of. The scholar kept his crossbow mostly trained on P'talan, but stood ready to easily and quickly target Caulter if need be. The weapon was fully loaded, its multiple bolts ready to fly forth at the touch of his finger upon the trigger.

"Now let's discuss this like civilized people, shall we. Before someone gets hurt," he said, pleasantly.

The weapons of both inquisitor and raider eagerly quivered in response.

"I wouldn't try the stew either," the scholar added, pulling a bowl from the surprised hands of one of the Tekni soldiers. "They say meals like that sit heavily on the stomach— hardly the time and place for that."

"They were poisoned?" P'talan asked.

"Not poisoned necessarily. It's amazing what you can whip up in the kitchen."

"You? After all your talk about a Koda?" P'talan hissed. His face contorted in outrage as he turned on B'lantra. His fist curled as if to strike her. Cyrus drew his sword. One of the Tekni soldiers pointed his musket at him.

"As long as I do no harm to you, the Koda remains unbroken," B'lantra insisted. "You would have slept, but you would have been fine in the morning. I wouldn't have done it if I'd known there was some monster out in the dark."

"Cunning and subtle are the ways of women. I should have known better. You're stretching the definition of the Koda painfully thin," P'talan growled.

"So are you," she retorted. "The Koda doesn't say anything about dragging a healer off to God knows where."

"All this talk about who broke what part of the code is pointless. We're forgetting what killed Kafka. The enemy is out in the dark, not in here. Put away your weapon, and I'll put away mine," Cyrus offered.

"You expect me to just accept your word about some monster?"

P'talan asked, derisively. "Why should I believe you?"

Cyrus met his gaze without flinching and sheathed his sword. "Think about it. This house has been empty ever since we came. What happened to the family that lived here? Probably the same thing that happened to your men."

"Then how does the wise and noble son of Aeliraneth propose we kill it?" P'talan asked, and then cast a sideward glance at B'lantra. "Perhaps the monster would like some stew."

"We don't know what it is. You offered us your protection. Now make good on that promise if you think you can."

P'talan bristled. "You doubt my skill?"

"It doesn't matter what I think," Cyrus said, firmly. "It only matters what the monster thinks. Do you really want to kill the only experienced monster hunter here?"

"And what does the monster hunter have to say?"

"I'd need to examine the body. If it's intact, it rules out troika, and lupesku, as well as a kurikai cat. Fairies don't hunt at night unless you blunder into their nest. That leaves some sort of spirit, perhaps that golden owl you supposedly banished. I'd stay here tonight if I wanted to live to see dawn," Caulter said.

The raider considered for a long moment and then waved his hand dismissively. He put his axe back in his belt. "Be grateful I'm a man of my word, witchhunter. Be grateful the Koda has meaning. You're going to spend the night under guard. All of you. Give us any trouble and the monster will be the least of your concerns. We leave at dawn tomorrow."

❋ ❋ ❋

The I-We stirred, stretching out its wings to feel the breeze that wafted by the silent, lovely pool. It glided adroitly over the water, past the one captured prey thing that lay sleeping under the placid surface— still alive, still dreaming— until the I-We had need of it.

There was distant terror on the breeze, swirling through the trees and over the fields. The prey things were afraid. They would flee, taking the offspring of the Aeliraneth prey with them.

The I-We would not let that happen.

* * *

There were few words spoken as the company slowly moved through the trees, almost as if everyone was afraid the darkness would steal their voice away. No sound came from the night. No bird called or woodland creature stirred. Only the faint breathing of the people near him gave Cyrus any indication that he hadn't gone deaf.

Nine of the Tekni soldiers remained, along with P'talan and the four of them that had fled Ashenwall. Yet even with the others around him, the quiet felt brooding and oppressive, just as it had at the fortress before the fighting had started. A silent scream, B'lantra had called it. It had been the perfect metaphor then, and it was just as true now.

Even though his eyes could pierce the darkness, the sight he'd been born with gave him no comfort. It reduced the world to shades of gray, leaving him grimly checking each and every shadow. He'd kept B'lantra close to him, leaving her astride the horse while he walked beside it. She kept her lantern near, like a frightened child clutching onto its mother.

It had been a hard day and night of traveling, more a forced march than anything. The animals were thirsty. They all were. They'd taken water with them, but not enough, and had braved stopping at a stream just once in the long hours since they'd left the farmhouse. Whether they'd outdistanced the monster that stalked them, he didn't know.

Instinct told him they hadn't.

They were headed east towards whatever destination P'talan had in mind. The Tekni soldiers had kept a tight watch on them, though they had at least given him back his sword and pistols.

"These trees are too suffocating. It reminds me too much of the way they were when Matri and Patri died," B'lantra whispered.

He couldn't really argue with her. The dark had never really bothered him before. In fact, it was often enjoyable— seeing what others were blind to. It was one of the few times he could truly enjoy being a witch's son.

Not now though. The dark pushed against him almost like a living thing, ready to smother him whenever it pleased.

Was this how B'lantra felt every night?

"Where's Orley?" P'talan said, grabbing the reins of his mount. "He's gone!"

Everyone in the little company gaped at each other in sudden confusion and fright. Cyrus swiftly counted and found eight where nine had been before.

A large shape loomed out of the darkness. One of the Tekni soldiers was dragged screaming into the darkness. Another simply curled up and collapsed as if the night had siphoned the life out of him.

Their attacker seemed almost unreal, a blur of dark within dark, moving with unnatural speed.

B'lantra's song began, tentative and terrified…

…and died just as quickly.

There was no spark, no flicker or ember, only the ravening continuity of the night. B'lantra's eyes were wide and frightened, nearly maddened. Her horse reared. With a frightened scream she tumbled off and lay stunned on the muddy ground. Only blind luck saved her from being trampled by the other horses.

The creature continued its assault, scattering the Tekni soldiers. Cyrus had the vague sense of great black wings flapping, of talons gripping and tearing, though there was no physical form to give substance to the images.

Its shadow gobbled up those who weren't fast enough to escape its grasp. Cyrus instinctively reached for his sword and then abandoned the idea. There was no victory to be had here.

He pulled B'lantra to her feet and towards the large draft horse she'd been riding. It was a gentle thing, probably more used to leisurely days in green pastures than war. Given B'lantra's inexperience as a rider, he'd chosen it more for its demeanor than for its speed. Even so, it backed away as far as its tether would allow. He took hold of it before it could bolt, quickly pulling its head to the side and spinning it round.

B'lantra scrambled awkwardly onto its back while Cyrus did his best to hold the animal still. He tried to keep his voice soothing and calm, even though he expected to feel the shadowy creature's talons sink on him at any moment. He felt it closing in on them.

Cyrus barely had time to pull himself onto the horse. Its tether snapped. It sprinted away into the night, carrying them in the direction it chose. The creature pursued tirelessly.

No matter how fast the horse ran, their pursuer seemed always close behind.

Its talons lashed out. B'lantra cried out in pain. Cyrus felt her blood splatter across his face.

"Hold on," he called to her, though he didn't know if she could hear him.

They galloped on, ducking and dodging through the trees until at last they came to some open ground. The creature finally faded away into the night that seemed to have spawned it.

He thought he saw a glimpse of another rider heading in the same general direction they were. It was hard to tell as it flitted in and out of the shadows. After what had happened, nothing was certain anymore.

❋ ❋ ❋

"There's not a mark on you anywhere. Not even the clothing's torn," Cyrus remarked as he examined B'lantra in the flickering lantern light.

Dontarius got up from the log he'd been sitting on. "Maybe it was all in our imagination— some power of that monster in the dark. Wish we could imagine ourselves safe and sound."

B'lantra sat huddled, arms and legs pulled tightly against her body. There was a haunted look to her face. "It doesn't matter if it hurt me or not. The song's not mine anymore. She took it from me!"

"We'll get it back," he assured her.

"Will we?" she asked, wiping away a line of sudden tears from her face. "Maybe I'm not some broken thing you can just be glue back together."

"We'll just have to find some better glue come morning."

"I just want to sleep, but who knows what the morning will bring the way things have been going."

"You might as well try to get a little sleep," he agreed. There was nothing he could really do for her. "These horses were already tired, and if we push them any more we'll end up walking anyway."

"I wonder what happened to our inquisitor friend. And the others. Maybe the monster will finish with them and leave us alone the rest of the night," Dontarius mused.

"You're just overflowing with sympathy, aren't you? It could have been you just as easily," Cyrus replied, darkly. "You're lucky I didn't put a bullet through you with all the confusion. And you're lucky you were able to find us."

"I had quite a number of conversations with God about those very things. And I'm grateful for everything from not being shot to not being eaten to not being alone in the dark. I'd even be willing to go back and help if I thought it would do any good, but we can barely help ourselves right now."

Cyrus glanced off into the night. The trees were thinner here, but more importantly the ominous weight of the darkness had lifted. The woodland creatures had begun to scurry and rustle once more, and even a few of the night birds had begun to sing.

"It'll be a little while before dawn. I think we're safe for now. At least I hope so."

"I don't think anywhere is safe right now," Dontarius said. He shivered and then got up and began searching for a blanket.

Cyrus glanced over and saw B'lantra had already fallen into an exhausted, fitful slumber. He got up and morosely trudged over to gather some nearby deadwood for a fire. Hopefully dawn would come soon.

They were alive, and he knew he should once again be thankful, but it wasn't enough. There had to be something better than just surviving. There had to be some way to change the run of luck they'd had, the fate they'd been dealt. Luck and fate could be changed if he could just figure out how.

Still, as he carried the firewood back, he had no idea what they were going to do or how he was going to change anything.

CHAPTER 22

A WELCOMING EMBRACE

DONTARIUS WOKE TO THE FEEL of a rock poking into his ribs. He turned over, pulling the blanket up more closely around him, but then found a tree root digging into his leg. Finally, he sat up in disgust. The cold stars peered down at him, twinkling in and out of the passing clouds. Saranor had nearly completed its descent to the horizon, though its celestial followers, Gani, the silver moon, and Revka, the blue moon, were still fairly high in the sky. Dawn was coming, though it was as yet an unrealized dream to the night.

He shivered suddenly. The fire Cyrus had made was now nothing but cold ash. The nearby stream babbled happily to itself from the other side of the hill.

Strange. He didn't remember hearing a stream when he'd gone to sleep.

He glanced over at Cyrus and B'lantra lying curled around each other and felt jealous. Maybe it was because that they were still sleeping when he couldn't, or maybe it was because they had each other while he was cold and alone.

B'lantra stirred, and he felt more than a twinge of lust as he watched her slender form. How long had it been since he'd bedded a woman? It seemed like it had been forever, but it actually wasn't that long ago he'd left the gunsmith's wife behind. What was her name?

Pity she wasn't here now.

No, despite her charms the gunsmith's wife wasn't the one he really wanted. Tarja. He'd been thinking about her a lot lately. Too much. Such things were probably better left alone.

He soon found he was thirsty as well as cold. Slowly and stiffly, he got up and went over to fetch the canteen from behind the saddle. It was empty, just as he'd feared. He relit one of the lanterns and grudgingly headed in the direction of the stream, thinking again of Tarja.

She'd been radiant in the time he'd known her, tightly curled flaxen hair ever straining against the barrettes and pins she tried to secure it with. She was tall and fair, delightfully headstrong and charmingly cantankerous. There were plenty of more beautiful women, but none he'd met quite held her spark, and few had been more resourceful or more determined. Her mind had greedily devoured every scrap of ancient learning she could lay hands on. Her eyes, the pale blue gray of a winter sky, had lit up whenever she'd discovered something new and interesting. And like the gunsmith's wife, she'd been aggressively willing. He'd been hard pressed to keep up with her advances.

Three years. They'd been three good years too. As soon as he'd seen her walking through the quiet halls of the library in the cool air of that summer morning, he'd silently thanked the Soledain, the so-called Arakostrian Intelligence Bureau for giving him the assignment. In those three years, he'd never felt the urge to look at another woman's backside. It was a singular achievement Tarja should be justly proud of. Did she even care anymore? It was hard to say.

The entire passageway shudders. The steam golem roars in the distance. It's trapped— now and hopefully forever. He wipes a dirty hand across his brow. The crossbow comes out of his jacket in a smooth motion. She stares uncertainly at him as he points it at her.

"Give me the scroll," he says.

Her eyes widen in disbelief.

He pulls the trigger on the crossbow. The bolt grazes her cheek as it flies past her and embeds itself into the stone behind her. The clockwork loading mechanism slides the next bolt into place.

She hesitates, her hand hovering near the prize.

Her hands shake as she finally hands it over. They're come so far… worked so hard to get here…

He keeps his face calm. Inside he seethes. It was her research that led them here. They promised they'd find Marithandri together. They had so many plans. So many big things they were going to do together. He's done what a Soledain agent should never do: become too close to his assignment.

In Arakost, unearthing holy relics is a crime punishable by death. The other Soledain agents are close and their reach is long. But they can't do anything to her, not as long as he has the scroll as a bargaining chip.

He backs slowly away. She doesn't understand, and there's no time to explain. He'll find a way to make it up to her. Somehow. Just not today. Not today.

"I love you," he says.

Her glare sears him as he slips into the darkness.

He'd never found a way to make it up to her. Was there even a way?

He shook his head in annoyance. Some things couldn't be changed, and it was time he accepted that fact. Men had destroyed themselves in drink or the dull escape of the opium pipe over lesser things. He wasn't going to become one of them.

Maybe he was just lonely. When they reached a civilized town, he would definitely have to remedy that problem. There were plenty of barmaids willing to pull up their skirts for a handsome Illumentry scholar.

He came over the hill, but didn't find the stream he was expecting to see. Instead there was a clear, silent pool. The water circled sluggishly around the reeds and cattails.

He could have sworn he'd heard the babbling of a stream. For an instant he thought he saw an obsidian black owl watching him from a branch, but it vanished almost as soon as he became aware of it. Why would he imagine an owl? He'd seen more than enough of them lately.

He sensed her presence before he actually saw her. She was standing nearby, as if she'd always been there.

"Tarja?"

"Hello, darling," she replied sweetly.

Tarja was just the way he remembered her, fiery and determined, beautiful in her own way. She was wearing a blouse of red satin with tight sleeves. Her matching skirt had a slit along the side so it could easily be tied back out of her way if she needed. Around her belt she carried the various powders and elixirs that she used for everything from making explosives to making tea. Her rope and grappling hook, her near constant companions, peeked neatly out of her pack.

She was perfect. Why he'd ever wanted to leave her in the first place he couldn't imagine. She put the pack down, walked over to him and put her arms around him.

"Tarja," he repeated, relishing in the name passing over his lips. "What are you doing here? How did you find me?"

"I've been waiting for you, dear," Tarja said, running her hands up and down his back, seeming to know all the right places to touch to get the soreness out of his body.

She'd been really good at that…

"I never wanted to let you out of my sight. It was… unfortunate the way it worked out."

"I forgive you. I've missed you."

His eyes narrowed. She shouldn't be here offering up forgiveness. That wasn't Tarja's way. In fact, she shouldn't be here at all. It made no sense to the logical part of his brain, the part that reveled in the intricacies of gears and turnings, schemes and plans.

He felt her breasts press against him through their clothing. She'd always had such lovely breasts. He ran his ran down her back until it settled comfortably over her ass. Maybe there wasn't anything wrong after all. She was like a present just waiting for him to unwrap.

Her Erendel perfume clung to her body, rich and intoxicating.

He never remembered her wearing it during the time they'd spent together, though he'd suggested it many times. Tarja had been as likely to smell of charcoal and gunpowder as anything else. Still, the fragrance suited her beautifully now.

He tried to collect his thoughts. "Maybe… maybe we should go to the camp. I have… friends waiting."

She kissed him deeply. He ran his hands down over her as their tongues battled. He was vaguely aware of his lantern sliding out of his hands and dropping onto the sandy soil beside the pool. His lions began to bulge.

A burning grew in the back of his mind, both painful and pleasurable at the same time, a dull sensation of something going through his memories like a librarian going through an archive. No, more like a diner looking over a fully set table before sitting down for the feast. Father, as stern and harsh as stone in winter. Mother, more interested in the contents of her wine glass than the world around her. A childhood spent immersed in machines and in books. Adulthood spent reveling in taverns and in gambling dens before a Soledain agent saw the potential in him. Each morsel of memory was carefully sampled, tasted by a delicate tongue to see if it were bitter or sweet before moving onto the next.

It began to hurt.

A tentacle. Long tentacles wrapped around him like tree roots growing around a stone. *A shape.* The writhing, filmy shape oozed through the water. *A thought.* Strange hungry thoughts filled his senses.

He was standing in the pool now, though he didn't remember wading into it. The water was stagnant and slick.

There were bodies in the water around him: white, puffy lumps of slowly putrefying flesh floating on the surface. A man looked up at him from the water, his eyes bulged and eaten away. Fish came up, nipping at the skin that was starting to fall away from his face.

For a brief moment, Tarja's flesh was cold against his. He had a brief flash of looking into the bloated eyes of a dead woman, of holding her moldering, wet body.

The smell of rot hammered at him.

He screamed.

But then Tarja was with him again. The warmth of her body was next to his. Her arms were clasped tightly around his back.

Maybe it wasn't so bad.

"Hush, dear. Don't struggle so. It will be fine. Everything will be fine," she whispered.

✳ ✳ ✳

"Son of Aeliraneth," Lyra said. "The I-We have been waiting for you."

Cyrus opened his eyes and bolted upright. The sound of a scream— someone's scream— cracked his dream and reverberated in his ears. He looked around but saw nothing except the gray shades of the night and the cold ashes of the campfire. B'lantra lay beside him, tossing fitfully in her sleep.

Dontarius.

Casting aside the blanket, he jumped up, grabbing for his weapons and frantically digging in his pack for the witchbane Caulter had made for him. Then, without dwelling on it anymore, he sprinted off in the direction the scream had come from.

✳ ✳ ✳

There was something inhuman about the cast of Tarja's face now. She reached up and gently caressed Dontarius' cheek. Her hungry thoughts began to rip through his mind. There was pain at first and then a growing numbness. He tried to escape her embrace, but knew it was already too late. Even if Tarja would have released him, he couldn't have gone anywhere. His legs were leaden, and his scream was now barely more than a whimper.

"Dontarius! Was that your scream I heard? Are you bewitched or something?"

P'talan and the surviving Tekni soldiers were coming towards the edge of the pool, looking at him curiously. They seemed to stare right through Tarja, seeing only him standing in the water. The lights of their lanterns bounced eerily off its stagnant surface.

"Too many. The memories will run together, and the taste will be spoiled," Tarja whispered. "Aeliraneth's son is coming, but it's not yet time for those by the pool."

One of the Tekni soldiers cautiously poked the surface of the water with his sword and then, believing it to be safe, waded a few careful steps from the shore.

It was hard for Dontarius to really care much about what he knew would happen. He felt Tarja near him. Over and over again he replayed the tangled memories of their bodies intertwined in the night.

He was numb to the world around him, even when the water began to swirl around the legs of the unfortunate Tekni soldier. Tarja's tentacles burst forth from the water, wrapped themselves around him and pulled him screaming under the waters. The pool barely rippled as it took the terrified man into itself.

Dull and distant shouts came. Several musket shots ineffectually splashed into the pool.

"Let him go!"

The voice was strong and clear. Dontarius tried to place the speaker from his tattered memories.

Cyrus.

It was Cyrus, Aeliraneth's son.

❋ ❋ ❋

The sun shines down harshly over a landscape that feels as parched and cracked as her throat. The few palm trees growing over the slate gray surface of the waterhole offer little in the way of shade. Beyond them, the barren cliffs and endless fields of broken granite and sand ripple in the sun. Only the thorny dokala trees and the brown wither grass growing in sparse, scraggly patches show any signs of being alive in the desolate expanse.

She's thirsty, but she has to wait until the tawny banuken camels of the caravan have slurped up their fill, and the watermaster says it is her family's turn. She holds the wooden bucket in her little hands expectantly. Patri stands beside her, his thick frame with its bushy eyebrows and beard partially shielding her from the sun.

Three more days.

Three more days until they reach Galado, and she can drink all she wants to out of the flowing fountains with their beautiful flowers set all around. Three more days of the Da'Gebron waste while their caravan moves north.

Something moved next to her. Cyrus? Her dream suddenly shattered around her. She had barely opened her eyes before he leapt to his feet.

What was wrong? He dashed off into the dark before she could even ask.

B'lantra got up, lit a lantern and began to follow him, trying to collect her sleepy thoughts as she went. It was hard to sort out reality from the dreams she'd been having. Even though she was awake they flared up again. She was back with the woods and the well, Matri and Patri, the trees and the troika. There had been the shadows and the noises of the birds, the creak of the old boards of the way-stop. There'd been running and running, with the horrible, hateful sounds of screaming flesh being torn apart ringing in her ears. And there had been a voice in the trees as she ran.

B'lantra stopped.

She stops in the woods, cold and thirsty, too tired to run anymore. But the troika doesn't. It pushes through the undergrowth and comes towards her. Its muzzle is soaked with Matri and Patri's blood. She's too afraid to move. She can't think of any words for the song.

The voice comes, cold and distant, and yet soothing at the same time. Green eyes and bronze skin. Hair the color of flame.

"Do you want to be safe?"

"Yes."

"Do you want the monster to go away?"

267

"Yes."

"I can help you. You want me to help you, do you not?"

"Yes."

"Then all you have to do is let me in. I have been looking for a little girl like you with such a pretty song. One with legs that walk and hands that carry and eyes that see. All you have to do is listen to me and do what I say. You will do that for me, will you not?"

"Yes."

"Then hold out your hand..."

The sigil writhes around her hand, and buries itself under her skin. It glimmers faintly: colorful swirls in the dark of the forest. Then it disappears. The bronze skin and green eyes and hair of flame vanish with it. The troika shambles away.

There had been only the voice, telling her which direction to go, where to find water, what to eat and what not to. It was the voice that had led her inexorably to Shrevnetska.

It had been that way ever since.

B'lantra looked down at her hand. At first, there was nothing. Then the faint outlines of the sigil showed through, swirling just as they had on that day in the woods.

Celaan's mark, a sign of the pact.

It had always been there, like the voice. Hungry, thirsty and frightened, she'd forgotten about it, and the voice had settled comfortably into her, guiding her the same way Patri had guided Thule, their jerukin ox.

Why hadn't she remembered before?

No, she already knew the answer.

The better question was why the Aeore empress hadn't wanted her to remember.

Celaan had said that memories had power. If so, could erasing the memory of something erase the thing itself? Perception was often reality. If she gained power over the memory, maybe she could regain power over her song.

✳ ✳ ✳

Putrid brown tentacles crept out onto the sandy shore toward Cyrus. The waters of the pool frothed and bubbled. Dontarius stood in the water beside what might once have been a woman—but more likely had never been human at all. Her arm was long, longer than any human appendage had any right to be. Starting from her shoulders, it changed gradually into one of the tentacles, wrapping around the scholar's neck.

Dontarius didn't even look like he wanted to run. His eyes were hazy. Part of him seemed to want to escape, but the other, greater part still gazed longingly at the woman's face and bosom, the only recognizably human parts of the creature in front of him. Below the woman's torso, the rest of the creature merged into a foamy mass of a body just underneath the water. The smell of rot nearly overpowered him.

He'd found the Bal-haegast.

Its face elongated, jaws stretching down until the last vestiges of its human features began to fade. Its mouth opened revealing row upon row of needle sharp teeth.

Cyrus didn't run. Whether from stupidity or stubbornness, he refused. He should be afraid. He was afraid, but he drew his sword anyway, and held his ground before the monster. With his other hand he readied the witchbane.

"I said let him go!"

The creature suddenly disappeared, and in its place the gentle, slightly wrinkled visage of Lyra appeared before him. Her hazel eyes greeted him.

"It seems the offspring of Aeliraneth has come to pay the I-We a visit. How thoughtful."

Lyra was so similar to the way she'd been. He could almost imagine her knitting or grinding up herbs for a morning's treatments. He could have been seven years old again, having her mend one of the endless cuts and scrapes and bruises he'd gotten.

He could have…

"No!" he said, a sudden fury rising within him. "Don't you

dare use her face! That's my memory, and you can't have it."

The image shimmered, and the monster returned. "The I-We know you. Perhaps you won't be devoured just yet. Then again, perhaps the memories of the son of Aeliraneth are worth tasting."

✳ ✳ ✳

As she hurried towards the pool, B'lantra was unsure what to make of the scene before her. The red light of Saranor broke through the granite veil of the clouds, shining wanly down on the still and stagnant water. In the light, the pool looked like a great puddle of blood. P'talan and his Tekni soldiers stood dully near the swaying cattails along the water's edge, their faces blank. The intensity and fiery determination that had so prominently blazed in the Surani raider's eyes was absent. He appeared more like a placid sheep than the ravening wolf she'd seen at Ashenwall. It was much the same for Dontarius, who languished in the pool's rank water, an idiotic grin draped across his face.

Then she saw the broken and ragged form lying amidst the tawny pebbles up from the shore, and everything else ceased to matter.

"Cyrus!"

She sprinted over to him, skidding to a stop beside his body. He was almost unrecognizable, a burned and blackened remnant of the man who'd been sleeping beside her.

No breath escaped his lips nor heartbeat drummed within his chest.

She stared numbly, not knowing what to do or think. It was several long moments before she even became aware of the toothy monstrosity right next to her, almost as though her mind had refused to recognize it until that point. It crystallized before her, a nightmare suddenly given shape and substance. It dwarfed even the largest jerukin oxen she'd ever seen. The bulk of its slimy frame lay beneath the pool, yet it was still massive enough to reach well beyond the confines of the waters to where Cyrus lay. Its scum-covered skin was chalky and tough, pierced through with spiny knobs of misshapen yellowish bone. Dozens of long tentacles snaked out of the water wrapping around Dontarius and the others. From its thick body, a long, skeletal neck protruded outwards, holding up a triangular head dominated by a wide, flat nose and two narrowly set sulfur tinted eyes.

The monster stared down at Cyrus' body with the intensity of a vulture waiting for its next meal to finally expire. Its tentacles hovered over him, quivering impatiently.

B'lantra gasped and fell back onto the sandy ground before turning and scrabbling frantically away. The monster cocked its head at the noise. A puzzled expression passed across its face, as if it hadn't been any more aware of her than she had been of it.

It peered around dimly. Its tentacles issued forth, slapping at the sandy soil around her like a blind beggar feeling around for a coin some passerby had tossed at him. A hideous grin broke out across its jaws as it finally registered her presence. Its dead yellow eyes lit up.

She called the song to her almost instinctively, but just like the night before, no answer came to her summons. She let out a despairing curse and pulled out her paring knife. It was pathetic defense.

"There it is. Yes, the I-We feel the faint crumbs of the memories now. They linger like shadows."

The voice was soft and raspy, almost soothing. It certainly wasn't what she'd been expecting. B'lantra slowly backed away and then began circling around to try and get back to Cyrus.

The monster's head snapped around, tracing her movement. "A witch. A Kaulswyr child. Broken now, but not changed from the essence of what it is. The I-We see the echo. The I-We will find it."

No matter where she moved, the monster kept its body hovering over Cyrus.

"Leave him alone! Get away from him," she finally blurted out.

"And so now the Kaulswyr child reveals itself. It was foolish to come here. The I-We will not spare it out of kinship."

"What do you mean a Kaulswyr child?" B'lantra demanded.

"It is the machine in the nucleus of Asylum. It is the wellspring for all the witch prey, as it is for the I-We."

"I'm nothing like you."

"In that, the witch prey is mistaken," the monster said, smiling a fanged smile. "But it will not be mistaken for much longer."

CHAPTER 23

JOURNEYS OF FATE

H E WAS SEVEN YEARS OLD AGAIN. He knew he was seven because of the wind blowing briskly down the cobblestone street. It swirled round the shops and warehouses along the Ossan Canal that ran through the heart of the city of Targus, scooping up the drifts of snow along the water's edge and hurling them at him in glittering, chilling sheets.

Mother walked purposefully along the street, forcing him to hurry in order to keep up with her. Kassun and Bruel marched dutifully behind them.

He did his best to make his teeth stop chattering and wished for what seemed like the thousandth time they could just go home. Everything around him— the buildings, the bridges, the street, everything— was a dull slate gray, covered by speckled patches of snow. Even the sky, soot-filled and smudged as ever from the nearby foundries, was more dour than usual.

A carriage, stamped with the blue and ochre insignia of the rising Pyrasine Trading House, carefully clacked by. Beyond that, there were few people out. It was Tenth Day, the day of rest, and most of the shopkeepers and laborers were indoors. The colorful hot air balloons that sometimes floated overhead, with their daring riders precariously suspended in baskets were nowhere to be seen.

Mother's silken voice droned on, continuing the lessons she constantly inflicted upon him. He wasn't really listening to her. A flock of swans was weaving its way through the islands of ice atop the canal's frigid waters. Occasionally, they would call to each other in their harsh, grating voices and dive momentarily under the water, perhaps in search of fish in the icy waters.

Mother abruptly stopped. "We've arrived at our destination."

It didn't look like they'd arrived much of anywhere. The street wasn't much different than it had been a few blocks back. A stone bridge ran across the canal, icicles hanging down from the underside of its arched belly. The ice was more solid, covering the canal in the opaque grayish blanket.

There must be a reason they were here. Mother never did anything without a reason. She'd even had Lyra mark this day on her calendar.

"I want you to find the sun."

He stared at her blankly. The sun was in the sky, hidden behind a bank of white-gray clouds. Surely she knew that.

Mother's green eyes burned into him. He shifted nervously from one foot to the other, waiting for the movement of her fan.

"All right," she said at last. "Let's try something a little simpler. Can you see the ley lines around us?"

He looked around, trying to find them. Ley lines were hard to spot— for him anyway. Mother claimed he'd get better at it as he grew older. There was a cluster of them in the sky above: red ones, purples ones, even a green one, all crisscrossing overhead. And there was another one. A deep, strong blue one ran directly across the canal, gently glowing underneath the ice.

"Now that you've finally noticed the one going across the canal, follow it and see where it leads you. The sun should be waiting for you," Mother said.

"But... but it goes straight across the ice!"

"And?"

Mother asked the question as if the task she'd set before him was no more treacherous than walking through a spring meadow.

"If it breaks—"

"If you have the skill, you won't need to worry about the ice."

Now he knew why Mother had left Lyra behind. Lyra would have put up such a fuss about the whole thing that even Mother might have been forced to reconsider what she was asking him to do.

Lyra wasn't here though. Even if they'd cared, Kassun and Bruel weren't brave enough to challenge Mother either. From behind him, Mother's lacquered crimson fan stirred.

He miserably set out. However bad the ice might be, Mother's anger was ten times worse.

He found the ice less dangerous than he'd expected. The surface had cracked and thawed several times during the winter, but on a day like this it merely crackled and crunched instead of giving way.

His confidence slowly grew. He was like Father, an explorer bravely setting out to chart new lands. The ley line glistened underneath him, a faint but definite trail for him to follow. As he grew more relaxed, he found it became easier to see.

He stopped when he reached the center of the canal. The ley line continued on, straight as ever, disappearing under the street on the other side. How would he follow it then? He scratched his head, pondering what he was supposed to do.

He was about to give up and ask Mother, when the clouds suddenly parted. The sun burst forth in a golden wave of light and heat. The ley line met the sun's light with a brilliant blue of its own. He stood dazzled as the ice glittered all around him. It was like he was standing in a field of gleaming diamonds.

A sharp cracking sound interrupted his joy. His heart began pounding in sudden fright. There were fractures in the surface of the ice, spreading out all around him until he was standing at the center of a spider web of fault lines.

"Use the ley line," Mother commanded. "A warlock can draw on the lines. Use them to save yourself."

He frantically looked down at the ley line. Was this why she'd brought him here? He wasn't a warlock. There were no such things anymore. Witchcraft was for girls. Why would Mother think otherwise?

The ice rumbled. He staggered, trying to maintain his balance.

"Beckon it while you still can. Make it obey you," Mother said.

He could feel the ley line coolly regarding him. There was energy within, just waiting for him to tap into it. It was like a fire, only cold instead of hot.

He called to it, and for an instant he felt as if he'd touched it somehow. The sensation quickly faded, and the ley line turned away. It continued to ignore him, despite his pleas. He might as well have been asking a rock for help.

Mother cried out to him again, but he couldn't hear what she said over the sound of the splintering ice. He abandoned all thoughts of the ley line and ran back towards her.

Widening avenues of chilling, flowing water spread out around him, blocking his path. The field of diamonds broke apart before his eyes.

He weaved and dodged, leaping, sometimes blindly, from one island of broken ice to the next. His thoughts pounded at him in a barrage of sound and color.

The shoreline was closer now. There was only a single sheet of ice left to cross. It looked solid enough.

It wasn't. His foot slipped, and then his leg plunged through its thinning skin. He threw his hands out as he toppled forward. The sharp edges of the ice chunks sliced into his cheek before the cold bite of the water tore into him. The current took him.

There was nothing more. Only the cold.

Lyra wouldn't be very happy with him when she found out. Would Mother care? He'd probably disappointed her once again.

His heart pounded pitifully.

These were his memories. He'd been here before and hadn't drowned. Why? What was different this time?

Was this a dream? Were his memories being twisted?

The water didn't seem to care what he remembered. The cold and the current felt plenty real.

He was going to drown!

For a long, horrible instant it was all he could think of.

His arms and legs frantically flailed.

No, why wasn't the memory right?

Because of the green scarf around his neck! That was why. Lyra had knitted it for him for his seventh birthday, insisting the coming winter was going to be a nasty one.

He'd worn it that day, even though it was an itchy abomination. That was the way it should have gone. That's what he should have.

He demanded it be there. The dream— or whatever it was— yielded, and a moment later he found it around his neck.

The dark form of the bridge foundation loomed at him through the gloom of the water. He swam upwards, fighting against the current. He only had a vague sense of his arms and legs. He could barely feel them.

The surface of the water above him was like a hazy, warbling mirror. The shadows receded as he drew closer to the surface. At last he reached it, punching through the thin skin of ice. The mirror shattered. He gulped for air.

The current grabbed at him, unwilling to lose its prey. He was about to be pulled under again.

He flicked the scarf out towards an iron hook embedded in the icy stone so boats could moor there. The fabric of the scarf caught on the hook, and he used it to pull himself from the grip of the water.

The cold air above hit him like a hard slap to his face, taking his breath away. He couldn't move, couldn't think. The cold seemed to go on and on, seeping inside his sodden clothes. Around him he saw the water freeze back over. Mother came walking across the ice towards him. When she reached him, she removed her velvet wrap and bundled him up in it. There was no gentleness to her touch, only efficiency. Her contempt was almost colder than the winter wind.

He was alive. He'd beaten the current, survived Mother's test. It was so cold. He wanted to sleep.

"It has earned the right to survive a little longer," Mother said. "Very well. The I-We will put off devouring it for a time."

The great clock in the High Market tower rang out through the morning, striking one lonely toll before going silent again.

He tried to still his frantic thoughts.

"The tolling of the clock?"

"It has used up one of its lives in the Inbetween Lands. Its possibilities are lessoned. Its essence is diminished."

"I came here for answers. Tell me what I need to know!"

✳ ✳ ✳

He was eight years old again. He knew he was eight because of the carpet underneath his feet. Mother had left for the night in the company of one of the young men she fancied, and that meant he could explore like Father would have. The house was large, with all sorts of interesting rooms and alcoves. They changed sometimes too, so even if he'd been somewhere before, it was always worthwhile to investigate again.

He walked down the new corridor he'd discovered on the bottom floor. His feet made no sound on the plush burgundy carpet beneath him. The dark oak panels along the wall seemed to swallow up the light from the lantern he'd brought with him. The arched ceiling seemed impossibly far above him.

There was a massive mahogany clock standing along the hallway. Its face looked like a grouchy old man. The numbers glowered down at him angrily, and the clock hands looked like Janus the Gardener's drooping mustache. Its carved lion's feet looked like they were sinking their claws into the carpet.

Farther down, he noticed a beautifully woven tapestry map of all the known lands of the Lanternlit. Why did Mother keep it here and not in her art gallery?

There was cold, snowy Nurengar in the north, right across from Arakost and its huge fortress at Manmar along the Backbone Mountains. To the south were Trafaria and the mysterious Surin deserts. Then there was Erendel, the Island City, in the west, with tall blue waves and white breakers surrounding it. There were monsters too, serpents and gryphons stitched into the unexplored places of the map where monsters ought to be. Their embroidered bodies glimmered like they were ready to come to life.

In fact, the glittering green serpent that had its tail wrapped around one corner of the map did move. He blinked his eyes and held the lantern closer.

It was just a map, and the monster was just woven thread. Even he was old enough to know it couldn't move.

The serpent twitched its tail and stared at him with hungry, reptilian eyes. Slowly it oozed closer. The edges of the map bulged and rippled. Its scaly head and body pushed their way out of the confines of the tapestry, growing larger as they filled the hallway. Water dripped from its chiseled coils. Its forked tongue flicked out to catch his scent.

He dropped the lantern in terror and backed away. The serpent slithered forward, opening its jaws wide. Poison dripped from its ivory fangs.

He cried out for Lyra. For Mother. For anybody.

No one came.

These were his memories. He'd been here before. But this wasn't the way it had happened.

The serpent came closer. It's reptilian eyes glittered coldly. It didn't seem to care what he remembered.

But this wasn't how it happened. It wasn't!

Why wasn't it right?

Because of his wooden sword.

He'd begged Lyra to read him stories about the brave adventures of Sir Bennon night after night for over a month before his birthday, and he'd kept the sword by his side for weeks after, ready to be brought forth at a moment's notice— or whenever Mother wasn't watching. After all, he never knew if he might find himself unexpectedly facing off against the Lion of Kasha like Sir Bennon had.

He found the sword by his side because his mind demanded that it be there. He drew it forth. The serpent stopped. There was uncertainty somewhere in its scaly brain.

He let forth a battle cry. The serpent struck too quickly for him to parry. Its fangs tore through the blue shirt he was wearing and drove into his shoulder. His arm threatened to go numb.

It hissed in triumph and struck again. This time he was quick enough to dodge out of the way. With the monster exposed, he brought his sword slicing down in a clean stroke across its neck—just like Sir Bennon had done! The wooden blade bit through the serpent's scales. Black ichor splattered across his face.

It was over in an instant. The serpent lay vanquished before him. Its body still writhed, but the hellish yellow light in its eyes had gone out.

His shoulder burned like fire.

He'd won.

The tall clock on the wall sent two dull tolls echoing down the corridor.

"The witch's son has the weapon it sought, but at a price."

The wound on his shoulder continued to bleed.

"I came here for answers. Tell me what I need to know!"

"The Aeliraneth prey sought much from the I-We and earned the right to know. Can the offspring do the same? If it cannot, then it will feed the I-We."

※ ※ ※

He was nine years old. He knew he was nine because of the looming green walls of Mother's hedge maze. Mother would often take him to the fountain for his lessons. He would study by the dancing figures and the flowing water, the motion and the music constantly tempting him to look away from his book. Mother's fan would always be there to stop any straying from his task. Why did she always bring him here if she knew the fountain would only distract him? Would he ever understand why she did the things she did?

Right now she was asleep, and this was his chance to see the fountain without her standing over him.

There were obelisks of worn black stone set along the route to the center of the hedge maze, each paired with a colored lantern that lit by its own power each night. At the base of the obelisks, an etched Iriethan character pointed the way forward. Once he'd learned the characters, navigating the maze was fairly simple.

He smiled to himself. For once he'd actually found a use for Mother's stupid lessons.

It was a warm, sticky night, deep in the heart of summer. He brushed the sheen of sweat off his forehead and tugged at the thin gray nightshirt that clung to his clammy skin. The fireflies were out, bobbing about just above the tops of the hedge walls.

He drew nearer the center and came across the first of the hedge lions set into the green walls. They were elaborately shaped, each one perfectly groomed and cut. It felt like they were watching him in the moonlight, even though they never moved.

At last, he passed the final obelisk and heard the faint music of the flowing water. Before him was an iron gate, and beyond that he knew the fountain lay.

The gate creaked open, more loudly than he'd imagined it would. He stepped breathlessly through and found himself in a small courtyard with the fountain in the center. At its base, a set of golden gears turned in perfect harmony. Their teeth were finely chiseled, their turnings intricate and delicately balanced. The bronze figures in the fountain cavorted and danced in the moonlight, just as he'd hoped they would. He drew closer, eager to see what stories they would tell.

He was immediately disappointed when he noticed that the tales they acted out weren't the great battles and epic legends he'd been expecting. Instead they were mostly about ordinary things. The figures went about their daily lives just as if they were real people. They laugh and cried. They lived and grew old— or at least some of them did.

A pattern became clear as he watched life after life unfold before his eyes.

Betrayal.

The main character in each story was betrayed again and again: by lovers, by friends or even by their own children. The scenes changed, and the music of the water took on a more somber note. Each life ended horribly. By drowning. By hanging. By beheading. He didn't know it was possible for a person to die in so many different ways.

And there was another story unfolding before him. A tall woman in glimmering battle armor stood regally, spear in hand, in front of one of her attendants, a shorter woman with an elaborate headdress and a curved staff. He recognized the taller woman immediately as Ansala, but couldn't figure out who the other woman was.

Ansala clutched her throat and fell, clawing at the air as if poisoned. The attendant stood over her in triumph. He watched them argue back and forth in their muted voices as the water cascaded around them. Finally Ansala struck out with her spear, cutting through the attendant's robes and leaving a long and jagged tear on her forearm. Molten bronze blood oozed from the wound. The attendant fell back. Ansala regained her footing. She angrily pointed her spear and spoke a silent proclamation. Tears of horror streamed down the attendant's cheeks before she fled, the wound on her arm glistening.

He stared in puzzlement and stepped closer to the fountain before he even realized he was doing it.

The wound that Ansala had left on the attendant's arm stuck in his mind. Mother had a similar scar. She always covered it in public, and even as her son, he'd only glimpsed it a handful of times. Was it somehow the same scar? It couldn't be. Ansala had lived and died nearly a thousand years before Mother had been born.

He must have missed some part of the story. Maybe the figures would act out another part of it so he could understand.

He had to be careful not to touch the water. Mother had told him many times that it was poisonous, and he didn't doubt she'd meant it. It might look cool and inviting, but it wasn't.

He reached out with a tentative hand. Surely it wouldn't hurt to touch one of the figures.

In unison, they stopped what they were doing and turned their gaze upon him. He tried to back way, but it was already too late. The figures' gaze held him as surely as a set of shackles. His legs were moving forward whether he wanted them to or not. He drew nearer and nearer to the poisoned water. The figures seemed to nod their approval at his fate.

His hand entered the water. A burning erupted through him, as if his bones were being boiled from the inside out.

He had a memory of being here, of events unfolding. Only now it was different.

Mother had once said memories were powerful things. But this was his memory, and it wasn't right!

The figures didn't seem to care what he remembered.

He'd been here before and hadn't died. What had he done then? How was it supposed to go?

The gears. The beautiful golden gears that drove the figures, drove the water, drove everything!

The water splashed over his arm, searing him up to the shoulder. His skin warped and blistered.

He reached for the gear box. The gear teeth snapped at him, tearing his fingers. They turned on, slick now with a red sheen of his blood.

The water engulfed his face, choking him. He closed his eyes and shut his mouth, but it did little good. He couldn't smell anything now but his own burned flesh and hair.

He blindly stretched out his hand a final time, willing the gear to be there. He grasped it because his mind demanded that he should. He held it, refusing to release his grip, no matter how much the teeth gnawed into his hand. The fountain stuttered.

With a cry, he wrenched the gear free.

All at once, the figures stopped moving. The music of the water abruptly ceased. He tumbled away from the fountain and lay in a writhing, smoldering heap.

Searing waves of pain splashed over him like the tide coming in. In twitching hands, he held the gear tightly to his chest.

He'd won.

"The prey thing has endured. But it is not done."

The gears in the fountain lurched forward once more. The golden teeth clacked against each other.

Once. Twice. Thrice. And then they were still.

He forced himself back to his feet and staggered over to the dead fountain. The figures watched him, cold and lifeless now. The water lay hushed and serene, the moonlight reflecting on its surface.

"The son of the Aeliraneth prey thing has earned the right to reclaim that which was given unto the I-We."

"A gear? What's it for? What does it do?"

"It has the tool to find the answers it seeks. Its time is up. Can it return? The I-We will feed soon."

CHAPTER 24

FACES OF THE POOL

S HE STARED DEFIANTLY AT THE MONSTER. If she was going to die, at least she could do it without blubbering. Maybe Heaven had a place for witches.

"You're a blighted, wretched thing, and I intend to make sure you pay for Cyrus' death."

"There are a few memories that it has not yet learned to shield. It lacks discipline," the monster replied.

Its form shifted and blurred. A moment later a burly man wearing colorful silks stood before her. He had a thick beard and dark, bushy eyebrows. His skin was a light brown, dry and chapped in places as if from long exposure to the sun. Jet black hair receded back from his stout face, curling up around his broad shoulders. A coin pouch dangled from the red sash around his considerable waistline.

B'lantra gaped at the sight.

"Patri—?"

Her dark eyes flashed with indignation.

"Pay for your lover's death? You're in a poor position to make threats, little one," the monster said through Patri's lips.

She shuddered at the voice. Every breath Patri took, every sound that came from his lips, every gesture he made was a wrenching, hateful reminder of everything she'd lost that day. It was like reliving the memory over and over again, and dying a little inside each time.

"I know you for what you are. Bal-haegast!"

"It is a name given by the prey, but the names they use are unimportant. The I-We are eternal. The Sunlit Owl and the

Midnight Owl. The I-We are fragments— wood scraps of the Carpenter's creation, given consciousness by the Kaulswyr."

"Cyrus came to you for answers and you killed him!"

Patri clucked his tongue chidingly at her. "Now, now. Your Cyrus isn't dead. Not yet anyway. The I-We gave him a chance to obtain the answers he sought. He simply wasn't strong enough to return with them. He lies caught in transition within his own mind."

"What are you talking about?"

"He journeyed to our domain within the Inbetween Lands, the spirit world that lies between Heaven and Hell. He found some of his answers. He was careless, and there is a toll to be paid for carelessness. And so he finds himself trapped."

"Then bring him back!"

"If he cannot survive such a trial on his own, he is not worthy of the involvement of the I-We. Unless you can somehow make up for his deficiency. What value can you add? What is it you think you have that the I-We cannot simply take?"

The smirk spreading across Patri's face revolted her.

There was nothing she would be able to add. She had no treasure to give, no worth without her song. Even her life probably meant nothing to it. The creature would steal that from her as a matter of course.

"I thought not."

Patri's hand lashed out and caught her arm. He twisted his grip, forcing her down to one knee. His eyes shifted from the kindly amber brown she'd remembered as a child to the sulfurous yellow of the monster.

"Shall we go to the pool?" he asked.

She struck at him again and again with her knife. His hide seemed like iron. Whatever nicks her blade made instantly closed over. He dragged her inexorably forward. The pool drew ever closer. Her hands raked the gritty earth, trying to find purchase.

She screamed, but none of the others seemed to hear or to care.

✳ ✳ ✳

He was alone in the obsidian sea that had become his world. Nothing and no one. A speck of dust floating in an endless, watery void. There was no sun, no sky. He had only his thoughts, and they would be subsumed soon enough.

A light in the distance beckoned him, the only chink in the void's otherwise perfect armor. Perhaps some part of his mind demanded that it be there, but it was too far for him to reach. He was too exhausted and beaten to swim any farther, and soon... soon he would probably fade away.

Maybe it was best. It didn't seem the most unpleasant way to die.

The scream came floating suddenly to him, breaking on the silent waves. He snapped his head around and again peered off into the distance towards the light.

The scream was important. It was meaning, when all meaning was falling away from him.

He swam towards it, though he didn't have any hope of reaching his goal. The waves fought against him, pushing him back the way he'd come. Every injury he'd suffered—the bone numbing cold of the water, the fangs of the serpent driving into his shoulder, the horrid burning at the fountain— conspired against him, trying to drag him under.

He railed at the waves, cursing their existence. To his surprise, he found they yielded to his will.

He gasped.

That was his answer to what had become his final trial. It was his void, his ocean. Just like the sword and the gear and the portal, the void existed because he allowed it to.

The world he saw around him was nothing more than his will made manifest.

It was understanding— so simple he'd never even considered it before. He existed because he willed it. The light could be reached because he desired it.

He rushed towards it, skimming atop the wave crests because he demanded that it be so.

Had Mother once done the same long ago?

His eyes snapped open.

The wounds that had covered his body were rapidly retreating. In one hand he clutched a bubbling flask of some unidentifiable liquid. A golden gear about the diameter of his hand lay beside him, shimmering faintly.

B'lantra's scream still lingered in his ears. He grabbed up his sword and careened toward the sound.

The Bal-haegast had one of its tentacles wrapped around her arm and was dragging her towards the pool. He raised the blade and brought it down in a gleaming arc. The cut was clean. Dark ichor stained the ground. The tentacle writhed for a moment and then was absorbed into the soil.

B'lantra quickly got to her feet and staggered away. Cyrus stood at the water's edge, sword in hand.

"Don't ever touch her again!"

The Bal-haegast shed Patri's form with no more effort than taking off a coat. It watched them from its pool, its tentacles poking up through the slimy skin of algae that floated atop the rancid water. If there was any trace of fear on its monstrous countenance, it was hard to tell. But it wasn't advancing towards them either.

"And so the son of the Aeliraneth prey thing is resurrected from its own memory. It has what it came for," the Bal-haegast rasped.

Cyrus tentatively held out the flask. "This is the witchbane, isn't it? It changed somehow."

"The prey altered it by an act of will. It felt a need to avenge itself, to destroy, and so it found a weapon in its memory and made it manifest."

"This will kill Asa?"

"It will do what the Cyrus prey has given it the power to do.

The prey thing called Asa is bound to another of the Creation's children: Nysse of the Waters. The weapon will break that bond for a time and let the Cyrus prey do what needs to be done."

Cyrus put the flask in his coat pocket and held out the golden gear. "And what of this? I know where it came from, but why give it to me? I asked for answers, not a keepsake."

The monster's form shifted. In an instant Lyra stood before him again. He shuddered at the sight, but managed to hold his temper this time.

"Celaan told you that memories were powerful things. To hold the memory of a thing is to hold power over it. Your mother had the fountain made many years ago, so she wouldn't forget. The stories it tells are reminders of things that were. Meaningful things. Insignificant things. When everything starts to fade from your dreams, then insignificant things become meaningful."

Cyrus frowned. "What dreams? What things? What is so damned important about that fountain?"

"The fountain exists in this world and in the world beyond. The spirit world, the Inbetween Lands, the Realm Beyond— call it what you like. Such words are empty shadows of the real thing. Aeliraneth anchored it there so time would never touch it— so it would be there for the one to succeed her."

"You mean me, don't you?"

To his surprise, Lyra shook her head. "No, you are her son, but you are not her successor. If you were, then the water wouldn't have harmed you."

"Then what is the gear for? I remember Mother taking it away from me after that night. She was furious. I thought she would beat me half to death. The fountain never worked after that."

"She warded the house on that last night as the flames raged and the rain fell. The Heart of the Great Machine will be there. The fountain is the gateway inside as the gear is the gateway to the fountain. Your mother gave the gear to the I-We to keep it safe."

"Mother made deals with you, didn't she? For knowledge

and for power." His face darkened. "What did she promise you in exchange?"

Lyra grinned, though it was a grin he could never have imagined Lyra having. The sight of it was enough to turn his stomach.

"You would not like the answer."

Cyrus' fists clenched in sudden outrage. Mother had been cold, sometimes cruel, and always unpredictable. What could have been a pleasant afternoon with her could just as quickly become chaotic and miserable when her temper suddenly and inexplicably flared. But even Mother couldn't have… wouldn't have…

"Those were people with their own lives and their own worth!"

"Her reasoning was quite simple, dear," Lyra said. "Places like Targus are teaming with people that no one will miss. What are a few lives in exchange for knowledge that could save everything? If ten die to save a hundred or a thousand, is that not a worthwhile transaction?"

Cyrus' face was hot and pinched. "No, it isn't."

"You say that because you do not yet understand the magnitude of what is to come. Simon Barros, your mother's great rival, made his way to Asylum despite her attempts to kill him. He fought a war that wasn't his to fight. Because of the knowledge she gained, she was there, you in her belly, when he cracked open the Kaulswyr and stole the machine's heart. All over the love of a woman he could never truly have. If the empress Celaan had been allowed to take her place as Keeper, the Wynding would not be endangered. But that was not the intention of Simon Barros. He would have made it his own then and there if not for Aeliraneth. He would have become God that day— rewritten everything, including the I-We. That is what the Heart is capable of. It is for that reason the I-We regard her as superior to the other prey things."

"She saved you and you still demanded tribute?"

"For everything given, a price is paid. Such is the law of the world we live in."

Cyrus' eyes widened. "Celaan said Mother intervened. They fought over the Heart of the Great Machine and lost it, and now I'm expected to clean up their mess! This isn't my fight. I'm not some goddamned savior!"

"No, you're not. You were simply in the wrong womb at the wrong time."

All at once, Lyra was gone. The conversation seemed like it had dragged on, but as he glanced around, it seemed almost no time had passed at all.

"It has learned what it needed. The debt of the I-We to the Aeliraneth prey is satisfied," the Bal-haegast said as it resumed its monstrous form.

"A debt? If you owed Mother a debt, then why not tell me these things outright? Why put me through all that?"

"Because the prey thing had to prove itself worthy of collecting on the debt. It is weak, but has demonstrated that it may be barely capable of the task before it."

Cyrus took a deep breath, trying to let his anger and resentment fade. Every answer he received only led to more questions. He'd set his sight on a horizon only to find it kept moving farther away from him with each step.

"Now, begone from this place," the Bal-haegast said. "Your time here is at an end. You have things to do, and the I-We have prey things to process."

Cyrus tensed. He'd forgotten Dontarius and the others, but the Bal-haegast had kept them very much in its thoughts.

"I already said let him go!"

He brought his sword up.

The monster turned on him in irritation. "The Cyrus prey is unwise to interfere in things that are beyond it. The I-We spoke with it to satisfy a debt. But nothing more is owed to it."

"I'm going to do a lot more than interfere," Cyrus said.

"Wait," B'lantra frantically called to him.

It was too late.

The surface of the water exploded in a sea of writhing tentacles. They lashed out, flattening the cattails and grasses in their wake. The Bal-haegast slid its bulk out of the water and slithered towards him.

❋ ❋ ❋

B'lantra called, and again the song refused to answer her.

"There are a few memories that it has not yet learned to shield."

That's what the Bal-haegast had said. Could she shield her memories from it? It hadn't been able to find her at first, not until she'd revealed herself. Momentary carelessness had allowed the monster to learn enough of Patri to assume his form. Was she a blind spot to it? She was a witch— a child of the Kaulswyr. Maybe she really did have something in common with the monster.

"You're not feeding on anyone today," she stated boldly, stepping between Cyrus and the advancing monster.

The Bal-haegast loomed over her, its bulk shading out the sun. Its neck snaked down, bringing its head within a hand span's length of her face. The breath issuing out between its slavering teeth smelled of carrion and death.

"The witch prey should leave while the I-We still allow it."

She didn't retreat. "No, you need to leave while I still allow it."

She thought back, forcing herself to relive the memory of the troika and the forest, of Celaan and the pact she'd made. She let the memories flow outwards— just a portion, just enough to pique the monster's interest.

"This is not something the I-We foresaw— an eddy in the current. The water is cloudy, and the empress' flesh puppet has arrived," the Bal-haegast said.

She could detect a hint of uncertainty in its voice now. "Shall I show you another memory? Shall I show you the destruction of Ashenwall so you know the wrath you face?"

In a moment, Patri stood before her again. "The empress used you to save herself. She was left without form after the machine was cracked open, so she found a Kaulswyr child to give her the arms and legs she no longer had. If you fully release her, there may be nothing left of you in the end."

B'lantra held up her arm. The markings on her hand swirled in the morning's light. "I remembered when Celaan first came to me. It was a dream I had this morning. I still have her mark on me from the pact we made. It was always there, but I couldn't see it before."

"The thoughts of the I-We and its prey sometimes cross paths. In dreams, people will sometimes relive old memories," Patri said. He chuckled to himself. "It is seasoning for the meal to come."

B'lantra took a deep breath. Celaan had to have known this moment would come. She'd anticipated it, planned for it. Taking the song was but the first step in a chain that had led B'lantra inexorably here, and to a decision the empress must have known would happen.

From somewhere in the depths of her mind, she could feel Celaan's sense of impending triumph.

"Very well," Patri suddenly growled. "The I-We do not see the purpose in a war with the empress. But the I-We do not fear her either. The lives you value so much would be destroyed in any contest, so your threat becomes meaningless. The I-We will consider a bargain, however. What will you provide in exchange for the lives of the other prey things?"

"You talk about them like they're nothing but a transaction!"

"There is no difference for the I-We. They are food to the I-We, no different from the chala and spiced rice you have for breakfast."

"And what guarantee do I have that you'll honor your part of any bargain?"

"The I-We are bound. Such was the nature of the Creation. You can accept the word of the I-We or not. Agree or do not."

"You like memories. Feelings. You helped me remember the day when Celaan first came to me— the day Matri and Patri died. Take the memory of that day for your very own. You can search this world, but you won't find another like it," B'lantra said. "And if you kill me, then it will be forever lost to you."

Cyrus stared at her. "You can't—"

B'lantra's body went rigid, almost if an invisible hand had grabbed onto it. Her teeth clenched in sudden pain. Sweat beaded up on her forehead.

"If you think you have suffered up until now, then wait and see what happens. You will only make me stronger. And in the end I will still win. No matter what you do, you are mine still."

The words pounded at her, a hammer striking an anvil.

"No, Celaan," B'lantra whispered. "I figured it out. I'll forget you and that day. Without that memory there is no pact, and you have no pathway to my mind. You're right. Memories are powerful things. And to remove a memory is to remove its power over you."

Cyrus surged forward, but a wall of tentacles sprung up to block his path.

"Leave her out of this! Your trials were for me not her."

Patri ignored his protests, fixated now on B'lantra. "So you seek your freedom as well. You will give the I-We that one day, those last fleeting heartbeats with your precious Matri and Patri in exchange?"

Her body shook. The pain in her mind intensified until she thought her skull would burst. The iron hand around her squeezed, smothering and crushing her.

A tear wound its way down her cheek.

"Yes."

"It is not enough," Patri told her. He glided over to caress Dontarius' face. "This one has a lived a full life already. His memories are rich. The others as well. You would have me trade several lifetimes of memories for a single day? It is a poor exchange. Give me your Matri and Patri, completely and totally, and the I-We will consider it acceptable."

An instant later Matri shimmered into view before her. She was unchanged from the way B'lantra remembered. Patri had once said she took after her mother, and looking at her as an adult,

B'lantra could see why. In many ways, her own face and body were reflected back at her when she gazed at the woman before her. Matri was a little taller than she was, her eyes a little more widely set and her figure a little fuller, but there was far more similarity than difference. Matri's ochre dress was the same as it had been that last day. The sky-blue bead in her hair glittered just as it had before. Her face had the tired lines and the touch of road dirt that always seemed to cover it whenever they'd traveled anywhere.

"You've grown up. And if you're willing to do this, then my memory has grown cold indeed," Matri said.

It was the last time she would see them, the last time she would even acknowledge their existence.

Matri's soft hands braiding her hair each morning. The bulky form of Patri shielding her from the desert sun. The shrill call of Matri's voice barking over the market crowds. The jingle of Patri's coin pouch.

Gone.

A hundred other little things. Gone. A thousand other little moments. Gone.

That is the price of her flame.

"Your offer is acceptable," she said to the monster.

CHAPTER 25

BARAKAHN

D ontarius and the others were thrown away like old refuse, while a Tekni soldier that had been enveloped earlier by the pool now burst to the surface, coughing and gasping for breath.

Cyrus cried out, but B'lantra didn't seem to hear him. The Bal-haegast brushed its monstrous tentacles across her cheek and then licked its thin lips.

"Matri...Patri..." she whispered in confusion.

The tentacles fell away before him, and he frantically raced over to her. "Your parents. Your Matri and Patri. Do you know what happened to them? Do you remember?"

B'lantra gaze was unfocused at first. "I went north. I don't know exactly why. I remember being carried into Shrevnetska. I remember growing up, doing things. Selling wares from a back of a wagon. Carnivals and color. Lots of time on a wagon. But there are holes when I think back... so many holes that don't make sense."

Cyrus turned on the Bal-haegast in sudden fury, but it was already disappearing. Its bulk seemed to flow away into the depths of the quiet pool like water draining from a gutter after a rainstorm. Above them, the pale morning sun started to break through the clouds.

It was hard to believe the monster had actually gone. The void its absence left ached against his consciousness, the sudden quiet after a cacophony of noise.

B'lantra grew flush with excitement. "Thank God! I can feel the flame again!"

"God had nothing to do with it! Do you have any idea what

you've just done?" Cyrus demanded, redirecting his fury onto her.

"I wanted my song back. I wanted it to be like it was," B'lantra said, startled at first by his vehemence. Then her eyes narrowed in anger. "I did what I had to do. I couldn't live with it like it was before!"

"And you put trust in that thing before me? Dammit, Bel! I would've come up with something. I wasn't going to just let it kill everybody. I would have found a way to get your song back. If you'd only waited…"

"What? What would you have come up with?"

"I don't know… something," he stammered. "You didn't give me a chance. You let it rip part of your soul away instead."

She thrust an irate hand in his direction. "You made your deal with that abomination. I made mine."

"I never gave it part of my soul! Even Mother, for all her arrogance— all the horrible things she did— never did that. You have no idea what you've done."

"I made the bargain that had to be made. We need to start thinking more practically. We're not going to stay alive much longer if we don't!"

He gripped her shoulders. "You wanted this! You hated the idea of the Bal-haegast when I first brought it up. But then you agreed. Now I see why!"

Her face contorted angrily. She pulled his hand off her before shoving him away. "No, Cyrus. I didn't want this. It's about saving me, saving you, saving everything."

"How convenient! That's exactly the kind of thinking that brought Mother to that monster."

❋ ❋ ❋

P'talan was nearly reeling as he approached her. "Not to interrupt such a delicate moment, but we're alive and it seems we have you to thank for it. I take it the demon has returned to whatever hell it spawned from."

"You knew it was there?" B'lantra asked, ignoring Cyrus for

the moment. She'd had more than enough of him for the day.

His musket shook in the raider's hand. Cold sweat beaded up on his forehead. "I knew... something. Like a dark dream that wouldn't go away. It is banished, isn't it?"

"I... made an arrangement in regards to your lives, and it seemed satisfied with what it received," B'lantra replied.

"You gave up something for it in exchange though, didn't you?"

"Yes."

"We'll arrive at our destination in a few days. I'm sure the Tekni council will wish to extend their appreciation, as well as compensate you for anything you may have given up."

"There would be no adequate compensation. Not now. Not ever," B'lantra said, bitterly. "And we're not going with you."

His gaze hardened. "I'm afraid I must insist. Need I remind you of the terms of the Tamaka Koda that you declared?"

"Then I invoke it again. By your own admission, you owe me your life. And by Tamaka that grants me certain freedoms, including the right to politely decline your request. We're going to Targus, and you're going to let us go in peace. Your honor demands no less than for you to accept my condition."

"You put me in an awkward position," P'talan said. "The Council will not be pleased. Nor will they like my particular brand of honor in this case."

B'lantra didn't waver. "I'm sure you'll think of something to say to appease them. Did not the great Fa'boule once say: a man's honor extends only as far as he is able to convince others of it?"

After thinking for a moment, P'talan bowed before her. "Well played. Go in peace if you wish, and may Brakeem and all the Faces of God bless your path."

"And yours. *Dola a'makant, koa-P'talan*," B'lantra replied with exaggerated formality.

A mischievous grin crossed his face. "You never know. Our paths may cross again."

He turned away and began to organize his ragged collection

of soldiers. Cyrus and B'lantra stood quietly watching them until they departed.

✳ ✳ ✳

The scholar was a sorry sight, and Cyrus couldn't help but feel sorry for him. Dontarius slowly waded back out of the water and onto the shore, feet dripping. His eyes were clear of the haze that had hung over them, but his shoulders slumped like a tired and beaten down old man.

"We're probably one of the few to meet a monster like that and live to tell about it. Better than those poor sods back in the water," he said.

B'lantra looked over and gasped at the tangle of bloated, water-logged bodies now visible for all to see.

"The farm family. That's where they went," she murmured, tugging uncomfortably at her dress.

"Seems it fed on their minds and left the husks to drown," Dontarius said, sadly.

"And that's why you don't make deals with monsters. We could have found another way. You can't just give away memories," Cyrus said under his breath.

She heard him regardless. "You couldn't just leave well enough alone, could you? They're my memories. They're mine to do with what I want!"

"They're part of you. They're earned, both the good ones and the bad ones. Hell, I never had a father. I don't even know what he looks like. You did. You don't throw something like that away casually."

"God above, save me from fools! Do you think I did that casually?" B'lantra snapped, her voice echoing through the trees. She grabbed the front of his shirt, shaking him. "When was this other way of yours going to show up? Was it going to just drop from the sky? I've been waiting. What has it gotten me? What has it gotten us?"

She released him and stormed off in the direction of their

camp. Cyrus watched her go, grinding his teeth, willing himself not to say anything more. He was right about the bargain she'd made. There was no doubt that he was right.

"It will come back to haunt us," he muttered.

"It's already haunting us. You saw the look on her face. You should go apologize to her," the scholar said.

Cyrus whirled to face him. "You as well? Why should I apologize? I'm right and she knows it. That's why she walked away without saying anything else. If she would've waited—"

"Winning an argument with a woman isn't the point. Trust me, in the long run it isn't worth it."

"What are you blathering about? That's the whole point of an argument."

"Maybe you'll learn better in time," Dontarius said, shaking his head. "She has faith in you, but the opportunity was right there. You can't blame her for taking it when you did the same. She did it for you just as much as for the rest of us."

"I didn't ask for any of this. I just bargained with that filthy abomination. Everything I hated Mother for doing, I just did myself. I might have doomed myself for all I know. The last thing I wanted was for her to be doomed with me— to be part of this."

"If you wanted a woman to put on a pedestal while you mired in the muck, then you picked the wrong one. She's going to kick that pedestal over and mire right alongside you. You might as well accept that now."

Cyrus began to pace along the water's edge. "There's a hollow space inside her where memories used to be. Something will fill that space, and it won't be good."

"I know she gave up something precious, and it wasn't casual."

"Why do you care anyway? And why didn't you leave with P'Talan when you had the chance?"

Dontarius shrugged. "You mean other than the fact that he makes most troika seem personable by comparison? I've made it my life to study ancient things, and unless I miss my guess, you're going to be stirring up a lot of them on your way.'

"In order words, we're the broom and you're the dustpan."

"That's one way of putting it. Don't be so suspicious. You could use the help, and it's not like there are people lining up to offer their services."

"What are you after?"

"Marithandri, if you really want to know?"

"The old Iriethan city? It's a myth piled onto a legend."

"I thought the same thing about the Bal-haegast until you showed up."

"Surely there must be easier graves to rob."

"Perhaps. But none quite as interesting. I promised someone we'd find it years ago. It's a promise I'd like to keep if I can."

Try as he might, Cyrus couldn't help but be impressed at the scholar's dedication. It was possible that Dontarius was only play-acting in order to illicit that exact response from him, but the earnestness on his face seemed more than genuine.

Dontarius patted him gently on the back. "Marithandri is a secret that can keep for a while, I think. In the meantime, don't you have an apology you need to make."

Cyrus' shoulders slumped. "I'll go say something to her. God knows what," he conceded. "I'm still right, but her intentions were good at least."

"When it comes to women, being right isn't all it's made out to be," Dontarius said.

Cyrus reluctantly trudged back up the hill to where they'd camped. B'lantra was sitting hunched up by the cold embers of last night's fire. She barely acknowledged him as he came near. Her hand flashed out, slapping his away when he tried to put it on her shoulder.

She still wasn't pleased with him it seemed. He hadn't imagined she would be. He wasn't particularly happy with her either at the moment.

He paused and then wearily ran his hand over his face.

The sun had barely cleared the tree line, and already he knew it was going to be a long day.

※ ※ ※

Dontarius' feet squished in his waterlogged boots as he followed Cyrus away from the pool. He'd need a new pair. Even after they'd dried, they would still smell of muck and death.

The sun had risen, and the day was warming, but the chill running down his spine refused to go away. Some hot, sweetened chala would be nice.

No!

He needed a stiff drink: Targanese whiskey, Erendel spiced rum, the vilest concoction from the seediest tavern in Targus or any other city.

How could God let things like that roam the world?!

He'd been through so many taverns. There had been so many buxom barmaids, gamblers, fleshmongers and conmen he'd dealt with over the years. The Bal-haegast could have masqueraded as any one of them.

He shuddered violently at the thought and quickened his step away from the pool.

From the top of the hill, he looked down the slight slope to the camp and saw B'lantra and Cyrus awkwardly talking. He was still too far away to hear what they were saying to each other, but he really didn't need to. B'lantra seemed like a heartbroken schoolgirl whose great love had callously cast her aside. She wasn't used to being criticized, not by Cyrus at least. For his part, Cyrus appeared the cocksure young nobleman trying to form an apology to a lady of the court when he really didn't believe he'd done anything wrong. He suddenly reminded Dontarius of a boy who'd been caught stealing a pie, and was now sheepishly trying to prove it really wasn't his fault.

They were both still children in a lot of ways. What was in store for them? More importantly, what was in store for him if he continued his association with them?

What was certain was that big and important things needed doing, and both Cyrus and B'lantra, whether they wanted to be or not, were key parts of what was going to happen.

And those things had already started. The golden gear had sparkled in the sun like a shining beacon, calling out to be studied. It was a gateway to something far beyond his ken. He'd felt the same way standing in the presence of the steam golem he and Tarja had encountered years ago.

The steam golem was out of his reach now, but the gear... well the gear was something he could obtain. The link it provided might even lead him to the gates of Marithandri. He just needed to see it, to hold it. He needed to possess it long enough to learn its secrets. Proper scholarship demanded nothing less.

Cyrus yelled out his name and motioned to him. He and B'lantra had kept their conversation short. From the language of their bodies, the two hadn't completely worked out their differences. They really weren't used to fighting with each other, not seriously at least, so it would probably take a while for the wounds to heal.

It was ironic. Two people who could barely resolve the problems between them were at the heart of something that might affect the whole of the Lanternlit.

They weren't ready.

He cast a quick glance back at the pool.

Maybe it wasn't just Cyrus and B'lantra who weren't ready.

Tarja.

He had a growing feeling that he'd end up seeing her again one way or another.

Cyrus called his name again, more impatiently this time. Dontarius nodded and slogged down the hill towards them.

❊ ❊ ❊

Cyrus swiftly drew his sword and stepped forward, thrusting the blade out straight and true. He backpedaled.

One step. Two. Three.

The sword was merely an extension of the arm. He drew the blade back into a guard position and then executed a swift riposte against a would-be attacker.

"You've left the air eviscerated and bleeding," Dontarius said to him. "I'm sure it regrets whatever it may have done to offend you."

Cyrus gave the scholar a dark look. "Would you like to volunteer as a sparring partner then?"

Dontarius shook his head. "I never carry swords. Miserable, heavy things."

Cyrus did his best to pretend the scholar wasn't there and went about gracefully executing a series of sweeping, careful strikes, just as he'd seen Caulter do.

One step. Two. Three.

The key was maintaining his balance and not overextending. That was the mistake he'd made when he'd faced the inquisitor the first time. Well, one of them anyway. It was hard to point to anything he'd done right that evening. He probably wouldn't be facing Caulter again, but there would be plenty of other menaces before the end.

The list seemed to grow by the day.

"You're probably going to need some more gunpowder," Dontarius said, once more interrupting his concentration. "The village of Flaxen is to the north, and we'll be passing right through it. They have a gunsmith from what I remember."

"I don't know what we'll do yet. We still need to stay clear of the roads as much as possible."

"We can't avoid them forever. Not if we want to get to Targus. We'll have to cross the Maidenskar Bridge at some point. There's really no other way around that."

"In case you haven't noticed, we're not exactly flush with coin. We're low on food and everything else. I assume you like eating."

"Yes, it does have a certain appeal," Dontarius agreed. "You know, we'd be in Flaxen already if you two hadn't wasted time looking for Caulter. He's fine, wherever he is."

"And you know that how? Dead or alive, I'd at least like to know what happened to him."

"Somehow I very much doubt we've seen the last of him. "

"I guess we'll find out," Cyrus said, irritably. Was it some sort of unholy compulsion that drove Dontarius to fill every spare moment with pointless chatter?

"While you're busy giving the air the thrashing it no doubt deserves, would you mind if I took another look at that gear?"

"Why?" Cyrus asked, reaching into his pocket almost protectively. "Surely you've examined it every way it can be examined by now."

"It's an artifact— a glimpse into another way of doing things. It's almost alive in its own way. If I can get it to respond somehow, there's a lot we can learn from it," Dontarius replied.

"It really doesn't work that way. The gear is a thing of witchcraft, and you're not a witch or a warlock. There's only so much you're going to be able to gather from it," Cyrus said, doing his best to remain patient.

"I see," Dontarius said, his voice dripping with disappointment.

Cyrus pursed his lips, trying to force down the twinge of guilt he suddenly felt. Dontarius was a scholar. He wanted to explore and to know, but it was like a blind man trying to figure out how to see. There was a whole world he would never know.

He fetched the scholar a distrustful look, and then reluctantly handed the gear over. There was something in Dontarius' manner that bothered him. It wasn't lust or obsession. The look on Dontarius' face as he examined the gear was subtler, like that of a child playing with a treasured toy. Indeed there was something almost childlike about the way the scholar eagerly went about, measuring, weighing and sketching the gear from all angles.

On the surface, the scholar's interest seemed harmless, even useful. They were searching for answers, and any information Dontarius could glean from his studies would be a blessing.

Better yet, with the scholar absorbed in examining the gear, there might be a small chance he would quit talking. At the moment, that was probably the best blessing Dontarius could bestow.

As the scholar continued his experiments, Cyrus sighed and stared at the ground trying to regain his concentration. It was futile. The sword hung limply in his hand.

He grudgingly put it away and turned towards the stream they'd stopped at. B'lantra had made herself at home near a large stump, well away from the water's edge. She'd said little beyond what was absolutely needed, and he hadn't felt the need to pry any conversation out of her.

Talking to her right now was like trying to plug a leak in a sinking boat. Given her mood, no matter what he said she'd likely find some fault in it.

He sat until he couldn't stand it anymore and then motioned the others towards the horses. Dontarius seemed loathe to part with the gear. For an instant Cyrus thought he would put up a fuss about handing it back over, but whatever resentment Dontarius might have felt was quickly covered over with a practiced smile.

They mounted without saying anything more to one another. B'lantra hesitated before accepting the hand he offered to pull her up onto the horse's back. She wrapped her arms around his waist to steady herself as they cantered away from the stream. There wasn't any affection in her grasp.

It was a small thing, but it gnawed at him nonetheless.

If B'lantra didn't want to make any effort to reconcile, then he didn't have to either. No, he would simply improve— find some way to be more skillful, more diplomatic, more… whatever the hell it was she expected from him. He'd already come as close to an apology as he was going to.

Besides, he was still right.

She gripped his side.

He irritably grimaced and turned back to her. "It's not like I'm going to let you fall."

"It's not that. I thought I heard something just now. Like voices carrying."

His hand reached down to his sword hilt, though if there were enemies lurking nearby, the legs of the horse would serve them far better. He guided the animal to the top of the grassy hill and looked around. At first he didn't see anything amiss, but then he spotted the distant figures riding in single file in front of a line of trees.

There were two of them, though they were too far away for him to be able to tell exactly who they were or what they wanted.

"Get out your spyglass," he said to Dontarius.

The riders disappeared into the trees before the scholar could oblige. Cyrus didn't know whether to be relieved or not.

B'lantra shifted in the saddle behind him. "Do you think—?"

"I don't know. They didn't come after us. Let's not wait around to see if they change their minds."

CHAPTER 26

AWAKENING

THE MISTS SWIRLED AROUND HER, slowly healing her shredded flesh. Pale, nearly perfect skin was rewoven overtop reforming muscle and bone. Eyes blinded by the white flash of hateful light gradually regained their sight. Hair burned away by the blast of energy regrew until it was long and lustrous. Fingers and toes twitched, testing themselves. The body renewed itself in the healing womb of the mist.

"Awaken."

The word was as quiet as the gentle babble of a stream. It was as loud as the ocean waves pounding against the rocks. Nysse wasn't quite ready to give up the body and soul it had bargained for. There were still sights to be seen, pleasures and agonies to be experienced. The body wasn't so damaged that it was beyond the water spirit's ability to rejuvenate.

Thoughts returned to a dead consciousness that had been both drowned and reborn in the water's embrace.

The annoyingly shrill sound of a child crying pricked her dreams. It was often there when she slept, nipping at her.

She raised her hand.

"Stupid little whore. I'll give you something to cry about."

The sound abruptly faded, leaving only an aching silence in its wake.

Asa opened her eyes.

She hurt.

The screaming, maddened hordes of the Tainted pour through the broken streets. The airships rain fire down, but still they come. The pavement crackles and pops from the heat. The air ripples.

From a window sill high above she waits. The Aeore gunners open fire. Beams of light stream out, tearing through the Tainted's shadowy bodies. It's not enough to slow the advance. She leaps from the window.

Her sword cuts into their ranks. One of them cries out to her. She doesn't recognize the language. Its jaws seem too long and distended to form speech. It doesn't matter. With a sweep of her blade, its head tumbles from its shoulders.

She hacks. Stabs. There is only to blur of blackened bodies. There is only the exhilaration of the kill.

They surround her. They cut her. So fast she can't heal. One of them leers at her as it runs its dull blade through her chest.

Pain. She feels pain.

The beams stop. A quick glance tells her the Aeore gunners have been overwhelmed. She slices through her enemy. Its entrails spill satisfyingly out onto the pavement.

She pulls the blade from her body and retreats.

She'd healed then and come back stronger for it— as she was doing now in the sheltering folds of the mist.

"It's time."

Asa stepped into the mist. It parted like a curtain because she willed it to be so, and she gradually re-emerged into the world. It was almost like being born all over again.

The marsh was much the same as when she'd left it. Birds flittered about. Frogs croaked from the stream nearby. From a short distance away, a small herd of deer stopped nibbling on the spring flowers and regarded her in alarm.

She ignored them for the time being. Her blue eyes flashed in anger.

"Susanna!"

The doll sat near the stream, soaked and soiled, the faint outline of a boot print on the front of its calico dress. Asa picked the fallen doll up, and cradled it to her.

"There, there. It's alright. I'm here now. Don't worry. We'll make him pay. We'll make him pay for everything we've suffered."

She began carefully wiping off the dirt. "Your dress is all dirty. We can't have that, Susanna. How many times do I have to tell you that you can't go out with a dirty dress?"

Once the doll had been properly cleaned up, she walked gracefully over to the stream and knelt down, stretching her hand out to touch the water's surface. She closed her eyes, seeing as Nysse had taught her to see.

The water flowed. It touched everything in its wake. All water eventually joined together. And it carried a memory of everything that had passed through it. Stream and brook, leaf and land. Her senses carried with the water, ranging ever farther.

What had the water seen? Where had her quarry gone?

The trace she was looking for finally appeared to her. The witch's son was revealed to her sight. The charm he'd had was gone, just like the weapon his mother had given him. He had no defense.

She sat up and smiled, pleased with herself.

"Come along, Susanna."

She would start with the deer, but they would be far from the last things she would catch.

✳ ✳ ✳

One of the flies buzzing around the dead rat rose from its feast and mockingly hovered near his face. Caulter resisted the urge to swat at it. He didn't dare move, not yet anyway. The rat's bloated corpse was an inconvenience, a fact that the rat would have probably agreed with had it still been able. But then Caulter really hadn't had time to be very choosy about his hiding place. One of the cats from the nearby village of Flaxen had ended the rodent's life, judging by the puncture marks on its throat. The 'cats' Caulter now sheltered from were perhaps more civilized, but no less deadly. From the golden thicket of forsythia, he peered out, warily watching them and hoping they would depart soon.

Sentinel Etmos of the Inquisition and his unwilling charge, the Illumentry sister Kierahne, hadn't taken notice of his presence so far. For the moment, their interest was focused on the line of newly captured Tekni prisoners standing bound and miserable along the Red Road leading into the village. Behind them waited a nervous gaggle of townsfolk and an equally nervous contingent of Arakostrian infantrymen.

Etmos and Kierahne were most likely after the Trafari witch. Caulter couldn't imagine any other reason for them to be here. Searching for her had been problematic at best after the shadow creature's attack. With it likely still prowling, he'd been left guessing as to her fate. His intuition had told him she was still alive, which meant she would either go east with the Tekni or turn north to Targus.

Caulter had gambled on north. The boy was really the key to her actions. Where he went, she would follow.

Aeliraneth's son would go north— back to whatever fate lay in store for him at his mother's old estate. And if so, they would have to pass through Flaxen. It was a tenuous theory at best, but his instincts had served him well over the years, and they told him he was right.

Unfortunately, it seemed Etmos and Kierahne harbored similar thoughts. They didn't seem to be in a hurry to leave either, leaving him helpless to warn the Trafari girl.

Etmos seemed determined to stretch the interrogation of the Tekni prisoners out. It was his way. The man was far too much in love with the sound of his own voice. Dark skinned and gaunt, his face almost skeletal, he was Southern by birth, if no longer by belief. In many ways Etmos was an older, more sophisticated version of Bregna. He was more refined, his methods less reckless, his ambition better concealed, but at their rotten cores they were much the same.

Kierahne, Etmos' personal project and interminable headache, was even more of a threat than her handler. She'd never been properly broken. Even after all the punishment the Illumentry had inflicted on her, a spark of rebellion still flourished within.

She wasn't yet aware of him, but that would change quickly if he grew careless. The bulk of her abilities lay in shadow and in darkness, and with the day failing, she would only grow stronger.

Etmos drew his gloved fist back and brought it crashing into the face of the nearest Tekni prisoner. They were a nondescript and ragged lot, probably peasant recruits talked into the Tekni's ranks by promises of a better life.

Caulter was about to dismiss them from his thoughts, when the man at the end turned. Beaten and dirty much like his fellows, he was squat and thickly built. Nurengarn most likely. A scar ran down the side of his face.

Caulter silently cursed. He'd seen the scar when the Tekni soldiers had first burst into the farmhouse. He'd seen it at the campfire before the creature of the night attacked them. Like Caulter, the man had probably been separated from the others and overlooked by the creature's predation. Unlike Caulter, he hadn't been fortunate enough to avoid capture.

Caulter brought out one of his pistols. The movement of the barrel was subtle, nearly imperceptible, but it was still enough to draw Kierahne's interest. Caulter froze as she turned towards him. She slid a small charm made of interlocking white bone out of the folds of her robe. It was the focus of her witchcraft, much like the Trafari witch's song. Kierahne rattled it slightly. The sound was dry and crackling, like leaves rustling in the autumn wind. Caulter waited, not even daring to breathe. He couldn't see Kierahne's inked face under the hood she wore, but he knew she was intently studying the brush where he was hiding. It was an eternity before she finally turned away.

Damn her!

"Now let me begin again," Etmos announced to the Tekni prisoners. "We already know one of your commanders went out in search of the witch. Where was he planning on taking her? Surely one of you must know."

The men looked anxiously at each other, but didn't answer.

"Let's try a different tack then. The first to tell me what I what to know will be free to go. The rest of you will have to hope the next world is more forgiving of your sins."

When he was greeted again with silence, he brought out his pistol and placed the barrel against the forehead of one of the prisoners. His eyes flicked back and forth. He cocked the pistol. His finger edged towards the trigger.

"They went east," the scar-faced Nurengarn cried out.

Caulter winced.

The man was shaking, tears streaming down his face. One of the other prisoners awkwardly lunged at him, trying to quiet him, but the Arakostrian infantrymen quickly moved in to separate the two. They dragged the scarred man forward until he lay at Etmos' feet.

"Now, you were saying?"

"They— they went east, Sir. Our captain, P'talan… he led a company of men after the witch. They were going to take her to Deadman's Crossing, near the foot of the Backbone."

Caulter listened intently to the rest of the sorrowful account, though there was little said that he didn't already know.

"Now let me go. Please, sir. You said you'd let me go!"

Etmos put the pistol away and scratched thoughtfully at his short, dark beard. A cold, white-toothed smile spread across his dark countenance. "Deadman's Crossing. An ironic name, don't you think?"

He leaned down and yanked the man to his feet. "And you're certain the man accompanying the witch claimed to be the son of Aeliraneth?"

"Yes, Sir Inquisitor. He spoke her name several times that I overheard!"

Etmos shoved the man away. "You're a coward, but you're a wise coward. And thus, you'll be a coward who is still breathing when tomorrow's sun rises. Start running, little man. I have no further use for you."

The man stared blankly for a moment. He gave his fellow prisoners an agonized, mournful look before turning and shuffling away as fast as his legs would carry him.

One of the infantrymen raised his musket and took aim at his retreating back, but Etmos waved him off.

"There's no need," he said, quietly. "We have what we came for."

"Shall we head east or report back to Targus? If the witch made the shelter of Deadman's Crossing, she'll be hard to ferret out," Kierahne noted. Her voice was as dry and cracked as her bone charm.

Etmos shook his head. "Neither. The scouts reported seeing three people, two men and a woman, moving north and trying to stay off the road. With what we now know, we can guess it's our quarry riding straight into our jaws. We were right to come this way."

Kierahne turned away as if disinterested.

"Does this strategy displease you?" Etmos asked, his voice rising in irritation.

"It neither pleases nor does it displease me. It simply is," she answered. There was just a hint of disdain lurking within her dry tone.

Etmos frowned and looked over to the commander of the Arakostrian infantrymen. "Thank you for your cooperation in this matter, Captain. We have no further need of the prisoners here. Kill them or release them as it pleases you. In the meantime, may I request that you have men stationed near the road and in the town? We'll have guests arriving soon."

❊ ❊ ❊

Asa prowled around the yard outside the farmhouse, searching for signs of her quarry. Aeliraneth's son had fled, though it hadn't been that long ago. She could still feel the echo of his presence carried on the moisture of the morning air.

The oaken front door hung open, gently flapping on its hinges. Noiseless as a cat, she slipped through and entered the kitchen.

The room was still and empty. She found a broken sword and
traces of gunpowder amidst the scattered leavings on the floor.
Soldiers had been here… and an inquisitor, judging by the scraps
of black cloth lying nearby.

She turned over a few bits of crockery and examined a crumpled, bloodstained blanket before a cracked glass bead, rolled
into a corner, caught her eye. She picked it up, studying it in the
streaked light slithering its way through the shuttered window.
The faint odor of herbs and ointments still clung to it.

A woman. A healer. Another witch.

It seemed her quarry had assembled quite the little band.
Aeliraneth's son likely imagined they would somehow be able
to protect him. He would quickly find out how wrong he was.

She went back outside to search the rest of the farm. Sensing movement from over her shoulder, she turned. The chimera
fluttered towards her, wretched harbinger that it was.

Simon Barros wouldn't be far behind.

Asa barely had time to collect her thoughts before he was
upon her.

"Why have you not returned as I bid?"

Violet eyes sparkled, the only trace of color in his gray-black
translucent form. His voice was commanding. Cold. The almost
friendly tone he had used the last time he'd spoken to her, like
he was speaking to a trusted friend, had vanished. Now it was
that of a ruthless superior demanding respect and obedience.

It wouldn't be easy to soothe him this time. Her convalescence
had taken several days, and she hadn't bothered to report in to
him.

"I suffered a small mishap," she said.

The violet eyes flickered in suspicion. "Tell me what happened.
Was this one of your loose ends that was supposed to be tied up?"

"It was the son of Aeliraneth," she said, quickly. Subterfuge
wouldn't benefit her. "He resisted when I tried to take him."

A blast of cold, dead air swept across the farmyard. "I wiped

Aeliraneth's blight from the face of this world in retribution for the years of suffering she caused me. I seared her with fire. Her son is dead as well. Burned!"

Asa shrank back from his sudden anger, but refused to concede her point. "The boy fled and was taken south by the witch's handmaiden. He lives."

"You would be willing to swear your life on this? You know how I dealt with traitors and liars in the past. My condition has changed. My methods haven't. Not even for you, Asa."

She remained resolute. "Yes, upon my life I tell you he lives."

"Then he is a threat. Where is he?"

"He escaped me, though I hunt him even now. I will have him soon."

Simon's anger faded like a sudden gust of wind. Disappointment crept into his voice instead. "And why did you choose not to tell me any of this? Information is critical in war, Asa."

The tone cut though her. His wrath she'd been prepared for. The disappointment almost hurt. She bowed her head, trying to look sorrowful. "I… I had thought to present him to you as a gift. I'm sorry if I have displeased you. I only wanted to bring you happiness."

"Happiness is irrelevant to us right now, only success matters," Simon stated. The violet eyes gazed at her and then past her. "I told her that once long ago…"

Asa tensed. She'd known that she somehow reminded him of Celaan. She'd even used it to her advantage, preying upon the one weakness he'd ever shown.

"This son of Aeliraneth must be destroyed," he concluded.

Asa relaxed a little. Her Simon had been placated, and any punishment would wait for another day. "Would it not be wise to keep him alive and question him?"

"The golem I created tore Aeliraneth apart. I have undone what she made. Even her successor in the chain will soon be in my hands. Only her spirit remains now and I'll take care of that soon enough. That is the only thing keeping the barrier in place. What is there for one misbegotten son to know?"

"It has been said that a live and unhelpful prisoner can always be made dead. The reverse is somewhat more difficult."

Simon considered for an instant and then nodded his approval. "Very well. Find him and bring him to me then. Eliminate him if he resists you. And be cautious. I would hate for you to suffer another mishap."

Asa smiled for the first time since Simon had come before her. Her plans had been momentarily hindered, but not crippled.

"He won't escape."

Simon didn't reply. He simply turned and walked away. His feet made no sound on the ground. The grass didn't bend under his weight. It was as if the world refused to acknowledge him. A moment later he had vanished.

Asa looked about the farmhouse one more time, trying to decide how best to proceed. A line of hoof prints leading off into the trees beyond the yard drew her attention. She went over to briefly examine them, but quickly decided against following.

Instead she made for the stream she'd seen as she'd approached the house. Following a set of prints was beneath her dignity. Tracks in the ground could sometimes lie, especially if one's quarry was clever. The water in the stream would tell her truly.

She was close now. Aeliraneth's son would watch his new friends die first, knowing all the while there was nothing he could do to save them. Perhaps she would start with the inquisitor.

Perhaps the witch.

❋ ❋ ❋

Caulter waited while the soldiers led the Tekni off to their fate. When both the captives and the infantrymen had disappeared from sight, Etmos fiercely turned on Kierahne.

"Don't ever defy me in front of others, witch! How many times do you need to be told? Shall I have Jakarti deal with you when we return? Shall I have her throw you into the dark again?"

"No," Kierahne croaked from underneath her hood.

"I'm glad we understand each other."

The sentinel and the sister were alone, but Caulter decided against attacking. Even now, the odds didn't favor him. Besides, he really didn't need to bother. Once he was no longer in danger of being spotted, he could leave the village and intercept the Trafari witch before she arrived.

"Come on, Kierahne. Let's be off," Etmos said.

Whatever look Kierahne gave him in return was hidden under her cloak. She suddenly tensed, spinning round to again face the undergrowth where Caulter crouched.

"What is it?" Etmos asked, reaching for his pistols.

"There is… there is…"

The bone charm began rattling.

Caulter remained still. The dead rat beside him twitched as the charm continued its rattle. Its decaying head lifted off the ground as if buoyed by an invisible hand. Its jaws, formerly locked together, now parted. Its sightless, bloated eyes stared off into the growing night, searching, until at last they fixed upon him.

Kierahne's voice sounded almost gleeful. "Lurker. Watching. Waiting. I see you!"

Her hand lashed out.

Caulter quickly rolled away, more out of instinct than anything else. Kierahne's witchcraft couldn't hurt him directly, though a clever witch could often find other ways, as the golden-haired woman had so ably demonstrated.

Gray streamers of energy slithered across the ground and latched onto the vegetation around him. The forsythia twisted and curled. Golden flowers shuddered, withering and dying on the branch until nothing remained but blackened stems.

He came up into a crouch. His pistols came out in a smooth motion. Recognition flickered in Kierahne's eyes. He held his fire. Maybe he could avoid a fight altogether, though he doubted the encounter would go that smoothly.

"I might have known," Etmos sneered. "Still trying to staunch your growing failure?"

"There is no failure. And this isn't your hunt. Why are you here?" Caulter coldly demanded.

"A witch on the loose. Inquisitor Captain Bregna dead, along with your entire company. A fortress nearly leveled by arcane energy. I'd say that is quite the failure."

"This hunt was assigned to me directly by the Conclave. It wasn't assigned to you. As such, I demand that you—"

"Don't waste your breath, Caulter. You know perfectly well I don't answer to you!" Etmos declared. His face twisted in thought. "But to whom do you answer to these days? Is it the Illumentry or some other need now? Vladimir reported some questionable orders you gave just before the Tekni attack on Ashenwall. Petru's body was found with a bullet wound."

"If Vladimir has questions concerning my leadership, he can bring them through the proper channels. I'll answer them once my hunt is completed."

It probably wouldn't matter what he said. He was a rogue now, and the Inquisition wouldn't hesitate to punish its own.

In the fading light, Etmos' face looked even more ghoul-like. "I think you have plans of your own for this Trafari witch. You know where she is, don't you?"

"No," Caulter answered coldly. "No more than you do."

"Ahh, but you do know quite a bit about her. Care to share that information?" The sentinel's tone suggested it wasn't a request.

There was no point in dealing with either of them any longer. In truth, there never had been. He was as much a fugitive now as the Trafari witch.

"No," he repeated again.

He slipped into the growing night, regaining the cover of the nearby trees before they could react.

He hurried through the underbrush, his mind awhirl with plans and contingencies if those plans failed. None of the ideas seemed particularly appealing. There had to be some way of warning the Trafari witch away from the village before it was too late. A cold sweat began to bead on his forehead. His injured leg ached painfully, slowing him down.

The silverworm was continuing to work its way out of his system, allowing emotion to creep back in to cloud his thinking. He was genuinely afraid for the first time in years. In another place and time, it might have even felt liberating. Now it was just another problem he'd have to contend with.

CHAPTER 27

INTO THE VEIL OF NIGHT

CAULTER USED HIS BODY WEIGHT to bend the tree over long enough for him to awkwardly wrap the rope around the peg. He'd been fortunate enough to find the materials in an old shed, and it was time to put them to use. He pulled the trip line tight and placed one of his pistols on the far side of the line before shuffling some leaves and dirt on top of the noose. The light from Saranor shone down through the treetops, glinting off the pistol's silver inlay.

A suitable lure.

It was an elementary trap that any experienced hunter would have scoffed at, but Etmos was far more at home in the narrow, suffocating streets of a city than out in the wilds. It was simply a matter of whether his arrogance overrode his native caution.

Caulter shook his head. Arrogance was a trait he derided in others and now his life depended on it. It was yet another gamble he'd taken. His life seemed to have more of them by the day.

The land grew rocky on this side of the village, rising up into sheer cliffs that unexpectedly narrowed into nasty little ravines choked with scrub trees. If the trap didn't work, he would be hemmed in. The sentinel's chase had been relentless. Silverworm coursed through Etmos' body, giving him speed and power Caulter could no longer match. Kierahne had held the full extent of her powers in check for the time being, though Caulter doubted she would hold off much longer. It was the perfect setting for someone like her. Saranor was rising over the trees, giving her a perfect army of ruddy shadows to work with.

Caulter's only real advantage was that neither of them were

experienced witch hunters. The Illumentry used them in other ways— intelligence gathering and assassination most likely.

He peered out into the moon-streaked night, watching and waiting.

Footsteps came, quiet and confident against the spongy green moss and new spring grasses pushing their way out of the damp earth. Caulter pressed against the side of one of the overhanging trees. Etmos moved inexorably forward, without fear or concern. Caulter recognized the look. He'd had it himself during his first few hunts, before experience had taught him that not all witches were frightened and helpless.

Etmos tensed. He'd seen the bait. The sentinel crept forward, pistol in hand.

Just a little farther. Another few steps.

Etmos stopped. A grin broke across his face.

Caulter pursed his lips and aimed his remaining pistol. Etmos spotted the movement and rolled away just as Caulter pulled the trigger. The bullets streaked past the Sentinel and tore into the tree trunk behind him.

"Nice try. But not good enough," Etmos hissed.

Caulter was already moving. His sword came out in a clean motion, slicing first at the pistol in Etmos' hand. The Sentinel was too fast. He let his pistol drop and unsheathed his sword in time to parry Caulter's attack.

Caulter pressed. Etmos expertly countered each blow and then launched a furious assault of his own. He was swift and certain, and soon Caulter found himself on the defensive.

He feinted. Etmos stepped in. Caulter leaned down grabbing up a chunk of loose earth and stones.

"Where are the witch and the witch's son?" Etmos demanded.

"I don't know where they are. I told you that," Caulter replied.

"Unfortunate."

Caulter flung the dirt up into the Sentinel's face. Etmos staggered back. Caulter leapt to his feet and blindly threw himself upon him. Where subterfuge and trickery had failed, brute force would suffice. It wasn't graceful or heroic, but it served his needs.

He pummeled Etmos mercilessly, and before the man could recover, Caulter shoved him toward the trip line. The line broke, and the noose constricted around Etmos' ankles. He cried out as he was jerked off his feet, dragged across the ground and heaved up into the air.

In another place and time, Caulter might have even found some amusement in watching Etmos helplessly dangle. The only question was whether to kill him or not. Caulter decided against it. Sentinels and witches were bonded together by the Illumentry. Part of the markings on Kierahne's body represented her link with Etmos. He was the muzzle for her fangs, ensuring she didn't bite anyone the Illumentry didn't want bitten. Without him to contain her, it was hard to tell what she might do.

He'd let one witch loose in the world. He wasn't about to release another.

Caulter slammed his fist into Etmos' face. He took more joy in it than he really should have. Afterwards, he stripped the man's coat from his unconscious body and then slipped back into the darkness.

There was still Kierahne to contend with. He patted the witchbane he'd made back in the farmhouse. With luck, she would prove easy enough to dispatch.

❋ ❋ ❋

It was the scream that had first caught her attention: a bright, piercing cry of terror that cut through the chill of the evening. It called, drawing Asa inexorably to it.

The hunter still twitched under the seething horde of purple and black bodies covering his frame. His cries had descended into whimpering by the time she arrived. The storm fairies gnawed freely on his hapless form, pulling little bloody chunks away and greedily devouring them. Already white bone was showing through the tangled mass of partially charred entrails and fluids. The charged air buzzed with the excited tremor of their scaly wings. The acrid scent of ozone intermingled with that of burnt flesh.

Asa watched the scene with the wry detachment she usually reserved for the bawdy comedies and epic tragedies she occasionally amused herself with. There was a certain justice to it as well. Any hunter foolish enough to wander close to a storm fairy hive deserved his fate. The fairies home stood just beyond the blood-soaked ground where the hunter lay. It was a tall, willowy structure of woven onyx stone and resin, rising above the scorched and blasted trees that surrounded it. Saffron markings twisted and curled around the hive, matching the swirling bands on the fairies themselves.

It was plain enough for anyone with the eyes to see. Foolishness had its price, no matter where you went or who you were. The hunter had simply failed to learn that lesson quickly enough.

A mild tingling went up her arm. Asa regarded one of the fairies hovering near her, readying itself to plunge its tiny spear into her once again. A puzzled expression crept over its banded, delicate face when she showed no sign of fear or panic at its presence.

With a determined chirrup, the fairy attacked, driving the spear into her arm once more. Asa's amused smile began to fade. Hearing the noise, some of the other fairies flittered up from their feast, the hunter's blood dripping from their tiny frames. In an instant, Asa found herself surrounded. The vague pinch of their spears came. Her mood darkened. The ending to the play had been spoiled.

"The hunter isn't the only foolish thing out tonight."

She called the mist to her. It obeyed, sweeping across the ground like the advancing tide. Its tendrils wrapped around one of the fairies and crushed it to death. The sound of its tiny bones cracking brought a smile to her face.

A tiny spark of lightning glanced off her. It stung more than she had expected. Asa glared at the perpetrator. The fairy returned her gaze with a look of determined triumph. The mists ripped it apart at her command.

Undaunted, the rest of the storm fairies bore down on her. Asa calmly stood her ground. The mists lashed out, striking again and again into their flitting ranks. Their cries of pain were almost as delightful as the hunter's.

She advanced towards the hive, stepping across the mutilated bodies in her wake. The fairies refused to provide her a clear path, no matter how many of the little beasts she slaughtered.

From the arched entrance, reinforcements poured forth until a buzzing wall of defenders barred her way. She had to admire their tenacity if nothing else. It wouldn't help them. Nothing short of divine intervention could save them.

Unless...

She laughed as the idea percolated.

Her quarry had hurt her once, and the fairies might prove useful in making sure it didn't happen again.

"Take me to your queen. I have an offer for her."

In response, the fairies set another sortie after her. She sent the mists tearing into the clustered creatures. It was like a hurricane shredding through a fisherman's flimsy wooden shack. Fairies scattered and died, their reddish ichor staining the ground. The mists battered the outside of the hive until cracks showed in the stone and yellowish bile seeped forth.

"I know you can understand me. You vermin aren't quite that stupid. Take me to your queen, or I'll exterminate you to the last."

The fairies hovered uncertainly. Finally, a mournful wail of acquiescence came from somewhere within the hive. The entrance creaked open. The fairies parted ranks, allowing her an unimpeded track inside.

Asa boldly strode past them, a victorious imperatrix taking stock of a nearly conquered city and its people. The fairies' faces weren't quite human, but they were close enough for her to be able to relish in their resentment and their fear.

She flashed them a bright smile. "Don't worry. We're going to have fun together, you and I."

❀ ❀ ❀

The shadows near the stone wall leapt and danced at her command. Gray streamers of energy crackled. The bone charm's rattle filled the night. A burly dog came out to investigate, growled and then slowly backed away. All the doors and the nearby houses were shuttered, the doors locked and barred. Kierahne moved down the lane by the wall, quietly and calmly. The etchings on her scarlet cloak gleamed in the pale lantern light.

Crouched on the other side of the wall, Caulter nervously awaited her approach. His knife was ready, already coated with the witchbane. Even a scratch would be enough to cripple Kierahne and end the hunt once and for all. The attack would have to be quick and certain. It wasn't a frightened, half-maddened girl he was facing, but a full-fledged witch, confident and well in control of her powers. Even with the witchbane, he couldn't afford to take any chances.

Kierahne came nearer, pausing just on the other side of the wall. Caulter gathered his nerve and then slithered quietly over the wall.

He crouched in the shadows behind her. She hadn't seen him yet. The knife trembled a little in his hand.

Why? It wouldn't have been the first throat he'd cut.

She turned in alarm.

He'd waited too long.

Damn!

He leapt forward. Her bone charm started to rattle. He slapped it out of her hand. His fingers knotted around the loose folds of her cloak. He slammed her up against the wall and swiftly brought his knife up. Her eyes were wide with sudden fear, her aura of invincibility diminished. Perhaps he'd overestimated her. She was just another witch come to the slaughter.

He hesitated just before the blade reached the soft flesh of her neck. He didn't know why. Maybe it was the lingering spark of life in her eyes. Maybe as he looked on her broken face he felt some scrap of pity somewhere in his heart. Maybe he was simply tired of killing. There was something mechanical in the act. He'd done it so many times that it felt rote. Empty. He might as well have been a machine, a murderous counterpart to a grain thresher or a wind-up toy soldier.

Kierahne's reaction was swift and surprisingly vicious. Her knee came up, slamming into his groin. As he doubled over, she shoved him violently away from her. He lost his balance and tumbled backwards, landing hard on his back.

The knife slipped out of his hand.

Kierahne pounced on him before he could move. In an instant she sat on top of him, knees straddling his chest, the very knife he'd intended to use now poised just underneath his chin. Her face was a mask of unsurpassed fury.

"What do you want with her?" she demanded.

"I don't want her dead," he replied.

The blade pushed against his skin.

It was hard to tell what Kierahne intended. Her face was a symphony of rage and resentment. Discordant and conflicting emotions rose and fell across her face.

"That doesn't answer anything!"

"I have a daughter whose life depends on the Trafari witch staying free. Is that a sufficient answer for you?"

"I saw her. Bruised. Beaten. Locked in that cage like a circus animal. She deserves better than you! We all do," Kierahne said. She reached into his coat and took out his vial of witchbane. With a quick motion she shattered it against the ground. "You and your poisons. Your self-righteousness. Passing on judgment like you're gods. She deserves better than you!"

He waited. Kierahne might as well have been asking for the sun to set backwards or the world to stop turning. Witches served the Illumentry or they burned. It was the way of things, and had been for centuries. No amount of rage would change it. Nor should it.

Kierahne withdrew the knife from his throat and stabbed it down beside his head. Again and again she brought it down, furrowing the earth with her rage. Angry, bitter tears glimmered in her dull brown eyes.

And then her fit passed, and she suddenly hopped off him, still holding the dirty knife in her hand. The bone charm was back in her grasp before he could even blink.

"Keep her free."

He sat up and then uncertainly got back to his feet. Kierahne watched him closely. His hand slid down towards his pistols. The bone charm rattled in warning.

He moved his hand away from the pistols. It was pointless. Her spell could wither his weapons as surely as it had withered the forsythia.

"Go! I'm giving you your life. Don't waste it."

"You don't want your freedom? Why not take it while you can?" he asked.

"Don't torment me. I can still feel Etmos' loathsome stench, which means you didn't kill him when you had the chance. I'm still bound. Still shackled. Damn you! I'll tell him you fled to the west. That will give the girl time to slip through. Now get out of my sight!"

Caulter edged slowly away. Somewhere in the back of his mind, angry, broken pride raged at him for his failure. He'd been spared by a witch, something that should be servile and bound. He was grateful though it galled him. It was a strange feeling, unworthy of an inquisitor.

Leaving his broken pride behind him, he slunk away.

✻ ✻ ✻

Crouched atop a low grassy rise that overlooked the village of Flaxen, they anxiously waited. It seemed a peaceful place:

pristine, well-maintained white buildings shimmering faintly in the moonlight. Lanterns flickered in tune with the cold stars overhead. In the center of town, an enormous oak tree cast its grandfatherly shadow over the streets below. The Red Road ran through the village like a ribbon strewn out across the rippled landscape. It was a quaint, happy scene that would have inspired any artist worth their paints to set up and attempt to capture it.

"I don't like it," Cyrus said. "There's something wrong."

There really wasn't as far as he could tell, but the feeling nagged at him nonetheless.

A couple of town watchmen milled around the large gray stone pillars that marked the entrance to the south side of the village. From the looks of them, they were far more interested in getting to the end of their shift so they could partake in the pleasures of the sprawling red brick inn nearby than they were in their job. The faint sound of both lute and flute, interspersed with laughter and the clinking of tankards, gently carried up the slope. It was achingly reminiscent of the many nights back in Shrevnetska when he'd strolled by Olaf's tavern.

"You're imagining things. It looks safe enough, and that tavern is probably a hell of a lot warmer than this ridge," Dontarius chided him.

"We're down to a few hard tack biscuits and a couple of apples. We didn't come to Flaxen just to stare at it," B'lantra said. It was one of the few times she'd spoken to either of them all day. She shivered and pulled her cloak more tightly around her as the evening breeze picked up.

"Exactly," Dontarius said. "There's a perfectly good inn down there with warm beds and hot food. Why you would want to spend yet another night camped out in the cold and the wind is beyond me."

There was nothing Cyrus could really say to dispute their claims. "Those honeyed words of yours had better be good if we run into trouble."

"The guards look friendly enough— more bored than anything. Besides, at their worst, they're still better than monsters in the forest."

"Not all monsters have tentacles and fangs, Dontarius."

They led the horses down the hill until they came to the Red Road and then turned northwards towards Flaxen. The lanterns twinkled at them as they drew closer.

Maybe it would be all right. Cyrus could only hope it would be.

He suddenly saw the figure out of the corner of his eye. He stepped in front of B'lantra and unshouldered his musket.

"Damn it! I knew we shouldn't have come here!"

B'lantra gasped.

The figure regarded them from the top of a nearby rise. It was an inquisitor, its black coat plain to see, the emblem of the Illumentry shimmering faintly in the moonlight.

Cyrus' breath froze in his throat.

The figure remained. Unmoving. Still as stone.

Cyrus warily circled. What was the inquisitor waiting for? Were there more of them?

They drew closer. Had the man not seen them? Maybe they could slip past. B'lantra's hand squeezed his in a near death grip.

They waited. The wind whispered hauntingly in the trees. The night seemed to stretch into eternity.

Cyrus suddenly relaxed. A nervous laugh spilled out of his lips before he could contain himself.

"It's a goddamn jackstraw!"

"Are you certain?" B'lantra asked.

"I'll show you."

Cyrus strode forward until he was face to face with the figure. Its blank, painted eyes stared back at him. Its ragged, tattered clothes rippled in the moonlight. The black leather inquisitor's greatcoat, so menacing when he'd first seen it, lay innocently draped over the jackstraw's shoulders, a threat to nothing but his frayed nerves.

B'lantra and Dontarius warily moved up to join him.

"I don't know whether to be thankful or embarrassed. It did gives us all a turn, I'll say that much," the scholar said.

"What's the coat doing here? Surely they can't have left it," B'lantra said.

Cyrus' expression hardened. The nervous tension that had just now begun to ease returned in full force. "It's a warning. They're here, waiting. Flaxen is closed to us."

"Who put it here? Caulter? Someone else?"

Voices burbled out from the distant town. Lanterns shimmered in the dark and began to weave their way towards them.

"We need to leave while we can," Cyrus said.

He took B'lantra's hand and hurriedly pulled her into the sheltering darkness.

As they fled, he turned and looked back at the town. It sat just as serenely as it had before, a shining beacon of warmth and light huddled in the vastness of the night.

He said a silent thank you to the night and then did his best to lose himself in it.

CHAPTER 28

AN UNEXPECTED CARNIVAL

AT FIRST THE JARRING FROM RIDING had helped keep B'lantra awake, but as time had gone on she'd become more and more used to it. Twice now, sitting behind Cyrus, legs dangling uselessly over the horse's flanks, her eyes had closed almost by themselves, and she'd ended up banging her chin on the back of his bony shoulder blades.

He'd been taciturn with her all morning, and that didn't show any signs of changing as the sun climbed ever higher on an otherwise lovely spring day.

She wasn't particularly pleased with him either. The paltry few hours of sleep they'd gotten the night before hadn't done much to help either of their moods. Avoiding the trap set for them in Flaxen had been a relief, but relief hadn't made the ground any softer or the chill in the morning any less biting.

The choice she'd made still preyed on her thoughts. Lyra had once told her that second-guessing would be the death of her, but it was hard not to wonder. The bargain with the Bal-haegast had seemed like a practical and necessary sacrifice to make on the face of it, but it increasingly felt like there was an empty, hollow space inside her.

Matri and Patri were just names now, people that Cyrus had told her should be important to her, yet had no meaning. There was no image, no feeling associated with them. It was almost easier to think of herself as an orphan. She could feel the song within her again, clear and confident. Surely that made it worth what she'd given up.

The silence of the day began to wear on her nerves. She tried humming to herself, but when even that didn't help, she stretched her hand and gave Cyrus' hair a gentle yank.

"Ow!" he complained. "Get off!"

She wasn't about to be put off, and sat up from the horse's back, reached around his shoulders and gave him a kiss on his scruffy cheek. It was a concession, a kind of middle ground that hopefully signaled she didn't want to fight with him anymore, but stopped short of offering an apology he didn't deserve.

"What is it?" he asked.

"Talk to me," she requested.

"About what?"

"I don't know. Tell me about this bridge we have to cross to get to Targus."

"The Maidenskar? It's just a big stone bridge that crosses over the Casimir River."

"With a name like Maidenskar, there's got to be some sort of story to go along with it."

He shrugged. "There was once a beautiful princess. And there was a hunchback that fell in love with her and kept trying to court her. After a while, she realized he really loved her for her, and not for her beauty like so many other men did. She came to love him too. Naturally, the king wouldn't allow her to marry him— not with so many princes competing for her hand."

"So what did she do?"

"She went to a witch that lived near the bridge and had the witch cast a spell on her to make her appear scarred and ugly. No one wanted an ugly princess, so her father wouldn't bother searching for her. She could be with her true love."

B'lantra grimaced. "I don't suppose the story has a happy ending. Let me guess: the hunchback rejected her now that she was scarred and ugly and she threw herself over the bridge in despair."

Cyrus smiled for the first time since the sun had topped the horizon. "No, nothing gloomy like that. They got married and lived happily ever after. Probably had lots of hunchbacked children together. The bridge has been called the Maidenskar ever since."

"I'm glad I'm not a real princess. It's apparently more difficult than people realize," B'lantra said. "So is this Maidenskar the only way to get to Targus?"

"There's some marsh and swamp country you'd have to go through, and a horde of old battlefields. They're supposed to be haunted now, so nobody tries going that way anymore. These days, unless you can fly, you either cross the Maidenskar or you don't get to Targus from the south."

"What if they have the bridge cut off?"

"I doubt they have it closed. Too many merchants and pilgrims coming north for Greenleaf."

"Ugh! I had forgotten Greenleaf was coming up. Lyra used to complain about all the mess and the drunkards, and I can't say I blame her."

"Well, it's supposed to be holy— thanking God for surviving the winter and all. That, and Ansala defeated the Aeore this time of year, I think," Cyrus said. "I don't mind it that much. It makes Shrevnetska less dull for a few days anyway."

"Greenleaf's still an annoying festival." She shifted uncomfortably and reached down to massage a cramp out of her leg. "I wish Targus were closer. I'm getting tired of just sitting like a sack of meal, and this horse isn't helping."

"If it makes you feel better, we'll probably have to get rid of them before we get to the bridge."

"The horses? Not that I'm complaining, but why?"

"They'll attract attention. I should have thought of that before we even dreamed about going into Flaxen. These have that spice merchant's branding on them. If they catch us with them, they'll lock us up for stealing."

"Well, Dontarius stole them actually. Maybe they'll just lock him up and leave us alone," B'lantra said in Trafarga.

"That might help. After a day or two of listening to him talk, they'd probably pay us to take him back. We could use the coin," Cyrus whispered back.

They continued on, shadowing the Red Road like thieves tracking a rich mark. The road was mostly empty except for groups of pilgrims marching steadily northwards in devout procession, their colorful lanterns held aloft.

B'lantra started to brood again. Everything just seemed too big for them somehow. Maybe she was thinking about it the wrong way. The Trafari custom was to take the road one marker at a time. One marker at a time made you pay attention to what was in front of you, and then you were less likely to break a wagon wheel on a rut or run across a clutch of skish or a den of bandits.

It made sense, though it didn't completely lighten her mood either. For now, all they really could do was concentrate on crossing the Maidenskar.

❋ ❋ ❋

Getting across the Maidenskar Bridge wasn't going to be as easy as he'd hoped. From the top of a small rise, Cyrus stared down on her. She was a huge stone monster, solidly built, crossing the chasm in one great span of skillfully hewn granite and mortar. It was as though the rock on both sides of the gap had simply made up its mind to stretch out and grow together, two lovers reaching out to each other high above the rushing waters that crashed below.

To say that the situation at the bridge was an unruly mess would have been an understatement. There were people, horses and wagons backed up on both sides as far as he could see. The flickering lights of a hundred or more campfires dotted the landscape, lighting up the twilight sky with an unholy reddish glow. Soldiers roamed throughout the gaggle of people trying to keep order, even as some enterprising merchants, seeing the chaos and general lack of movement over the bridge, had set up shop. It even had the atmosphere of a carnival in some places.

He looked uneasily out over the crowd and saw that the soldiers had already set up a makeshift gallows as a warning to any potential thieves. No unfortunate soul was hanging from them yet, but that didn't provide him a great deal of comfort.

It wasn't hard to figure out how the whole mess had gotten started. The Illumentry had put out holy writs and had gathered an army to move south and counterattack the Tekni at Ashenwall. Their movement was being choked up at the bridge. Pilgrims and merchants were trying to move north, and couldn't because of the soldiers.

The real heart of the problem lay on the Maidenskar herself. A wagon train, carrying one of the Illumentry's massive artillery pieces had broken down in the middle of the bridge. Behind it, several more wagons carrying oil, powder and what looked like explosives had been stalled. Some of the oil had even spilled out and covered the surface of the bridge.

The situation was a nightmare. If the Tekni were somehow able to mount an attack, the result would be a disaster for the Illumentry.

He had no idea how they were going to get across. They'd tethered the horses a ways back to avoid drawing attention, but now it seemed pointless. There would be no easy, quiet crossing, horses or not.

"We may have to take that other way you were talking about," B'lantra said from beside him.

"You may be right," he agreed. "But if it were that easy, most of these people would have gone around already."

"We should wait. Maybe blend into the crowd and wait for the bridge to clear. That golden-haired woman you're so worried about wouldn't dare try attacking with this many people around," Dontarius said.

"You're the one who said Flaxen was safe. Look how that almost turned out," Cyrus said. "Besides, they didn't set up those gallows just to look at them."

"The gallows are for thieves, and we're not planning on stealing anything. Those soldiers have more on their plate than witch-hunting right now. We're just three more peasants to them," Dontarius replied. "All we have to do is wait, and they'll eventually sort this all out. Then we can cross just like we planned."

"He does have a point, I suppose," B'lantra conceded.

"Of course I do," Dontarius said. "And we might as well go down and be friendly."

Cyrus glowered at the scholar. "That's a terrible idea."

"I don't know," B'lantra said. "It would be nice to look and talk and maybe even haggle a little bit."

He looked at her quizzically. "Since when do you haggle?"

"Just because Bertrand wouldn't hear of it back at that old store in Shrevnetska doesn't mean I didn't try. It's one thing I've never understood about you Northerners. The merchant's price is just the starting point. It's not set in stone, no matter what they say."

And there it was: the desire for the normal life she hoped to have showing through. Maybe it didn't sound so bad. He could only hope he'd be able to give it to her one day.

They descended into the chaotic mass of people, and after a time Cyrus found he didn't mind mingling with the various merchants, pilgrims and simple travelers. It brought him back to his days of jumping up and down in excitement when hearing of a merchant caravan coming to town. He'd stared in awe at the colorful men and women with their outlandish clothes, strange accents and equally strange wares standing in the dusty Shrevnetska streets. It had been a wonderful change from the nearly endless summers punctuated by the droning of the grii-is-griis flies, trees that seemed to shut out the entire world and whatever task Lyra had assigned him.

B'lantra seemed to find as much enjoyment in it as he did, maybe more. Her obvious delight was heartwarming, even if her ruthless bargaining with some of the merchants did unnerve him a little. She'd always been the quiet, calm Trafari girl who mended hurts and had enough patience to put up with him, a far cry from the boisterous traders that had come through the village.

Apparently he'd been wrong about that.

She went from booth to booth, talking to each merchant, sometimes harshly, sometimes sweetly, but each time coming away with the better end of the deal. Their scant silver sparrows and copper crows were converted into food, clothing, medicine and even a new pair of boots that he got whether he wanted them or not. By the time she was done, there were still a few coins jingling together in her purse.

"What do you think?" she asked him, holding up an ornate brass hand mirror with etchings of rose petals and ivy running up its short handle. "That man had the nerve to try and charge me three sparrows for this. I got him down to one and a few crows."

"It's nice," Cyrus said. "No wonder Bertrand didn't want you in his shop."

B'lantra grinned. "It's just a matter of reading people, really. Look what else I found."

She held a chunk of golden wood out for him to inspect.

His eyes widened. "Waidenwood? How did that get here? Do you know how hard that is to find? It must have cost a fortune."

She gleefully shook her head. "No. He was trying to get rid of it. He practically begged me to take it off his hands. I can't wait to start carving it."

"Not more animals, I hope."

"I haven't decided yet."

He couldn't help but smile at her. She was happy, something he'd seen far too little of in the last days.

"Thank you for the boots, though I think there's still some life left in the ones I have," he said.

"No," she said, waving a finger at his dilapidated footwear. "I never want to see those things again. They look like a dog chewed them up and spit them out."

"They're comfortable."

"They're disgusting!"

Cyrus started to laugh, but then tensed when he saw a patrol of soldiers working their way through the crowd toward them. B'lantra was Trafari, and that had probably drawn some unwanted attention— just what he'd been afraid of in the first place.

He turned her quickly away, watching the soldiers carefully out of the corner of his eye. It was the worst thing he could have done, almost as if his reaction sent up a bright, brilliant flare signaling their guilt. The soldiers caught up to them before they could blend back into the crowd.

"What's this?" one of them sneered, seizing his arm. "This one looks like he's been up to something."

"I didn't do anything! Get off me!" Cyrus said, angrily, struggling against their grip. He glanced around to see if Dontarius and his quick words were around the talk them out of their predicament, but the scholar was nowhere to be seen.

Typical.

His efforts to free himself only agitated the soldiers further.

"And what about those new boots and those weapons then? Where'd you steal those from?" the soldier asked.

"We bought them in Shrevnetska. We were coming north and were worried about bandits on the road," B'lantra interjected. "We didn't steal anything."

"Traveling with a damn *straik* gypsy this far north?" the man said. "Now I know you're both thieves. You're both going to the gallows. The judge there can decide your fate."

"I said we didn't steal anything!"

Cyrus slammed his fist into the man's jaw. B'lantra cried out as another soldier grabbed her. He heard the sound of musket being cocked even over the murmurs of the crowd that had gathered to watch the excitement.

"That's enough! Leave the Trafari girl to me. And the boy."

Caulter?!

"This is a simple matter of justice being done. There's no need for your help here," one of the soldiers said. "Now be on your way."

"I think not. You'd best leave these two to me," Caulter said.

"And who are you?"

The look on Caulter's face was hard. There was no hint of emotion, only a promise of quiet, impending menace. Even wearing the worn clothes he'd scavenged from the farmhouse, he still looked every bit the inquisitor. "I'm Inquisitor Captain Caulter. I've tracked these two quite a ways, and I intend to take them into custody."

"With respect, Sir, these are our prisoners," the soldier insisted.

"These two may have some knowledge of a witch I pursue. I've seen a witch burn a man's immortal soul from his body. Is a little diversion from your duties really worth that?"

Cyrus could almost feel the men pale once Caulter's words took root. In short order, they released both Cyrus and B'lantra and hastily retreated.

"What the hell are you doing here?" Cyrus asked, brushing himself off.

"Saving you from your own stupidity it would seem," Caulter replied, coolly.

"I didn't know I was trying to impress you."

"You survived the Bal-haegast then?" B'lantra asked.

"It followed me for a time and then it gave up in search of easier prey. I tried to find you, but we'd gotten too far separated. I took a chance that you survived and continued north. Since this is the only crossing to Targus, it made sense that you would end up here."

"You left the coat, didn't you?" Cyrus demanded.

"They had set a trap for you in Flaxen— another inquisitor, soldiers and even an Illumentry Sister. Fortunately, they were unable to spring it."

"Coming here was a huge leap of faith. You couldn't have known we'd come this way," B'lantra pointed out.

"It was the only choice available short of searching the entire countryside. Obviously you were able to get rid of that strutting fool of a Surani raider and elude the creature that attacked us."

"No. We didn't elude it. We ran right into it and had a long talk. We were even able to make a bargain with it," B'lantra said, straightening up and looking at Caulter with sudden sternness.

His eyes narrowed. "What kind of bargain?"

"One that insures I don't need you quite as much as you seem to think."

"Don't think to change the terms of our agreement. You'll need my good will before all is said and done."

"I'll still help you, Caulter. But it will be on my terms now."

"And just what are those terms? I can easily turn you back over to those soldiers," Caulter warned.

"It's so nice to be reunited with old friends, isn't it? You know, I just heard some of the soldiers talking," Dontarius said, suddenly appearing out of the crowd and gracefully interposing himself between Caulter and B'lantra before their disagreement went any further. "They say they'll have the wagon unloaded and cleared by morning."

"And now he shows up," Cyrus said in annoyance. "We could have used your forked tongue just now."

Dontarius took stock as Cyrus told him what had happened. "I took a moment to talk to the soldiers to find out some things. Pardon me for imagining you two could stay out of trouble for even that short amount of time. We'll have to stay out of sight now, but all we really have to do is wait."

"Then just blend in with everyone else all the way to Targus," Cyrus agreed.

B'lantra shook her head. "I'm starting to think Targus is some mythical place people talk about but can never actually get to. It's like…"

Murmurings and whispers swept through the crowd. The voices of the criers and the barkers died down, replaced by a nervous quiet.

A fog was rolling rapidly in, coiling around people and animals, campfires and merchant's booths alike.

Caulter grimly checked his pistols.

"What is this?" Dontarius asked glancing anxiously around.

Cyrus didn't bother trying to explain to him as he reached into his pocket for the glass flask he'd earned from the Bal-haegast.

The mist overran everything in its path with unnatural speed, swallowing the land up in a thick haze. In mere moments only the campfires and the lanterns were left, each like its own tiny isolated island of light drifting in a sea of fog. The throng of people all around them a few short moments ago vanished, leaving vague outlines nearby and nothingness beyond.

"Get out of here, all of you," Cyrus said. "She's only after me."

"Don't be such a damned fool," B'lantra snapped back, her brown eyes wide as they moved closer to the pitiful shelter of light provided by a nearby torch.

"There's no point in putting all of us at risk."

"We're already at risk. Getting separated right now won't help," Caulter said.

Crackling and popping sounds erupted from the fog. Several small saffron sparks pierced the billowing gray-white veil. Malevolent high-pitched laughter filtered down from above them. A tiny winged creature, warty with bulging purple eyes, whirled by, cackling to itself before flying back up into the mist and disappearing.

"That was a storm fairy. They can't possibly be causing this," B'lantra said.

"They're not. This is her doing," Cyrus replied.

Dontarius' face was pallid. "We need to get out of here. Get the horses. Try to outrun her!"

"She waited till we got rid of them," Cyrus growled. "How are we going to find the horses in this?"

Tendrils of the fog wafted by his cheek, gently touching him, almost like the caress of a soft hand. He clutched the flask closely as he searched around. Only the mist stared back at him. What was he supposed to do with the flask? It had never occurred to him to ask the Bal-haegast how to use it. He'd simply imagined he'd know when the time came.

Should he open it now? Should he wait?

What was supposed to happen?

"I can't take this anymore. I won't," B'lantra declared.

Her song began. It was an angry and frightened melody, the notes shrill and hurried. The song began to build until the mist suddenly lashed out and seized her. Its wispy coils constricted around her throat as they lifted her up in the air and sent her careening violently against the side of a nearby wagon like a doll tossed aside by an overwrought child.

"Bel—"

"No, pretty pretty. We can't have that," the voice said from the fog.

Cyrus stopped, a knot growing in his stomach so intense he could barely move.

Asa of the Mist stood before him, as beautiful and terrible as he remembered her.

CHAPTER 29

FALL OF A MAIDEN

MIST SEEPED AROUND HIS BODY, chilling him with its cold caress. Cyrus' arms and legs felt stiff, almost like they'd suddenly been set in stone.

Caulter leapt forward. His sword came around in a clean sweep that would surely have separated Asa's head from her shoulders had it reached its mark. The mist flared, turning aside the blade and then ripping the weapon out of the inquisitor's hands. He fared no better with his knives and pistols.

Asa turned briefly to Dontarius, and an instant later rogue scholar was swept aside.

Cyrus willed his numbed fingers to obey him and open the glass flask. Asa's baleful gaze now fell back on him. The mist knocked the flask out of his hand. It bounced uselessly away.

"A potion," she sneered. "Is that truly the best you could do?"

Using the mist, she slapped him across the face like a scorned woman striking a wayward lover. It even felt like a slap, the mist merely an extension of her body.

His eyes watered. "Go to hell, you murdering bitch!"

"Now that's not very nice. You won't get very far in life with those manners," Asa purred in response. "Let's see… where were we when we last left off? I believe you were about to volunteer to retrieve the Heart of the Great Machine for me."

"It won't answer to you even if you found it. It's not yours to take!"

"I understand it's quite fond of you though. If you're a good boy and use it as I dictate, then we can avoid any… unpleasantness. We know all about unpleasantness, don't we?"

"I'll die before I help you do anything!"

Asa looked over to where B'lantra had fallen. "If you cooperate, I might not have to hurt your little pretty pretty quite so much."

A feeling of nauseous dread gripped him. His eyes flicked around, but the glass flask was nowhere to be seen. In desperation, he pulled his sword from its sheath and charged at her. The mist buffeted him away before he even got close. He got up and attacked again. The mist effortlessly shoved him away once more. He shook his head to clear it and then finally spotted the glass flask lying nearby. He dived for it, but the mist intervened, gripping him and casually tossing him back.

"Naughty, naughty."

He staggered to his feet, bruised and bloodied. Asa stood relaxed and amused before him, playfully twirling her golden hair around her finger. She was playing with him now, just as she'd done with Bregna, the inquisitor captain.

From behind her came a sharp click, followed by a roar that echoed through the fog. The acrid smell of gunpowder filled the air. Asa momentarily lost interest in him, a surprised squeal erupting from her ruby lips. The smug smile on her face momentarily vanished. She ran her hands over the hole the passing bullet had torn in her chest. No blood flowed. Only water.

"The pretty pretty's not going anywhere with you."

On rickety legs, B'lantra stood near the wagon where she had fallen, holding a musket in her trembling hands. She was still coughing, both from the gun smoke and the aftereffects of the mist's grip around her neck. Her face was flushed, her eyes bloodshot.

Seizing the opportunity, Cyrus stepped forward. Asa's pale hand shot out and grabbed his sword arm. Her grip was surprisingly strong, twisting and squeezing until he was forced to let go of the hilt. She drew back her hand. The mist hammered him to the ground.

"Do you think that's going to stop me, whore of Celaan?" she said to B'lantra. "I can feel her stench on you. You have her inside you, don't you? Hiding there all this time."

The mist struck, knocking B'lantra to her knees.

"You're here for the Heart of the Great Machine, aren't you? But all you have is now is a pretty pretty."

"Celaan's gone. It's just me now. Just B'lantra."

The Trafari witch's song followed. A ring of crimson flame erupted from the ground, lighting the area in a flickering, hellish glow. The mist shriveled away. At B'lantra's urging, the flames began advancing.

Asa let Cyrus go and warily backed away. "You might want to be careful. You wouldn't want a repeat of what happened at that fortress, now would you?"

The flames hesitated.

Asa snapped her fingers. Storm fairies flew into view, flitting frenetically around her head, cackling like some demented choir of angels.

The satisfied smirk returned to the golden-haired woman's face. "The bridge is soaked with oil by now, and those idiot men still haven't gotten that wagon full of powder and explosives off it. One spark— one little spark from my servants— and it all burns. Quite the lovely plan on my part, don't you think? Men, women and children all delightfully incinerated if you don't cooperate."

The song wavered. Uncertainty crept into the melody.

"That's right. The pretty pretty doesn't like the idea of all those poor people dying, does she Susanna?"

Cyrus slowly rose to his feet. How many times had he been knocked down? How many times could he get back up again?

"Cyrus."

He turned his head and saw Dontarius peering out from the shelter of a wagon. The scholar was shaking all over. "I'll see if I can get the bridge cleared off if you give me some time. That'll be one less weapon she has to use."

"What do you expect me to do? I lost the flask," Cyrus asked.

"Figure it out as you go along."

Dontarius disappeared into the fog.

Cyrus stood in helpless frustration. The flask, his only real weapon, was out of reach. Asa wouldn't give him a chance to find it. What did that leave?

Figure it out.

B'lantra's flame had been the only thing he'd seen so far that had given Asa pause. It made sense. The mist was as much a part of her as were her arms and legs. There had been no real difference between the feeling of the mist against him and her actual grip. She was the mist, and mist was essentially water.

He looked over to the torch. Sure enough, he saw the mist circling the flickering flame like a wild animal being kept at bay.

✳ ✳ ✳

The gear called to him, a shining jewel amidst all the chaos around it. Dontarius stopped and stared at it for a moment before quickly picking it up.

Its golden surface seemed to grow warmer in his hand as if it were welcoming him. It was his now. His prize— won through sweat and toil on the battlefield. Sharp eyes, a steady nerve and a sense of the moment. That's what enabled you to survive and prosper in life.

It was meant to be.

He put it in his pocket and continued on, trying to avoid falling over the toppled carts and scattered goods. A group of soldiers loomed out of the mist, nearly impaling him on their bayonets in their panic. He held his hands up, trying to show he wasn't a threat.

"You have to clear the bridge. Get everyone away from it."

They looked at each other anxiously, but made no move to do as he requested. They probably thought him mad, and he really couldn't blame them. How to convince them? He needed the authority to command them. It would have been so much easier if Caulter were here.

"I'm Inquisitor Captain Caulter. The Tekni are planning an attack on the bridge while the oil and powder are still on it. I need you men to follow me and try to get the bridge clear before they get the chance," Dontarius said, straightening up and doing his best to imitate Caulter's sound and bearing.

The soldiers looked to each other and then quickly fell in line. Even Dontarius was a little surprised. Maybe it was his manner or the thought of the Tekni. He didn't question his luck any further.

"Some of you men go back the way I came. There's a Tekni agent— a golden-haired woman— back there. See if you can stop her. The rest of you come with me," Dontarius ordered.

He continued towards the bridge, the remaining soldiers in tow. His ruse gained momentum as he went. He brought more and more men under his command, almost like a proper general. How far could he push his charade? In one sense, it really wasn't all that different from convincing a noble's wife he was someone he wasn't and then enticing her into his bedchamber. Inquisitor was just another guise, after all.

The span of the Maidenskar rose in front of him. He found her completely clear of fog, almost as if the golden haired woman didn't want the mist damaged by the upcoming fireball. From the middle of the massive bridge, he spotted workers and soldiers alike still toiling to unload the broken wagons. They were working by the light of lanterns and torches, even while the sheen of spilled oil glistened on the Maidenskar's stone.

Stupid.

The golden-haired woman might not need the storm fairies after all.

❊ ❊ ❊

Cyrus could see B'lantra wasn't going to be able to last much longer. Her ability to bring so much flame into being all at once was a new thing to her. She probably hadn't even known she could do it until the moment came. The flames ebbed, sputtering now as her energy waned. They needed new substance to feed on.

B'lantra didn't dare unleash them for fear of turning the entire camp into a blaze. It would be like Ashenwall all over again.

The mist continued to shy away from the torch as he picked it up. Asa's attention shifted to him. He advanced on her, holding the torch in front of him.

"You came for me, so either fight me or begone from here."

The mist lunged at him. It seemed to snarl and snap before being singed and retreating. Asa hissed like an angry cat. A long, curved sword appeared in her hand. Pale runes glowed along the length of the blade.

"All right," she said. "If you want to play some more, then Susanna and I will indulge you."

The flock of storm fairies scattered at first, and then reformed into a cackling gaggle above her. The movement of the blade was almost a blur. Asa wasted no time, each strike precise and clean. He could only guess she still wanted him alive. It was hard to be sure as he weaved and dodged around the blade, barely managing to keep it from piercing him.

Asa never seemed to flag. Her movements were flowing and relentless. He fell back. It was like trying to avoid getting wet while dancing in a waterfall. Every once in a while he was able to get close enough to try and strike at her with the torch, but although she seemed to dislike the flame, she never stopped coming at him.

How could anything move so fast?

In mere moments, the torch was sputtering feebly on the ground, well out of his reach. He lay exhausted and battered before her, blood leeching out from a dozen or more shallow cuts. They were painful, but not deep. If she wanted it, he'd have been dead a hundred times over.

B'lantra was no better. The flame around her had burned out, and her voice was little more than a croaked whisper. She clutched onto the splintered railing of a nearby wagon, barely able to keep her feet.

She was beaten.

They both were.

"I've wasted enough time with you," Asa said. "But I'll give you one last present before we go."

She motioned with her sword, and as one, the flock of storm fairies raced off towards the Maidenskar. Their laughter filled his senses before they whisked off into the fog.

She'd won. Ruby lips curled, reveling in his despair just as they had by the stream. All his preparations, all his plans had come to naught. He'd fought so hard to forge a weapon he couldn't even use. Maybe it would have been better if she'd just snapped his neck years ago.

He tried to force himself back to his feet. Asa's sword flashed slicing neatly across his neck. He gasped and fell back, clutching at the shallow wound the tip of her blade had left. If her sword cut had been a little deeper, she'd have flayed his throat open.

"Not so fast. We have a show to watch before we go."

"That's her. That's the one."

A group of soldiers emerged from the mist.

He tried to warn them away, but even as the words tumbled out he could see it was pointless. Asa turned on the soldiers in delight, and there was nothing Cyrus could do other than be momentarily grateful her gaze was elsewhere.

The mist mercilessly devoured them, suffocating and crushing them within its folds. Swords snapped. Muskets splintered. Bones cracked. They tried to flee, but even that didn't satisfy Asa. She let out a long scream of rapture as she slaughtered them, sending their bodies flying. In a grotesque chorus of wet sound, their broken forms smashed and splattered off the merchant's cart and stalls.

Cyrus turned away, unwilling to watch. More wasted lives.

"The flask," Caulter called to him.

Cyrus looked to where the inquisitor pointed and saw the etched glass flask lying on the ground nearby, revealed by one of the dead soldiers as his careening body had knocked it back out into the open. Cyrus' eyes lit up. Maybe the soldier's lives hadn't been for nothing.

He lunged for it, securing it in his grasp before Asa noticed him. The flask was scarred and battered, perilously close to spilling its contents on the damp ground.

He loosened the lid slightly. The mixture hissed and popped in anticipation. There was a sense of horrible rage within, as if a ravening beast had somehow been shoved inside and was eagerly awaiting the opportunity to feast upon its captors.

Asa's cruel ecstasy faded suddenly. The mist lunged at him.

"Run!" Cyrus screamed to B'lantra and Caulter.

He loosened the lid before she could stop him. The liquid inside burst forth. It was unlike any potion he'd ever seen, certainly far different from the elixirs Lyra and B'lantra mixed up or the concoctions merchants sold in their shops.

It was his creation, powered by the will and desire for vengeance that had gone into its making.

The liquid seemed to hover in the air for an instant. Its form shifted, changing into a glowering shadowy figure of rage and of hate. Red tinged eyes bore into Asa. It was a long and angular shade, a reflection of the pain he'd felt staring at Lyra's crumpled body by the stream.

He saw himself in its dark form. It held no mercy or compassion, only a writhing need to seek and to kill. With a piercing shriek, it called out to the heavens and then launched itself at Asa.

It hammered into her, enveloping her in an obsidian embrace before disappearing in a cloud of searing black energy. Asa began choking and retching and then collapsed in a twisted heap. Her mist darkened to the same shadowy hue. Shadows danced gleefully over her prone form, ripping and tearing at her flesh. Chunks of her skin fell away. Blackish water bubbled out underneath.

Vengeance! Vengeance for Lyra. For everything!

Yet he suddenly felt no triumph. Seeing Asa like this wasn't satisfying. It wasn't heroic. It was just empty. It joined a myriad of other images over the last few days that he wished he'd never seen.

Had he been that angry? Had he hated her that much?

He was capable of more than he knew.

He was his mother's son.

He wrenched his gaze away, unable to bear it any more.

Where was B'lantra?

His heartbeat slowed just a fraction when he spotted both her and Caulter heading for the bridge.

So far, it seemed the Maidenskar was intact, but the purple flashes of the storm fairies shimmered ominously on and off nearby. Smoke rose in disjointed columns over the cowering crowd of people.

The fairies were coming for the bridge. Only the distracting wealth of potential targets below them had kept them from reaching it already, but it was simply a matter of time.

"Kill you. Kill you," Asa whispered.

Cyrus jerked his head back around.

She rolled over and started to rise: a ravaged, nightmare thing of blistered skin and bone. Her golden hair had been eaten away. The perpetual smirk had vanished. The ruby lips were a faint memory.

His weapon had taken the mists from her. It hadn't killed her.

He quickly snatched up a sword from one of the fallen soldiers and held it before him. Asa paused and cocked her head at the sound of his footsteps. He took a few uncertain paces towards the Maidenskar. She bent down to sniff the ground where he'd just been.

"You can't get away," she croaked. She felt around until her fingers found the hilt of her sword. "I don't need to see you to catch you."

There wasn't time to finish with her. He didn't want to. He wanted to run, to never see her again.

He turned and fled. A moment later she began to follow.

❋ ❋ ❋

The first round of musket shots was nearly deafening. The foul smoke that hovered around them made her eyes water. B'lantra knelt beside the stone guardrail of the bridge, trying to get her breath back and find her voice.

They'd made it this far, but the battle was far from over. The storm fairies came ever onwards. The soldiers on the bridge held their ground. In the darkness, many of the shots failed to hit their targets.

Where was Cyrus? Damn him, where was he?

Caulter took hold of her arm. "We can't stay here. We'll all die if those fairies reach the bridge."

"I'm not leaving," she snapped, her stare withering. She struggled against him. "Cyrus is still coming."

"These men can't hold this bridge," Caulter said, his voice an icy whisper. "This isn't some tale about a noble last stand. Those belong in story books, and you're too old for that foolishness."

B'lantra's jaw set in tight determination. She called the song to her again, withered and weary thing that it was. She stretched out with the melody, feeling the inner fire of the fairies, tiny candles in the night. The lullaby she began was as gentle and soothing as she could make it, despite her apprehension. It was as sweet sounding as she could conceive it, despite her cracked voice.

The fighting stopped. The men paused, and the storm fairies hovered, held in seeming rapture.

"We have to leave! Now— while we still have the chance!" Dontarius said.

Concentrating on the song, she was barely aware of Dontarius and Caulter pulling her towards the far side of the bridge.

Where was Cyrus?

❋ ❋ ❋

Cyrus reached the Maidenskar and started across. Behind him, Asa burst through the crowd of people. She stopped, searching around with matted, puss-covered eyes. Finally she sniffed the ground, bringing a handful of dirt close to her ruined face, snuffling to herself at it poured through her fingers.

She howled and rushed after him.

As he reached the apex of the Maidenskar, Cyrus heard the tones of B'lantra's song still in the air. Through the smoke that clung to the area, the storm fairies drifted like they were in a pleasant dream.

"Bel! Bel, where are you?"

"I'm here. I'm here."

From the far end of the bridge she motioned emphatically to him.

Asa leapt over the wagon, snarling in triumph and pounced down upon him.

"Found you!"

He stumbled backwards, barely avoiding her. Her sword tore through one of the wagons, nearly taking his head off in the process. She slipped in the oil, allowing him time to scramble away. He turned and sprinted with all his remaining strength for the far side of the bridge.

❄ ❄ ❄

Even from the stout stone pillars that marked the far end of the Maidenskar, B'lantra could see the toll Cyrus' potion had taken. Asa's cold beauty had been shattered, leaving only a bestial shell. The golden-haired woman stood in the center of the bridge still, turning round and round.

The mixed odors of the lingering smoke, the oil and the bodies of the soldiers seemed to confound Asa's senses for a moment. Then she regained her bearings and began to move deliberately forward, following Cyrus' scent like a bloodhound.

He was coming.

Cyrus was getting closer and closer, but the span of the Maidenskar went on forever like some endless nightmare of stone.

The cracked melody wavered. The storm fairies began to stir back to life.

B'lantra tried to adjust her song to pull them back into their stupor, but the power had faded too much.

She paused. A detached part of her mind studied Asa's position on the bridge, trying to gauge how far away Cyrus had managed to run.

Finally, B'lantra couldn't wait any longer.

Fire. Fire had first taught her she was different from the other children. It had been her first taste of witchcraft, given form then by her voice. With the last bit of her voice now, she called upon it again, willing the flame to form on the oil-soaked surface of the Maidenskar.

It flickered to life, ravenously seizing upon the abundance of ready food, gaining in strength with no one there to stop it. Asa stopped, unsure which way to run. The flames greedily encircled her.

"Burn. Burn for Lyra," B'lantra softly whispered.

An instant later the flames touched on the gunpowder. The world shook. A fireball erupted from the center of the bridge, racing out into the darkness beyond. A wave of force knocked B'lantra back, but not before she caught a glimpse of great gouts of fire rising angrily into the sky like harbingers to the birth of some god.

If Asa's screams came at all, they were lost in the massive roar. The center of the bridge splintered, twisted and then plummeted into the waters below.

The Maidenskar began to die.

It should have stopped there, but it didn't. She'd underestimated the ferocity of the flames and the strength of the blast. The rumbling and cracking went on and on. The stone pillar she'd been standing near swayed wildly and then collapsed in a heap of rubble and dust before her.

She yelled out for Cyrus, but her voice was devoured in the din of shattering stone and the hiss of the waters below as they accepted the bridge's offering of burning rock.

❉ ❉ ❉

Cyrus was barely able to keep his footing. Cracks were forming in the stone beneath him. The surface torqued amidst the bridge's death throes. An entire section gave way. He fell back, narrowly avoiding joining the chunks of granite and masonry plummeting down into the river. The remainder of the bridge threatened to topple. He ran. The drumfire of fragmenting rock seemed to go on forever.

He had to be close to the end of the bridge. Stone crashed down around him. Flame chased him.

He leapt blindly.

The slippery rock wall of the far side of the chasm loomed out at him. He tried to grab onto it as he slammed against it. He started to slide down into oblivion before he seized upon a tree root growing out of the rocks and managed to arrest his fall. Clinging fervently onto it, he tried to find a foothold to steady himself.

His grip started to slip.

The Maidenskar continued its collapse, shaking the rock wall he clung to. Below him the rushing water circled like a hungry predator waiting for him to fall into its jaws.

"Got you."

An arm reached down and grabbed at him just before the tree root slipped from his grasp. He cried out.

Asa. It had to be Asa. She'd survived!

Dontarius' head popped over the edge of the cliff and looked down on him.

"He's here. Help me pull him up!" the scholar called out.

Caulter appeared a moment later and with their help, Cyrus was able to scramble back up onto the top of the cliff. He stood there, trying to stay upright, willing every muscle in his body not to give out.

"Cyrus!" B'lantra cried, running out of the dust and smoke to wrap her arms around him.

He held her tight to him, tears coming despite his best efforts.

"We got her. I hope to all the heavens we killed her this time," he finally said.

"I don't care about her anymore. You're here and we're safe and I don't give a damn about anything else right now," B'lantra replied, her head nestled against his chest.

CHAPTER 30

THE FOUNTAIN

THE GOLDEN GEAR WAS GONE. He'd frantically searched for it, throwing a lifetime's worth of epithets to the sky in the process. The joy he'd felt barely a day ago had been dashed against the rocks and battered into oblivion. His rage had cooled, and now he sat morosely on a damp log, trying to figure out what they were going to do next.

The gear had been lost during the battle at the Maidenskar. With that knowledge came the certainty that there was no getting it back. Even assuming it hadn't been destroyed in the fireball, someone had surely picked it up. It was probably adorning some merchant's booth even now.

His fingers dug into the rotted skin of the log. There wasn't even any way to go back and look. The destruction of the bridge would bring inquisitors swarming into the area like buzzards greedily flocking to a bloated corpse.

"You know, you're still Aeliraneth's son. That's got to count for something," B'lantra said, sitting down beside him.

"It's a cruel twist of fate to have to be grateful for something like that."

"Not really. You might not have thought much of the life you had there, but it was yours. It's your house we're going to. You have just as much right to it as Aeliraneth did."

"I doubt she ever saw it that way."

"She's gone, so it doesn't matter what she thinks anymore. Only what you do."

He shook his head. That there would be any advantage in being Aeliraneth's son was a strange thought. It was a burden, a

358

curse. He was going home, but not really. The estate had always been home, but it had never been his.

Still, he was his mother's son. The image of Asa writhing on the ground in agony filtered back to him. It had occupied his thoughts, despite all his efforts, reminding him of the monster he was capable of being.

Maybe, just maybe, there was some good to be found in it. Would the barrier Mother had erected around the house part because he demanded it to, because he shared the blood of the woman who had created it?

He sighed. At this point, it really was their only hope.

"It will be whatever it is no matter what you want it to be," B'lantra said.

His brow wrinkled. "I think you lost me somewhere during the 'be' and the 'is' part."

She gave him an indignant look. "See if I try to cheer you up again. You know what I meant."

"I'm guessing it meant that I shouldn't worry about it, because there's not a damn thing I can do about it anyway. And you're probably right."

"Of course I'm right. We'd fight a lot less if you just admitted that sooner."

"That doesn't mean I'm going to do it. It's hard not to think about tomorrow. It keeps coming up in my head whether I want it to or not. Honestly, I don't know what we'll find."

"Since when has not knowing something ever stopped you?" she asked, arching her eyebrow. "You leap and half the time it's to somewhere angels would think twice before following. In fact, they don't follow. They just send me in to scrape up the pieces. So quit brooding. If there's any brooding to be done around here, I'll do it."

"Nice of you to look out for me that way," he said.

She gave him a kiss. "Always. We'll leap together tomorrow."

❋ ❋ ❋

A few blackened stone columns and walls still stood like decaying bones amidst the piles of rubble marking the carcass of the house of Aeliraneth. The ground around lay naked, its clothing of green grass and trees still absent, though the fires had long since burned out.

Statues of angels and other figures still clung to life in the forsaken expanse. Seemingly angered by its rejection near the house, the overgrowth had taken out its fury on them, and most of the forlorn statuary lay toppled and broken. The survivors almost wept; their faces and wings slowly crumbling away under the combined siege of both time and nature.

Farther away from the house, the once lush pine trees that had marked the border of Aeliraneth's sanctuary now stood languid watch over the landscape, whispering to each other in cowered, hushed voices as a chill breeze blew through.

The air was thick and hazy, pregnant with the feel of things long past, of memory and of reflection. The sun shone meekly down, its yellowish light giving off far less warmth than it should.

Standing amidst the pines, Cyrus shivered, dolefully taking measure of the place he'd once called home. There was a sense of loss everywhere. In everything. He looked from the desolate stone to the ravaged angels to the piles of seared rubble and couldn't help but remember what had once been.

Here, beside an overturned statue, he'd played soldier against imaginary foes. There, near the scorched bodies of splintered timbers, Mother had drilled lessons into him until he was on the verge of tears.

He almost expected Lyra to come up and greet him as she'd done so many times.

"I almost didn't believe you when you said nobody came here anymore. I can see why now," he said to Dontarius.

"The Illumentry spread the stories that the fire was Talast's retribution on Aeliraneth for her wickedness. It served their purposes well enough, I suppose. And not everyone that comes here returns, so that tends not to encourage many visitors," the scholar replied.

"I wonder if the ward is still in place."

"You're her son. I don't imagine the ward, if it exists, would be any hindrance to you."

There was a slyness in the scholar's tone that struck Cyrus as somehow wrong.

"Let's look around and see if we can find the fountain. I don't want to linger here," B'lantra said.

She stared out onto the grounds, her voice nearly as hushed as the pines. Her face and body were pensive, though she did her best to conjure up some semblance of an encouraging smile for him. She didn't like it here. He didn't either. Any comfort he might have taken from familiar things had departed as soon as they'd topped the hill.

Cautiously, they made their way from the trees and moved closer to the house.

He saw no sign of the hedge maze that had once sheltered the fountain. Had it been burned away? An empty, nervous gulf began to form inside him. If so, then where was the fountain? There should be some trace. It was a thing of metal, not of wood. There should be ruins at least. He surveyed the eastern part of the grounds where he knew it to be, but saw nothing other than choked weeds and twisted shrub trees.

The wind picked up, still whispering to itself even though they were farther from the pines. It was almost speaking to him, carrying cries and laments in its wake, hints of turmoil and longing that pricked at him, but frustratingly stayed just at the edge of hearing. His brow furrowed. There was no source, no reason for the wind to give voice.

And then it grew louder and more distinct, and he couldn't deny it any longer. He caught tone and purpose, though he still couldn't make out the words. He froze. The very air felt like it was trying to grapple him.

Mother!

The others stared at him expectantly. Caulter's hand drifted down to his sword and the set of silver pistols he'd recovered. B'lantra instinctively stepped closer as if to protect him. He ignored them both, and turned in the direction he'd heard the voice come from.

The shadow that flitted by the broken angel was vague, a feeling more than anything. It was a tall figure, graceful and elegant, a long dress flowing behind. The phantom held no color, but he thought he could detect the leaf pattern on the brocade layers of the dress. Mother had worn it on that last day as night had settled over the house.

"What is it?" B'lantra asked worriedly, putting her hand on his arm.

He madly dashed towards the ruined angel.

The apparition was gone long before he could reach it. He came to a stop beside the stone angel, his face and arms scratched from forcing his way through the brambles. He really didn't notice, still awash in the excitement and apprehension the shadowy figure had stirred within him. The voice still played on the wind.

Mother. Here somehow?

He looked around the area beside the angel, expecting to find some evidence that what he'd seen was real. There was only the uneven weed-streaked earth and the angel. Vines grew up over the statue, their roots digging into its stone skin, giving it a diseased appearance. Through dilapidated, crumbling eyes, it looked morosely out to the ruins of the house.

Maybe it was trying to lead him somewhere.

He walked a few paces towards the house... and abruptly found himself right back beside the angel. It was as if he'd never moved at all. Puzzled, he started forward once more. Again he made no progress. The angel looked at him sadly, but could offer no comfort or solution.

This was the ward Asa had spoken of. And it seemed that it

was just as much an obstacle for him as for anyone else.

"What are you playing at?" he demanded. "It's me. Or have you forgotten? This is my house just as much as is yours. Now let me pass!"

Again and again he tried to move forward, but each time his advanced was checked. Mother's voice continued to whisper on the wind, crooning words he still couldn't make out.

"Have you gone mad?" Caulter admonished him when he finally caught up.

"Who are you yelling at?" B'lantra asked him.

"Mother. Who else would I be yelling at? She's here. Watching. Probably laughing at us this very minute thinking how smart she is!"

"Your mother is dead."

"No, she's not," he insisted.

He kicked at a loose stone in disgust, closed his eyes for a moment and then forced himself to calm down long enough to explain. They gave him a quizzical look until they too tried to pass through the ward and found themselves blocked.

"There's got to be some way in," B'lantra said.

Cyrus walked back towards the angel, muttering curses under his breath, pondering what to do. Maybe he was missing something. Mother had never been one for simply giving out answers. She'd enjoyed her intrigues and her aura of mystery, even with her own son.

He almost stepped on the burned book lying innocently in the weeds before he noticed and stopped to pick it up.

Fire had ravaged it. The thick leather cover that had bound it together was now badly seared, bubbling up in places, flaking off in others. The lantern and the long, seven-pointed star of the Illumentry were faintly visible, stamped in faded gold on the front cover. No matter how gentle he tried to be, the vellum pages nearly crumbled in his hands. The ink had run together or been boiled away to the point it was mostly illegible. In places he could still make out a few traces of the Iriethan characters.

Why had she left this here? It was Mother's writing without a doubt, but the book was clearly of Illumentry make. Mother's relationship with the Illumentry had been cold at best. They'd been mortal enemies behind the veil of polite ramblings they'd made at each other. The Illumentry would have cheerfully burned her if they could have, and Mother would have been more than happy to wipe them from existence in turn.

Why would Mother pen a book with an Illumentry stamp?

The last page was intact, though blank. He glared at it, willing words to come to the page, willing a simple clear resolution to be given to him. None seemed to be forthcoming. He could almost imagine Mother walking behind him, just as she'd done years ago. There had been many silent afternoons like that: a problem to be solved, and the only sounds around him the ticking of the clock and the soft scrape of Mother's shoes on the carpet as she impatiently paced, waiting for an answer so obvious to her to finally come to him.

The book had been put there for a reason. The last page was intact for a reason. And Mother had clearly intended for him to find it, meaning there was something on the page that only he was supposed to see.

The voice on the wind seemed to take on a harsher tone, as if growing restless.

Mother was a witch. How would a witch hide something on a blank page?

"Mirrormelle. That's how she would do it," he whispered to himself, suddenly understanding. "Bel, get me that hand mirror you bought at the Maidenskar."

"It's cracked it at least two places. Why would you want it?" she asked, curiously, before digging the mirror out of her pack and handing it to him.

"Mirrormelle," he repeated. "Mirror letters. Witch script some call it. They're letters that you can only see when looking at them through a mirror. There's all kinds. Rain script, moon script. The Iriethan witches used them to leave messages for each other in the days before the Illumentry."

He held the mirror in front of the blank page and then grinned when he saw the golden, wavering Iriethan characters shimmer into view upon the faded surface of the vellum page. He'd beaten Mother at her own game, figured out her little puzzle.

He had no desire to see any more Iriethan characters. The lessons by Mother's enchanted fountain had been endless. Her red lacquered fan had stood ever vigilant, ready to come slamming down on him if he made the slightest mistake interpreting them.

They were magical, she said.

They were power, she said.

He probably would've ended up chained to the fountain with only the lesson book for company if not for Lyra's intervention.

Cyrus closed his eyes for a moment, willing himself to relax. Slowly he forced the characters to form order and meaning for him. His grin vanished as he finished reading. To his dismay, they began to fade away, as if having been read, their purpose had now been served, and they were free to decay away like everything else around them.

"There isn't anything useful, is there?" B'lantra asked, seeing the expression on his face.

He let out a slow breath through clenched teeth and allowed the book fall out of his hand. "It's worse than nothing. There's a mention of spirit dancers and water. And there's an account of her search for the Heart of the Great Machine— a few scraps of it anyway. She contacted a welkin spirit to help her. It told her:

'North where the snow falls and the silence dwells.
A mirror that hangs above still waters.
Crystalline.
The star will light the way.'

It just ends after that!"

"That's at least something, isn't it?" B'lantra said. "And we might find some more clues if we look around the grounds."

He already knew they wouldn't.

The wind had gone silent. The voice that had carried on it had disappeared into the emptiness from whence it came. Mother had departed, and he was on his own once more. She'd abandoned him years ago, foisting him off on Lyra the night of the fire, and now she'd done it again. Mother wasn't going to reveal anything more to them.

Not when he'd lost the golden gear.

"There's nothing here. Nothing! And that's exactly what we've ended up with," he ranted, all his pent up fears crystallizing. "There's nothing that's going to help because she doesn't care about us. She never did, just her damn obsession. We're the arms and legs she doesn't have any more because she died."

B'lantra's face grew stern. "You don't know any of that. You're just guessing what she thought and felt. You don't even know if she's still here."

"She's here. Her spirit… some part of her is," he insisted. "I know what I saw and what I heard. Dammit! The cursed witch didn't even have the decency to die properly."

"This isn't helping!"

His eyes lit up. "She's playing with us. The answers we need are here, but she won't let us have them. Damn her!"

He turned away in fury. After a few moments, his anger faded and a disparate emptiness set in. It was pointless. Everything was. The angel watched him, the despair in its stone eyes a mirror to the despair he felt inside. He walked over to it and laid his head down on the cold surface of its pedestal, trying to think.

There had to be an answer.

There had to be.

What was it?

※ ※ ※

The gear grew warmer, nearly burning his fingertips when he drew it forth. Dontarius stared over at the elaborate hedge maze that had seemingly sprung up out of nowhere on the far side of the grounds. Where it had come from was a mystery, but investigating it seemed far more productive than watching Cyrus waste his energy on a ward that showed no signs of fading away. Even dead, it seemed some legacy of Aeliraneth remained.

He'd assumed the ward would simply part for her son, that Cyrus would be the one person who wouldn't need a special talisman to pass through. It appeared that idea had been wrong.

What truly puzzled him was that none of the others could see the hedge maze. Maybe they weren't meant to. The gear was his. He was the one meant to go on, to see and to know.

He'd studied Aeliraneth's work ever since he was a boy. He'd been excited beyond belief to actually meet her, even if only briefly. Cyrus had been more fortunate than he knew. To spend an entire childhood surrounded by all that secret learning. To be raised and educated by a mind the quality of Aeliraneth's. Cyrus was blind to the special opportunity he'd been given. That much was clear from his ravings.

The hedge maze was a test to see if Dontarius was smart enough and skilled enough to find his way through it. It made sense that a woman like Aeliraneth wouldn't simply give away her secrets to fools. It would take someone with both intelligence and persistence to make it through the maze, and that was exactly the kind of person who would properly appreciate Aeliraneth's work. Viewed that way, the hedge maze made perfect sense.

He moved towards the hedges. Soon the thick wall of foliage obscured Cyrus and the others from sight. As if responding to his inner desires, a section of the hedgerow parted for him. He stepped through, trying to take into account every little detail he could. It was a maze, and that was how the game was played. The would-be player simply memorized the location of landmarks to keep himself from getting lost and then preceded meticulously onwards. At first it would be trial and error, but a pattern would soon emerge.

He walked confidently along, scribbling notes in his journal to document each landmark. The hedgerows towered over him in all directions, becoming his entire world. Black stone obelisks had been set up along the way, almost like trail markers. He didn't recognize the Iriethan character etched into each one, leaving him to his own devices. He'd have to pry more insight into reading them from Cyrus. Aeliraneth's son could be useful for that at least.

As he moved deeper into the maze, he could hear birds chirping and the sounds of animals rustling. He saw no signs of them though. A bee buzzed near his ear, but when he turned to swat it away, he found nothing but the heavy air.

Farther along, there were elaborate lions carved from the hedge plants. Sentinels maybe? Each beast was perfectly manicured and sculpted as if by the hands of an expert gardener.

It was hard to imagine a gardener or anyone else coming here. It wasn't that sort of place. It was a quiet place, a hidden place. His were probably the first eyes to see it in years.

The sad state of decay that seemed to afflict everything else in Aeliraneth's domain finally started to manifest. Dead plants began to mar the otherwise solid blanket of green. Thorns grew up into the hedgerow walls, their points sharp and wickedly curved. The sculpted lions started showing signs of neglect. Their faces and bodies became distended and wild looking. In a few places the foliage on their forms had withered away altogether, leaving the naked branches underneath showing through like bones. He suddenly noticed all the animal and bird sounds had died away, leaving an uncomfortable silence in their wake.

Should he even be here at all? It was the first time the thought had occurred to him. He could hear his own breathing and the beating of his heart, and both of them almost felt like an unwelcome invasion of the somber stillness. What should have been a lively walk amidst the spring verdure now felt like he was treading through a tomb.

The music that reached his ears when he rounded the next

corner did nothing to soothe his nerves. It was off key somehow, but not the way it would be in the hands of incompetent musicians. It was a more calculated wrongness, as if the music were being played by experts who understood precisely what they were doing, but perceived the piece and the world around through a warped lens.

Ahead of him lay a wrought iron gate, flanked on both sides by another set of lions. The gate was closed, rust showing along its twisted frame. The music played on, coming from somewhere beyond it.

He gathered his nerve, walked up and pulled the gate open. Beyond it, he found himself in a large courtyard, surrounded on all sides by the looming walls of the hedge maze.

The massive brass and stone fountain in the center drew his attention almost immediately. A horde of small golden figures moved and twisted around the elaborate structure in a complex, rhythmic progression of form and movement. The water poured forth, splashing as it tumbled down from basin to basin, adding its own character to the music that filtered through the air.

He studied the figures as they deftly danced around each other, fought each other with detailed brass weapons, or merely went about their daily lives like they were real people.

And for while he saw them without really seeing them, maybe as he had inwardly wished to see them— until he finally spotted the decay that had set in. He blinked and looked again.

An illusion?

Through new eyes, he saw now that the fountain was still, the dancers inert. Many of the figures were dented and tarnished, their bodies bent at awkward angles. Ivy grew over the fountain, its strangling tendrils reaching out like some voracious predator. The water flowed sluggishly through the basins, dribbling down from one algae choked platform to the next.

A longing grew within him to see it working once more. The gear burned in his hand. At the base of the fountain he spotted the elaborate gear box that had once given it power and life. Its once ornate front cover, with its leaf filigree and gently curving etched trim had been torn open, exposing the workings inside. Other cogs and gears, much like the one he held in his hand, sat impotent and muted. There was a hollow space in the mechanism, like an open wound. The fountain seemed to cry out to him to mend its hurts and make it whole again. The gear pulsed in anticipation of being reunited with its fellows.

He should have felt trepidation, but he didn't. He should have approached the situation calmly and rationally like a scholar, but he didn't. He simply stretched out his hand and slipped the gear back into place.

CHAPTER 31

THE SCION RETURNS

CYRUS SAT CROSS-LEGGED, his eyes downcast. The ground didn't change no matter how intensely he stared at it, though he really wasn't seeing it. In some part of his mind he was sure he'd counted a dozen times over the exact number of pebbles in the patch of ground before him, and studied in exact detail the thorny swirl of the tangled brambles growing by his feet. But both seemed distant at the moment.

There was blade grass growing here, its gently hued purple and blue spikes a contrast to the rocky gray earth they grew in. It was a tough plant, supple and durable like leather— almost beautiful in its own way. Wise peasants sometimes used it to craft makeshift armor for themselves when they were conscripted by the nobility.

He took his knife and idly cut several of the leaves away. They were easy to weave and gave his hands something to do while his mind roamed lost in a desert of his own making. Maybe weaving was all he was really cut out for.

The blade grass persisted even in the harsh conditions in which it found itself. Why couldn't he?

He was a failure. He ran the thought through his mind over and over as he tried to find some way to make himself believe it wasn't true. They'd come through so much, suffered so much. It couldn't have all been meaningless.

The ward remained, and the fountain they'd come all this way for was nowhere to be found. He'd never wanted to see either the house or the fountain again, but now that he needed them, he was barred like some unwanted beggar.

He was Aeliraneth's son. He'd fought and struggled because of who and what he was. Both Asa and the inquisitors had sought him because of it. The Bal-haegast had paid a debt to him because of it. Supposedly, he was special— the one person who could prevent the Wynding from failing.

But when it came down to it, he wasn't special at all. "Born to the wrong womb at the wrong time," as the Bal-haegast had said.

It took him a moment to realize B'lantra had pushed through the brambles to come and sit beside him. She put her arm around his back and continued to sit there quietly for a moment, before reaching over and giving him a kiss on the cheek.

She set the crumbling book in his lap. "Maybe it's useless, maybe it's not. But it's your mother's. She put it there for you to find, and I don't think you should just idly throw it away."

He stared dejectedly at the book for a moment and then finally looked up at her. "Sorry I yelled at you earlier. It's not your fault."

"Well, that's a start. You were acting the fool not too long ago."

"I know."

"Shouting at the air was pretty pointless too."

"I know that too."

"Well, if you can figure out that much, then maybe there's hope for you."

"Not enough hope to get into my own damn house it seems."

"You tried. You'll keep trying. I can't ask much more than that right now," she said, and laid her head on his shoulder. "We'll find a way."

"I don't know what we're going to do," he replied, turning to her.

"We didn't know what we were going to do to at Ashenwall. But we escaped. We didn't know how we were going to survive Asa. But we're here, and she's not. We'll find a way," she insisted.

"You seem awfully determined to cheer me up."

"You did it for me often enough when we were growing up."

"I don't know about cheering you up. I usually wound up

getting hurt trying some stupid stunt to impress you and take your mind off of it."

B'lantra smiled. "It worked, didn't it? It was hard to be upset and sad when I was busy trying to put you back together."

"Fine, you win," he said. "I still don't know what we're going to do though. Seems like in the stories they always knew what they were doing."

"I doubt they knew any more than we do. They just had good storytellers along with them to make it look like they did."

"Then we're doomed. The closest thing we have is Dontarius."

B'lantra looked around. "Speaking of that lecher... I wonder where he's gone off to. Caulter went back to the pines to wait for us, but I haven't seen Dontarius anywhere."

"That's it!" Cyrus exclaimed, becoming suddenly animated, his despair melting away.

"That's what?" B'lantra asked. "Dontarius?"

"Not just him," he said, shaking his head. "Dontarius... Illumentry. The Arentine. Don't you see?"

"No," B'lantra said, flatly.

Cyrus tried to collect his thoughts. "Mother wrote the book, but it has an Illumentry stamp on it. That means they worked together, no matter how much they hated each other. She must have told them about the Heart, recruited them as allies. They were there on that last night before the fire started... before everything burned."

"The Illumentry came to visit your Mother?"

"Yes, important people too. Scholars and matrons and the like, experts on the Aeore lands in Asylum.

"How does that help us?"

"Where there's one book, there's more. I doubt this was the only copy. The knowledge was valuable. And the Illumentry locks valuable things away."

"So they sealed the other copies away? In this Arentine place?"

"Under it. It's a huge building in Targus. You can see it even over the wall. There are archives down there. If we can't get into Mother's house, maybe we can get in the Arentine and find an undamaged copy."

"It has to be guarded. They're not going to just let us in to look around."

He grinned at her. "We'll find a way."

✳ ✳ ✳

The fountain sprang to life. The brass figures around the fountain jerked into motion. Gears turned. Cogs spun. From the depths of the fountain came a screeching, piercing wail.

Dontarius stood rigid, frozen in fear as the noise reverberated throughout the courtyard. All the tolling of all the bells of all the towers in Hell couldn't have sounded any worse.

It had been foolish to come here. In the back of his mind, the voices of caution and of reason, voices that he'd callously cast aside, berated him in shrill harpy tones. He'd had such a high regard for Aeliraneth the scholar, that he'd forgotten she was also a witch. She'd seen the world in ways he couldn't imagine. All witches did.

Had he learned nothing from his encounters with the golden-haired woman and the Bal-haegast?

He felt a sudden presence in the courtyard. A hand fell on his shoulder, gently caressing him, soft but palpable. It stung, as if little needles of electricity were jabbing into him. He cried out and whirled around. A shadowy figure— a tall woman in a long dress— stood nearby staring malevolently at him. She was gone almost instantly, but the feeling lingered all through the courtyard of baleful eyes watching him. The look told him all he needed to know. It was the look a teacher might give a particularly pathetic student. But it was more than that.

There was a disdain contained in the brief stare that would have torn the heart from his chest and ground it underfoot if it could have. He would have gladly crawled into the deepest, darkest hole he could find if it would have averted it.

What had he called forth?

The ground rumbled beneath his feet, then splintered and cracked. From the depths crawled a hundred or more metallic spiders. Spiders were the only way Dontarius could think to comprehend them. It was hard to tell whether they had eight legs or many as they swarmed out of the ground. Each was larger than his hand. Their bodies were the flat dead gray of a winter's morning, interspersed with bands of swirling colors. Red, purple, green— they shifted too quickly for him to determine.

He cringed as several of them skittered towards him. Their chittering hum began to overwhelm the fountain's plaintive wail. The smell of gear oil and of blood assaulted his senses. Beady, mechanical eyes locked in on him.

His legs refused to work. The fearful pleas from his brain became muddled in his terror. His feet remained rigidly planted in the fractured earth.

Perhaps they would dissect him, study him, the way a young physician might take apart a cadaver. The flitting talons at the ends of their segmented legs looked well suited for such things.

It was the damned gear. It was all the gear's fault. He should've let the cursed thing lay!

The spiders suddenly turned away from him, as if he weren't worth bothering with. Almost as one, they fell upon the fountain. In an instant their bodies covered it. Their claws flashed, slicing through the fountain's brass body as if it were little more than paper.

❋ ❋ ❋

The distant wail ripped through the desolate expanse like a hurricane, tearing away the silence of the afternoon. Cyrus flinched at the sheer force of the sound.

The hedges sprang into being before his eyes, mocking him, as if they'd always been there, but only now were debasing themselves enough to be seen. The wail continued, echoing through the grounds. There was a desperate tone to it, a pleading, clarion call for succor. Somewhere, amidst the anguish and fear mixed into the sound, he could detect a hint of the music that had enraptured him as a child.

The fountain.

And it was dying.

He leapt to his feet and dashed towards the hedges, heedless of the brambles that lashed and grappled at him.

✳ ✳ ✳

Dontarius let out a scream and then found what little courage he had left. It was enough to force his legs to finally carry out the urgent orders his brain had been sending them. He turned and fled, racing out of the courtyard and back into the maze, frantically turning this way and that, disregarding the careful strategy he'd used to get in.

The sculpted lions seemed on the verge of life. The crackling of their wooden skeletons came soon after, along with the rustling of their leafy coats. The sculpted creatures stirred from their slumber. Even as Dontarius ran, they sprang from their pedestals, mouthing a silent roar to the hazy sky before giving chase.

He could hear them closing in from behind. No matter how fast he ran, they relentlessly grew nearer. Leaves, like the caress of hot breath, brushed across the back of his neck. Thorns, like claws, tore at the back of his jacket. Brambles, like grasping paws, swooped in to take his legs out from under him.

He fell, landing hard on the spongy grass that grew between the hedgerows. The lions pounced.

✳ ✳ ✳

"Stop it. Let off him!"

Cyrus did his best to make his voice sound strong.

The lions, their jaws poised just over the scholar's face, their thorny teeth lightly brushing against his flushed skin, turned. A scowl formed across their bushy faces. They advanced towards him without any sign of fear or hesitation.

Cyrus couldn't claim to feel the same. His throat was dry.

The thrum of his pulse was nearly deafening. The look in the lions' hollow eyes was intense and deadly. They were predator. He was prey. They were guardians. He was an intruder waiting to be devoured.

Every instinct he had told him to draw his sword, to fight desperately for his life. He stifled the urge.

From behind him, B'lantra's song began. He recognized it—an angry song, a burning song.

"No, don't!"

He forced his heart to calm and his hands to steady.

They were his. The lions were his. He was Aeliraneth's son, and the lions were his.

He was Aeliraneth's son. God help him.

This was his home, though he was no noble prince returning to claim his heritage. He was little more than a beaten, beggarly urchin crawling back to the nest. It didn't matter. Whatever his state, whatever his condition, he'd returned.

The lions were his. He had to believe that.

"Enough!" he commanded.

The lions stopped.

"You know me, just like you knew my mother," he continued, his confidence growing. "I walked by you a hundred times or more. I watched you being shaped and pruned. Don't you dare turn on me! Know me and obey!"

He waited for an instant and wondered for a moment if it would be his last instant. Would it really make a difference to the lions whose son he was? Then one of them cautiously approached him, and sniffed at his hand. It bowed its head. The wind whispered through its leaves. He walked over and touched it, stroking it as he would a cat.

The wind came again, almost like a purr.

They were his.

"Get up, Dontarius. You're not going to be eaten, at least not yet. Now what mischief have you been up to?"

Dontarius rose to his feet, abject terror still washing over his face. "Nothing. I saw the hedge maze and followed it in. Nothing more than that. I found the fountain you were after, but you'd better hurry if you want to save it."

Cyrus looked at him inquisitively, but then dismissed him. The scholar could be dealt with later. Whatever else Dontarius might be withholding, his statement about the fountain rang true. The fountain's wail still echoed, weaker now and more pitiful.

He motioned the lions onward and headed toward the center.

The spiders turned as he burst into the courtyard. Their chittering increased in intensity. The fountain lay thickly coated in their bodies. Whether any of it remained, he couldn't tell.

He drew his sword and charged. The blade sliced through the spiders again and again. The lions joined him, ripping and tearing through the spider's ranks. B'lantra's song began and this time he did nothing to stop it. Small sparks of fire pierced the hazy afternoon, searing the spiders away.

The numbers seemed infinite and the fountain's cries inexorably became weaker. Pistol shots rang out. Caulter. But even the inquisitor's intervention did little to change the outcome.

Cyrus fought. The spider's claws nipped at him. He struck again, lifting the sword and bringing it down. Time after time the blade cleaved through their skittering bodies until his hands were wet with both his own blood and their oily, acrid ichor.

It took him a moment to become aware of the quiet that had settled in behind the cacophony of sound all around him.

The fountain's scream had faded into nothingness. It was dead despite all his efforts to save it.

The spiders gave it no quarter, continuing to tear at its remains. The remains of the fountain stood bare and bleached. The dancers had vanished, picked clean by the creature's greed, their trials and tribulations, their untold, ever-unfolding stories brought to a swift end. Water leaked away like blood, soaking into the soft grass. The music that had so enticingly played was a distant memory. The golden gear he'd lost still lay entombed in the fountain's carcass. It pulsed once, a last heartbeat, and then was still.

He leapt forward to seize it before the spiders could reach it. They sliced and stabbed at his hand as he drove it between their bodies and clasped at the gear. It resisted at first, as if even in death the fountain was unwilling to give up its prize. His fingers burned. The oil from the spider's bodies seeped into the gashes their claws left in his hand.

He cried out, willing himself to maintain his grip. With a last frantic tug, he finally jerked it free and toppled backwards, the blood-slickened gear still clutched in his torn and trembling hand.

Enraged, the spiders surged after him. B'lantra's song rang out again. A tenuous wall of flickering flame burst into being, blackening the grass and momentarily stalling the spider's progress.

Caulter roughly pulled him to his feet. "Come on. She can't hold it for long. There's nothing more to be done here."

Cyrus fought against the inquisitor's grip. "I can't just leave. We came all this way! This is our chance—"

Caulter's face was hard. "You'll have no chance if you're dead."

The flames ebbed. The first spider pushed its way through, singed and smoldering, but still very much alive. Emboldened, a dozen more followed.

Cyrus reluctantly retreated. Caulter was right. It was too late to do anything.

The fountain was one more thing. One more thing he'd grown up with that was now lost to him.

"I see you, son of Aeliraneth. You will be undone just like your mother was."

The voice was deep and commanding. It tore at him almost as surely as the spiders had.

He didn't recognize it, but its intent was clear enough.

The lions leapt past him to stem the spider's advance, and he used the opening they'd given him to retreat.

They fled the hedge maze. They ran until they could run no

more, until the lions, the hedges and everything else melted away. In nearly an instant, they found themselves back in the weed streaked grounds of the ruined house of Aeliraneth.

Cyrus fell to his knees, tired and bloodied, dirty and defeated.

✳ ✳ ✳

"He's gone. That wretched, worthless *skish!*"

B'lantra's voice threatened to shrivel the already blighted pines.

Cyrus wearily glanced over. Sure enough, the scholar's belongings were nowhere to be seen. He'd gone.

"If the scholar has fled, then good riddance I say," Caulter said.

"I'm almost sorry to see him go," Cyrus said. "I thought... I thought maybe after the Maidenskar that he'd changed a little bit. I guess not."

"He never changed. He just allowed you to think that he had. It's how his kind operates," Caulter said.

"You've plenty enough lies of your own," B'lantra said, disapproval flashing in her dark eyes.

If he hadn't known better, Cyrus could have almost sworn Caulter looked wounded by the accusation.

"You know who and what I am. I've never hidden it," the inquisitor said. "You can't say the same for our former traveling companion. Something put the fear of God into him, and I don't think it was the spiders or the lions. Perhaps your late mother paid him a visit before the fountain was destroyed."

"I wouldn't put it past her," Cyrus agreed. He shook his head. "He must have had the gear all along. He picked it up during the battle at the Maidenskar or just flat out stole it. Either way, we have it back. There's nothing else left for us here."

"That's the first sensible thing you're said since we came to this cursed place. Our path takes us to Targus."

"Don't worry. We'll take care of your daughter," Cyrus replied, irritably.

"You have your own needs in Targus. You're going to try to break into the Arentine, unless I miss my guess."

"How could you know—?"

"I overheard you, for one. For two, it would be the most logical step. You need to figure out a way past that ward, and the Arentine provides you with your only hope of learning how to do it."

"What do you know about the Arentine?"

"Precious little. That's one area where the scholar would have actually been useful."

The inquisitor said nothing more and impatiently went over to gather up his scant belongings. Cyrus looked out over the desolate ruins before following. It was hard to believe the scrub-choked expanse could have ever been home. It was his now, though he still felt as much intruder as owner. Maybe the Heart of the Great Machine lay somewhere beyond the ward Mother had set up, but it was out of his reach for the time being.

There had to be a way to restore the fountain.

How?

He nearly gasped as the answer came to him. The words the Bal-haegast had spoken filtered back to him, almost mockingly: *'The fountain exists in this world and in the world beyond. Aeliraneth anchored it there so time would never touch it— so it would be there for the one to succeed her.'*

"The true fountain is in the spirit world," he exclaimed.

"What are you talking about?" B'lantra asked.

Her expression remained skeptical, even as he explained. "It's not a place for the living. You went there once when that monster was testing you. You'll die if you go back. Besides, it's not a place you can just travel to. Only the dead go there."

"It's in that book I found. That's what Mother meant when she talked about dancers and water. It has to be. She found a way, and the knowledge is somewhere in that book. We find it and we find a way to the fountain and past the ward," he countered. "See, I told you we'd find a way."

Her eyes flashed angrily. "You go where angels won't and then expect me to follow you. The only thing there is death."

"What would you have me do? Just wait for the end? You heard that voice with the spiders. Someone knows we're here, probably that Simon Barros," he said, his frustration growing.

"Then we find another way," she said.

"What way? Do we go crawling back to the Bal-haegast and ask for help? We'd have to sacrifice a lot more than memories."

"Of course not! Don't even talk like that." She closed her eyes and took a deep breath. "You said memories are precious. Well, I don't want mine filled up with fighting with you. Not over this. Promise me you'll find another way. I'm not losing you again. I still see you lying dead on the shore beside that pool. I can't go through that again."

There was a gravity to her tone that felt like she'd taken a hammer to his skull.

"Fine," he said, quietly. "I promise. We don't know what the book will say, but it's the only lead we have. Can we agree on that?"

The trace of a smile creased her tired face. "Agreed."

An impatient grunt came from behind them.

"Come on," B'lantra said. "Caulter will probably shrivel and die on the vine if we stay here much longer, but I'm going to look at your hand before we go."

He gave her a quizzical look and then regarded his torn hand. "I'd almost forgotten about it."

"Good thing for you that I haven't," she said, dragging him towards her physician's satchel.

He grinned in spite of himself. Despite their world being turned upside down and inside out, some things hadn't changed much at all.

CHAPTER 32

TO LOSE THE RAIN

THE ROAR OF THE RIVER became almost unnoticeable after a while. It blended into and became one with the pain that coursed through her. The water, chillingly cold, splashed over her as it made its mad dash through the huge boulders that lined the bottom of the chasm. Rain poured from the sky, tears from a Heaven that had never wanted her.

Asa clung grimly to the wet rock of the small ledge she'd landed on when she'd plummeted from the Maidenskar, more out of an instinctive will to survive than anything else.

She was shattered beyond all recognition. The mists had failed her, any attempt to use them to heal her body thwarted by the effects of the flask the witch's son had opened.

The madness that had taken her had passed, and her sight had returned. Neither one seemed any great gift. Her thoughts were dark. The world around her was harsh, holding only the promise of more pain. She didn't know how long she'd been there. Pain had been her constant companion throughout, dimming her sense of the passage of time.

Nysse hadn't come for her quite yet, even as the waters that pumped through her body leaked away to join those of the rushing river. Perhaps the water spirit had abandoned her like so many other things, too caught up in its nature to be bothered with something so pitiful and broken.

She held Susanna in her other hand. The doll was as ravaged as she was. Her hair had been seared away by the fire on the bridge. One of her button eyes was missing and part of her face had been burned away. Her sawdust stuffing spilled out from great gashes in her cloth body and was carried away by the waters.

"Beautiful Susanna. Ugly Susanna. I'm sorry that I let them hurt you."

The effort of moving her jaw to speak sent a fresh surge of agony shooting down her spine.

Asa felt the presence coming towards her.

Nysse?

No.

It was difficult to see the translucent form of Simon Barros through the haze of the rain and the spray of the foaming water. His feet barely touched the rapids as he walked atop them. She willed her body to move in response, stretching out a crushed and blackened arm. It took most of her energy to hold her head up enough to look at him.

The expression on his face was nearly impassive. She found some pity there, but no compassion. There was no look of concern for her battered condition to be found anywhere on his ghostly features.

"So this is where your fate has brought you. It would seem Aeliraneth's son still lives and runs free," he said, coldly.

"I tried," she whispered. "I tried so hard…"

Simon nodded and turned to leave. "I'm sure you did."

"Wait. Don't leave me here. Don't go," she wailed.

Simon turned. "I can spare no resources, no power to help you. Not when we're this close to achieving our goals."

"You can't leave me! You can't—"

"You've been a strong ally and a good friend, sweet Asa. You will be missed."

She tried to focus, willing herself to stay alive. "No… I fought beside you. For you. I meant something to you once. I…"

Simon bowed his head. "That time is past. War is coming. It's inevitable once the Wynding falls. Sacrifices will have to be made. You understand that."

Asa laid her head back down on the wet rock, too feeble to

hold it up any longer. This wasn't how it was supposed to be.

"Go in peace, Asa. May you find comfort in another life. I have none to give you anymore."

She cried out to him again and again, but there was no answer, only the crash of the water. Susanna slipped out of her fingers and was soon swept off, tumbling away downstream into oblivion.

She felt numb at first. Then the warmth of anger and of hate began to flow through her.

He'd left her to die, just like the others had so long ago. He might as well have tied another rock around her neck.

He'd left her.

Abandoned... unwanted.

Liar! Betrayer! Just like all the others.

Asa's broken body shook with outrage. Her eyes narrowed and burned through the spray of the river, gazing intently in the direction of Targus. She'd take her pain and revisit it upon him a thousand times over! She'd squeeze the life out of him until there was nothing but ash and misery.

She tried to rise, but her body refused to obey despite all her efforts. It had nothing left to give her, no matter the fury that welled up within. Her grip on the rock began to slip.

"Come home. Susanna is waiting."

The waters were cold against her skin.

She finally lost her hold, and they claimed her.

Her body floated. Flotsam in the current.

❋ ❋ ❋

The rain hadn't let up. B'lantra had decided that in some ways it was worse than even the fae storms. Despite the destruction it brought with it, at least the fae storm came with the knowledge that the dawn's light would bring its end. The drizzle held no such promise.

As evening set in, she stood huddled underneath the paltry shelter of a stout oak. This early in the spring, its leaves were barely formed thoughts on its gnarly branches. She muttered a curse as a cold droplet penetrated the defenses of her cloak and wound its way down her back.

Nearby their campfire hissed and sputtered as it attempted to eat its way through the damp wood they'd been able to gather. Beyond the stand of oaks, she knew Targus lay. They were still half a day away. Already she thought she could smell the hint of sulfur and soot on the sopping air.

"Here," Cyrus said to her as he emerged from the rain. He wasn't soaked, but he was close to it. In the fading light, with rivulets of water snaking their way down over his face and clothes, he looked like a shaggy, damp wolf come to stand beside her.

"Maybe this will help."

He shook out the battered parasol that he'd found and awkwardly held it over her.

She arched an eyebrow in surprise. "Where on God's green earth did you find that?"

"There's a rubbish dump a little ways down the hill. Looks like it used to be a stopover for the caravans."

The faded yellow fabric of the parasol had seen better days, but even so, it still looked far too fancy to have been simply left. Maybe the people who came to Targus were wealthy enough to afford it. It seemed strange given what Cyrus and Caulter had said about the city. It was the smithy for the Lion's League cities and for much of Arakost and the Northern lands. It was also a dirty and dank place, filled with desperately poor souls and a privileged merchant class. Ryvenne the Dowager ruled the city and from the description, she sounded about as a welcoming as a hungry troika.

The wind and rain picked up, and B'lantra immediately saw why the parasol had been abandoned. It was nearly as leaky as the tree branches they sheltered under. Its only real contribution was helping shield some of the damp evening from her sight.

She glanced at Cyrus and gave him a gentle smile as he twisted and turned the parasol about trying to find the best angle to combat the rain. It was a sweet gesture, even though it was mostly futile. It was so like him, in so many ways— trying so hard, but ultimately falling short of perfection.

"Thank you. Actually, I have something for you too," she said. "I was going to wait, but now is as good a time as any. God only knows what Targus will throw at us."

She reached into her satchel and pulled out the waidenwood carvings she'd been working on: two wide-eyed identical owls, each perched on its own sculpted branch. They weren't finished to her satisfaction, but then, knowing her, she'd never have been quite satisfied regardless of how much time she spent. They were ultimately short of perfection, just like the parasol. Just like Cyrus. Just like she was.

They were quite the pair, she and the witch's son.

"They're beautiful," he said, holding one up to study it.

"They're a matched set, so I thought we could each have one. They might even be magical. They feel that way for some reason. Though if they turn out to be, then you can thank the waidenwood more than me."

He shook his head. "They're magical because you gave them to me."

She smiled at the compliment. "Happy Greenleaf, by the way. Let's hope the new year turns out better than the last one."

His eyes widened. "It is Greenleaf, isn't it? It crept up on me. As it turns out you're not the only one with presents this evening. I happen to have more than just a used parasol."

The woven bracelet he presented to her was surprisingly beautiful. The blade grass strips were elaborately woven with a delicate crosshatched pattern, the native purple and blue of the tough grass expertly blended together. Even after seeing the silksteel ring he'd made, it still amazed her to think there was such artistry in his rough hands.

He handed her the parasol and then quickly tied the bracelet around her wrist before she could examine it further. She stared at him, momentarily taken aback. Did he understand what he'd just done? Or was it like so many other things he did, well-meaning but unconsidered?

"I know exactly what it means for a man to tie a bracelet around a woman's wrist," he said to her in Trafarga. "I did learn a few things since we left Shrevnetska."

She smiled again and then suppressed a giddy giggle that threatened to well its way out of her. It was a strange sensation.

"In that case, then yes," she said, giving him a lingering kiss. "The answer was yes before, and even after everything it still is."

"I have to admit I like the Trafari way of proposing better. Less words."

"Trafari have their advantages... in that and in other ways."

"So you've said."

They drifted into silence, but it was different from the brooding and worry that had consumed them over the last days. It was a silence because there was no need for them to say anything more.

She was with him, and he with her.

It was a moment— a fleeting, flitting thing that fled almost before she could even acknowledge it— but it was enough.

The rain finally eased, tapering reluctantly off into a fine mist before stopping altogether. It was a miracle in and of itself. The clouds parted for just an instant, and a faint bit of purple and gold peeked through, the faint, the last embers of the day.

It was gone before she could savor it, but it too was enough.

Lanterns twinkled through the trees from the darkening city of Targus. It was probably glowering at them, lurking like a spider in its web, just waiting for them to come near. She brought out her lantern to combat the deepening dusk that pressed closer to her, half expecting Cyrus to tell her it was just dark, and that there was nothing to worry about. But he remained silent. His confidence had been badly shaken at his old house, though it seemed to be returning. It might not be enough for whatever they were walking into, but it was at least a start.

She did her best to put thoughts of Targus out of her mind. Savor the moment. It was all they had. Targus would keep, and tomorrow would show the way.

One part of their travels had come to an end. A new one was about to begin…

The journey of Cyrus and B'lantra is continued

In the Warlock's Grasp

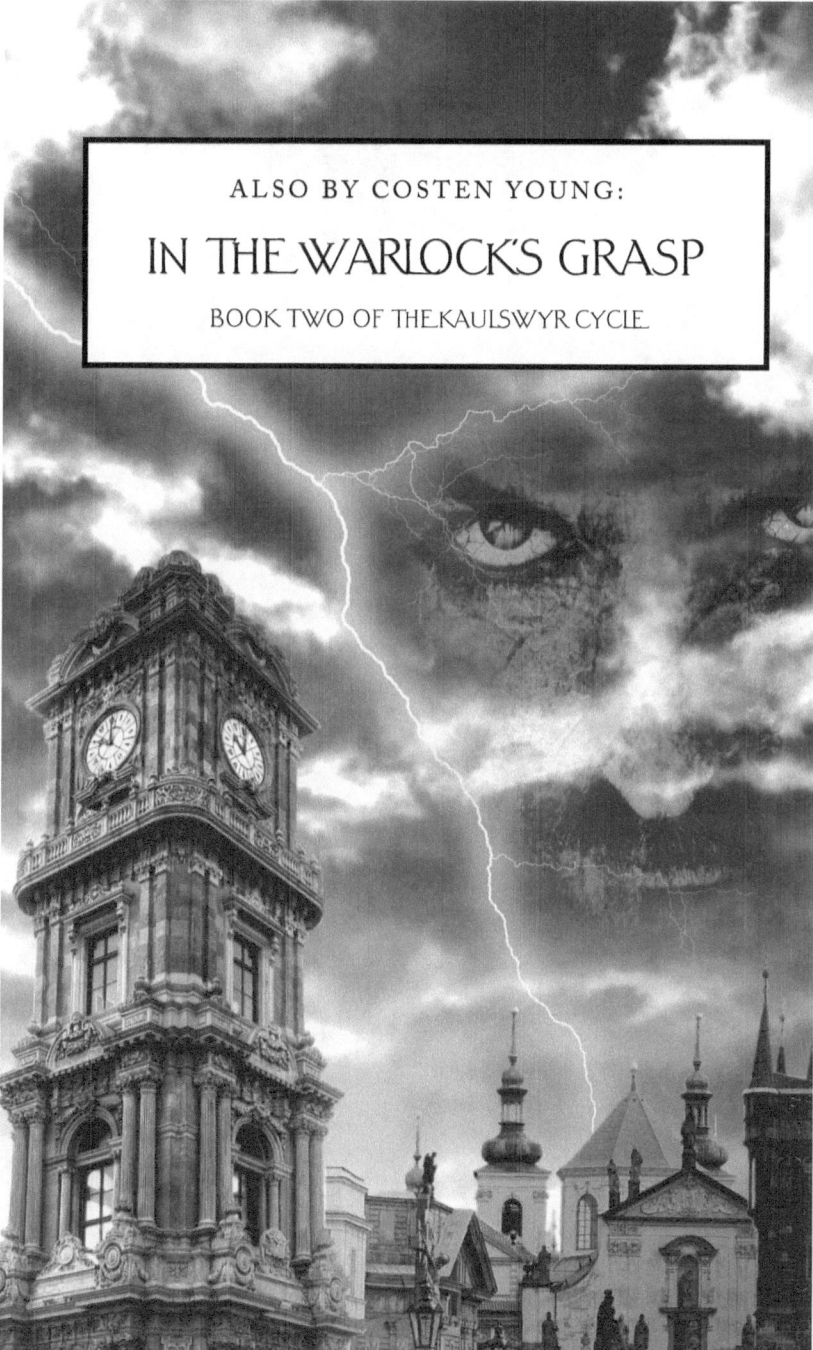

ALSO BY COSTEN YOUNG:

IN THE WARLOCK'S GRASP

BOOK TWO OF THE KAULSWYR CYCLE

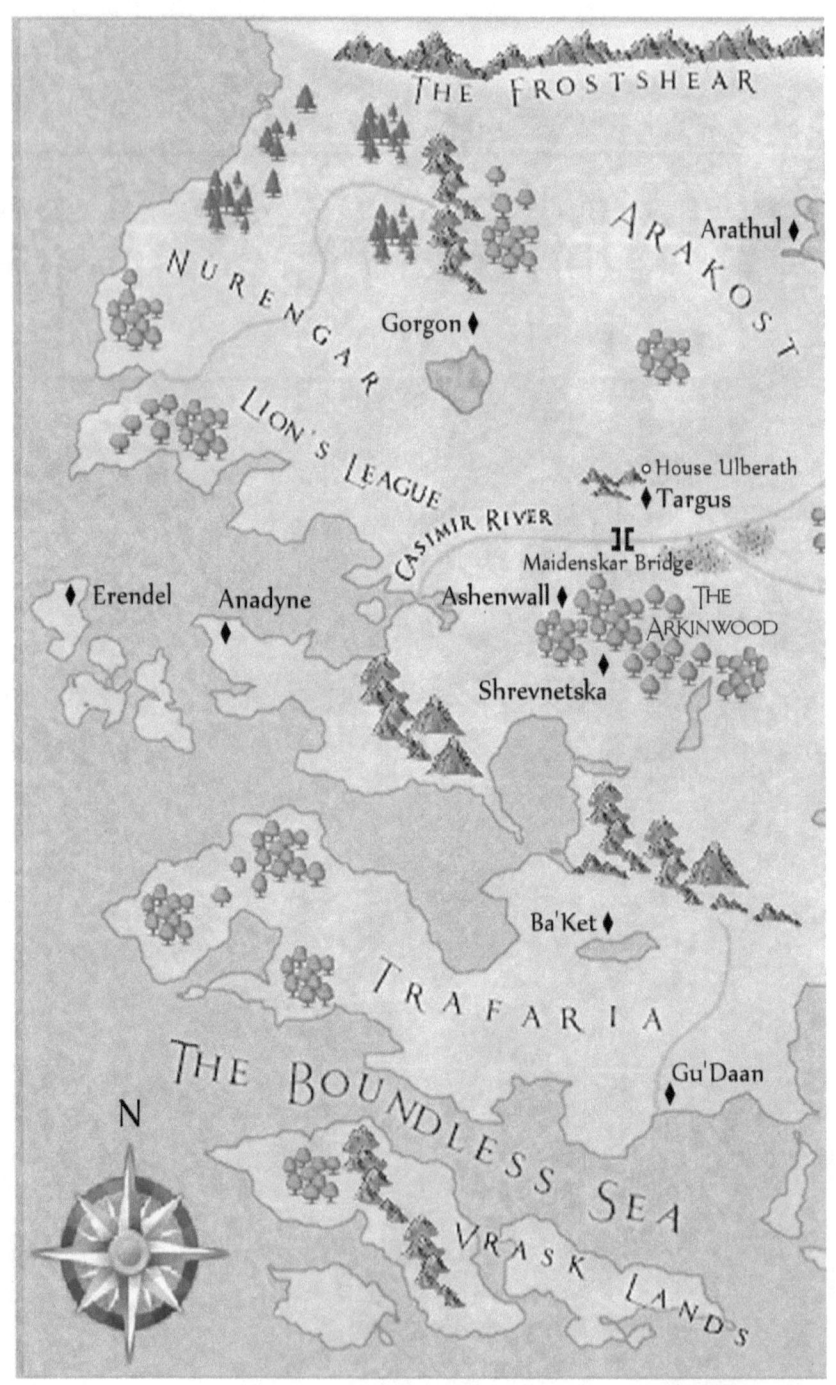

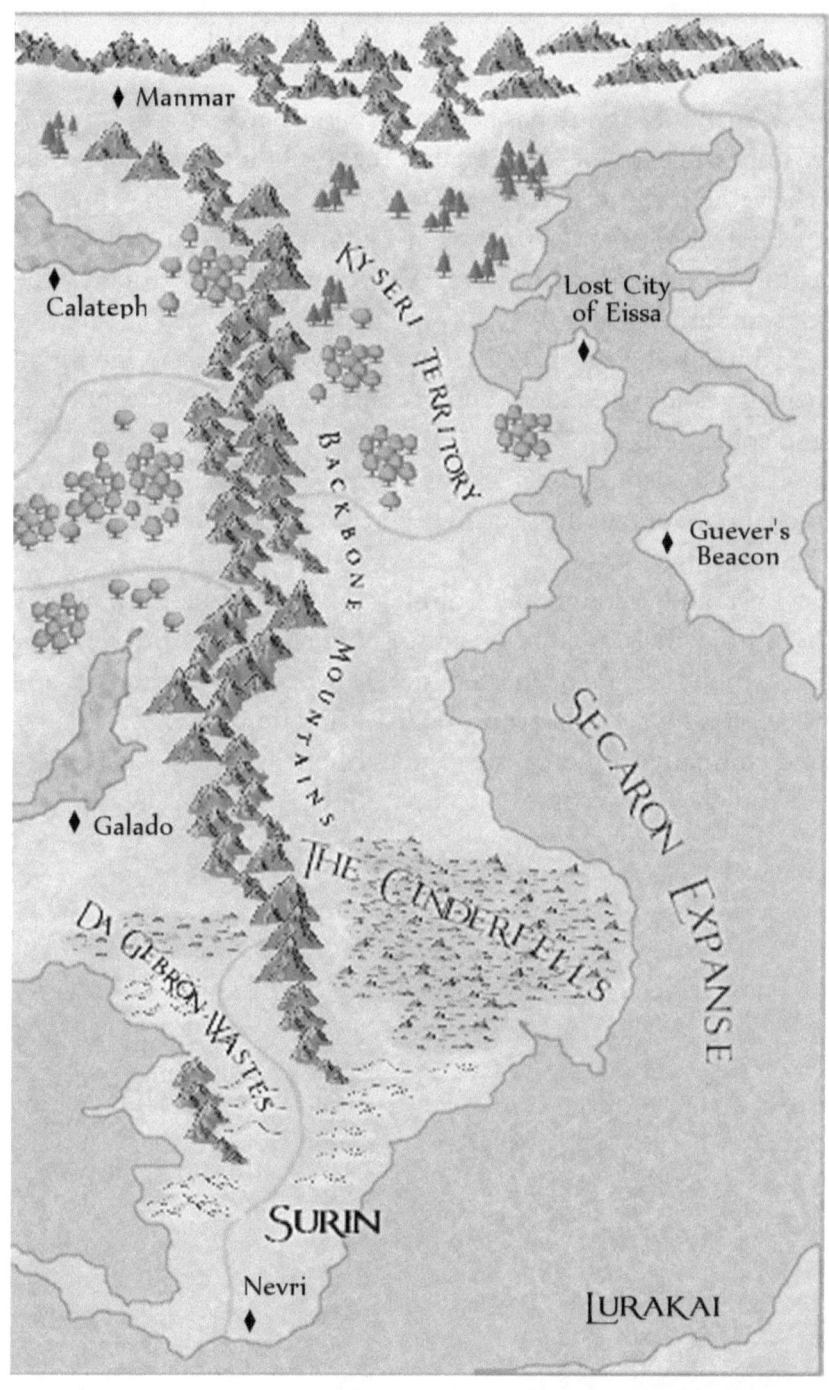

Manmar

Calateph

Ky·seri Territory

Backbone Mountains

Lost City of Eissa

Guever's Beacon

Secaron Expanse

Galado

The Cinderfells

Da Gebron Wastes

Surin

Nevri

Lurakai

Acknowledgements

Writing this book has been a long journey forward. It would be impossible for me to adequately thank all the wonderful people who've helped me along the way.

First of all, thanks to my family for putting up with me as artfully and as long they have. We writers can be a troublesome lot sometimes.

I'd like to give a special thanks to my sister Katherine for all her suggestions and ideas, and of course her inspiring front cover and spine designs.

Thanks also to David Young and Raina Romero for their modeling work, and to Rachel Pierce for her timely loan of the 'badass Conan sword.'

Last, and certainly far from least, I would like to thank my beautiful wife Marla for her editing, her comments and certainly her patience. She's been there nearly every step of the way, and there is no way in heaven or earth the tale of Cyrus, B'lantra and company would be the same without her.

You are all awesome.

About the Author

As a precocious five-year-old, Costen helped Luke Skywalker and company take down the Death Star— in his young imagination anyway. Not long after that, he went on a fateful journey with a hobbit, a wizard and thirteen dwarves to separate a dragon from his ill-gotten hoard.

He went on to snare a degree in Communications from Shepherd University, and later returned to add another in accounting. Over the years, he's worked as a machinist, an accountant, a news reporter and a little bit of everything in between.

Costen currently lives near Shepherdstown, WV with his wife Marla, three loyal (if demanding) cats and as yet unfulfilled plans for world domination.

You can find out more about Costen and the world of the Lanternlit by visiting WWW.COSTENYOUNG.COM or by email at COSTENYOUNG@GMAIL.COM

REVIEWS

"You can consult ancient texts, contact eldritch sprits or enlist an army of willing informants to find out what you want to know... or sometimes you can just simply ask."
— Lady Aeliraneth Ulberath, infamous witch

We like hearing from you, so if you'd want to let us know what you thought about the first part of Cyrus and B'lantra's journey, please feel free to stop by Amazon to leave a review. Otherwise, we'll have to call up the eldritch spirits, and you know how they are.

Thank you for your support.

www.ingramcontent.com/pod-product-compliance
Lightning Source LLC
Chambersburg PA
CBHW050901250626
47155CB00001B/56